PENGUI.

Mother's Love

Daisy Styles grew up in Lancashire surrounded by a f.
and community of strong women. She loved to listen to the
stories of life in the cotton mill, in the home, at the pub, on the
dance-floor, in the local church, or just what happened to
them on the bus going into town. It was from these women,
particularly her vibrant mother and Irish grandmother, that
Daisy learnt the art of storytelling.

A Mother's Love

DAISY STYLES

PENGUIN BOOKS

PENGUIN BOOKS

UK | USA | Canada | Ireland | Australia
India | New Zealand | South Africa

Penguin Books is part of the Penguin Random House group of companies
whose addresses can be found at global.penguinrandomhouse.com

Penguin
Random House
UK

First published 2022
001

Copyright © Daisy Styles, 2022

The moral right of the author has been asserted

Set in 12.5/14.75pt Garamond MT Std
Typeset by Jouve (UK), Milton Keynes
Printed and bound in Great Britain by Clays Ltd, Elcograf S.p.A.

The authorized representative in the EEA is Penguin Random House Ireland,
Morrison Chambers, 32 Nassau Street, Dublin D02 YH68

A CIP catalogue record for this book is available from the British Library

ISBN: 978-1-405-95043-5

www.greenpenguin.co.uk

For Claire Birdsall – beloved friend and patient counsellor

1. Ward Rounds

With her long, mahogany-brown hair swinging in the light spring breeze, Ada hurried up the farm lane from the cottage where she had just left her husband and baby daughter, on her way to start her shift at Mary Vale Home for Mothers and Babies. Much as she loved the Home, her patients and staff, Ada's heart ached; she had yearned to stay with her little family this morning. It was Jamie's daunting first day of looking after Catherine on his own.

He hadn't been there for the birth, stationed as he was with the Front Line medical corps in Tobruk, and it was there that he had suffered the accident that cost him his left hand. After being shipped home for a long period of hospitalization and convalescence, Jamie was mercifully recovering, and also due imminently to return to work as Resident Doctor at Mary Vale, fitting his working hours around those of his wife, who was Senior Ward Sister in the Home.

As usual, the minute Ada walked into Mary Vale, domestic preoccupations flew away, quickly replaced by thoughts for her patients and their needs. She had read when she first arrived that Mary Vale had once been a stopping point for pilgrims crossing the Irish Sea, seeking refuge en route to Furness Abbey. A thousand years ago on these very foundations an abbey had stood, and it was here that monks offered a bed and a simple supper to any who arrived asking for sanctuary. 'So it has been, and so it is now,' Ada thought. The ancient abbey, now transformed into a refuge for unmarried mothers and babies, was still a place of sanctuary. 'And long may it stay so,' Ada prayed

Removing her nurse's cape, Ada briskly walked down the corridor that led to the wards and Matron's office. The mornings were always busy with the endless cycle of feeds in the nursery, skilfully handled by Dora, an older, vastly experienced midwife who had been at Mary Vale for years and was primarily responsible for the care of all the babies in the nursery. Morning ward rounds were always conducted with Matron, these days accompanied by the new Senior Sister who had recently been appointed to accommodate Ada's wish to work part time. The interviewing panel, just Ada and Matron, had been surprised when the glamorous, commanding Renee Short had applied for the job. On paper she was more than qualified, coming from St Thomas's Hospital in London, with a vast experience of midwifery nursing. Unlike her cold, rather aloof predecessor, Sister Renee, with her long, curling, jet-black hair and green eyes, seemed relaxed, bright and breezy.

Ada's only question about her application had been why an apparently dynamic young woman seemed in such a hurry to leave London. Wouldn't she miss the social life that still thrived in the capital even during wartime? But Renee had waved a dismissive hand in the air: she had had more than her fill of all that; what she yearned for these days was peace and quiet and the beauty of the Lake

District. Here was something that Ada completely identified with: her passion for fell-walking and the splendour of the mountains were what had attracted her to the area in the first place. Nevertheless, Mary Vale – on the very edge of the vast sweep of Morecambe Bay – was a far cry from a bustling city hospital on the banks of the River Thames. Oddly enough, so far, Ada had seen no evidence of Renee's passion for the great outdoors: there had been no sign of a pair of stout walking boots or a rain jacket, no questions about the best routes to take up to the higher fells, not even a request to borrow an ordnance-survey map.

'Not everybody is as mad and impetuous as you,' she had firmly chided herself. 'Let the poor woman get her feet under the table before you start criticizing her lack of adventure.'

Ada found Dora in the nursery, with a chubby red-faced baby balanced across her knees. Dora deftly changed the baby, expertly sticking safety pins into the terry-towelling nappy before popping the little lad over her shoulder and winding him.

'How was Catherine when you left her?' Dora immediately enquired.

Ada suspected that the subtext of Dora's question was: How was Catherine when you left her alone with her daddy this morning?

'They were counting the flowers in the garden,' Ada smiled. 'She barely noticed me leaving, to be honest.'

Dora gave a cheerful smile, but Ada knew just how much she missed little Catherine, who had been under her

3

care in the nursery when Jamie was away and Ada was trying to work full time. Dora had loved her like a daughter. Since the day Catherine was born, the two of them had formed such a special bond, to the extent that sometimes when Ada arrived in the nursery to pick up her daughter Catherine clung to Dora, who, though firm about handing over her charge, was nevertheless touched by the little girl's devotion to her.

'I know you two will miss each other,' Ada started sympathetically. 'But it's really important that Catherine gets used to Jamie looking after her; sharing the child-minding will allow us both to work part time at Mary Vale but still give us lots of time with our baby, time that Jamie really needs after missing out on Catherine's first months.'

Dora nodded. 'Yes, I understand that.'

'Plus,' Ada added firmly, 'Jamie really has got to get back into practising medicine; the longer he's away from it, the more his confidence drains away.'

Dora gave a tight determined smile. 'It'll be good for the little lass to be with her daddy, and it will be good for Mary Vale to have their Resident Doctor again.'

As Ada recalled Jamie's arrival at Mary Vale as the new doctor she had fallen madly in love with, her big blue eyes sparkled; Dr Reid had certainly set the residents buzzing; but, as the girls got to know him over the length of their pregnancies, it was his professional skill and expertise they valued the most.

Dora dragged Ada's wandering thoughts back to the here and now. 'Do you think Jamie will, er . . . manage, like?'

Ada rephrased her friend's question. 'Do you mean,

will he manage with only one hand?' Ada gave a little sigh. 'I'm sure eventually he will be fine, especially as it's the left hand he lost, though, to be honest, he's not as convinced as I am.'

'You can hardly blame the poor fella,' Dora answered. 'How long has it been now since the accident, six months?'

'About that,' Ada agreed. 'Poor lamb, no sooner has he got to know his daughter than he's left on his own to feed and change her.'

Now it was Dora's turn to comfort Ada. 'I wouldn't fret yourself,' she soothed. 'When I saw Dr Reid pushing the little 'un down the farm lane in her pram the other day, the pair of them seemed happy enough, chuckling and nattering away they were.'

Ada smiled. 'Luckily Catherine's still enough of a baby to take each new experience as it comes; whether it's being looked after by Daddy or a new toy, she seems to take it all in her stride.'

'Aye, you're right there: she's a confident lassie. Catherine certainly ruled this nursery,' Dora recalled. 'I miss her sweet smiling face,' she said with genuine affection.

Ada threw her friend a reassuring smile. 'Don't worry, you'll be seeing her soon. Jamie's bringing her up here when I finish my shift this afternoon.' Glancing at her fob watch, Ada headed for the nursery door. 'Better get on with the ward rounds – don't want to keep Matron waiting.'

'Look out for little Polly: she's been getting herself into a right state,' Dora called after her.

Stopping at the door, Ada turned. 'When has Polly not got herself into a right state?'

'Sixteen's too young to be carrying a babby,' Dora said sympathetically. 'Poor kid's frightened to death most of the time.'

'I know – I'll do my best to calm her down,' Ada promised.

'Good,' Dora responded. 'You're one of the few she'll listen to.'

On her way to the ante-natal ward, Ada grew thoughtful. Dora was right: poor little Polly was way too young to be carrying a baby. Hers was an all-too-familiar story: walking out with a local lad, things had gone too far, and Polly, ignorant of the facts of life, had fallen pregnant. The families – who knew each other – were immediately at loggerheads. The boy's family, who had money behind them, urged Polly's family to pack the girl off right away, 'get her sorted', as they phrased it. As far as they were concerned, a dangerous and illegal termination was preferable to bringing shame on the family; the very idea had sent Polly's parents, devout Catholics, into a lather of righteous indignation.

'Abortion's against the law and a mortal sin in the eyes of our Church – Polly's poor little baby would live forever in Purgatory,' they claimed.

The concern of both families to conceal Polly's situation from the public eye resulted in the girl being booked into Mary Vale very early on in her pregnancy. Having taken no part in any of the decision-making, she'd arrived in a state of shock and bewilderment.

'The more they fought it out, the more invisible I

became,' Polly had wept after Ada had brought her a cup of tea that she couldn't drink and a slice of bread and butter that she couldn't swallow. 'In the end Ted's family said they'd cover the cost of getting me out of the way on condition that I have the baby adopted, which my parents were in favour of.'

'And what, if anybody had taken the trouble to ask, would you have liked, Polly?' Ada gently enquired.

'ME?' Polly asked in surprise. 'Well, if it had been down to me, I would have married Ted and had our baby and been one happy little family in Rochdale . . .' Her sad voice trailed away. 'That didn't happen, especially when Ted turned eighteen and got his call-up papers: he was off sooner than I could blink.'

Ada smothered a sigh; if she could have had a shilling for every time she had heard this same tragic tale, she would be close to having a few hundred pounds in the bank. It was one of the oldest stories in the book, an unwanted pregnancy that could have been avoided if only mothers were prepared to educate their daughters about the real facts of life instead of talking about birds, bees and storks delivering babies. Hiding menstruation, conception and childbirth behind gawkish sentimental images and puerile explanations helped nobody, especially the girls themselves, who alone dealt with the consequences of an inadequate sex education.

Ada having joined Sister Renee and Matron in the hospital corridor, the three women swapped notes before starting the ward rounds.

'Dora's already mentioned that Polly's in a state,' Ada said, as they made their way to the ante-natal ward.

Sister Renee Short managed to look both smart and attractive in her starched white uniform with the belt pulled tight, emphasizing her curvaceous figure and slender legs, with her jet-black curly hair tucked under her Sister's cap. Impatiently she rolled her eyes. 'Really, the girl does herself no favours at all, panicking about every little thing that comes her way.'

Matron gently reminded Renee of Polly's immaturity. 'Her age and lack of knowledge certainly don't help, but with patience and understanding we can prepare her for the months ahead.'

Renee gave a blasé smile. 'I'm aware of that, Matron. I just think it's a pity the poor kid reacts to every physical change in her body with tears and drama.'

Ada quietly added, 'I actually think she's getting a bit better.'

Renee's astonishing green eyes widened in surprise. 'Really?'

Ada nodded. 'Yes, really. She listens more these days and reacts less.'

Renee raised her perfectly manicured eyebrows as if to say, 'Well, that's certainly not something I've noticed.'

'There is some small improvement,' Matron acknowledged.

Renee gave a little laugh. 'Let's hope it stays that way.'

Ada was well aware of the problems that could accompany pregnancy at a young age: premature delivery and pre-eclampsia were top of her list, along with the risk of anaemia and bleeding during pregnancy – the latter had already happened to Polly. When Ada found Polly – looking more like a child than a young woman – lying pale and limp on her hospital bed with her mousy-coloured lank hair plastered around her face and her eyes red rimmed with crying – her heart ached for the poor kid. Nevertheless, she maintained a cheery presence as she pulled the curtains around the bed.

'Morning, dear. How are we feeling this morning?'

Polly gave a weak smile. 'Sick,' she answered briefly.

Polly complained of feeling sick most of the time, and Ada always did all she could to alleviate her condition, though she did occasionally wonder if some of the nausea might be psychological. But she knew telling Polly that (which she suspected Renee might be inclined to do) wouldn't help the girl one little bit.

'I could get you a drop of barley water,' Ada suggested, as she leant over to take Polly's temperature. 'If you sipped it slowly, you might keep it down.'

Devoted to her favourite nurse, Polly gave a feeble smile. 'I'll try,' she promised.

Before Ada left her bedside, Polly clutched hold of her hand. 'Is my baby really all right?' she asked for at least the tenth time.

Ada gave her a bright smile. 'Yes, we've heard a good strong heartbeat – try not to worry, dear.'

'But bleeding's like a period,' Polly fretted. 'How can you keep a baby when that happens?'

'Trust me, dear, bleeding during pregnancy can happen

with girls your age – we're keeping an eye on it,' she assured her agitated patient. 'The best thing you can do for now, Polly, is get some rest.'

Polly gave a grateful smile. 'Thank you, Sister Ada. I know I've got to give my baby up for adoption, but, while I'm in charge and the baby is growing inside me, I want to do my best for it.'

Seeing the lingering sadness in the girl's eyes, Ada gave her a sympathetic smile. 'Pregnancy is a strange experience: sometimes it quite overwhelms you, not just your body but your mind too,' she said softly.

'I never thought I'd feel so much concern for a baby I'm not going to keep,' Polly murmured tremulously. 'I feel protective and responsible and full of love for the poor little mite.' Sighing, she added, 'God only knows how I'll ever have the strength to give it away.'

2. An Usherette in Blackpool

Holding her torch at an angle so that her customers could see the sloping aisle that led to the semi-circular rows of cinema seats, Lillian Latham whispered as the light from the big screen softly faded.

'You and the little lad should be able to see all right here.'

The older woman, obviously the boy's granny, gave a toothless grin as she barged her way along the row, disturbing all she passed, treading on toes or bashing people with the big leather handbag that swung from her wrist. Lillian smiled to herself as she watched the granny, once settled, take a bag of sweets from her handbag. As she and the lad noisily chomped on nut-brittle slabs, a young man who was trying to kiss his girlfriend in the dark muttered, 'Eeeh, bloody hell, you'd think they'd go somewhere else to eat their bloody toffees.'

Lillian smiled as she skilfully negotiated her way back to the darkened entrance, where she stood against the faded velvet curtains that draped the doorway to watch (possibly for the ninth time that week) the opening titles of *The Jungle Book* unfold.

'That kid is going to be bawling his eyes out in ten minutes' time,' she thought, as she lit up a Woodbine.

The film was an absolute sell-out, to the extent that a

number of customers sat through a second showing as the film looped over and over again throughout the day and night. The moustached, Brylcreemed manager of the Regal Cinema in the centre of Blackpool bristled at the audacity of some 'Bloody cheeky folk', as he put it.

'Fair enough, they've paid for the A film, and the B film, plus Pathé News, but sitting through another showing for free is bang out of order, don't you think, our Lillian?'

Even though they weren't related, the manager had called her 'Our Lillian' since he had given her the job as the Regal's usherette. Lillian, who didn't care one way or another how many times people watched the films for free, just shrugged. 'It's nice to see the picture house so full,' she answered diplomatically.

In truth, just like the punters, she could happily spend all day long watching films. Since she was a kid, she had adored going to the cinema and being transfixed by the latest pictures, and now, as the Regal's usherette, she could do exactly that all day long. Admittedly, she often left work looking like a tired owl after being in the dark all day, and she smelt of cigarette smoke all of the time, but it was a price she was willing to pay for watching movies for a living. Lillian lived in a world of perpetual drama, with her emotions permanently teetering on the edge as she watched box-office film releases unfold on the big screen. *Mrs Miniver, Casablanca, The Jungle Book* (presently showing), *Yankee Doodle Dandy, In Which We Serve* were just a few of the most popular, money-making shows playing these days.

Lillian's long wavy hair was naturally a soft light brown, but she had dyed it blonde and curled it to look as sexy and fashionable as possible. The little pocket money remaining after she obediently handed over her pay-packet every Friday evening was spent on make-up and clothes – a long raincoat with a turned-up collar, heeled button-up brogues and cloche hat that she pulled down over her long, blonde bob, slanting the brim provocatively over her big honey-brown eyes. Dressed like a film star, with her glossy red lips pouting just like Joan Crawford's, Lillian felt herself the perfect match for dark, moody, brooding Humphrey Bogart, with cigarette smoke curling from his lips. There were other heart-throbs too: Robert Mitchum, Cary Grant, Laurence Olivier, James Stewart and Frank Sinatra, who took it in turns to feature in her romantic fantasy world.

'That job at the Regal will be the undoing of you, Lil,' her mother had admonished. 'You've always been a daft romantic dreamer, but these days you live in a world of your own.'

'Mam!' Lillian remonstrated. 'You know I've loved the pictures since I was a kid.'

Her mother raised her eyes towards the ceiling. 'Tch,' she clucked disapprovingly. 'Falling for a different film star every week and putting on airs and graces like you were Ginger Rogers. You'll soon be forgetting where you come from if you're not careful.'

Though she would never have admitted it to her mother, Lillian knew in her heart that she had definitely become more fanciful since she had been working at the Regal. Like the little boy she had escorted to his seat, now (as she had predicted) bawling like a baby as he watched

The Jungle Book, she too had wept at every showing of *Reap the Wild Wind*, *Valley of the Sun* and *Mrs Miniver*. She had also hidden behind the thick velvet curtains, trembling with terror, when she first watched *The Ghost of Frankenstein* and *The Corpse Vanishes*, and laughed herself silly at the first showings of Gene Tierney's *Rings on Her Fingers*. Every week one spectacular film after another unrolled for her delight, and every week she loved her job more and more.

Wearing a frilly red pinafore arrangement over her short black skirt, Lillian became accomplished at gliding up and down the carpeted aisle, guiding stumbling customers to their seats. Occasionally she had been called upon to part a couple petting too heavily on the back row, and she regularly had to stop naughty children from throwing toffees at the screen during the Saturday-morning performance when children were allowed inside the picture house for knock-down prices, which the manager always referred to as 'The Tuppenny Rush!'

'Step back or you'll get trampled to death,' the caretaker would warn as he flung open the double doors, narrowly avoiding a stampede of crazed children, all intent on getting to the front seats first.

The particular occasion that had really matched up with her fantasies was on the day that she had been forced to ask two rather drunken gentlemen to leave the building. After they insulted her, they chose not to cooperate, at which point a tall, well-built man in naval uniform stepped in saying, 'Do as the lady says, lads.'

After growling and swearing, the more drunk of the two men staggered to his feet and took a swipe at the sailor, who deftly caught him in an arm lock and promptly escorted him and his friend out of the building. Trembling so much the beam from her torch wobbled erratically, Lillian followed her rescuer to the exit.

'Thank you, thank you so much,' she babbled gratefully, catching her breath when the stranger turned and she saw how handsome he was.

'My pleasure, miss. Trevor Hughes at your service.'

Tall and dark, with a mop of thick hair that fell in a sweep over his deep blue eyes, this stranger was a combination of all Lillian's heart-throbs. Broad-shouldered, he had high cheekbones, a dimpled chin, a smile that made her heart skip a beat, and all of that was enhanced by his dashing uniform. Holding out a broad hand, he gripped her small one in his.

And Lillian, full of romantic yearnings and tales of heroic servicemen, fell in love with Trevor Hughes right there and then.

Trevor's leave was short, but the infatuated couple spent every minute of it when possible together, either inside the Regal (cuddling like other lovers on the back row when she wasn't working) or on Blackpool Prom, walking in the bright summer sunshine with seagulls wheeling overhead and warm breezes carrying the tantalizing smell of fish and chips and fresh cockles and mussels. Lillian, lying in Trevor's strong arms on the sandy beach or cuddled up on a breezy bench at the end of Blackpool Pier, kissing her boyfriend until her lips were sore, was totally infatuated. She was glad that she had splashed out on the sweetest little crêpe summer dress, mauve and printed with forget-me-not blue flowers that clung to her short, shapely body in all the right places, emphasizing her narrow waist, high breasts and slender hips.

'You're the best-looking girl in Blackpool,' Trevor had said proudly on his last night of leave.

Reluctant to go home, desperate not to be parted, they had made their way on to the beach, where the tide scraped against the pebbles as it made its way out. Under the starlight they found a sheltered spot, and Trevor pulled Lillian down on to the ground – and, wrapping his arms around her, for the first time in their brief courtship their kissing began giving way to much more. Through the silky crêpe material of her skimpy summer dress, Lillian felt Trevor's hands skimming over her body, making her gasp with pleasure, and she crushed against him as he cupped her breasts. Then, with her pulse racing, she was unable to resist his advances as he went on to stroke the silky softness of her inner thighs. Limp with desire, she felt all resistance drain from her, and by the time Trevor's hands reached her underwear Lillian could barely breathe; she would have unquestionably abandoned herself and all her principles right there and then if a torch hadn't suddenly blazed in their startled faces.

'Hello, hello, what's going on here?'

Pulling down her dress and straightening her underwear, Lillian leapt to her feet, while Trevor struggled to buckle up his trousers. Blushing and hot with shame and embarrassment, Lillian could hardly speak. Luckily Trevor managed a few words. 'We'll be heading off now.'

'Good idea, son,' the bobby had agreed. 'See the lady home nice and safe, eh?'

The following day Trevor reported back to base, and Lillian returned to the familiar routine at the Regal, where now, as she watched passionate love scenes on the big screen, she fully understood how lovers got carried away in the heat of the moment. Though she had been upset when she parted from her boyfriend, Lillian had been comforted by the fact that they would write to each other regularly and meet up again on Trevor's next leave. She dreamily imagined where they would go on their next date: if the North Pier was open maybe they could walk hand in hand down the length of its decking and stand on the very end as the waves crashed against the stout wooden posts and seagulls dive-bombed the surging waves for small fish and clams. Blackpool's Pleasure Beach, considered to be a morale booster by the powers that be, was fortunately still open. She and Trevor could have fun on the Big Dipper, the Waltzer, the Ghost Train and all the slot machines selling silly toys and goldfish. They could end their day with fish and chips loaded with salt and vinegar, eaten straight out of the bag as they sat on the beach watching the sun go down. She had penned all this to Trevor and urged him to apply for leave as soon as possible, when an event happened that turned Lillian's happy world completely upside down. In a rush and late for work, she had picked up a letter which she had shoved into her pocket and which she only remembered to open halfway through the first showing of *Captain Marvel*. Standing at the back of the picture house, she used her torch to read the letter, which shocked her to the core.

'No!' she gasped out loud as she dropped her torch on the floor.

Customers in the nearest seats turned around to glare at her. 'SHHH!' they hissed.

Pushing her way through the velvet curtains, she entered the brightly lit box-office area, where she reread the letter from His Majesty's Government, instructing her to report for conscripted work at a farm just outside Keswick in the Lake District within the week. Lillian had stared incredulously at the words.

'Land Girl,' she exclaimed. 'A *Land Girl*,' she repeated in horror.

When there was a break in the day, Lillian bolted into the manager's office and blurted out her news.

'Aye,' he said lugubriously. 'Churchill wants all able-bodied lasses helping out with the war effort.'

'But I never applied,' Lillian cried.

'You don't have to, love, you've been conscripted: it's the law, just like it is with all the fellas that get called up – there's no bloody choice.' Looking at Lillian's face, smudged with make-up and running with tears, the manager felt sorry for the poor kid, who was clearly in shock. 'Don't tell me you're the only girl in Blackpool who's never heard of female conscription?'

'Course I've heard of it,' she replied crossly. 'I talked to somebody about it down at the Labour Exchange last year . . . I think,' she added vaguely.

'And what did they say?' the manager asked patiently.

'They asked me if I wanted to join the armed forces.'

'And what did you say to that?'

'NO!' Lillian actually laughed. 'I'm not clever enough to be a Wren or the likes of them bossy Army women doing Morse code and tracking enemy planes.'

The manager shook his head as he considered what she had just said. 'Sounds to me like you've been watching too many war films and got your wires crossed,' he concluded.

On the defensive, Lillian demanded, 'What do you mean, got mi wires crossed?'

'Women do plenty of war work,' he explained. 'It's not just about the WRNS and the WAAF. They're working on the buses, in the hospitals, building bombs – surely you know that? It's on Pathé News nearly every night,' he pointed out.

Knowing he had caught her on the back foot, Lillian answered hotly, 'Of course I've seen that stuff on the news.'

'So you'll understand it's your turn now,' the manager reasoned.

'But I never actually chose to be a Land Girl,' she protested again.

'Well, I'd say, our Lillian, that the government's made the choice for you. You didn't make your own mind up fast enough – no lass, unless she's sick, can skip conscription.'

Lillian returned to her work, ushering customers in and out of the picture house, but, in between, hidden by the swathes of velvet curtain that overhung the entrance, she sobbed her heart out. She would have to say goodbye to all of this: the Regal, watching films and meeting people all day long. And there was Trevor too. Being a Land Girl in the far-flung Lake District had to reduce her chances of seeing her handsome sailor boyfriend to near zero.

'CUMBERLAND!' she groaned.

Wasn't it miles away, almost in Scotland? Knowing she had only herself to blame for the mess she was in, poor Lillian started to weep all over again.

3. Coming Home

By the beginning of June, Jamie was ready to go back to work, but, for all of Ada's upbeat determination that he would soon get into the swing of things once he started practising again, she could see on the morning that he was due to start that the poor chap was white with nerves. Fortunately, Catherine eased the atmosphere around the breakfast table. Grabbing the little spoon from her mother's hand, she smeared baby cereal on to her hands, then wiped them all over her face. The sight of his pretty daughter's cheeks splodged with gloopy mess brought a smile to Jamie's tense face.

'I shall miss you, poppet,' he said, as he tenderly wiped Catherine down.

'I'm sure she'll miss you too,' Ada assured her husband.

Settling Catherine on his knee, he jiggled her up and down. 'It's silly feeling this nervous,' he confessed.

Desperate to comfort him, Ada said encouragingly, 'I know the staff are all looking forward to seeing you back.'

'It's not the staff that trouble me,' he admitted. 'It's the residents who don't know me – what will they think when a disabled doctor walks on to the wards?'

Ada answered his question robustly. 'Jamie, for a child who struggled all his life with the effects of polio, which you never allowed to get the better of you, you surely must know that you have it in you to handle this?'

'The other thing, to be blunt, is these days I'm used to men with burnt faces, lost limbs, nervous disorders, shell shock – not pregnant women with ailments that I've almost forgotten about.'

'It will all come back the minute you walk into the Home, especially after you've been briefed by Matron, who can't wait to see you by the way. And you'll also get to meet glamorous Sister Renee too,' Ada teased.

'Ah, yes, the new member of staff.'

'She appears to have bags of experience,' Ada told him.

Jamie smiled at his wife over the top of his daughter's blonde curls. 'Sounds like you, my darling: a good nurse, with bags of experience.'

At his words of praise Ada's lovely face lit up. 'Here, let me take her,' she offered.

As Catherine was passed to her mother, she protested loudly, 'DADA!'

'See, she doesn't want me to leave,' Jamie joked.

'Off you go, Dr Reid,' Ada laughed. 'You have patients waiting for you and a ward round to do.'

'Wish me luck,' said Jamie, as he picked up his doctor's bag and headed for the door.

'Bye, Dada,' Catherine burbled as he went.

'Bye bye, darling,' Jamie said, and he blew the baby a kiss. 'Look after Mama.'

Standing on the farm track holding Catherine in her arms, Ada could barely believe that everything she had hoped and prayed for had come true. Her husband was strong and healthy again and, better still, at this very moment he was on his way to work. It sounded so normal it made her want to laugh with joy.

'Daddy's gone to work, Catherine,' Ada chanted, as she jiggled her daughter up and down.

Was it possible that this man swinging down the lane on a perfect summer's morning was the same man who had been sent home in a hospital ship with horrifically grave injuries? She would never forget that terrifying morning only eight months ago when she had received a telegram informing her that Jamie was mercifully alive but in serious need of specialist care. Out of her mind with worry and fear, she recalled how she had rushed to show Matron, her dearest friend and confidante, the telegram.

'Why can't the Army tell me more?' she had cried. 'Is he suffering from burns, shell shock, has he picked up an infection out there, can he walk, or God forbid – has he lost a limb?' Ada (still ignorant of the extent of Jamie's injuries) had gone through the gruesome list of possibilities with tears in her eyes.

Sitting Ada firmly down in a chair in her office, Matron had hurried to the nearby kitchen to make a pot of strong tea, which she urged her friend to drink.

'Darling, the most important thing of all is that Jamie is coming home, he's alive.' With her deep dark-brown eyes full of concern, Matron continued. 'You must focus on the positive, dear, you have a husband and little Catherine still has a father. Once Jamie's hospitalized back here, you can visit him and make your own judgement on his condition.'

Taking Ada's free hand, she'd squeezed it softly. 'Until then we shall all pray for Jamie's health and swift return.'

Grateful for her advice and support, Ada had squeezed Matron's hand in return, calling her by her first name, the name she often used when they were alone together.

'Thank you, Ann, you're right as usual – at least he's coming home.' Then, suddenly side-tracked by another alarming thought, she cried, 'But what if he's hospitalized in London, or Portsmouth? I can't take Catherine all the way down South on a troop train – it could take days.'

Matron shook her head and smiled. 'Don't be silly, Ada,' she soothed. 'Little Catherine will stay with us, of course, if that happens. Dora's with her every working hour of the day in the nursery, Sister Mary Paul babysits at the slightest opportunity, and Sister Theresa takes her out in the pram whenever the sun's out. Plus – as you well know – I myself am your daughter's greatest fan, so I can safely say that Catherine will be perfectly all right here with us at Mary Vale.'

'I am so lucky to have my dear Mary Vale family,' Ada said fondly.

'And we're lucky to have *you*,' Matron replied.

In the weeks of waiting for Jamie's return, a desperate Ada had continued to worry about everything imaginable: was her beloved getting enough food and water, was he seasick, losing weight? If he had wounds, would they become infected below deck in unsanitary conditions? Her worst fear had been that the ship would get torpedoed by enemy fire and all on board would go down with the vessel. By the time Ada received the news that Jamie was in Preston Hospital she had lost nearly half a stone in weight and had barely slept through the night for weeks on end. Fortunately, Catherine, thriving under Dora's doting care in the nursery, had been a bundle of smiles and giggles, and even cutting her first teeny milk teeth didn't appear to be too much of a hardship for the happy little girl.

'She's such a brave soldier,' Ada cooed, as she cuddled her baby during a snatched moment in the nursery.

Dora smiled adoringly at her charge. 'She's a little treasure, for sure.'

Seeing the familiar glimmer of sadness in Dora's kind eyes, Ada knew exactly what she was thinking. The loss of her twin boys at the beginning of the war had all but broken Dora's brave spirit: if it hadn't been for her return to work on Mary Vale's maternity ward, poor Dora, deranged with grief, would surely have taken her own life in order to stop the pain that tortured her every waking moment. Mercifully, Mary Vale's babies, lined up in their little white canvas cots in the nursery, had quite literally been Dora's lifesavers. Her passion for babies and her instinctive understanding of their needs: whether it was as simple as a nappy change or relieving colic to detecting a more serious ailment like mumps or measles, Dora could spot them all. Babies responded to her unconditional love, blossoming like flowers in the sunshine under her care, and she in turn gratefully drew life from them.

Kissing her daughter's silky pale fingertips, Ada had said, 'She's besotted with you, Nurse Dora. I'm certainly second fiddle when you're around.'

'Don't be daft, woman,' Dora had chuckled. 'Every babby loves their mammy best in the world.'

'I agree,' Ada conceded. 'But there's a lot of competition when you're close by,' she finished with a teasing smile.

Safe in the complete confidence of her friends and colleagues, Ada had left her daughter in their care as soon as she heard she could visit Jamie, whom she found looking shockingly thin and pale. Fortunately, before she actually saw her husband, the Ward Sister had informed Ada of the amputation that had been performed on Jamie's left hand. Hearing the terrible news, Ada had swayed in shock and gone weak at the knees.

'Your husband's young, he's strong, I'm quite sure he'll cope.'

But seeing her darling man so weak and wasted in his rumpled bed had brought a rush of tears to Ada's blue eyes, and, swallowing hard, she'd hurried to Jamie's bedside.

'My darling,' she whispered.

Jamie's eyes fluttered open and a weak smile had creased his haggard face.

'Sweetheart,' he murmured incredulously.

Quickly pulling up a chair, she'd positioned it as close to his bedside as she could.

'It's so wonderful to see you, dearest,' she'd blurted out, taking hold of his good right hand. 'I've been so worried,' she confessed.

'I'm sorry, my darling.'

'Don't be sorry,' she quickly said. 'You're home; safe and sound. I can look after you now.'

'Can you?' he asked. 'Can you really?' Struggling to raise himself higher on his pillows, he'd given his wife a long, level look. 'I'm not the man I was,' he said bluntly. 'How can I practise medicine with only one hand?' he demanded with angry tears in his eyes.

Seeing the look of abject despair on his face, Ada answered with renewed vigour. 'Jamie, *of course* you can practise. I'm not saying it will be easy, at least not to start with, but you still have your right hand, the one you favour and write with. As the wound heals, we might be able to consider the possibility of a prosthesis,' she said with growing confidence. 'The medical advances in that area are improving all the time. Let's face it, darling,' she added bluntly, 'many men like you will need similar treatment when this wretched war is over.'

Her glowing eyes, brimming with hope and determination, had brought a smile to Jamie's face, which visibly relaxed in her presence.

'My lovely brave girl,' he'd sighed. 'Trust you to find a positive in a ghastly negative.'

They talked and talked until Ada saw Jamie's eyes droop with fatigue.

'Dearest, I'm going to let you get some rest,' she said softly.

The visitors' bell clanging out sent Ada packing, but not before she had promised to visit Jamie just as soon as she could – which she did as often as possible until Jamie was finally discharged.

Ada had driven her husband home one bright late winter afternoon, a day that was melodic with birdsong and vibrant with bobbing yellow early daffodils and snow-drops shining in the cottage gardens lining the roadside. From the passenger seat Jamie had gazed in rapture at the passing landscape.

'Sometimes,' he had admitted, 'I thought I would never see the mountains again. I used to say their names – Glaramara, High Stile, Catbells, Honister, Skiddaw, Sty Head – chant them like a rosary when I couldn't sleep. The naming of precious things always ended with you and Catherine. My entire world is right here in this beautiful valley.'

As they neared Mary Vale Cottage, Jamie's mood grew sombre. 'She won't know me,' he had said anxiously. 'I'll be a stranger walking into her life, claiming her mother's attention – how scary is that going to be for a baby?'

Ada, who had already considered this prospect, had an answer ready. 'You're right, darling, she won't know you, but really how many thousands of other babies know their fathers in wartime? We look at photographs of Daddy every night before bedtime,' Ada continued with a smile. 'We always say, "God bless Mama and Dada."'

'You talk about me when I'm not there with you?' he had asked in amazement.

'Oh, yes,' she had laughed in reply. 'Catherine might not know you, Jamie, but believe me she certainly knows your name!'

Catherine, standing on the path tugging at her mother's long glossy brunette hair, brought Ada back to reality.

'BAA-BAAA!' she chanted.

Popping babbling Catherine down on the ground, Ada extended her hand to her daughter.

'Let's go and see Farmer Arkwright's sheep, sweetheart.'

Holding tightly on to her mother, excited Catherine took a few wobbly steps.

'BAA-BAAA!' the little girl chuckled, as they made their way up the lane to the farm.

4. Back on the Job

Jamie's heart lifted now as he approached the familiar building of Mary Vale, its old brickwork bright in the morning sunshine, the gardens abundant with delphiniums, peonies and, best of all, fragrant roses in abundance everywhere; and, beyond the rolling green lawn, the marsh and the vast stretch of the sea. Inhaling breaths of sweet fresh air that carried the tang of sea-salt on the breeze, Jamie smiled at the gambolling lambs in Farmer Arkwright's fields. Only the other day he had leant on the drystone wall with Catherine in his arms and together they had watched the lambs frisk and play around the reclining mothers, who occasionally bleated to their young if they strayed too far. Stopping briefly to stare up at the ever rising hills which rolled north, Jamie promised himself a good long walk on the fells on his first day off. Passing Cartmel Woods, Jamie heard the distant cackle of a green woodpecker followed by the ratcheting sound of a busy great spotted woodpecker hammering at tree trunks in search of worms and insects.

Turning his thoughts firmly to the job in hand, Jamie recalled Ada's warm but firm words. 'The sooner you're back working at the coal face, using your medical skills and helping women in need, the better you'll feel.'

'Darling Ada,' he said out loud.

As ever, his wife was right: he could do this work and he would do it well.

The first person he met was Sister Mary Paul, who bustled him into the hall, talking nineteen to the dozen.

'Oh, Doctor, it's wonderful to have you back among us.'

Though he had seen the old nun several times since his return home, Jamie nevertheless enjoyed her enthusiastic welcome.

'Morning, Sister Mary Paul.'

'Come along, then, follow me,' she said, as she headed off down a corridor.

Though Jamie knew his way around both the Home and the hospital, he allowed Sister Mary Paul to guide him on to the wards, where he found Matron and the glamorous new Sister.

'Good morning, Doctor,' Matron enthused. 'Let me introduce you to Sister Renee Short, recently arrived from London.'

No wilting violet, Renee gave Jamie a bold stare, taking in his tall physique, broad shoulders and strikingly good-looking face. Surprised by her directness, Jamie cast an almost shy glance at her pale elegant face, dominated by stunning green eyes and jet-black curly hair that escaped in tendrils from her starched cap.

'Hello,' he said, and he extended a hand to her.

Shaking his hand, Renee smiled widely, revealing perfectly white teeth. 'Pleased to meet you, Doctor,' she responded.

'Your coat is washed and ready for you in your office,' Matron added. 'And your patient list is on your desk.'

'Righty-ho,' Jamie said briskly. 'Give me a minute to fetch my coat, then I'll be with you.'

The morning round went well and proved to be both interesting and informative. In the post-natal ward Jamie made the acquaintance of a young woman who was recovering from a Caesarean delivery and another who was suffering from an intra-uterine infection. In the ante-natal ward Jamie examined a nervous young woman in the early stages of labour. Promising to return to check on her progress, Jamie popped into the nursery, where Dora was thrilled to see him.

'All bouncing bonny babies,' she announced, as she tucked the baby she had just changed back into his little crib, where he promptly fell fast asleep. 'They're a lot smaller than your little Catherine is these days,' she added.

Gazing at the rows of pristine white canvas cots containing the latest arrivals, Jamie shook his head in disbelief. 'I can't imagine my daughter was ever this small,' he said.

'Indeed, she was,' Dora exclaimed.

'With a healthy appetite too,' Matron added.

Seeing Sister Renee looking slightly bored by their affectionate exchange about his daughter, Jamie changed the subject. 'Anything to report, Nurse Dora?'

'No, not at the moment, Dr Reid,' she answered in professional mode. 'Though it's good to have you on call again, and close by too if we do need advice.'

'Don't hesitate to get in touch,' Jamie answered with a winning smile.

After they had finished the rounds, Jamie hurried to his office, where his patient list was laid out on the polished desk. A gentle knock on the door heralded Sister Mary Paul, bearing a tray with a pot of coffee on it and slices of fresh bread spread with a scraping of Mary Vale Farm butter.

'You'll need this before you start on your list,' she said with a knowing smile and laid the tray on the desk.

'You are an angel, Sister!' he exclaimed.

Blushing in delight, Mary Paul chatted on. 'It's a mix of chicory coffee, but the milk's fresh and the bread's warm, it'll get you through the morning; then there's a nice mince-and-onion pie for lunch, and jelly and custard too.'

'You're spoiling me,' he teased.

Sister Mary Paul gave him a critical look. 'You need building up, Doctor,' she said firmly.

'Looks like I've come to the right place, then,' Jamie replied. 'There's no better kitchen in the North-West than yours, dear Mary Paul.'

The most difficult part of the day was lunchtime, when, after seeing quite a number of patients in his morning surgery, Jamie finally met the rest of the residents. It was clear the second he entered the dining room that word had got around about the new doctor. No matter how polite the residents tried to be, averting their eyes, trying not to stare too obviously at his wounded limb, Jamie knew exactly what they were all thinking. Recalling Ada's words about how he had never given in to weakness throughout his polio-crippled childhood, Jamie spoke to himself firmly. 'If I could fight prejudice at ten years old, I can certainly fight it as a grown man.' Smiling more confidently than he actually felt, he took his place at the large dining table and, turning to his neighbour with a charming smile, said, 'I'm Dr Reid, I don't believe we've met yet.' He extended his right arm and shook the nervous girl's hand. 'Tell me,' he continued amiably, 'when is your baby due?'

After Sister Mary Paul, assisted by young Sister Theresa, had served the surprisingly hearty dinner, given rationing, the atmosphere relaxed, and, as the residents' chatter filled the room, Jamie began to relax too. It was going to be all right, he thought. They seemed like a good bunch of girls, who would be grateful for non-judgemental care and professional medical advice, both of which he could give. Finishing his dinner (as the midday meal was always called), Jamie lit up a cigarette and took a stroll around Mary Vale's garden, which was brimming with early-summer blooms. The climbing roses that draped the old red-brick building were heavy with buds that would flower up until October, if he remembered rightly. Heavily perfumed, dense creamy pink petals blended with a white rambling rose that threaded its way all along the gable end of the Home. The flowerbeds were ablaze with all the brightest summer flowers, banks of heady lilies, alongside pink peonies, lavender and trailing geranium. Flanking them was a blaze of stunning blue blooms, tall larkspur, delphinium and agapanthus with golden crimson honeysuckle lacing the old walls that provided shelter from the often cold winds blowing off the Irish Sea.

Sitting on a garden bench, smoking a second cigarette Jamie closed his eyes in order to inhale the combined summer fragrances that surrounded him.

'My God,' Jamie thought. 'This is a world away from the Front I was rescued from.'

Only a year ago he had been on the Front Line in Tobruk, attending to men who cried out for water when there was none to give. The Germans had made sure they cut off the supply, not just of water but of food too, and vital supplies for the hospital stores. Their biggest problem in the raging heat had been the flies and the desert dust, both of which contaminated any food they had and were a serious cause of infection in open or healing wounds. All of that notwithstanding, the camaraderie he had shared with his colleagues out there was something Jamie would never forget: brave men and women who worked as a team, supporting each other in good times and bad. Smiling to himself, he recalled announcing the birth of his daughter to the unit, who had sung 'For He's a Jolly Good Fellow' before wetting the baby's head using a brew mixed with some brandy filched from the medical stores.

Things had certainly improved since he was discharged: only recently the Germans and Italians had surrendered in North Africa, which had made Jamie cheer for joy. Montgomery had done a first-class job of not only rallying his Eighth Army but retraining them too, so they could take on the might of Rommel's disciplined troops. Inevitably guilt filled Jamie when he thought of his comrades; it felt all wrong for him to be well fed and smoking a cigarette in a peaceful English garden when men and women were still battling in Europe and the Far East for his freedom. Thinking of them and the sacrifices they were making, Jamie vowed that he would do his absolute best for the Mary Vale residents.

'They might not be fighting on the Front Line, but they carry a great burden and need all the help they can get,' Jamie thought, as he stubbed out his cigarette and returned to his patients on the wards.

5. Stella Isles

To the strains of Joe Loss's orchestra on *Workers' Playtime*, Stella Isles scrutinized the sheets of pastry she had just rolled out and wondered if it would be enough for ten huge mince, onion and carrot pies. Knowing that the workers in the munitions factory had colossal appetites, Stella started to roll the pastry even thinner. Laying the pastry, made with leftover dripping and thick white lard, into the large trays she had already greased, Stella ladled the cooled meat mixture, enhanced with gravy browning and wild herbs gathered locally from the moors, into the pastry cases, then very carefully laid a pastry crust on top of each pie. After nipping the crust tight around the edges of the tin, Stella cut a couple of slits in the lids to let out the steam, then popped the lot into the vast industrial cookers which dominated her kitchen.

That done, Stella, hot from the heat of the oven, wiped her brow, then surveyed her empire with a steely critical eye. Before being conscripted to the Dove Munitions Factory on Pendle Moor in Lancashire, she had been a cook in a cotton mill in Burnley, so was more than qualified to cook for hundreds of people, working in shifts around the clock. The big difference these days was that Stella now cooked using only rationed food, which was quite a challenge. Her natural flair for imaginative cooking was certainly cramped, but she always tried her best to add a little something extra, even if it was only a sprinkle of any fresh herbs she could get her hands on or a dash of mustard. But no matter how hard she tried with extra seasoning and good stock, it was nothing like the cooking she did before the war.

In those days, good-quality beef, mince and stewing steak, ham shanks, neck end of lamb, pork sausages, liver, tripe and bacon were always delivered fresh on the day they were served. Stella gave a little sigh; it had been so empowering to handle good produce and create quality meals. These days things couldn't have been more different. One egg, two ounces of tea and butter, an ounce of cheese, eight ounces of sugar, four ounces of bacon and four ounces of margarine was the rationed amount of food per person per week, but when you were feeding hungry workers doing tough manual jobs three times a day around the clock, there never seemed enough to go around. Stella thought of the war-time slogan she had recently heard on the radio: 'Go easy with bread, try potatoes instead.' That was all well and good, provided you had potatoes, Stella thought wryly.

'Swings and roundabouts – and a lot of imagination,' thought Stella as she checked the corned-beef hash, which was the alternative on the menu to the meat pie. Leaving Nellie, her young assistant, to keep an eye on the pies and get on with the cabbage and sprouts that would accompany the lunchtime meal, Stella set about making the pudding, apple fritters, a regular favourite with all the workers. As she whisked the vat of batter, Stella allowed her mind to wander: a works dance was scheduled for this coming weekend and the canteen, with all the tables and chairs shoved back to the wall, would be the venue. A bar would be set up, not manned by Stella, who was intent on dancing the night away, but she would pre-bake some pasties and mushy peas that could be served up at some point in the evening.

As the music on the big old radio in the canteen boomed out Glenn Miller's 'Little Brown Jug', Stella's feet beat to the rhythm of the drums and saxophone. Next to cooking, dancing was her passion. It came naturally to her: the minute she heard an orchestra strike up, Stella could barely stand still. In fact, when nobody was looking, Stella would turn the radio on full belt and swing around the canteen, dancing to the latest popular songs. Duke Ellington's 'Take the A Train', the wonderful Andrews Sisters singing 'Boogie Woogie Bugle Boy' and Glenn Miller's 'Chattanooga Choo Choo' and 'String of Pearls' were her absolute favourites, but she loved Tommy Dorsey too, and the Ink Spots. And who could resist Frank Sinatra's silky seductive tones?

As far as Stella was concerned, there was nothing in the world to beat that magic moment when she took to the dance-floor. Under the shimmering light of the twirling silver orbs and the roving spotlight, it was possible to forget, if only for five minutes, the horrors of war. The lives that had been lost, the families broken and the never-ending heartbreak briefly receded in that dreamy, gilded moment of spinning around the dance-floor lost in the beauty of the music.

'Shall I wipe down tables?' Nellie called out loudly, interrupting Stella's romantic thoughts.

Startled from her reverie, Stella gave a quick nod before continuing to daydream about the forthcoming dance. The Canadian airmen were already a presence in the area, but now there were Americans too and all the female hearts were racing. Stella had never seen an American, never mind an American serviceman, in her whole life, but she had heard that they were bigger, taller, stronger and bonnier than lads at home. Apparently, it was down to all the good grub they'd been fed most of their lives, as opposed to her generation, born during the depression and growing up in poverty. Stella had heard that the Yanks were often great dancers who could sing, jive and bebop till they dropped.

'My kinda guy,' Stella said, recalling a line from an American movie she had recently watched.

Yelling loudly, Nellie once again intruded into her wandering thoughts. 'Pies are out.'

'Righty-ho,' Stella replied, and she hurried back to the steamy ovens, having run out of time to dream about American servicemen.

When Saturday dawned, Stella woke up with a spring in her step. Usually weekends were no different from the weekdays in the munitions factory: food had to be served and cleared, then more prepared; it was an unrelenting cycle. But not today, Stella thought.

'Tonight, I'm going dancing!' she chanted out loud, as she almost skipped to work. With breakfast over – tea and

toast with a scraping of marg accompanied by the manda-
tory two or three cigarettes, which most workers seemed
to need to kick-start their day – Stella quickly opened the
canteen windows in order to get rid of the cloud of dense
smoke the workers left in their wake. Keen to get her work
done so she could go home and prepare for the dance,
Stella set about the midday meal: corned-beef rissoles,
veg of the season, right now spring greens and mashed
parsnips, followed by an adapted recipe for spotted dick
and a very weak version of custard. Fortunately, weekend
tea-times were kept simple: usually an assortment of
meat- and fish-paste sandwiches, followed by some sort
of cake – this week Nellie had made a fresh batch of
Brown Betties in order to use up all the stale breadcrumbs
that had mounted up during the week.

Leaving her young assistant in charge of the cake-
making, Stella swiftly assembled a batch of pasties, the
refreshments to be served with mushy peas during the
dance interval. After rolling out vast sheets of pastry which
she cut into circles, then filled with mince and onion (made
the day before), Stella simmered the dry peas that she had
soaked overnight in salted water on the hob. Finally, when
all her chores were done, she removed her pinafore and
the turban that held back her long, golden-red hair.

'I'm off; don't forget the sandwiches for tea,' she told
Nellie, who was slicing the Brown Betties into neat little
squares. 'Are you coming to the dance tonight?' she asked.

Nellie shook her head. 'No, mi mam's properly poorly.
I promised I'd get the bus into Manchester and spend a
bit of time with her,' Nellie replied.

'See you on Monday, then,' Stella said with a cheery wave.

Back in her digs, a cramped little prefab on the munitions complex that housed herself and her best friend, Doreen, Stella had the luxury of the place to herself while Doreen worked her shift. Slipping into a warmish shallow bath (a pleasant change from bathing in somebody else's scummy bathwater), Stella lathered off the smell of the kitchen and washed her long red hair too. After wrapping a towel around her dripping body, she dashed into the bedroom, mercifully not as cold as it had been in the arctic winter months, to dry herself down and brush out her unruly curls. The mirror over the chest-of-drawers reflected back her flawless creamy-white young skin, and a face dominated by large, pale-blue dreamy eyes, and a wide, generous mouth. Tall and slim, with hips like a boy's, a narrow waist and small pert breasts, Stella rarely had the chance to show off her young body, shrouded as she often was in white kitchen overalls. But not tonight, she thought excitedly, tonight she would dress up in the hope that she would meet a handsome Yank who would hold her in his arms and swing her round the dance-floor until dawn broke over Pendle Moor.

By evening the factory's canteen, freshly swept, with all the tables and chairs pushed back against the walls, was transformed into a temporary ballroom: huge silver diamanté globes twirled from various points in the ceiling, reflecting the ever-changing glowing colours of the roving spotlight. The subdued romantic lighting, combined with the swing band tuning up – the swish of the snare drum, the mellow sounds of trumpet and saxophone and the tinkling piano – immediately set Stella's pulse racing. Catching sight of her friends at the makeshift bar, Stella hurried over to join them.

Handing her a shandy, Doreen, who had just finished her late shift and changed into her dancing glad rags in the ladies' toilet, said, 'Thank God! The Yanks have landed,' nodding towards the opposite side of the room.

Sipping her shandy, Stella gave a surreptitious glance at the young Americans in their distinctive smart uniforms, relaxed, sitting at tables or standing, chatting and smoking.

Throwing a look at the factory's male workers, who were gathered in a dour clump on the other side of the room, Doreen continued: 'Our lot don't look very happy with the competition. No wonder,' she chuckled, 'the Yanks are a lot better-looking, taller too.'

Though she too was struck by the difference in stature and style as well as how damn healthy the Americans looked in comparison with the Brits, Stella replied, 'To be fair, they were probably brought up on a better diet than us.'

'That would explain the teeth too: they dazzle from a hundred yards,' Doreen joked.

'Stop eyeing them up like prize race-horses,' Stella giggled.

'They're doing just the same to us,' Doreen pointed out. 'Not shy there, eyeing up the local talent.'

Everybody was waiting for the music to strike up and the dancing to begin, and when it did there was a surge

43

across the floor as the American servicemen converged on the munitions girls before they could be snapped up by the local lads. As a foxtrot sounded out, Stella's sparkling bright eyes locked on to one of the tallest men; laughing and confident, he was walking straight towards her with the ease of somebody who knew exactly what he wanted and was determined to get it. As he approached, Stella saw that his short, cropped hair was golden-blond, and his tanned handsome face contrasted vividly with his golden-brown hazel eyes. Standing before Stella, he politely extended a hand, then, with a smart bow, he asked in the sexiest voice she had ever heard in her life, 'Ma'am, could I have the pleasure of the next dance?'

Overcome with nerves, Stella found herself simply unable to speak; in answer to his request, she simply laid her hand in his, causing a sensation almost like an electric shock to zip through her entire body. Cradling her slender waist, the stranger literally spun Stella on to the dance-floor, where he caught her smoothly in his arms and held her firmly as they glided under the glittering lights. Responding instinctively to his expert dance moves and trusting his timing, Stella lost herself to the music and the moment. As the rhythm slowed and changed to a dreamy waltz number, Stella closed her eyes and swayed in sync with her partner, abandoning herself briefly to the heady sense of romance and escapism. When there was a break in the music, Stella opened her eyes as if from a dream and focused on the man who had swept her off her feet.

'Hi,' he said in that soft drawling voice that made her

heart skip a beat. 'I apologize for not having introduced myself before. I'm Bill Austin, serving officer in the United States Army Air Forces,' he said, and clipped his heels and smilingly saluted.

Feeling suddenly shy and self-conscious, Stella replied, 'Pleased to meet you. I'm Stella Isles, and I work here.'

'No way!' he mocked. 'You are way too pretty-looking to be building bombs.'

'I'm not a Bomb Girl,' she explained. 'I'm the canteen cook.'

'Then I'm sure you'll know where we can find us a drink,' he joked.

Just as they were approaching the bar, the band struck up with 'In the Mood' and everybody on the dance-floor went wild, so they abandoned their trip to the bar.

'This is my kind of dancing,' Bill cried, as once again he caught her up and whisked her into a jive such as Stella had never danced before; the man was just *sensational*.

Skilfully guiding her through the steps while keeping perfect time with the music, he turned her from left to right, caught her lightly only to spin and turn her again and again. Circling the floor, they moved faster and faster, with Bill always taking the lead. When he snatched her up, she gasped in amazement; then, when his strong arms lifted her and turned her in a full circle before lightly putting her back on the ground, Stella laughed in sheer delight. They romped through five jazz pieces, including Stella's absolute favourite – the Andrews Sisters' 'Boogie Woogie Bugle Boy'. Later, Stella, limp and breathless, needed a break.

'I'll get you that drink,' Bill volunteered, as he joined the line up by the bar.

Starving hungry from all her physical exertions, Stella took the opportunity to pop into her kitchen, where she helped herself to a pile of pasties, which she and Bill wolfed back.

'Did you really make these?' he asked in amazement.

'It's an old-fashioned Lancashire recipe, nothing fancy,' she told him.

'They're so rich and flavoursome,' he said, and sank his perfect teeth into the warm crumbly pastry. 'I don't think I've ever had a pasty in my whole life,' he added.

'Then you don't know what you're missing,' she joked.

After they had both refreshed themselves and in Stella's case drunk a pint of cold water, he suggested that they take a stroll during the interval.

'To cool down,' he said.

Leaving the factory behind them, they walked out into wild countryside, which on a warm summer evening was still not entirely in darkness. Squeaking bats zipped around the old barns and outbuildings, foxes barked across the valley, and owls hunted in the nearby wood.

'This is beautiful,' Bill sighed, as he leant back against an ancient drystone wall to gaze up at the twinkling stars that were just beginning to peek out through the scudding clouds.

'Come here,' he said, extending his arms to Stella, who needed no second bidding.

Shy as she was, she simply couldn't wait to feel his strong arms around her, and, yet again, his touch on her

46

skin sent a spine-tingling sensation sizzling through her body. Though Stella was well above the average female height, Bill towered over her, and the shoulder she was leaning against was hard and muscular. Peering down at her pale face nuzzled against the cloth of his uniform, he picked up a strand of her golden Titian-red hair and let it fall silkily through his fingers before tilting her chin and staring into her pale sky-blue eyes.

'The second I saw you walk into the room, with your hair tumbled all around your shoulders, I knew I had to dance with you,' he gushed. Picking up another handful of hair, he buried his face in it. 'I've never seen hair like this,' he exclaimed.

Overcome with the pleasure of his compliments, Stella smiled. 'It's the result of my Irish heritage.'

'So now you're telling me you're a dancing Irish colleen?' he teased.

'More of a Lancashire lass!' she corrected him.

Pulling slightly away in order to look up into his face, Stella asked, 'Tell me about you? Where do you come from?'

'Seattle. That's on the West Coast of the States. I live by the ocean, the Pacific to be precise.'

Places like the Pacific, the West Coast and Seattle, Stella had only read about.

'Tell me more,' she urged, fascinated.

To her delight Bill didn't hesitate, in fact, he seemed eager to talk of home.

'Seattle's a wonderful place,' he said passionately. 'The sea on one side and the Cascade Mountain Range on the other. In the winter we ski; in the summer we swim. Dad's a fisherman; I grew up with fishing and joined the business just as soon as I left school. The business is downtown near the docks, where our boats are moored, but we live in the city.'

'It sounds amazing,' she exclaimed.

'It really is amazing,' he agreed. 'But this' – he turned to survey the moor – 'is altogether another country, soft and wooded, wild and rugged all at the same time.'

Stella turned to take in his view of the moor, illuminated by a half-moon that was slowly rising over the highest peaks. She had loved this landscape from childhood, but, seeing it for the first time through his eyes, she appreciated it more than ever. Hearing strains of music floating out on the night air, Stella looked up. 'Shall we go back in?'

'Not yet,' he whispered, bent his face close to hers and kissed her long and deeply.

Bill's touch had been electrifying, but his kiss was simply explosive. As her lips parted to his, Stella felt weak with desire: the touch of his stubbly chin against her pale cheek, the texture of his golden-blond hair as she ran a hand through it, the line of his high cheekbones enhanced by the slanting moonlight – all took the breath out of her body.

Slowly pulling away, Bill looked like he too was coming up for air. 'Wow! Lady, you pack a punch,' he murmured; then, cradling her smiling face, his lips sought hers once more.

Stella had no idea how long they were outside, utterly lost in their kissing and cuddling; in the background she could hear jives, waltzes and foxtrots playing out, adding a wonderful atmosphere of music to their embraces. Nevertheless, they eventually made it back to the dance-floor, locked in each other's arms, circling to the dreamy tones of 'I'll Never Dance Again Till I Dance with You'. As the music faded and the lights went down, the couples on the floor held the moment, hardly daring to move in case they shattered the magic. Clinging on to each other, Stella and Bill shared the last kiss before the bright lights came up

'Beautiful Stella, my evening star,' Bill whispered. 'When can I see you again?'

Winding her long slender arms around his neck and standing on her tiptoes so she could reach his lips, Stella softly replied, 'Soon please, very, *very* soon.'

6. Domesticity

As the summer progressed, Jamie and Ada enjoyed sharing their working arrangements.

'It's just like the old days,' Ada recalled.

'When I fell in love with beautiful Sister Ada with the flashing eyes and devastating smile,' Jamie replied with a cheeky wink.

Because of Catherine's sunny nature and offers of help from friends and colleagues, the pair could be fairly flexible. If they were needed for an urgent consultation while they were on babysitting duty, they had their choice of several minders, who in Catherine's world were called Sissy Merry, Sissy Ann and Sissy Trees! When Jamie and Ada weren't working, they took advantage of the long summer days, when they went for walks, with Catherine perched on her daddy's shoulders or sitting in her pram, waving at the gambolling lambs and burbling at the Muscovy ducks clustered around the farm pond.

'She is wonderful!' Jamie announced at least three times a day.

In the adoring stakes, Ada wasn't far behind her besotted husband, but she always tried her best to keep a balance.

'She's a good little girl,' she agreed.

'And very clever too,' Jamie insisted. 'She notices

everything – birds in the treetops, new flowers in the hedgerow, she even pointed to one of Farmer Arkwright's cows the other day and went "Moo".'

Ada, who loved seeing her husband revelling in his daughter's progress, smiled indulgently. 'She's always loved animals,' she replied, as they walked through the fields towards the beck, across which stepping-stones had been thoughtfully placed to provide a short cut to the forest on the other side of the meadow. Smiling, she added, 'But then she was born next door to a farm, so she might think the sheep and cattle are part of the family!'

'You couldn't wish for a better start in life than to be surrounded by all of this,' Jamie said, as he carefully lifted Catherine out of her pram and dangled her little pink feet in the clear shallow stream. At the touch of the cool water Catherine shrieked in delight, and, safe in her father's hands, she confidently splashed her feet.

'Splish, splash, splish, splash,' Jamie chuckled, while his giggling daughter bounced up and down.

At moments like these, caught up in their love of their child and the natural beauty of the forest and fells all around them, Jamie and Ada experienced exactly the same stabbing sense of guilt. What right had *they* to be so happy, so fulfilled, so content, when most of their generation were battling it out in Europe, North Africa and the Far East? Admittedly Jamie, losing a hand in combat, had certainly done his bit for his country, but the pay-off was that he now lived a life safe in the bosom of his family, in a corner of England that had always been heaven on earth to him. As for Ada, she constantly thought of the women, like herself only a year ago, desperately waiting for good news, or any news, in fact, of their beloved. How many thousands, millions of wives, mothers, sisters, lovers, had not experienced the joy of seeing their loved ones return home alive and safe? But, Ada firmly reminded herself, the war was going well in Italy, and that was something the entire nation could celebrate. The Allies' bombing of Rome and Palermo, followed by the arrest of Benito Mussolini, had to be a sign that the tide was finally turning against Hitler, who earlier in the year had ordered the brutal liquidation of the ghettos in Poland, where over half a million Jews had died. The shocking news had prompted the nation to wonder what other horrors Himmler and his Nazis thugs might have inflicted on the Jews, what other atrocities were yet to be revealed?

There was one niggle in their working life, which Jamie and Ada occasionally discussed, and that was Sister Renee. Both had experienced an increasing feeling of disquiet when it came to her professional behaviour. She was bright and breezy enough, nobody could doubt that, and the majority of the residents responded to her cheeriness, but slowly, like water dripping on stone, Ada and Jamie (in their own separate ways) began to worry. As far as Ada was concerned, it started when Dora mentioned the breathing and exercise classes that Renee had taken over from Ada.

'Don't worry, I'm familiar with the routine,' Renee had assured Ada. 'We ran a similar course at St Thomas's, which I assisted with.' Renee had, in fact, exaggerated her role, which had consisted only of her escorting pregnant patients across the site to the exercise area, where she watched the proceedings, before escorting her patients back to the ward.

Expressing her relief and gratitude, Ada had taken Renee at her word, but sometime later, while mopping down the sluice room with Dora, her friend had asked, 'When you were in charge of the exercise classes, did your ladies ever complain of bad back pains?'

Ada paused before she answered the question. 'Not that I recall, and anyway I wouldn't have been happy if my classes resulted in my ladies suffering back pain,' she reflected. 'The entire purpose of all the exercises I used was about improving breathing techniques useful in child-birth. Nothing strenuous or pain-inducing, which would entirely defeat the purpose of the exercises.'

Dora cocked a quizzical eyebrow. 'I thought so,' she muttered grimly.

'Why?' suddenly anxious, Ada enquired. 'What's wrong?'

Dora looked awkward. 'Well, little Polly mentioned she had a terrible back pain after her class,' Dora explained. 'She came to see me because she was worried. I gave her a hot-water bottle and told her to take it easy at the next class. I only started worrying when another lass turned up shortly after with the same complaint.'

Ada's hand flew to her mouth. 'That shouldn't happen, Dora,' she cried.

'The upshot, lovie, is most of the girls have stopped attending the classes, which, as far as I'm concerned, is a bit of a relief, given the way things were going.' Looking Ada in the eye, Dora added pointedly, 'They didn't drop out when you were in charge.'

Though she hated the idea of spying on a colleague, Ada made it her business to find out first hand what exactly was happening in Renee's ante-natal classes. Knowing they were held after dinner every afternoon in the garden when it was fine, Ada chose her moment to observe Renee in action, and what she saw put the fear of God in her. Determined not to make her presence known, Ada watched Renee teaching the few residents that still attended the class from certain vantage points in the garden.

'Oh God . . .' she sighed as the class unfolded.

Renee didn't teach and explain, soothe and inspire – she just went hell for leather as though she were on some sort of Outward Bound course. From where she was secretly observing, Ada could see the poor girls grimacing as they tried to follow Renee's instructions.

'Hold your legs up just a bit longer – go on, you can do it, good for your tummy muscles.'

'It hurts, Sister,' one girl wailed.

'Go on, push yourself,' Renee urged.

'OW! OUCH!' the same girl exclaimed.

'All right, all right,' Renee quickly called out. 'Take a break and we'll start again.'

Seeing how badly it was going, Ada simply couldn't stand by and do nothing a minute longer. Hurrying forward, pretending she was just breezing by, she stopped to smile at the residents. 'Hello there,' she waved.

'Lovely day for exercise,' she said, as she smiled up at the bright-blue summer sky.

This group of girls had never known Ada's teaching techniques and moaned out loud at her words.

'Bloody route march,' one poor resident muttered.

'I thought these classes were supposed to be relaxing,' another scoffed. 'Mi stomach's aching so much I feel like mi waters might break any moment now.'

Feeling panic rising in her, Ada feigned a smile at Renee, who waved her hand in a cheery 'Don't be silly!' dismissive gesture.

'It's all about limbering up for childbirth,' she announced energetically. 'The tougher you are, the stronger you'll be when the time comes.'

Struggling to their feet one by one, the girls waddled off indoors, leaving the two nurses alone on the sunny lawn. Worried that she might appear intrusive but also desperate for the safety of the residents, Ada said carefully, 'Is it wise to be quite so strenuous?'

Renee gave a bright beaming smile. 'I'd say so,' she replied confidently. 'It doesn't suit some of the feebler residents, but the tough girls always come back for more.'

Wondering how she could put an end to the classes before serious damage was done, Ada hurried off to have a word with Dora. In the empty delivery room, behind closed doors, she whispered, 'Renee's classes have GOT to stop.'

Dora gave a curt nod. 'The sooner the better, I'd say,' she declared.

Putting her head in her hands, Ada gave a low groan. 'Oh, WHY did I ever ask her to do the wretched classes in the first place?'

'Because somebody had to and you thought you could trust her,' Dora reminded Ada. Seeing her friend's desperate expression, she continued, 'Look, why don't I quietly have a word with the few remaining girls in the class?'

'You mustn't put your foot in it, Dora!' Ada cried.

Dora gave a wry smile. 'It wouldn't be the first time.'

'Be serious, please,' poor Ada begged.

'I could just suggest that if they weren't, well, enjoying the classes, they could bow out. I could even furnish them with a few polite excuses.'

'Like what?'

'Oh, stuff like, it's nearly my time, I've had a bit of a bleed, I'm going to the lavatory a lot,' Dora suggested.

'But what if Renee finds out?' Ada continued to fret. 'I would take it very personally if everybody in my class suddenly dropped out.'

Shaking her head, Dora replied, 'Sister Renee's skin is as thick as a rhino's; mark my words, she'll take it in her stride.'

And to Ada's astonishment that's exactly what happened. Not long after her furtive conversation with Dora in the delivery room, Renee waltzed up to Ada on the ward, where she jubilantly announced, 'Looks like my classes have come to an end; my ladies tell me they're quite happy to stop now that they've got the exercises under their belt. Must be the way I teach, fast and furious,' she joked.

Stunned, Ada couldn't believe that Renee thought finishing the classes so abruptly was something to be pleased about. 'It's a shorter course than usual,' she said cautiously.

Renee shrugged. 'Doesn't trouble me, just so long as

they got the drift of things and remember the routine when it comes to delivering.'

Torn between relief and incredulity, Ada was rendered almost speechless. Standing watching her colleague breeze off down the ward, Ada shook her head as she thought, 'She just doesn't get it; she *really* doesn't get it.'

7. Dobb End

When the local bus dropped Lillian off in Rosthwaite village, she could barely believe her eyes. Greystone walls flanked narrow winding lanes that led seemingly nowhere. Before the bus driver (lugubriously puffing on a smelly pipe) pulled away from the stop where Lillian had disembarked, blind panic gripped her. 'He must have dropped me off in the wrong spot,' she thought. This place simply couldn't be her destination.

'Where's Dobb End?' she cried, before she lost sight of the bus driver, her only link with civilization.

Pointing to a narrow alleyway, the driver called out, 'Down yonder snicket.'

'Snicket?' she mumbled.

'Yon ginnel?'

'Ginnel?'

God! Lillian didn't even understand the language he was using. Rolling his eyes as if she were a nincompoop, the driver yelled, 'Bloody yon alleyway.'

Then losing patience he pulled away, leaving Lillian, teetering in high-heeled suede court shoes and bearing two heavy suitcases (she had brought just about everything she possessed), to negotiate the narrow alley that was littered with fresh sheep droppings. At the end of it she emerged on to a farm track that wound up a slight rise to a farm-house; as she approached it, Lillian made out the sign on the gate, DOBB END. After making her way up the garden path, she knocked on the front door and, getting no reply, she knocked again, this time even louder. A dog barking loudly startled Lillian, who nervously glanced around, and saw a scruffy, grumpy-looking woman approaching.

'Nobody uses front door,' she barked.

Turning her back on Lillian, and certainly not offering to help with her luggage, the broad-hipped, untidy-looking woman led the way to the back door.

'Come on in,' the woman called over her shoulder.

Stepping over muddy boots cluttering the hallway, Lillian entered the kitchen, which was strewn with all sorts of clutter, from engine parts to rusty tools to animal feed. The vast kitchen table showed signs of a meal, which made Lillian's empty stomach rumble.

'You've missed dinner,' the woman told her. 'Your room's at the top of the stairs,' she added. 'You'll be sharing with three other lasses.'

Lugging her cases up a steep flight of stairs, Lillian stumbled into the bedroom, where she gasped in shock. Originally a bedroom that would have housed a double bed and wardrobe, it was now crammed with three ancient single iron bedsteads, while the fourth bed was simply a filthy-looking mattress that had been dumped on the floor. The sight of it and the smell of the sweaty clothes and dirty socks that were flung all over the room brought tears to Lillian's eyes.

'God help me,' she groaned, as she dropped her cases on to the floor. 'What a dump!'

By six o'clock Lillian, still wearing her smart travelling outfit, was starving. Tea was served when the other Land Girls arrived home, all wearing turbans and dungarees splattered with clods of mud. Sitting around the table, they introduced themselves to Lillian as Sal, Pat and Mo. When Mrs M, as the Land Girls referred to the farmer's wife, set the food on the table, they all but fell on the lamb hotpot that was dished up along with watery boiled cabbage and great slabs of hard bread.

'Ta, Mrs M,' the girls said dutifully, as they eyed the pot in hope of second helpings, which were not forthcoming.

Lillian, who was struggling to swallow the greasy lumps of fatty meat, pushed her serving of already congealing food towards the girls.

'I'm not hungry.'

'Ta,' they said again in unison, and wiped hunks of bread around their plates to mop up the gravy.

Upstairs in the privacy of their own room, the girls, lying flat on their backs on their beds, lit up cigarettes, at which point Lillian realized that the mattress on the floor was for her.

'Owd bitch,' Mo tittered as she blew smoke circles across the room. 'There was enough in the pot for seconds and another loaf cooling on the range.'

'She does well out of our ration coupons,' Sal grumbled. 'Watch out,' she warned Lillian. 'She'll have yours first thing tomorrow morning.'

Raising her head from the pillow she was propped up

against, Pat eyed up Lillian's short flippy black pleated skirt and her pretty cream silk blouse.

'I hope you've got a change of clothes in those suit-cases?' she enquired. 'Summat not so posh as what you're wearing now?'

'I've got some summer dresses, and skirts and jumpers,' Lillian replied.

'We wear fellas' dungarees,' Pat explained. 'There's a pile in't barn. I'll sort out a pair for you tomorrow before we start work in't fields.'

'Thanks,' said Lillian; then, eyeing the mattress, asked, 'Is there any bedding?'

'Only a blanket,' Mo replied, and threw an old grey army blanket across the room. 'When it's cold we all sleep together and pile coats on top of the blankets.'

Arranging the frayed blanket that smelt of horse muck on the mattress, Lillian cried in frustration, 'How do you stand it here? It's worse than prison.'

Sal shrugged. 'No choice: we're conscripted women. If we tried running away, we'd only be brought back or sent somewhere even worse than this hell-hole.'

Mo, who was a little dumpling of a girl, gave a throaty giggle. 'If you think this is bad, wait till you meet Mr M, Wilf, the farmer, randy old git. He'll have his hand up your skirt in no time.'

Getting into a more comfortable position on her bed, Pat gave a loud yawn. 'Time for shut eye.'

Gazing miserably out of the dirty window, which gave a smudgy view of the sun setting over the fells, Lillian exclaimed, 'Bed! It's only just going dark.'

Pat gave a shrug. 'There's nowt else to do round here,' she grunted. 'And we'll be up at five in the morning.'

'FIVE?' Lillian cried.

'Aye and in't fields by six, come wind, hail or shine,' Pat glumly concluded, before she turned her face to the wall and promptly fell asleep.

Lillian returned her gloomy gaze to the window, where the sky, now streaked red and gold from the slow-sinking sun, blazed briefly before it disappeared behind the mountain range. Only a week ago she had been in the Regal Cinema, on the back row with all the other amorous courting couples, watching *The Man Who Came to Dinner*. With Trevor's strong arms wrapped firmly around her, Lillian barely had time for the film – all she wanted was Trevor's lips on hers and his hand reaching for her breasts, which set her heart thumping. Within the space of a single week she had packed in her job, moved town and become a Land Girl, which she hoped by now Trevor would be aware of, after receiving the letter she had written in haste just before she left Blackpool. The memory of the velvety-dark picture house thick with cigarette smoke and loud with music accompanying the opening titles of the film rolling out on the big screen brought a lump to Lillian's throat.

Hurrying into the freezing cold bathroom, Lillian washed in the dirty cracked basin with taps that constantly dribbled rusty water. Shivering, she slipped on her nightdress, cleaned her teeth and brushed her lustrous long hair, which tomorrow would be wrapped in a turban stuffed on top of her head. Creeping back to the bedroom, she found her three room-mates still fully dressed, fast asleep and snoring.

Waking in the gloomy dawn light to the sound of heavy rain splattering the grimy window panes, Lillian shivered in her grim mattress bed, and, clutching the miserable blanket to her upper body, she tried unsuccessfully to arrange it around her cold legs and feet.

'God, it's supposed to be summertime, but I'm freezing,' she grumbled under her breath. 'I've got to get more bedding, or I'll die of pneumonia.'

'Wakey! Wakey!' Sal cried out from the other side of the room.

Breakfast was a heap of rock-hard bread smeared with white marg.

'This is the crap what's left over after the old bag has fed the hens,' Mo joked grimly, as she poured tea strong enough to strip paint into pint-pot mugs.

Later in the barn, struggling to get into the dungarees she had finally been given, Lillian got her first glimpse of Wilf, the farmer who had unbeknown to her been standing behind her, gazing raptly at her shapely bottom.

'Nice view,' he leered.

The sight of him eyeing her up made Lillian flush with embarrassment.

'You must be the new lass?'

Unable to speak, Lillian gave a curt nod. 'Bloody sight better-looking than t'others, who look like summat the cat dragged in on a dark night,' the farmer drawled. 'All set?'

Lillian gave another curt nod. 'Tek a mac,' the farmer

ordered, nodding to a row of coats and jackets dangling from hooks on the wall. 'You'll need it on't tractor.'

Shocked into finally talking, Lillian squeaked, 'TRAC-TOR? But I don't know how to drive!'

Seeing her startled expression, Wilf gave a throaty chuckle. 'Don't worry, lass – you soon will.'

8. Sister Renee Short

Renee closed her bedroom door and leant heavily against it. Christ, it had been a long day, a long week in fact, and she was desperate for a stiff drink. Grateful for her secret hoard of gin stashed away at the back of her wardrobe, Renee flung her starched white cap on to a chair, along with the belt that fitted tightly around her slim waist. Reaching into the wardrobe, she located the bottle of gin, a generous amount of which she poured into the water glass standing on her bedside table. Sighing with relief, she lay down on the bed and propped herself up against the pillows, gratefully sipping the strong spirit. After a few large mouthfuls Renee felt her body start to relax.

It had been her first week working alongside Dr Reid, and, handsome as he was, Renee kept at the forefront of her mind that he was her colleague's husband, a no-go area. In the past she had flirted with many good-looking doctors, married or otherwise, but this young man was definitely out of bounds. Playing around with Jamie Reid could cost Renee her job, she had firmly told herself the moment she had locked eyes with his. Never a wilting violet, she had instinctively held his gaze on introduction, but Dr Reid (being the uxorious gent that he was) had averted his eyes, sending out loud and clear the message: *I am a married man.*

'Well, at least we both know where we stand,' Renee muttered as she topped up her glass.

It was a good outcome, she thought; married men were the worst, especially doctors who these days rarely saw their wives and family after packing them off to the country for safekeeping. The ones she'd come across in London were unfaithful men, eager for swift, uncomplicated sex, always in a hurry and terrible fumblers – worldly Renee had known there were better fish to fry outside of St Thomas's Hospital. Even with a war on, London life was thrilling if you knew the right people, which she certainly did. There were shows, cabarets, new films out almost every week, plus the Ritz, Savoy and Connaught continued to serve excellent food and delicious wines – Renee was especially fond of the latter.

Renee, the only daughter of bons viveurs, had been brought up drinking wine (albeit diluted) from her father's excellent cellar, and a year in France perfecting her French after leaving school had enhanced her appreciation of a robust Bordeaux and a classic Chablis. She had developed a hard head for alcohol, which, once she started her training as a nurse, Renee had curtailed, drinking only on her days off, though occasionally after a really grim day she had been known to down a double gin before bedtime. That had been her little secret and it certainly hadn't hurt anybody, well, not until the awful accident that had nearly cost her her career.

After the incident she had made a clean break, immediately leaving St Thomas's Hospital, which she loved, and finding work elsewhere, far enough away to avoid news of her irresponsible behaviour making its way there. Using old references, Renee had applied for new positions and made a quick discreet exit from London. Still, it had to be said, she missed her friends and all the wild times they had enjoyed together, dancing till dawn and blotting out the horrors of war in what seemed like never-ending glasses of sparkling champagne. Leaning out of her bedroom window, Renee murmured, 'That kind of gallivanting would never happen here.'

Funny old Mary Vale was a far cry from London; it was like living on another planet compared to city life. Staring out at the vast full moon sailing out from behind a bank of dark wispy clouds, Renee breathed in the fresh night air. There were unquestionably perks to be had from living in a far-flung place like this, avoiding a full-blown scandal being top of the list. And the residents weren't bad; good girls, mostly young and ignorant, a few like Polly, scared to death of everything relating to their pregnancy, but, on the whole, they were sensible kids who accepted their fate and just got on with it.

The prospect of living next door to a convent had been the one thing that had nearly put Renee off applying for the post. Would they expect her to attend morning services, or get up in the middle of the night to recite the rosary? But, once she got used to the Home and the staff, Renee quickly realized how very warm and generous the nuns she worked alongside actually were; they smiled a lot, joked a lot and certainly cared a lot. Matron (Sister Ann) was a sweet smiling woman with the patience of a saint; in the short time that they had worked together

Renee had been impressed by Matron's obstetrics knowledge. Then there was sweet little Sister Theresa, who was a regular help in the kitchen and clearly a great favourite among the residents. In addition to completing her noviitiate, Sister Theresa was also in the process of training to be a midwife, and so far, Renee thought, she had the makings of a fine practitioner. Calm and experienced, she could soothe the most anxious patient with her gentle manner. Renee frequently wondered how a young nun could plumb the depths of human suffering as Sister Theresa did. It was Ada who in confidence told Renee something of Theresa's former life.

'Theresa fell pregnant when she was a young teenager; she came here to have her baby, then stayed on and eventually joined the Sisters in the convent. Her extraordinary gift for compassion comes from her own experience of pain and fear; it's from this she draws her strength too,' Ada explained. 'She is a wonderful nun and a wonderful nurse too,' she concluded.

Reaching out for the gin bottle, Renee limited herself to a small tot; she had had enough already, but, oh, she thought, it was nice to lie back and let her body go. Strenuous shifts hadn't been helped by Polly's constant snivelling, her fretting needlessly about one thing after another; then Ada having the cheek to question her about the relaxation classes that she had kindly volunteered to take on. Just the tiniest bit woozy, Renee mumbled, 'Honestly, you offer to do something as a favour, then get ticked off for not doing it the right way. Bloody nerve! But it has to be said,' Renee grudgingly conceded, 'Ada can handle Polly, which certainly eases my workload.'

Mumbling sleepily, Renee popped the gin bottle back in its hiding place.

'Watch your step with Ada,' she told herself. 'Behind that warm smile and those kind eyes there's a nurse who expects only the best from her team.' Shutting the wardrobe firmly, Renee set about getting ready for bed. 'I know her type, always on the high moral ground – I wouldn't want to get on the wrong side of her, that's for sure.'

The following morning Renee was up bright and early, joining the residents for a hearty breakfast of warm home-baked bread, a small amount of Mary Vale butter supplied by Farmer Arkwright from Mary Vale Farm and some of Sister Mary Paul's sugarless bitter-sweet gooseberry jam, all accompanied by strong hot tea poured from the big brown teapot that dominated the breakfast table. As always, the quiet chatter of the girls filled the room along with the sound of herring gulls wheeling on the incoming tide. After finishing her first Woodbine of the day, Renee pushed back her chair.

'Righty-ho, ladies,' she announced cheerfully, 'I'll be off to do my rounds.'

'Give my regards to the poor sods on the labour ward,' one perky girl joked. 'Rather them than me.'

Renee threw an appraising glance over the girl's swollen belly. 'Don't gloat, dear, it'll soon be your turn,' she reminded her patient.

'I wish somebody would just knock me on the head with a rolling pin when I go into labour and wake me up when it's all over,' the girl added.

Renee shot her a jolly smile. 'I'll do my best, dear, but you might have to supply the rolling pin!'

With her abundant hair pushed neatly under her starched Sister's cap and looking trim and shapely in her midwife uniform, Ada waited in the corridor for Sister Renee, who arrived smiling and breathless.

'Shall we start?' Ada asked brightly.

Their first patients, three women on the ante-natal ward who were all near their time, greeted them warmly.

'Morning ladies,' Ada said cheerily, as she and Renee took their temperatures and checked their pulses.

'You're doing well,' Renee said breezily to one of the women. 'Hopefully you'll be heading home very soon.'

Ada, knowing that the patient in question had been thrown out of her family home and had, so far, nowhere to go once she left Mary Vale, cringed at Renee's crass remark. Seeing the girl flush with embarrassment, she firmly said, 'Not too soon, dear, I'm sure you'll be with us for a bit longer.'

Seeing the exchange between Ada and the patient, Renee could have kicked herself and thought, 'Damn it, I haven't updated myself on her notes.' Sensing she had put her foot in it, Renee quickly reined back her comments. 'That's right,' she beamed. 'None of us are in a rush to see our girls go, are we, Sister Ada?'

At the end of the rounds, Renee tried to cover her

tracks. 'Sorry about that slip-up, Ada, I obviously missed something.'

Typically, Ada didn't beat about the bush. 'Yes, you did. The poor girl's dreading leaving Mary Vale because she's got no home to return to – it's all in the notes, Sister,' she added pointedly.

'Yes, as I said, I obviously missed something,' Renee apologized, flushing. 'Now, if you'll excuse me, I need to collect some instruments from the sterilizer.'

Looking busy and practical, Renee headed off to the sluice room, chiding herself for her carelessness. She really had to set aside time at the start and the end of every day to go through patients' notes; her obvious ignorance of a touchy situation had not gone down well. From now on, she told herself, she had better pay more attention to detail than to the gin bottle hidden away in the back of her wardrobe.

9. Land Girl

Nothing in Lillian's entire life could have prepared her for the work of a Land Girl. Arriving in the summer as she did, the list of jobs was unrelenting: sheep-shearing, hay-making, lamb-worming, and baling and carting straw were just some of the seasonal high-priority tasks she, Mo, Pat and Sal were expected to do. And all in the summer months, when it was either baking hot or pouring with rain. Wet, muddy dungarees dried as hard and crispy as a biscuit once the sun came out, making climbing on and off the tractor or bending to shear sheep cramped and uncomfortable.

Of all the jobs they had to do throughout the farming year, milking the cows was not one of their chores.

'That would involve us getting up at four in the morning instead of five,' Mo pointed out.

'It's Mrs M's job,' Sal said sourly. 'At least it gives the old cow something to do apart from sup tea and smoke fags all day.'

'She'd dump it on us if she could,' Mo growled. 'Luckily Wilf needs us out in the fields; otherwise we'd cop that job too.'

'Let's be grateful for small mercies,' Pat reminded them all.

Lillian for one was deeply grateful for small mercies: the

thought of having to face a cow's bottom at dawn every day, then having to worm lambs, bale hay, cast straw and lay bedding, plus drive the tractor, was utterly overwhelming.

There was no question that she had been terrified of driving the tractor to start with, especially after she had landed it in a ditch during her first week on the farm. Trying to make a turn, she clumsily let the wheel slip from her hands, and the tractor rolled out of control on to its side. Scrambling out covered in stinking ditch water, Lillian was almost hysterical.

'Christ!' she gasped.

Knowing that she and her friends couldn't pull the bulky machine out of the ditch, she ran like the wind back to the farm, not to find Wilf (who would have been livid) but one of the farm lads whom she had grown friendly with. After gabbling out what had happened, she begged, 'Please, Tom, you've got to help me before Wilf finds out.'

'Go back and wait for me,' the lad instructed, before he dashed off towards the stable block.

When he reappeared, he was leading two magnificent shire horses with ropes attached to their harnesses. Seeing them approach, clip-clopping over the cobbles with their silky manes lifting in the breeze, Lillian backed away.

'They're twice the size of me,' she thought.

Ignoring her nervous expression, Tom fondly said, 'Meet Major and Daisy.'

Lillian gazed in awe at the magnificent animals. Major, the taller of the two, was seventeen hands high with a shiny black coat and flowing black mane; at sixteen hands, Daisy was smaller than her companion, a pretty grey, with a shimmering silver mane and tail. With impressive large heads, dominated by dark-brown kind eyes, and their deep shoulders, wide chests and muscular hindquarters, they left no one in doubt of their enormous pulling power. As if reading her thoughts, Tom said, 'Between 'em they could pull up to forty tons, and they'd never hurt a fly,' he added tenderly. 'Though, really, Daisy will be laid off heavy work soon,' Tom added.

Tentatively laying a hand on Daisy's long neck, Lillian asked why.

'Take a look at her belly,' Tom laughed. 'She's in foal.'

Lillian gazed in amazement at gentle Daisy, with her silky mane framing her young pretty face.

'That's wonderful,' she whispered.

'Aye, she was covered last autumn, little 'un's due October or November. Aren't you a clever lass?' Tom said softly, as he patted the mare's shiny flank.

To Lillian's surprise Tom suddenly thrust the horses' lead ropes into her hands.

'Hold on to 'em while I fix some chains round yon tractor.'

Shaking like a leaf in the wind, Lillian did as she was told, thinking, if these animals bolt, I'll be dragged to my death. Instead the trusting shires, standing on either side of her, dipped their heads to nuzzle her hair, then they nudged her in the tummy. Panicking, Lillian cried out to Tom in the ditch, 'Will they bite?'

'Nah,' he called back. 'They just want a cuddle.'

Gazing up at the shires so much taller than she was, Lillian squeaked, 'How do you cuddle them?'

Laughing now, Tom replied, 'Just stroke their noses, or tickle their ears, that'll keep 'em happy.'

Gripping the ropes in one hand, Lillian used her free hand to stroke the shires' velvet-soft muzzles, but, as she turned her attention from Major to Daisy, the former snorted into her hair. Amazed by their teasing gentleness, Lillian started to smile and relax.

'I've only got one free hand,' she explained, as if they were over-eager children. 'I can only stroke you one at a time, so please wait your turn,' she said firmly.

Climbing out of the ditch, Tom hitched the chains on to the shires' harnesses, then, clicking his tongue, he called, 'Giddee-up there.'

In unison the patient horses moved forwards and, straining their haunches, they dragged on the chains secured to the fallen tractor, which righted itself as they slowly towed it out of the ditch. Impressed, Lillian patted them both on their gleaming necks. 'Good work, well done,' she cried. 'I'd be in big trouble with Wilf but for you two beauties.'

Grinning, Tom took a couple of carrots out of his jacket pocket and handed them to Lillian.

'Them's for the horses,' he told her.

Over-excited, Major and Daisy tossed their heads and neighed. Lillian laid the carrots flat on her palm and carefully fed them their treats, giggling at the feel of their silky muzzles tickling her palm.

'They like you,' the lad announced.

'I like them,' Lillian enthused. 'They're beautiful animals.'

'Aye, they're that indeed,' he replied proudly. 'I'll leave

you to your tractor, then. Hope it works,' he added, as he led the horses away.

Mercifully the tractor started after a couple of turns, and Lillian drove it back to the field, where she helped the three other Land Girls load baled straw into a cart attached to the tractor. Lillian then trundled back to the barn. After stacking the straw in the dry barn, they all slumped on to the prickly bales, utterly weary and with aching backs.

'Jesus! I'm knackered,' Sal declared.

A shrill neighing sounding out from the stable block opposite caused Lillian to stagger to her feet and, peering out, she laughed with pleasure when she saw Daisy's and Major's heads poking out over the stable's half-door. Unable to resist them, she hurried over to stroke them again, but this time with confidence and pleasure.

'Major and Daisy,' she whispered. 'Hello again.' In answer the faithful shires softly whinnied. 'I'll fetch you some treats tomorrow,' she promised before heading for the farmhouse and another disgusting meal served up by Mrs M with a fag dangling from her mouth.

Lillian appreciated the ready advice and friendship of her fellow Land Girls – as Pat said, they were all in it together, against Hitler, the Huns and Wilf in that order. Shirking a job or doing it badly meant you dumped extra work on your pals, which was unacceptable behaviour, given that they all worked till they dropped seven days a week.

'Work our arses off,' as Mo so succinctly put up. 'For a pittance too, £1.17s a week, a bloody joke if you ask me!'

'You should have joined the Wrens and married a toff,' Pat mocked.

Lillian soon understood why her companions sparked out like faded fireworks at the end of every working day; sleeping fully dressed and barely taking time to wash their faces, they literally collapsed into their dirty beds, where they slept like the dead. Even Lillian (with the worst sleeping arrangements) stopped moaning about the mattress on the floor, though she did insist on being given some sheets, which she washed in the stream along with the grubby blanket and hung out over a nearby drystone wall to dry.

Ever fastidious, Lillian couldn't imagine why her friends barely washed. 'Don't you feel filthy?' she enquired one early morning, as she cleaned her teeth and brushed her long hair, which after weeks in the open air was slowly returning to its natural light-brown colour, streaked blonde in parts by the summer sun.

'It's not like any bugger cares!' Sal shrugged. 'We smell of cow muck and sheep from dawn till dusk. Anyway, the water's stone cold in the tap, and rusty too; there's not a bar of soap anywhere. And, as for the company, friends excluded,' she added diplomatically, 'Wilf stinks worse than the dogs and Mrs M looks like summat that's just crawled out of the cesspit.'

'And there's no decent fellas about,' Mo glumly concluded. 'So what's the bloody point anyway?'

That nobody cared didn't stop Lillian doing her best as far as personal hygiene went; using the small perfumed bar of soap, talc and a teeny bottle of 'Evening in Paris' she had brought along with her, she never failed to wash the sweat and grime from the farmyard off her body every single night.

'You'd think Laurence Olivier was going to turn up for cocktails,' Sal teased.

'Oh, I wish,' Lillian sighed.

Those dreamy long-ago cinema days were well over; in fact, she didn't even know where the nearest picture house was these days. And, even if she did manage to find one, she knew that once she was inside the all-consuming, seductive velvet-darkness, she would close her eyes and sleep for a week.

As high summer set in and the temperature soared, it was bliss to discover a natural deep rock pool in the fold of the steep grey fells where the sheep grazed. After hours of shearing panting sheep with thick woolly coats stinking of lanolin, the girls made a beeline for the pool to escape the scorching July heat. Lillian, desperate to cool herself off, reached the place first one particularly hot day, abandoned her dungarees and the rest of her clothes and whooped like an excited child as she leapt into the deep clear pool stark naked. Floating flat on her back with her hair streaming out behind her, Lillian flipped her slim, lithe body under water, where she swam until she ran out of breath. When she surfaced, she sensed she was no longer alone and looked eagerly for her friends. But she saw, to her utter dismay, that it was a leering Wilf who was standing on the rocks surrounding the pool, holding her dungarees, drinking in the sight of her small slender frame, half of which was submerged under the crystal-clear waters of the pool.

'Thought you might be needing these,' he said with a lecherous wink. 'Though if you fancied it I could rub you down first, sweetheart?'

Hugging her breasts and making sure she stayed well under the water, which now felt freezing cold against her skin, Lillian tried to behave as normally as she could, given that she was alone and stark naked with an over-sexed farmer.

'Yes, thank you,' she answered stiffly. 'Please leave them there.'

'If I did that, I'd miss the view,' Wilf mocked.

With her heart pounding, Lillian was wondering whether it would be better to freeze to death or reveal her body to the loathsome farmer, when she was saved by the arrival of noisy Mo, Sal and Pat. Swivelling her eyes from Lillian in the pool to Wilf on the edge of it, Pat immediately grasped what was going on.

'Hello there, Wilf, are you coming in too?'

Much as he yearned to see the lovely new arrival rise like a goddess from the water, Wilf had no desire to see the other three clod-hopping women starkers, so he dropped Lillian's dungarees.

'I'll be off – some sheep have run on to't fells and need rounding up.'

The girls didn't even try to conceal their mocking laughter as Wilf scurried off.

'Dirty bastard!' Mo scoffed.

Throwing off her clothes, Pat chided Lillian, 'I told you

to wait for us, Lil. You've got to have eyes in the back of your head with a bastard like Wilf around.'

Grabbing her dungarees, Lillian held them close to her body in an attempt to get warm. 'Next time I'll take your advice, Pat,' she promised. 'I was so hot I just didn't think. He gave me the fright of my life,' she admitted. 'Towering over the pool, waiting for me to get out.'

Plump, pale, freckly Mo inched into the water. 'Jesus! It's bloody freezing,' she wailed.

After the girls had had their dip, they lay in the sunshine on the cool slabs of rock to dry themselves off. Staring up at the duck-egg-blue sky, where a pair of hen harriers glided on the warm spirals of air, calling out to each other as they hunted over the high rocky crags, Lillian sighed, happy and relaxed for the first time in weeks.

'This is so beautiful.'

'Aye, so long as Wilf hasn't got his binoculars out and is having a good gawp at us lasses in't nude,' giggled Sal.

Worried that the farmer might be doing exactly that, Lillian slipped back into her dungarees, then sat with her arms locked around her legs, thinking about where Trevor might be. Having only so far received one letter from him (compared to the half a dozen she had sent him with her present address clearly written in bold at the top of the page), Lillian was beginning to despair. Could such blinding passion go so quickly, like a flash in the pan? Their brief relationship, which had blossomed in Blackpool's dark picture house, seemed to be fast fading: though Trevor had promised on their last evening together that he was 'eternally hers', the only letter he had bothered to write was vague and rushed; he hadn't even mentioned his next leave or hinted at any desire to see her. Had Trevor played with her while he was home on leave? Had she been nothing more than a brief romantic episode? Had they both lost themselves in the magic of the motion pictures, imagining themselves to be Hollywood movie stars who found happiness at the end of the rainbow? Thank God she hadn't given herself to Trevor, as she almost nearly did that night on Blackpool Beach. What if he had left her pregnant? Being a Land Girl was bad enough but a pregnant Land Girl – Lillian shuddered at the thought – would be absolutely intolerable.

10. Observations

Jamie's concerns about Sister Renee centred more around her bedside manner than her teaching techniques. Technically she was a good nurse. He had seen her on the wards and in the delivery room: she was unquestionably competent and experienced, but sometimes he worried about the image she gave off. There were days when Renee's bright, upbeat demeanour lapsed into a sloppy dismissiveness which set Jamie's teeth on edge. The delicate likes of Polly she left others to nurse when she could get away with it, leaving Renee free to attend to the more robust noisy patients, with whom, Jamie thought, she was way too chummy and intimate. He regularly witnessed Renee's casual behaviour during mealtimes when, typically, she took things one step too far: putting her feet up on an empty chair, smoking and cracking jokes. Renee somehow managed to change the atmosphere into that of a bar or a tap room rather than a hospital. Jamie maintained that *they*, the staff, were the professionals – the grownups who kept their patients calm, informed and secure, not necessarily entertained. Energetic and often overfamiliar, her manner reminded Jamie of some of the students he had trained with who had tried to befriend their patients rather than treat them. Jamie believed that the best doctors and nurses did not need their patients to be their friends, but it became evident to Jamie that Renee certainly did.

From his own relationship with the residents Jamie knew that nearly all of them were concerned not only about themselves and how they would handle their advancing pregnancy but about their baby's health too. Over and over again he heard the same questions.

'Doctor, is my baby strong?'

'I want to do the best for my baby.'

'It's the least I can do before I hand her over for adoption.'

After hearing Renee's flippant responses to some of these genuine questions, Jamie became increasingly annoyed, to such an extent that finally, early one morning, when Renee was clocking on, he was forced to have a quiet word with her.

'Look, I hope you don't mind my saying this, but I'm a bit uncomfortable with how you sometimes address the patients,' he started.

Shoving stray black curls under her starched cap, Renee gave Jamie a rather bleary-eyed look. Uncomfortable that he might well come over as a prig, Jamie nevertheless explained his concerns.

'In my professional opinion I think it's very important to draw a line between patient and professional. On a couple of occasions, I've witnessed you ignore a request for information, or turn it into a joke, as if it's not worth the trouble of even answering,' he added. 'These young women in our care are very vulnerable and often very, very frightened.'

Renee's green eyes flashed dangerously. 'Are you implying I'm a bad nurse?'

'Certainly not – your technical skills are good – it's just that I've noticed that you have a tendency to be rather over-friendly on the wards. It's disrespectful to fob off patients with a joke when all they want is a straight answer,' he finished bluntly.

'And exactly how have I fobbed my patients off?' Renee asked huffily.

Jamie quoted some of the things he had heard Renee say to anxious patients.

'To tell them things like "Nothing to worry about" or "You're imagining things", when that isn't necessarily the case. That kind of response is disrespectful. When a patient is worried about intermittent bleeding or prolonged sickness, she wants a serious answer to a serious question. Casual behaviour in those circumstances is unprofessional in my opinion.'

Obviously annoyed Renee hit back. 'In my training at St Thomas's I learnt from my tutors and colleagues that the best attitude a nurse could have was one of cheerful optimism, and that's exactly how I conduct myself here at Mary Vale.'

Having worked with doctors and nurses from St Thomas's, Jamie was not for a moment convinced. 'Cheerful optimism is to be applauded,' he agreed. 'But if an anxious patient wants the truth, a smile or a joke won't cut the mustard,' he declared, then continued with a passion that simply got the better of him. 'Without any doubt the residents here have all been through some kind of personal hell; the least we can do is take their concerns seriously and treat them honestly,' he concluded.

'So, if a young girl says to me, "Will having a baby hurt?" what do I say?' Renee snapped. ' "Like hell it will", or "Don't worry, nothing worse than period pains"? Truly, what is going to calm her down the most?'

'Softening the blow with a throw-away remark might momentarily help the patient, but ultimately it won't help her through the long, traumatic experience of giving birth.'

Moving away from him, Renee said coldly, 'Thank you for your advice, Doctor, I shall take it on board.'

Looking thoughtful, Jamie watched her go. Had he gone too far and made an enemy? He hoped not.

Polly was turning out to be a real worry. She could never get enough reassurance about how her pregnancy would progress and where her baby would go after she had given birth.

'Have another chat with Father Ben,' Ada advised the highly nervous expectant mother. 'You've seen him before, and, as I recall, you liked him very much and felt you could trust his judgement,' Ada reminded the scatty frightened girl.

Polly nodded. 'Yeah, I remember he's the one that handles all the adoptions for the Mary Vale babies.'

'He's excellent at finding the right match for all our babies,' Ada assured her.

As the days passed, Jamie was relieved to see Sister Renee more supportive with their youngest patient.

'Maybe she did take what I said on board,' he thought hopefully, but by the end of the week he could see that Renee's resolve was slipping. Unaware that he was close by, Jamie overheard her impatiently telling Polly to stop flapping.

'You've months to go yet,' she said sharply. 'You'll wear yourself out if you carry on worrying about your blood pressure.'

'It's not just that, Sister, I'm worried about the size of my baby too. I saw Sister Ada measuring a girl's tummy the other day; she was using a tape measure. Can you do that for me?' she begged.

Renee gave a loud exasperated sigh. 'Really, Polly, I'm in the middle of doing jobs. I can't stop just because you've found something else to fret about.'

Nearly in tears, Polly cried, 'Can't you come back later, please?'

'I'll do my best,' Renee said, before she went on her way.

Jamie's heart sank; obviously the talking-to he had given her had hardly had any effect at all.

Hearing Polly weeping, he popped his head around the corner of her bed curtain. 'Did I hear something about measuring your baby?' he said with a winning smile.

Polly's desperate expression cleared and, clearly relieved, she smiled brightly. 'Yes, please, Doctor.'

As Jamie hurried off to fetch a tape measure, he thought crossly, 'If a tape measure is all that's needed to make a patient happy, why the hell didn't Sister Renee put herself out?'

*

86

Later Jamie glumly told Ada that he had had a few words with Renee.

'I'm afraid they didn't have much of an effect,' he admitted. 'Or not for long.'

'What did you say to her?' Ada asked.

After Jamie relayed the conversation, Ada looked concerned. 'Mmm, I bet she loved you?'

'She wasn't best pleased,' he admitted. 'She said that she was trained to nurse that way at St Thomas's.'

Ada raised a cynical eyebrow. 'I don't think so,' she retorted.

'Neither do I,' he responded. 'I thought it might be wise to mention my conversation with Renee to Matron; she said she would certainly have a word with her.'

'It's good that Matron's dealing with it,' Ada said.

'Well, I only hope she has more luck than me,' Jamie concluded.

After her meeting with Matron, Renee didn't appear for work the following day.

'She sent word down to the ward that she's got a tummy bug, something she ate,' Matron told Ada when she turned up for her shift. 'Odd, when you think about it; we all eat the same food at Mary Vale, and nobody else has reported a tummy bug.'

'It could be an infection she picked up on the wards,' Ada replied.

Crinkling her brow underneath her starched white wimple, Matron said realistically, 'Or it might well be that she's upset after I ticked her off yesterday.'

Knowing what a kind and gentle soul Matron was, Ada smiled reassuringly. 'I'm quite sure you didn't say anything too dreadful; it's not your style.'

'Renee said she felt picked on by the senior staff,' Matron admitted.

'That would include Jamie too,' Ada reminded her.

'She might consider that a good-enough reason not to show up for work,' Matron murmured.

Feeling suddenly irritated, Ada exclaimed, 'Instead of playing the victim, Renee should take on board what senior staff are advising. It can't be a coincidence that we're all concerned about exactly the same thing.'

Matron nodded her head in agreement. 'I don't want it to turn into an even bigger problem,' she said frankly. 'Perhaps one of us should pop in and see Sister Renee later this afternoon.'

'I'll call in on her after I've finished work,' Ada promised.

True to her word, Ada tripped upstairs to the top floor of Mary Vale Home, which housed the staff, at the end of her shift. Hurrying along the faded carpeted corridor to Renee's room, she heard a clinking-clanking sound, which was a relief, as Ada had been worried about waking Renee from a deep sleep. Tapping cautiously on the door, she called out softly, 'Hello, Renee, it's Ada.'

Hearing a scuffling noise, Ada waited, but the door didn't open.

'Can I get you anything, Renee – some tea and toast, an aspirin?' she suggested. When the door remained closed,

Ada thought she had better back off; clearly the patient was in no mood for company. Just as she was about to turn away, the door slowly opened an inch or two, and Ada was assailed by a strong stale smell that issued from the darkened room. Seeing white-faced Renee, still in her nightdress, with her hair plastered to her head, leaning limply against the wall for support, Ada immediately apologized.

'I'm so sorry, dear, we were all just a bit concerned. How are you feeling?'

'Still a bit sick and dizzy,' Renee answered in a low, cracked voice.

'Can I bring you anything?' Ada asked again.

'No, thanks – the thought of food makes me feel even worse. I'm just sticking to water.'

'Good idea,' Ada said cheerily. 'Well, I'll leave you in peace – don't rush back if you're feeling under the weather,' she urged.

'It's just a tummy bug,' Renee assured Ada, before she closed the door. 'I'll be back on the wards tomorrow.'

Hurrying downstairs, Ada headed to the back door, which she always used these days as it led into the yard, then directly on to the farm track, her route home. Passing the open pantry door, she saw Sister Mary Paul looking very agitated.

'What's the matter, dear?' Ada asked the old nun.

'I know my eyesight's failing,' Mary Paul replied. 'But I swear there was a good half-bottle of brandy in here a few days ago. For the life of me I can't find it now.'

Seeing her friend squinting as she struggled to locate

the brandy bottle, Ada stepped into the large pantry and had a quick look for it herself.

'There's some port and sherry but no brandy,' she told Mary Paul. 'I hope you've not been having a tipple?' she teased.

'Get away with you, child, it's the devil's brew! The vapour it gives off and the smell of the stuff turns my stomach,' Mary Paul cried. 'I keep a bit by just in case any of the residents gets a sore throat – diluted with hot water it can be quite soothing.'

Giving the pantry shelves one last look, Ada reaffirmed, 'It's not here now, for sure.'

Mary Paul shrugged. 'I'll ask Farmer Arkwright to get me a half-bottle from the outdoor off-licence when he's next in Kendal; you never know when we might need it next.' Checking the time on her wristwatch, she exclaimed, 'Shouldn't you be on your way home to that lovely baby of yours?'

'Yes,' Ada laughed, 'I just got waylaid by hearing you muttering away to yourself in the pantry,' she joked. 'And I also popped in to see Renee.'

'How is she?' the old nun enquired.

'Rough,' Ada answered honestly. 'She's still in her night-dress, so she's obviously been in bed all day.'

'I'll be blowed if I can think what's caused Sister Renee's illness; we all eat the same food day in day out, so I don't think it can be something she ate, and nobody else is being sick, which you'd expect from a tummy bug,' Sister Mary Paul fretted.

'Don't worry about it, darling,' Ada reassured her. 'I'm sure it's nothing to do with your lovely cooking.'

Walking home deep in thought, Ada recalled Sister Mary Paul's appalled reaction to the thought of drinking brandy.

'The devil's brew! The vapour it gives off turns my stomach.'

Recollecting the stale smell that had drifted out of Renee's room, Ada stopped dead in her tracks. 'It smelt of stale alcohol,' she suddenly realized. 'Could it be . . .' Guilty that she was being suspicious and judgemental, Ada ticked herself off. 'Just because Renee's been in trouble recently doesn't mean to say she hits the bottle.'

Then, hurrying down the farm track, Ada headed for Mary Vale Cottage, where on summer evenings like this she knew Jamie would be in the garden playing with Catherine: her two favourite people waiting excitedly for Mummy to come home.

11. RAF Burtonwood

Bill was stationed at RAF Burtonwood, just outside Warrington, on the edge of the Cheshire Plain. He proudly
told Stella on her first visit that it was the biggest airbase
in Europe, with the most aircraft and the longest runway.

'It also has the reputation for the most proposals of
marriage,' he laughed. 'Our guys just keep on falling in
love with you gorgeous British ladies,' he teased.

As Stella gazed up at Bill, with the summer sun glint-
ing on his golden-blond hair, catching the slant of his
high cheekbones and the softness of his golden-brown
hazel eyes, her heart did what was now becoming a
familiar sensation when she was with Bill – it skipped
several beats.

This was their third date; the two previous meetings
had been in Manchester, where they had met in St Ann's
Square to have tea in a Lyons' Corner House. Their meetings, based around their days off, which were few and far
between, had been tricky, and bomb-torn Manchester
turned out to be a bit of a grim venue.

'I'd love to see your Burtonwood base,' Stella said eagerly.
'I'm quite sure I can catch a train to Warrington.'

'That would be great,' he enthused. 'I could get a visitor's pass and show you around the parts that aren't off
limits.'

Travelling to Warrington was much less complicated

than deciding what to wear for the occasion. Much as she loved the blue satin dress that she had worn the night she first met Bill, Stella certainly didn't want to wear it for every date.

'He'll think it's the only thing I've got,' she declared.

Sitting on the bed in the room that they shared, Doreen lit up a Woodbine.

'You are a bit limited on the clothes side,' she observed wryly. 'There's your overalls of course, but you can't swan around Burtonwood looking like a dinner lady,' she teased.

'Be serious, Do,' Stella begged. 'I've got a couple of skirts and a few blouses, all a bit tired-looking, and too warm for this summer heat,' she grumbled.

'I've got a nice silky top you can borrow,' generous Doreen suggested.

Comparing Doreen's voluptuous bosom to her own pert little breasts caused Stella to bite her lip nervously. Reading her thoughts, Doreen laughed.

'It won't fall off if you tuck it into your skirt, though I bet Bill wouldn't complain if it did.'

After a press with a damp cloth, her old cotton skirt looked fairly presentable, but it was Doreen's bright, multi-coloured spotted silk top with strappy sleeves that enhanced the look. Wearing thick-heeled sandals that she had whitened with a chalky paste, Stella felt pretty smart, especially after she had washed her hair, which hung long and loose around her bare shoulders.

'WOW! Veronica Lake, eat your heart out!' Doreen enthused.

Blushing in delight at her friend's words of praise, Stella hurried to catch the bus that would take her into Manchester, where she would board the train to Warrington.

Stella was delighted to find Bill waiting for her in an army truck outside the station.

'Can I give you a ride, lady?' he called, as he waved at her from across the road.

Hopping out of the truck in order to help Stella into the passenger seat, Bill gently drew her into his arms and crushed her to his hard, muscular chest.

'You look beautiful,' he murmured as his hand swept over her silky shoulders. 'I can't wait to show my gel off to all the guys on the base.'

Walking hand in hand with Bill in the permitted areas of the airbase, Stella did indeed draw a great deal of attention; everywhere she went she was aware of eyes following her tall, willowy figure.

'I knew you'd cause a stir with those gorgeous long legs of yours, not to mention that glorious hair,' Bill said proudly.

Though she was thrilled by his compliments, Stella seriously wanted to know about the place where Bill spent most of his time. 'Please, let's stop talking about me,' she insisted. 'Let's talk about you and what you do here at Burtonwood.'

So, as much as he was authorized to do so, Bill gave his sweetheart a guided tour.

'Obviously, that's the runway,' he said, pointing to a strip where US planes were lined up ready for take-off. 'Me and my engineering team built that,' he added with a bit of a swagger.

'The longest runway in Europe,' she laughed as she reiterated his own words.

'The control tower is over there and those various red-brick blocks are the officers' quarters, guard house, hospital wing, theatre, cinema, operational buildings, latrines and supply stores – there's even a church,' he added. 'Over towards the runway, away from the domestic buildings, there's the oil storage, machine-gun range, parachute block and the repair sheds, which is where we fix the thousands of damaged planes that come limping back from nightly bombing raids.'

'Don't you find it demoralizing repairing planes every single day?'

'No,' Bill answered firmly. 'Anything I can do to beat Hitler, be it large or small, I do with all my heart.'

Impressed by his fervour, Stella cried, 'That's a splendid way of looking at it.'

'It's the plain truth of the matter,' Bill said, shrugging. 'I'm no different to you,' he pointed out. 'You feed munitions workers to help them build bombs to destroy the enemy; my job is building planes and runways.'

Stella smiled adoringly at his handsome face, presently suffused with patriotic zeal.

'I'm thrilled you're rebuilding thousands of planes – we certainly need them!' Stella exclaimed.

Suddenly as eager as a boy, Bill grabbed her hand. 'Come on, kiddo, enough of this war talk – we're going for a picnic.'

Startled, she cried, 'A picnic, where?'

'Rivington Pike,' he told her. 'I've got the truck – it won't take long to get there.'

Driving up the busy road north, Stella was thrilled to be going to one of the favourite haunts of her childhood.

'You know it?' Bill asked, surprised.

'I most certainly do,' she replied. 'It was one of my family's favourite walking spots when I was little, and when I was older my friends and I would cycle over the moors to the Pike, mostly on bank holidays. In my memory they were golden sunny days with larks rising over the heather, soaring higher and higher into the sky, always singing. The North-West is supposed to be one of the wettest spots in England, but I don't ever recall rain falling when we were up there. How did you hear about Rivington Pike?' she asked.

Bill grinned. 'The guys I work with in the repair shed come up here with their sweethearts, so I thought I'd bring mine.'

Stella was constantly surprised and delighted by Bill's open manner; he never seemed self-conscious like most of the young men she had known. Previously when she had been 'walking out' (as her mum called it) with a boy, there would be an awkward shyness, an inability to express emotions, or sometimes even voice an opinion. Bill was the opposite: easy in his own skin, curious about the world and everybody he met. Concentrating on the road ahead, Bill asked with a smile on his lips, 'So you rode a bicycle?'

'An old heap,' she confessed. 'But it got me up to the

moors and back on a regular basis.' Sighing, she added, 'It feels like all those carefree happy days of my girlhood have been subsumed by war, work and rationing.'

'Talking of rationing,' he interrupted with an impish grin, 'you're just gonna love the picnic I prepared.'

Thinking along the lines of meagre fish-paste sandwiches and Brown Betties, Stella, little knowing of the pleasures he had in store for her, smiled politely. After scrambling over moorland, they crested the peak and enjoyed the view from the top of Rivington Pike. Grateful for a chance to get their breath back, they stood hand in hand staring out over the rolling landscape that peeled away west towards Liverpool and the Irish Sea, and east towards the majestic Pennines. Bill was briefly mesmerized by the stark black monument buffeted for centuries by the harsh elements.

'How come an ancient pile of rocks got stacked up here?'

'It's one of a line of beacons built across the Pennines; they were lit to alert the people of an imminent French invasion by Napoleon,' Stella explained.

'A bit like smoke signals!' Bill joked.

Descending from the blustery beacon, they found a sunny spot and Bill opened up his rucksack, revealing the treats he had promised earlier.

'Chocolate, and pop!' she cried.

'Coca-Cola,' he clarified. 'We Yanks drink it by the bucketful.'

'And proper sandwiches!' Stella exclaimed.

'Beef and mustard for the lady,' Bill grinned as he gallantly handed her a round of sandwiches.

'Oooh, this is a feast!' she laughed in delight.

'Courtesy of the US government,' he declared.

Hungry after their walk, they consumed everything, including the Coca-Cola, which Stella had never tasted in her life.

'It's a bit like dandelion and burdock,' she announced, as the bubbles burst in her mouth.

Amused by her comment, Bill chuckled, 'Sounds more like a bunch of flowers than a drink.'

Later, after Bill had packed up his rucksack, Stella held out her hand to him. 'Come on,' she smiled. 'There's something I want to show you.'

They dropped height, until they were threading their way along narrow pathways lined with dense banks of rhododendron bushes. Curious, Bill asked, 'Where are we going, darlin'?'

'It's a surprise,' she promised.

It was undoubtedly a surprise when the myriad woodland paths cross-crossing the site opened up on to a lake dotted with little islands and charming interconnecting little bridges.

'Welcome to the Japanese Gardens,' Stella announced.

'Heck!' Bill gasped, as he turned full circle to take in the view. 'Who built this extraordinary place?'

'Lord Leverhulme, at the turn of the century,' Stella replied. 'He wanted to recreate some of the amazing structures he had seen on his travels overseas; he had money enough, so he commissioned a gardener to design an exotic landscape up here on Bolton Moors.'

Leading the way, she guided Bill across the lake over stepping-stones that led to secret caves and winding passageways, which opened on to waterfalls and rich foliage. Settling back against a sun-drenched rock, Bill patted the spot beside him. 'I need you here, beautiful,' he murmured.

Like a homing pigeon, Stella flew to his side, to curl up with her head pressed against his shoulder.

'I thought I was taking you for a day out but instead you know the place better than me,' he said, as he leant down to kiss her full red pouting lips.

'I might know it, but I could never have got here without your doing the driving,' she said, after their long, lingering kiss. 'Seriously, it was never as exciting as it is now, with you, Bill.' Emboldened by passion, Stella reached up to kiss him again, deeply on the mouth. 'You make everything special,' she smiled.

They stayed in the Japanese Gardens until the warm summer day drew to a close.

'We'd better head back before it gets dark,' Stella said. 'Otherwise we could be stuck in this place, going around and around in circles until dawn breaks.'

'I like the thought of being stuck in a place with you that I can never get out of,' he whispered in her ear.

Though Stella was finding it hard to resist the pressure of Bill's arms around her and the urgency of his kisses, she knew from experience that they had to get out of the maze of pathways, caves and bridges before darkness fell. Taking him by the hand, she led him along the interconnecting tracks and back to a glade of rhododendron bushes close to where they had parked the truck. The warmth of the summer night – with the silvery new moon shedding its light over the moor, where badgers, owls and foxes hunted – made them both reluctant to leave.

'Let's stay just a bit longer,' Bill begged.

Sinking on to a bed of dry purple heather, they found their kissing and petting exploding into something way beyond their former canoodling.

Concerned about his beloved, Bill cautiously held back. 'Are you sure about this, honey?'

Without a moment's hesitation, Stella answered softly, 'Yes.'

'I can use something,' he assured her.

She nodded and, again, without hesitation, told him she was sure.

'I love you, darling. I'm yours, and always will be.'

So it was there, on a summer's night, as the stars came out over moorland drenched in the perfume of wild-flowers, that Stella lost her virginity. Locked in each other's arms, they made love until the sun rose in the east, shedding its light on two young lovers sleeping in the exhausted blissful aftermath of their love-making.

12. Major and Daisy

Much as she loathed Dobb End, and Mrs M in particular, Lillian nevertheless settled into the rhythm of working life on the farm thanks to her new friends, who worked solidly from dawn till dusk through the long summer months. With the weather swinging from scorching heat to torrential rain, Mo, Sal and Pat never shirked from their workload, which, though undoubtedly tough, was their duty to the nation.

As the four of them lay sprawled out on their beds, smoking cigarettes after a long day out in the fields, Mo, typically not mincing her words, blurted out, 'If we all felt like you when you got your call-up papers, nowt would ever get done.'

Outraged, Lillian vehemently protested at her blunt choice of words. 'I came up here as instructed by the government,' she strongly pointed out.

'But you told us you didn't want to,' Pat reminded Lillian. 'I have some sympathy,' she continued. 'Who wouldn't prefer working in a picture house to shovelling sheep shit or castrating lambs?'

Tenaciously self-righteous, Mo added, 'But we just *have* to, it's the law – that's all there is to it.'

Defeated as she was, Lillian's shoulders slumped. 'All right, all right,' she groaned. 'It's true: I admit I never wanted to leave the Regal.'

'The trouble with you, Lil, love,' a sympathetic Sal added, 'is you worked too long in the make-believe world of the picture house.'

Bridling again, Lillian asked sharply, 'What's wrong with that – who wouldn't want to escape reality at a time like this?'

'It's make-believe, lovie, fantasy,' Sal persisted. 'All them soppy films about kissing and cuddling in the moonlight, wearing posh frocks, dancing till dawn, drinking champagne – it's just a distraction from the misery of war.'

'A distraction from reality never hurt anybody,' Lillian continued to protest.

'Fair point,' Sal conceded.

'But it's not helping the war effort, is it?' Mo demanded.

'I believe it is,' Lillian forcefully replied. 'Good films with a message boost the nation's morale – what's so wrong with that?'

Mo gave an indignant little swagger. 'Us Land Lasses feeding the country is more help than the pictures when it comes to winning the bloody war,' she announced.

Pat gave an irreverent giggle. 'Well, not just us *four* up here in't valley,' she joked. 'There's a whole army of Land Girls out there, all digging for victory.'

'Aye, it's our only way of fighting that bastard, Hitler,' Mo savagely added.

Her friends' stirring words galvanized Lillian, and her heart quickened: if this was her only way of fighting 'that bastard Hitler' (to quote loud-mouthed Mo), she would do it wholeheartedly. She yearned to live in peace once more, and if that meant digging for victory, then she would damn well dig till she dropped. Her friends were right – folks couldn't fight on empty bellies, so somebody had to dig up spuds, plough fields, feed sheep, milk cows, collect eggs, harvest the crops and chop down timber – otherwise the nation would starve. Dobb End, with a sloven for a housekeeper and an oversexed farmer forever waiting to grope a lass in the dark, was undoubtedly grim, but the Borrowdale Valley was breathtakingly beautiful. The high majestic fells rose steeply from the tiny hamlet consisting of a scattering of grey slated cottages, with Stonethwaite Beck gently gliding through the valley's fertile meadows. It was another world from Blackpool's noisy Fun Fair and packed pubs.

'Places like Blackpool and Borrowdale are just part of the bigger picture,' Lillian thought with an unexpected lump in her throat. 'In towns, villages, cities, hamlets – the entire country – north, east, south, west, there's a vast army of loyal men and women, of all creeds and ages, working to save the land they love. Making bombs, building planes, milking cows, driving tractors, putting out fires – never giving up, *never ever* giving in to Hitler and Fascism.'

A wave of patriotism flooded Lillian, making her spine tingle all the way down. Sal was right: she had looked upon conscription as a forced exile, but working alongside stalwart Land Girls in a beautiful part of England now seemed less of a punishment and more of a privilege.

As bats flitted in the fading light, Lillian settled down to sleep, thankfully on sheets that she regularly washed in the gurgling beck, then dried over the sun-drenched drystone walls that enclosed the farm. Inhaling the sweet smell of fresh air and wild thyme that clung to the sheets, Lillian fell into a deep sleep of complete exhaustion.

As dawn broke, bleary-eyed Lillian and her friends staggered down the rickety stairs to the kitchen, where they brewed strong tea and toasted the stale bread Mrs M had left out for them. There was no time for talk or pleasantries; it was a matter of fuelling up, then going on their way. Mo, Sal and Pat to the fields, Lillian to the stable. Being the tractor driver (which she had become quite skilful at) had led to her working these days with the horses too, which was a wonderful bonus as far as Lillian was concerned.

In late summer, when Wilf suddenly got laid up with sciatica, Tom the stable lad immediately suggested that Lillian should replace him in the stable yard, while he, Tom, took over the farmer's workload until Wilf was back on his feet.

Though thrilled at the prospect of spending more time with Daisy and Major, Lillian wondered if she was up to the job.

'Anybody would be better than Wilf,' Tom exclaimed. 'Heavy on the whip, never a kind word, he barely knows one 'oss for t'other. Not like you, Lil: their ears prick up at the sound of your voice.'

'I love working with them. I don't even mind mucking out their stable,' Lillian admitted, as she and Tom polished the old leather harnesses to a high shiny gloss in the tack room, which smelt of hoof oil, bran mash and linseed.

'Never in a million years would I ever have imagined that I'd finish up driving a tractor and working with a team of shire horses – I always thought that was man's work.'

'Aye, so it was till all't fellas got called up; I'm hoping I'll be next,' said an eager-eyed Tom.

'You're far too young for that,' Lillian exclaimed.

'I might be short and skinny, but I am nearly eighteen,' he answered with a cocky little swagger.

Lillian looked at Tom, who seemed barely more than a boy. Her heart sank at the thought of him being sent to the Front.

'I'll do my best with Daisy and Major,' she promised him.

Taking her word Tom gave a trusting smile. 'I know you will, lass.'

After hanging up the harnesses on the sturdy post in the tack room, Tom continued, 'You're going to have to take extra special care of Daisy when I'm gone; she'll be ready to give birth in the autumn,' he said knowingly. 'Check her teats regularly, watch out for swelling and tenderness there, and don't panic if you see discharge from her back end,' he advised. 'There's a really good vet in Seatoller, just up the valley, Robbie Allen; he's got a gift with the horses. I'll leave his number chalked up on the feed board, for when you need him.'

Tom was right about the shires' devotion to Lillian: the second they heard her step on the cobbled yard both Major and Daisy snickered softly.

'Morning, beautiful,' Lillian crooned as she stroked each in turn, running her small hands through their long silky manes, then sliding them down their smooth, glossy necks. 'Breakfast-time, then down to business,' she announced cheerfully.

After topping up their water buckets and refilling their mangers with fresh hay, Lillian left the horses in peace to finish their breakfast and made her way to the barn to help Tom drag the cutting machinery out. Returning to the stable, she found Major and Daisy impatiently pawing their cobbled floors, eager to get out and start the day.

'Hold on, you two,' she laughed, as she attached lead ropes to their head collars and led them out into the yard, where, at the sight of grinning Tom, they tossed their heads and neighed in excitement.

'Ready for work, eh?' he chuckled, tickling both animals behind their ears.

The shires allowed Lillian and Tom to attach the cutting machine to their harnesses; then, with Lillian on one side and Tom on the other, they made their way to the meadow, where they would spend most of the day cutting hay.

Those long summer days riding atop Major with gentle Daisy plodding steadily at his side were days Lillian would remember and cherish for the rest of her life. Working in harmony with nature and a pair of faithful trusting animals, reaping a harvest for a hungry war-torn country, was a pleasure which brought her great satisfaction. As she and Tom guided the steady horses up and down the line, Pat, Mo and Sal and a few locals collected up the hay, which they gathered into sheaves and, thanks to the fine weather, left stacked in stooks to dry out in the hayfield.

By dinner-time the harvest team were hot, thirsty and starving hungry; even the valiant Major and Daisy were flagging. Leading the sweating horses to a shady spot out of the blazing sun, Tom unharnessed them so they could relax, while Lillian hurried to the beck to fill up buckets of water, which the horses gratefully drank. Stroking their hot, damp coats, Lillian couldn't resist the urge to lean closer in order to inhale their sweet smell. Thinking of the glamorous Blackpool usherette she had been until recently, Lillian smiled to herself. 'I think you two beauties have stolen my heart,' she whispered into their manes. 'Which is just as well,' she continued under her breath, 'because nobody else wants it.'

Recalling how quickly Trevor's passion had waned once she moved North and he moved South, Lillian gave her equine friends a word of advice. 'Never trust a fella!'

When Lillian joined the cutting team in the field, she found them glumly eating Mrs M's miserable dinner.

'Yet again, more stinking stale bread and fish paste,' Sal seethed. 'I'm so bloody hungry I could eat the bloody hay we've just cut, smells sweeter than this shit!' she cried, and threw her share of food to the crows that were stalking around them.

Tom smiled. 'Just as well that I brought something else, then,' he said, as he unwrapped a knotted tea towel. 'A few little treats I found locked away in Mrs M's pantry – bought on our ration coupons, no doubt, and ours by right, so get stuck in!'

The entire crew gazed in wonder at his filched hoard – ham, fresh bread, cheese, sugar – and fags. Without asking any questions and barely pausing to speak, they set about eating chunks of bread on to which they piled the salty boiled ham and slices of tangy Lancashire cheese. Gorged and replete, they settled back and drank tea from Thermos flasks sweetened with the stolen sugar.

'Tom, you're a star, lad, that's the best meal I've had since war was declared,' Mo announced.

Intrigued, Pat asked the grinning boy, 'How did you manage it?'

'Easy – just broke the pantry lock behind Mrs M's back and helped miself,' Tom chuckled.

'You'll be in for a roasting when the owd bag finds out you've been nicking from her store,' Sal warned.

Cheeky Tom stuck two fingers up in the air. 'I don't give a bugger!' he laughed.

'She'll have the farmer whip you,' Mo cried.

'No, she won't,' Tom winked. 'I'll be well gone.'

Looking worried, Lillian said, 'You'll be in big trouble if you're planning on running away.'

Tom gave her a long, slow smile. 'I've been conscripted into the Navy. I'm off to fight the enemy.'

His friends were all so shocked they simply couldn't speak.

'Are you pulling my leg, you little tinker?' Mo asked.

'Straight up, I'm leaving Dobb End today, so Mrs M will have to follow me to Penrith if she's a mind to box my ears,' he joked.

With tears in her eyes, Lillian leant over to give young Tom, who had taught her everything she knew about horse management, a big hug.

'Take care, lad, and come back safe to us,' she said softly. 'Major and Daisy will miss you.'

Tom's expression softened. 'I feel better leaving them in your care – that old bugger Wilf don't know one end of a hoss from another. They'll do well by you, Lil.'

'I promise I'll love them just as much as you do,' Lillian assured him.

'Oh, another thing, Lil,' Tom added as he leant closer to whisper, 'don't trust Wilf to get the vet, Robbie Allen, out; he begrudges every penny spent on the animals, the old skin flint.'

'Stinginess seems to run in the family,' Lillian commented.

'If it's left to Wilf, he'll just give the horses a dose of some manky, years-old medication from one of the black bottles in the tack room – I've seen him do it many a time, and it gives the horses the runs,' he concluded.

Lillian nodded earnestly. 'Don't worry yourself – I'll call Robbie Allen if I need to.'

13. Whooping Cough

Polly, now in her fifth month, was not settling into her pregnancy as the nursing team had hoped. Renee, as usual impatient with Polly's semi-hysterical reaction to any changes in her body, left Ada and Sister Ann to deal with the young girl.

'My time is best spent elsewhere,' she said. 'Believe me, I have tried my best, but she always asks for you, Ada, or Matron, even Dora, in that order – not me.'

'Patients shouldn't be encouraged to choose who they want to nurse them,' Ada said sharply. 'This isn't an exclusive private nursing home with one-on-one nursing; we're a team at Mary Vale, and that's how it always has been.'

Renee was equally sharp in her reply. 'There are plenty of other needy patients to concentrate on while you and others tend to Polly's constant demands.'

Though Ada always defended Polly, she was nevertheless a little bit cross with the young girl. What would she do if Renee was actually the only nurse on duty – would Polly refuse to be nursed by her? Determined that she was not going to collude with Renee, who, Ada believed, was ducking her professional duties, she responded as calmly as she could to her colleague. 'Every patient is our responsibility.'

'Absolutely,' Renee said with the big bright smile that Ada was beginning to distrust. 'Of course, I'll be there when Polly really needs me.'

Towards the end of the summer, problems developed in the kitchen. Sister Mary Paul, who had ruled the domestic roost for decades, began to show significant signs of slowing down. It wasn't just the slowness of her old arthritic legs which were forever on the move from kitchen to dining room and back again, nearly a dozen times a day; it was the slowness of her reactions too. One morning, while the old nun was stirring a vat of custard on the hob, Sister Theresa (who split her working day between the wards and the kitchen) spotted Sister Mary Paul stumble as she tried to heave the heavy pot off the heat. Crying out in fear, the young nun rushed forward, just in time to save Mary Paul from stumbling and dropping the scalding hot custard all over the kitchen floor.

'Sister!' she cried, as she steadied Mary Paul and quickly relieved her of the pot, which she set safely down on the kitchen worktop.

'Glory be to God,' Mary Paul exclaimed. 'I don't know what came over me.'

Wiping her sweating brow on her handkerchief, she sighed. 'Mi eyes went all funny – one minute I could see as right as day, the next I could barely see a thing.'

After persuading the old nun to sit down for five minutes, Theresa enquired, 'How long have you had trouble with your eyesight, Sister?'

'Well, now, let's see,' Mary Paul answered, as she sipped

the strong sweet tea Theresa had made for her. 'It sort of comes and goes, but it's not good if I'm standing over anything steamy, like that custard just now.'

'Does it happen any other time?' Theresa asked.

Mary Paul nodded. 'Aye, I can get a filmy blur from time to time, like I've steamed up mi glasses when I've not.'

Looking concerned, Theresa continued, 'When that happens, will you tell me, then I can take over the task you're doing?' she implored. 'You could have really hurt yourself you know.'

'For sure I will, child,' Mary Paul promised and reassuringly patted her colleague's hand, then rose to recommence her work.

With a concerned expression on her gentle face, Theresa watched her set about rolling out a sheet of pastry – quite sure that the single-minded Sister Mary Paul would not confess to any weakness, especially if it meant saddling a colleague with extra work. Theresa was determined to be extra vigilant in the kitchen.

Shortly after Sister Mary Paul's near-accident, a number of residents also began to develop bad coughs, which was a cause of concern for Jamie.

'They're complaining that the cough settles on their chests and they start to feel a bit wheezy,' he told his wife. 'I think I might run a few tests and send them off to the lab.'

'Good idea,' Ada agreed. 'I'm keeping an eye on the nursery.'

Jamie gave a knowing smile. 'With Dora at the helm I'm sure that's all in hand.'

Jamie was right: Dora, as protective as a she-lion guarding her precious cubs, had banned mothers with coughs from the nursery.

'I can't have any infection in here – a bad cough could wreak havoc with the new-borns,' she told Ada, who was relieved to hear about her colleague's wise decision.

During their ward rounds, when Matron flagged up the increasing number of patients reporting bad coughs, Renee remained cheerful.

'No wonder! Living by the Irish Sea in a cold damp climate where there are twenty-six types of rain – it's a wonder we haven't all got pneumonia.'

Looking annoyed, Matron stopped in her tracks. 'It's not something I care to joke about, Sister,' she said sharply. 'As you know from your training,' she added pointedly, 'a debilitating cough can be indicative of other, more serious conditions. I expect my staff to be on high alert for any symptoms developing in their patients alongside a cough.'

Continuing down the ward together, Ada and Matron exchanged a knowing look – was there anything that Renee didn't manage to turn into a joke for her own personal entertainment?

Unfortunately, the tests that Jamie had sent off for analysis indicated that the cough was what they had feared: Mary Vale was soon in the grip of a whooping-cough infection which spread through the Home like wildfire. It was bad enough for residents to contract the highly infectious disease, but whooping cough was a potential death sentence for the new-borns in the nursery. Dora, fearful for her precious charges, instructed all staff to sterilize their hands in hot soapy water before entering her nursery, where she insisted that they wore masks and gloves.

'Sorry, I know it's a nuisance, but I'm not taking any chances with my babies,' she apologized to Ada.

'Don't worry, dear, we all completely agree with your strategy – it's essential we keep this wretched infection under control.'

'There's Catherine to think of too,' Dora pointed out. 'The further away she is from this place the better for the time being at least.'

Ada nodded. 'Thank God it's lovely weather and we're in beautiful countryside; at least she can safely play out in the garden or in the meadows.'

'The biggest risk is from infected residents coughing of course, when the bugs become airborne,' Dora fretted.

Ada sighed heavily. 'It's a menace: once they're airborne anybody in the vicinity could pick them up. The sooner a vaccine is developed to protect against whooping cough, the better. At least we have a small isolation wing where we can transfer any patient with a suspicious cough immediately.'

'Aye, you're right there,' Dora agreed, as she wiped a sanitized cloth over all the surfaces in the changing area. 'I'm obsessed with keeping everything clean,' she confessed.

'We're the same on the wards,' Ada agreed. 'We've been incinerating all rags and cloths infected with sputum.'

Looking sombre, Dora held Ada's gaze. 'You know all these precautions have doubled our workload,' she said.

Ada gave her a sympathetic smile. 'I know, Dora, it's hard work, but it absolutely *has to be done*.'

When three more infected residents were put into the isolation ward in another wing of the building, Matron sought out Ada for a word in private.

'Can we talk out in the garden?' Matron asked. 'At least the air is clean and fresh out there.'

Ada smiled. 'I'd be happy to take a turn around the garden with you.'

As she and Matron settled on a bench under a shady oak tree with a view of the vast Irish Sea sweeping in over Morecambe Bay, Ada's eyes scanned the empty lawn. 'No exercise classes these days,' she remarked.

'Not a bad thing, dear – heavy breathing and coughing are not something I want to encourage, even outdoors, at the moment,' Matron replied, before she earnestly added, 'What I wanted to say to you in private, dear, is that, with this dangerous infection in our midst, the entire staff – Sister Theresa, Dora, you, me *and Sister Renee*' – she pointedly stressed the name – 'will need to be especially watchful of all our patients.'

Knowing that it was Renee who was really troubling Matron and why she had purposefully asked to have this particular conversation in private, Ada quickly responded,

'Of course, Matron. Our patients and their babies have always been our priority; if anything, at a time like this, we need to pull together more than ever before.'

'I totally agree, Ada dear,' Matron replied. 'But you and I both know that not all of the staff are quite so committed as you are.'

'Don't worry,' Ada said with a small, determined smile. 'There are plenty of strong women working in Mary Vale who wouldn't flinch from putting a shirker firmly in her place.'

14. A Long Night

Predictably, Polly reacted badly to the announcement of a whooping-cough outbreak.

Terrified, she avoided all contact with fellow residents, took her meals out in the garden or in her own room, and repeatedly asked the staff (but not Renee) to check her temperature just in case she was spiking a fever. The staff obliged; as far as they were concerned, it was agreed that keeping Polly calm was a priority. Unfortunately, late one evening, when Polly thought the coast was clear, she slipped into the communal bathroom to clean her teeth before she went to bed. Too late she heard the laboured coughing of a resident, who emerged from the lavatory looking weak and flushed.

'Sorry,' the poor girl apologized, but the effort of speaking brought on another severe coughing fit. Gasping for breath, she leant against the lavatory door in the grip of an attack that convulsed her entire body.

Horrified, Polly ran back to her bedroom, where she flung open the window in order to gulp in deep breaths of fresh air. But, despite all her efforts, within days Polly fell ill herself, and Jamie, after confirming the diagnosis, quickly despatched her to the Home's isolation wing. It was very unfortunate that the night her condition deteriorated was the night Sister Renee was on duty. Ada, who had been nursing Polly during the day, settled her fretful patient down before she finished her shift.

'I'll be back in the morning, first thing,' she assured Polly. 'Now, dear, before I go, let me listen to your chest.'

Pressing the stethoscope to Polly's chest, Ada listened hard to the girl's laboured breathing, after which she took her temperature, which was still sky-high. Knowing she was handing over to Sister Renee for the next shift, Ada took particular care to record this in the handover notes.

'Please keep an eye on Polly's temperature, which has been consistently high throughout the day. Suggest you take her temperature every two hours just to be on the safe side and carefully monitor throughout the night.'

Feeling deeply uneasy, Ada headed home, praying that Polly's condition would stabilize in the night and that Renee would indeed keep an eye on her vulnerable patient.

Polly's condition didn't stabilize; in fact, it got distinctly worse. Hot and feverish, she rang the emergency bell in her room, and Sister Renee, who had arrived late for her shift and hadn't had a moment to look at the handover notes carefully left by Ada, bustled in to find her weeping patient tangled up in dishevelled bedding.

'Oh, Sister,' Polly sobbed. 'I feel sweaty and sick.'

Sighing, Renee suppressed her irritation – even in pre-whooping-cough times Polly had constantly complained of these symptoms – nevertheless she said calmly, 'Sit up, and I'll take your temperature.'

Feeling breathless, Polly struggled to sit upright, allowing Renee to pop a thermometer under her tongue.

'Your temperature's high,' she conceded. 'Hardly surprising in a room with no window open and you covered in bedding.'

'I was shivering earlier, but now I'm boiling hot,' Polly wailed.

Rearranging her pillows and straightening the sheets, Renee said, 'I'll top up your water glass and open the window – that should cool you down a bit.'

After she had completed her tasks, she added, 'Now settle down and try to get some sleep; you're sure to feel better in the morning.'

But in the semi-darkness of the ward, Renee (still ignorant of Ada's very clear instructions) failed to check Polly's temperature again overnight, and by morning Polly had a dangerously high fever and severe coughing spasms that left her drained and coughing up blood. Uncharacteristically quiet and now too weak to complain, Polly lay limp and listless on her bed. Ada did her best to make her patient comfortable before joining Matron, who was checking the handover notes from Renee.

'She reports that Polly had a mild temperature at eleven fifteen p.m.,' Matron read.

Now thoroughly alarmed, Ada quickly checked Renee's brief notes too.

'I specifically advised in my handover notes that her temperature was very high, and that she should be checked every two hours. It sounds like she checked only once! And how can the temperature have been mild when it was sky-high both when I went off duty and again this morning?' Feeling fear rising in her chest, Ada turned to Matron. 'I think we had better fully examine Polly right away,' she said urgently.

Examining Polly was difficult because of the prolonged coughing fits that convulsed her hot body. When they finally managed to take her temperature, it was once again high, and her face was covered in a sheen of sweat.

'Will I be all right, Sister?' Polly gabbled, before another paroxysm of coughing seized her, ending in the characteristic whoop.

Worried sick, Ada nevertheless kept calm. 'You'll be fine, dear; we just need to cool you down a bit and fetch you some nice clean sheets,' she soothed and helped Polly take a sip of water from the glass on her bedside table.

Looking across the bed at Ada, Matron whispered, 'You'd better check on the other patients, dear. I'll keep an eye on Polly for the time being.'

Leaving Matron to attend to Polly, Ada made her way back to the wards in order to examine the other patients who weren't in isolation, but who, in the circumstances, needed to be checked regularly for signs of fever and asked if they had spotted blood in their sputum. At the end of her ward round, Ada felt confident that there were no new outbreaks.

Later that day what they had all been dreading happened: Polly started to bleed. Shortly afterwards, her waters broke, and she went into early labour. Matron and Ada, working with the poor terrified girl in the delivery room, knew from bitter experience that the premature foetus stood no chance of survival. Convulsed with hacking coughs and terrified about what was happening to her, Polly had to be sedated in order for the nursing staff to deal with her contractions and deliver her still-born baby. By the time Sister Renee signed in for night-shift duty, Polly had miscarried and lay quiet and sedated in an isolated side room in the post-natal suite.

Surprised by the unexpected news, Renee was immediately on the defensive. 'The only discomfort I observed last night was a high temperature, but it wasn't dangerously high.'

Ada, now thoroughly roused, tried hard to control herself but failed. 'I left a specific comment in my handover notes to you. Did you follow those instructions?' she demanded.

Omitting to mention that she hadn't even read the notes, Renee quickly covered her tracks. 'I didn't want to wake the poor girl up once she had fallen asleep; she was exhausted. And the temperature wasn't that high at eleven p.m.'

Ada raised an eyebrow. 'And did you check for blood in her sputum and administer aspirin for her temperature or try to cool her down?'

Renee hit back forcefully. 'As I have just said, the temperature wasn't high enough to warrant that, and I certainly didn't rouse her every two hours. I actually thought it unnecessary, but I kept a careful eye on her.'

Ada threw her a sceptical look. 'I'll have to take your word for that, Renee. Did you examine her again before you went off-duty this morning?' Ada persisted.

Renee shook her head. 'No, Polly had had a broken

night. I thought she needed her sleep, so I left her in peace.'

Shaking her head, Ada repressed the urge to scream at Renee. 'I don't see the point of leaving handover notes if you ignore them,' she snapped.

Knowing that she had done far worse than ignore the notes – she had failed to read them at all – Renee was determined not to be cross-examined further.

'Now if you'll excuse me,' she said sharply. 'I have to start my shift.'

A few hours later Ada arrived home to find Jamie feeding their daughter her supper. Having heard the sad news, he gave his wife a long, level look.

'Yet another Sister Renee slip-up,' he murmured.

Slumping on to a kitchen chair, Ada poured herself a cup of tea from the pot that stood on the table.

'More of a disaster, I'd say. I've been trying all day to be fair-minded,' she confessed.

'But you can't, can you?' he asked knowingly.

Ada woefully shook her head.

'Dada, Dada,' Catherine gurgled. 'Poon, poon.'

Smiling, Jamie handed his daughter the spoon, which she used to bash the beans left on her high-chair tray.

Seeing Ada pre-occupied, Jamie said, 'You know, I doubt Renee even read your handover notes, darling.'

'I've been wondering the same thing,' Ada agreed.

'I've grumbled about Renee's attitude to patients in the past, but now I'm far more concerned about her nursing standards.'

Thoroughly upset, Ada blurted out, 'We've no proof that she didn't nurse her properly last night.'

'We could try asking Polly about what happened?' Jamie insisted.

Ada looked doubtful. 'The poor girl's in no state to be questioned right now, and anyway who would believe Polly? She's always so over the top and emotional. Renee could shoot her down in flames in no time.' Near to tears, Ada cried, 'Oh, where will it stop, Jamie?'

'I don't know, but my gut instinct is it can only end badly,' he replied, as he wiped his daughter's smeared face with a damp flannel.

'Play, Mama, play,' the charming little girl cried, grabbed her mother's hand and toddled out into the sunny garden.

As they watched Catherine totter up and down the garden path, Ada turned to Jamie. 'We've got to keep an even sharper eye on Renee now, Jamie – and double-check her notes for any misinformation or inaccuracy.'

'Sweetheart, we can't be her minders all the time,' Jamie pointed out. 'It's simply impractical.'

'We have to, Jamie, there's *no* choice,' Ada answered hotly. 'We're here to protect our patients and their babies, not expose them to the dangers of poor nursing.'

The following day it was Jamie's turn to face Renee. Knowing just how tough Renee was, Jamie's heart sank. It would be easy to let things go, but ethically he simply couldn't do that; he had to at least attempt to find out the truth.

'Polly says the only thing that you did on the night that she was sick was take her temperature once and open a window to cool her down – is that correct?' he stated without any preamble.

Renee's sharp green eyes flashed angrily. 'So you've been checking up on me, have you, Doctor?' she snapped.

'It's my duty, in fact,' he answered shortly.

Controlling her outrage, Renee said, 'Polly had a fever. You can hardly rely on a delirious girl to properly account for my nursing throughout an entire shift.'

After throwing him a contemptuous look, Renee swept off with her head held high.

'Well, that didn't get me far,' Jamie acknowledged to himself. 'Ada's right, as usual – Sister Renee's got it covered and she's showing no sign of dropping her guard even if she is in the wrong.'

After the premature birth of her child, Polly's body recovered over a period of weeks, and the whooping cough eventually left her, as it did many other infected residents. Once the outbreak had been successfully contained and life returned to normal, Polly's mother came to collect her daughter and take her home. Renee made herself scarce while Polly said her tearful goodbyes to friends and staff. When it came to saying farewell to Ada, whom Polly had always trusted, the girl wept bitter tears.

'I might have had a healthy baby but for Sister Renee not looking after me properly,' the miserable girl insisted. Dropping her voice, she added in a whisper, 'And there's something else you should know too. Now that I'm leaving, I can tell you what I've been afraid to say before – she's a drinker. I've smelt it on her breath.' Sighing heavily, Polly wiped her eyes. 'If she'd had a few on the night she was supposedly taking care of me, that would certainly explain any slip-ups.'

15. RAF Mildenhall

The sudden appearance of a letter from Bill explaining that he and his team were due for an imminent transfer to RAF Mildenhall in Suffolk reduced Stella to floods of tears.

'Cheer up,' ever pragmatic Doreen said after Stella told her the news. 'At least he's not being sent to Sicily or the Far East.'

Her words brought no comfort to Stella. 'I've barely seen Bill half a dozen times,' she wailed into her hankie. 'The longest time we've ever had together was the day he drove me to Rivington.'

Just thinking of that glorious day in the Japanese Gardens and the entire night Stella had spent locked in her lover's arms brought on another rush of tears.

Lighting up a Woodbine, Doreen enquired, 'When's lover boy off, then?'

Stella gazed once more at the letter clutched in her hand. 'Soon,' she replied glumly.

'Will you get the chance to say goodbye before he leaves?' Doreen asked.

'Oh, I hope so, I really hope so,' Stella answered earnestly.

By a stroke of luck, they managed to meet (albeit briefly) in a dingy pub just off St Ann's Square in Manchester, where Bill explained to his puzzled girlfriend why his transfer was so sudden.

'Stella Star.' He started by using his favourite nickname for her. 'Believe me it's the last thing I want right now, just after meeting the girl of my dreams, but there's not a thing I can do about it. RAF Mildenhall urgently need my team down there to mend their runway and fix their planes.'

Sitting beside Bill, sipping the tepid gin and orange that he had bought for her, Stella's lovely blue eyes clouded with tears and her small determined chin wobbled as she struggled to keep her emotions in check. Quickly putting down his pint of bitter, Bill drew her into his arms.

'Honey, please don't cry.'

Throughout the days that she had been waiting to see Bill, Stella's darkest fear had been that he would politely suggest that they split up – after all how could they sustain a relationship when he was on the other side of the country? She had even gone so far as to imagine how he would break the bad news to her.

'Gee, nice knowing you, but this just ain't gonna work, babe.'

Pre-empting the situation, Stella tremulously asked him if he would prefer it if they did go their separate ways. Completely flabbergasted, Bill gazed at her for several seconds.

'Do you really, *really* think that I would play such a mean trick on you, sweetheart?'

'No . . .' she started to say, then blurted out, 'Yes! You're American, and I'm English – how's that scenario ever going to work out?'

'Stella, calm down,' he soothed. 'I'm not from another planet,' he said, smiling. 'Sure, I follow my President's orders, but, hell, we're on the same side, fighting the same damned enemy, we're allies – surely we can work things out rather than create difficulties?' he reasoned.

Feeling like a fool, Stella dropped her head, and her long, tumbling hair fell around her flushed, embarrassed face.

'I'm sorry, I've been pent up with nerves for days now. I know I'm over-reacting.'

'Jumping the gun!' he teased.

'I don't know what's wrong with me,' she mumbled. 'I worry all the time that you might have gone off me, or you'll be sent back home, or get injured, or meet somebody else.'

Tilting her face, Bill kissed Stella gently on the lips. 'Stella Star, you are the light of my life. I've never felt this way before,' he told her. 'Sure, I've had other women, all of whom I cared about to some extent, but never anybody like you, my sweet,' he added tenderly.

Taking two cigarettes from his Lucky Strike pack, he lit them up before handing one to Stella. 'That night at Rivington sealed it for me – you gave yourself so completely to me, how could I ever break that trust and walk away as if you were one in a line of many? I'm crazy about you, babe,' he confessed.

'Oh, *why*, *why* do you have to go away now?' Stella cried in sheer frustration.

'Why? There's a war on, honey, we go where we're sent.'

Filled with guilt for thinking of only her own needs, Stella quickly apologized. 'I'm sorry, darling, I'm such a selfish cow. You're so much nobler than me.'

'Bullshit!' Bill laughed. 'My heart dropped when I heard

about the transfer, though to be honest a move was always inevitable – we're a crack team who will always be transferred at a moment's notice. But, hell, Stella,' he insisted, 'it's not the end of the world! Instead of snatching an evening here and a day there, we can apply for leave and have some quality time together with no deadlines and no interruptions.'

Cheered by his words, Stella's blue eyes suddenly sparkled. 'I'd never thought of it that way.' Then her smile fell as yet another troubling thought crossed her mind. 'But where will we meet? We could spend all our leave travelling across country just to snatch a day together.'

'We'll find a way,' he assured her. 'We'll meet up somewhere in the middle and have a ball,' he promised. 'Now come on, kiddo, stop dreaming up problems and let's make the most of our last date in Manchester.'

Later that week Bill and his team were transferred south, and it was quite some time before Stella received Bill's first letter from Mildenhall.

My dearest darling wonderful girl!

God, how I miss you. Lucky that they work us to the bone here in Mildenhall – if I had time on my hands, time to sit and dream of you, I think I would go crazy. As it is, we hit the ground running at dawn and only finish when the job's done (whatever that job might be, from tarmacking the runway to patching up planes that have staggered back from a Luftwaffe hammering). It's around-the-clock work, sometimes sleeping on the job. It's

hardly surprising that RAF Mildenhall has the title 'Bomber
Station' – apart from working on the Wellingtons, Lancasters
(my favourites – beautiful machines!) and Stirlings, the sorties are
more numerous than I had ever imagined – can't say more than
that or I'll be in trouble with the censors. It is thrilling to know
that we are physically close to the enemy, just across the North Sea
from us here on the base. The challenges have taken over my entire
life – there's barely a free minute in the day. I've put in a plea for
leave (I said I'd go crazy if I didn't see my gel! Joke), but my
charm offensive didn't work. To be fair none of the other guys in
my team have got leave either. It's one rule for all here, no favours,
pal. But I'll keep working on it, don't you fear, my Stella Star.
Until then I close my eyes and kiss your lips. Please send me some
photographs, and please, please keep on writing.

Your loving devoted
Bill
Xxxx

And so the summer passed, culminating in an autumn
that was full of the events in Italy. When the jubilant news
came through of the Allies landing in Salerno, Calabria
and Taranto, the nation's mood was high and hopeful.
What with their gains in North Africa and the increasing
numbers of daylight American air raids, the balance was
definitely shifting.

The production of bombs in the munitions factory was
now even more vital to the war effort, so much so that the
factory manager at the Dove called a meeting begging the
workers to extend their hours and build more bombs.

'Let's blow the Nazis to buggery!' he cried.

A patriotic cry that was echoed by the workforce a thousand times over.

More shifts meant more mouths to feed, and, with rationing getting worse by the month, Stella's culinary skills were stretched to the limit. Her weekly menu (posted up in the canteen) centred around tried and tested popular savoury dishes: curried corned-beef balls, shepherd's pie, potato hash, stuffed sheep's heart, mock roast with mince and spam, cheese-and-onion flan, spicy sausage casserole, tripe and onions, mutton stew and fish pie were followed by the workers' favourite puddings – jam roly-poly, Bakewell tart, sticky gingerbread, stewed apple and cinnamon, fruit pie, rhubarb crumble and rice pudding or sago. Fortunately, five o'clock teas were a lighter meal: beans on toast, macaroni cheese, smoked mackerel, toad in the hole, baked potatoes, spam fritters, sausage butties – all disappeared in no time.

There was little available to heighten the bland taste of most of the food, but Stella tried her best with sprinklings of fresh tangy herbs, gravy stock, dripping or just bog-standard sauces like HP and Lea & Perrins. Occasionally, a local farmer or one of the workers who shot game on the moor would turn up with a brace of pheasants, or wild rabbits, very occasionally a hare and plenty of pigeon, which helped enhance the flavour of cheap mince, corned beef and spam, even if it did mean Stella had to do all the plucking and disembowelling herself.

Whenever she had a free moment, Stella wrote to Bill, sometimes from the kitchen table in between washing, and preparing, cooking and serving meals. She poured out her heart to her lover while keeping him informed of the local news in her part of the world.

My precious love,

Summer's slipped away from the moors, the cool misty mornings are back, and the days are getting shorter. It's so long since we met – I count the weeks that we spent together, recalling every golden moment of our summer romance.

Life trudges on here, as we do our bit, building bombs to fight the enemy, but, as the air raids increase, many led by you brave Yanks, I can't help but think of all the German civilian lives that have been lost. They're humans just like we are; though their leaders are monsters, there are still women, children and babies suffering for something they never even started.

I wonder how you're settling in down South, if you're taking care of yourself, not getting into trouble? I hope not! I'm sure you're far better provided for than us Brits. If I have to cook one more mince-and-onion pie or another rice pudding (without milk!), there's a very good chance I might throw one or both of them straight out of the window. I'm quite sure you have got your Coca-Cola, chocolate, cold beer, Lucky Strike and gum. Keep a stash for when we meet, my darling.

The munitions factory still hosts dances on Saturday night. I only go now to help out in the kitchen, serving food to the dancers when the orchestra take a break. They always play our favourite songs, 'Boogie Woogie Bugle Boy', 'In the Mood', waltzes, foxtrots, jives, but I don't dance, except with Doreen if she's stuck for a partner. Remember the line from the song 'I'll Never Dance

Again till I Dance with You'? Well, that's me: there's no joy in dancing without you, my sweet Bill.

I enclose some photographs. I have yours in a frame next to my bed. I kiss your photo every night before I fall asleep. Stay safe, my beloved.

Your adoring Stella xxx

16. Keswick

With Tom the stable lad gone, and Wilf still laid up with sciatica (which didn't stop him dragging himself out of bed every Friday night to stagger down to the pub), Lillian took complete charge of Major and Daisy and all the accompanying work that was required of a stable girl. Hitherto unknown tasks – feeding, grooming, mucking out, cleaning tack, maintaining farm machinery – completely occupied Lillian from dawn till dusk. Fortunately, she had finally managed to get hold of a proper Land Girl's uniform: brown breeches, green jumper and leather boots, which she alternated with dungarees and cotton shirts, depending on the weather. With Lillian now firmly established with the horses, she had suggested that Sal take over the tractor driving. Mo and Pat, terrified at the thought of sitting behind the wheel, had insisted that they were both 'too numb' to handle the tractor gears, never mind steer a straight course.

'I'd finish up in't blody beck!' Pat had threatened.

And she meant it too. After Mo had cheerfully announced that she was as thick as two short planks, nobody even bothered to persuade her. Though funny and good-natured, Mo really was the dimmest young woman, with no ambition other than to meet the Italian prisoners of war who had recently landed in the valley.

'They all look like Frank Sanitary,' Mo had excitedly told her friends.

Puzzled, Lillian had asked, 'Who's Frank Sanitary?'

Sal shook her head. 'Frank Sinatra,' she explained. 'To this day Mo's never got his name right yet!'

In all weathers Lillian worked with her powerful horses; attached to their shafts, they turned the rich black earth which curled and broke under the sharpened blades. Later, after the earth had been exposed to wind, ice and rain, they would drill wheat and barley, but not before the Land Girls had weaned the youngest lambs and prepared the ewes for sale at Keswick market. No sooner was one back-breaking job done than another began, and it was the faithful horses that bore the brunt of the hard, slogging work, without complaint, steady, patient and reliable. They were the best example of selflessness and devotion Lillian had ever seen.

'They're more patriotic than we are,' she declared in a moment of passion, as she, Mo, Sal and Pat cycled the ten miles from Rosthwaite village to Keswick on their 'war agricultural' bikes to pick up personal provisions.

Knowing just how much Lillian adored Major and Daisy, her friends couldn't resist teasing her. Wobbling dangerously close to the banks of the gurgling River Derwent, Mo joked, 'Don't be daft, hosses can't beat Hitler.'

'Course they can!' Lillian staunchly exclaimed. 'They help us provide food for the nation. Like you yourself once said, nobody can fight on an empty belly,' she reminded her friend.

Pulling over to the side of the road by the Bowder Stone in order to allow a loaded farm cart – pulled by a fine pair of enormous shire horses, who tossed their heads and jingled their harnesses as they clip-clopped by – to pass, Sal agreed with Lillian's sentiments. 'You're right, Lil,' she joked. 'If it weren't for the likes of Major and Daisy, Wilf would saddle up us lasses and have us dragging carts and ploughs around the fields.'

'And whip us if we did so much as stop for a breather,' Pat joked.

When they got into Keswick, the four women made a beeline for the shops. Clutching their clothing coupons, which Mrs M had not managed to filch, they bought cotton knickers and warm vests, new socks, fashion magazines, cigarettes and strong thread to sew their ripped work clothes. Afterwards they went to a steamy hot café opposite the Moot Hall in the centre of town, where they ordered tea, rock buns and spam sandwiches.

'This is the life,' sighed Pat, as she sipped scalding hot tea. 'No filthy pots on the table, no stale bread and no Mrs M with a fag hanging out of her gob serving us rissoles that you could bounce off the wall.'

Helping herself to the biggest rock bun, Sal said with her mouth full, 'What will we all do when this rotten war is over?'

Taking the second biggest rock bun, Mo immediately answered. 'Get married, have kids and never so much as visit the countryside again.'

Lillian gazed at her in astonishment. 'Do you really mean that?'

'I bloody do,' Mo forcefully replied. 'I hate the great outdoors. Gimme a little terraced house, two up, two down, in Barnsley, with an indoor privy, running water and a nice fella to cuddle up to every night,' she said with a dirty laugh.

Thinking how hard it would be to leave the land and the horses that she loved so much, Lillian shook her head. 'I don't know whether I could go back to "normal" any more.'

Remembering her life in the plush interior of Blackpool's Regal picture house, Lillian couldn't equate that small, slim, glamorous young woman with the woman she was now. Over the months of lifting farm machinery and controlling two powerful shires, Lillian had developed muscles in her legs and arms she never even knew she had. Her delicate, heart-shaped face, previously always highly made-up, was now deeply tanned, which contrasted prettily with her sparkling honey-brown eyes. These days Lillian didn't even care what she wore; at the end of every day she always finished up covered in mud, rain, sleet and every kind of muck. Clean underwear was altogether another matter and vital to Lillian's sense of well-being – hence their trip into Keswick that afternoon.

Curious, Sal asked, 'So what will you do when the war's over – carry on working with horses?'

Lillian thought about what Sal had said. 'I'd love to, but I don't know how I could ever do that,' she answered honestly.

Mo gave a throaty chuckle. 'You could always marry a farmer like Wilf, who would land you with the horses and every other job going.'

Lillian grimaced. 'And turn into a sloven like Mrs M? No thanks!'

Lillian's care for Daisy was especially touching as the mare's pregnancy advanced.

Watching her development like a hawk, Lillian logged any changes in a little notebook which she kept in the tack room. Though she had never met the vet, she knew immediately who he was when she spotted him out in the farmyard checking the cattle. Wearing old tweeds, a crumpled felt hat and knee-high leather boots, he looked like a classic old-fashioned vet. Hurrying across the yard to introduce herself, Lillian smiled as she extended a rather grubby hand.

'Hello, I'm Lillian, the new stable girl,' she said.

Turning, the vet was struck by this young girl he had never seen before: young, strong and astonishingly beautiful, she exuded health, youth and energy.

'Pleased to meet you, Lillian. I'm Robbie Allen, from Seatoller.'

'Tom told me about you before he left,' Lillian explained. 'He said I was to get in touch with you if I have any concerns about Daisy's pregnancy.'

The vet's brow crinkled in concern. 'Is she having problems?'

Lillian quickly shook her head. 'No, she's healthy enough, as far as I know, though I have to admit I am very inexperienced, but I have been keeping an eye on her progress.'

'I'm happy to take a look at her while I'm here,' Robbie said kindly.

Lillian smiled in relief. 'Thank you, I'd be most grateful.'

Following Lillian to the paddock, where the shires were grazing in the fading light of the autumn evening, the vet confidently approached both horses, who raised their heads to snicker as he approached.

'Hello there,' he murmured softly, before stroking a firm hand first down Major's broad glossy neck, then Daisy's. 'How are you doing?'

At the sound of his soft voice Daisy's ears twitched and she pushed her muzzle into his chest.

'They really like him,' Lillian marvelled as she watched Robbie Allen bend down gently to examine Daisy, who was obedient to his bidding.

The only people Lillian had seen previously with the horses were Wilf, who was a brute, and young Tom; the vet was altogether different. It wasn't just Robbie's easy, confident manner; it was his knowledge that struck Lillian. He *knew* these beasts, understood them; they in return instinctively responded to his touch and voice. Major, jealous of all the attention that the mare was getting, gave the vet a strong nudge on the arm.

'All right, big boy,' Robbie smiled. 'I've not forgotten you.' Straightening up, he gave Daisy a gentle pat on the rump, then turned to stroke Major, who towered head and shoulders over the vet. Snorting down his nostrils, the horse blew into Robbie's thick, auburn-grey hair.

'They're playing you off,' Lillian chuckled.

'They're beautiful beasts,' Robbie answered affectionately. 'Let's get away from them for a few moments, then I can report on Daisy's condition,' he suggested.

Leaving the horses to graze in the paddock, they stood in the yard, the vet lighting up a pipe, which he puffed on for a few seconds before speaking. Inhaling the nutty dark smell of the burning tobacco, Lillian thought how much nicer pipe tobacco smelt than the cheap cigarettes she smoked.

'She's doing fine – on track to drop the foal sometime mid-November, so not long now,' Robbie told Lillian. 'Take it easy with her from now on, though,' he warned. 'Let Major do the work where possible or use the tractor, if you can. Daisy needs to rest, and eat well, as much as that's possible these days.'

Just listening to Robbie talking about the imminent birth made Lillian's pulse race, as she realized that she was both excited and nervous.

'I could leave Daisy in the paddock throughout the day when I'm working,' she suggested. 'The grass isn't as rich as it was in the summer, but there's still some there to graze on.'

Robbie nodded in agreement with her idea. 'Leave her in her stable on cold days; if she's out and it's chilly, she'll drop weight and that might affect the weight of her foal. Right,' he concluded, as he tapped his pipe on a fence post. 'I'll be off – nice to meet you, and keep in touch,' he said cheerily, before heading off to his mud-spattered old Jeep.

Lillian watched him go with a quizzical expression on her face. He had assured her that all was well with the mare in her charge, and the advice he had given her was sound and sensible; but it was Robbie Allen's way with the animals that lingered with her after his departure: the instant rapport between man and beast had deeply moved her. A shrill neigh from the paddock recalled Lillian to the here and now, and, hurrying back to the field, she nimbly leapt over the gate to attach lead ropes to Major and Daisy and take them back to their snug, straw-littered stalls, where, after a warm bran mash supper, they peacefully settled down for the night.

17. Peterborough

Dearest, darling Stella Star,

Good news! I've got leave in October, so get your gorgeous self to Peterborough, where I plan to meet you. I appreciate you'll have to get leave too, but, considering you've not had time off in months, I'm really hoping you can swing it with your factory manager. You'll never guess where I'm planning to take you for five days – just believe me when I say it's quite uniquely lovely. No more clues, so don't ask!

After reading Bill's letter, Stella danced around the canteen kitchen in sheer joy, so much so she didn't hear her young assistant, Nellie, enter the room. It was only after she had spun full circle, wildly waving her hands in the air, that she came face to face with her colleague, who gawped at her boss in disbelief.

'Is summat up?' she asked bluntly, as Stella came to a stumbling halt.

With a wide smile still on her face, Stella answered, 'Everything's fine. I've just had good news, that's all.'

'Shall I mash the spuds before they get cold?' Nellie continued pragmatically.

Trying to gather her thoughts, Stella answered, 'Yes, please,' just as the smell of burning assailed her senses.

Stating the obvious Nellie grumbled, 'You've burnt yon sausages.'

After smothering the sausages in onion gravy, Stella popped the heavy trays into the big industrial oven, and, leaving Nellie to mash pounds and pounds of spuds, Stella made several huge dishes of jelly, which she planned to serve with tinned peaches. All the time she worked her mind raced: what exactly was Bill planning for her? In truth she didn't care where they went, or where they stayed, just as long as she could see him, hold him, kiss him – nothing else mattered. But he had sounded so excited about his plans that now she couldn't help but wonder what they might be. Tapping her feet to the music blaring out from *Workers' Playtime* on the canteen wireless, Stella dreamily wondered if she and Bill might go dancing during their leave. The thought of being in Bill's strong arms, swinging around a ballroom-floor made her heart beat double time; he was such a wonderful dancer and could move to any tune, foxtrot, waltz, tango but best of all jive. Hearing 'Chattanooga Choo Choo' blasting out on the air waves, Stella itched to dance, and, quickly checking that dour Nellie was nowhere in sight, she jived around the large kitchen table, waving a dishcloth over her head.

Serving dinner to a long queue of hungry munitions workers, then clearing away, followed by a constant stream of washing-up, slowly brought Stella down to earth. Realizing that she wouldn't be going anywhere if she didn't get official leave, she decided to pop over to the factory manager's office. Leaving Nellie to start the teas (fortunately a simple meal of baked potatoes and beans) for the first shift of diners, Stella dashed across the site to the old mill building which housed the management. After considering the long hours Stella had worked throughout the summer, plus the overtime she had put in when the workers had been asked to voluntarily work a longer day in order to increase the munitions output, the manager kindly granted Stella five days' leave at the start of October.

'You'll leave everything in order before you go?' he asked sharply. 'We don't want the workforce starved to death in your absence.'

Knowing that she would prepare at least half of the meals before she left, and that Nellie would be helped by a young girl whom Stella had been training up as a junior cook, she was able to assure the manager that everything would be under control. Leaving the office with wings on her feet, Stella completed the teas, then, while Nellie cleared away, Stella, keen to catch the last post, quickly answered Bill's letter.

Darling!

I can barely think straight. Your letter put me in a flat spin and, though I've managed to prepare and serve food all day, my mind has been elsewhere. The thought that we'll meet soon makes me giddy with happiness, and I'm intrigued by your mysterious plans, but I won't ask any questions. Believe me, I want to, but I don't want to spoil anything. I was worried that I might not get permission to take leave at such short notice, but the manager agreed to the dates you suggested, so that's a huge relief. All I've

got to do now is arrange train tickets for the journey down to
Peterborough; as soon I have times I'll let you know but you know
how late trains are running these days, so please wrap yourself up
warm as you might be in for a long wait at a draughty station.
OH! I just can't believe I'll see you soon, my precious love. I'll
write more later but for now I must dash to catch the post.

All my love
Your Stella Star
xxxx

After securing her train ticket to Peterborough, Stella went into over-drive, frantically trying to organize what clothes she would need for five days away. Sitting on her bed in the chilly bedroom that they shared, cheeky Doreen lit up a Woodbine as she watched Stella pulling her clothes out of the wardrobe.

'With a bit of luck, you won't get out of bed for five days,' she teased. 'So clothes shouldn't be your priority.'

Stella, who had confessed to her friend that she had lost her virginity to Bill, blushed to the roots of her long golden-red hair.

'Stop it,' she implored.

'Well, it's true,' Doreen insisted. 'I'd be more concerned about sorting out birth control, unless you're planning on starting a family right away.'

'Of course we're not!' an indignant Stella exclaimed. 'I've trusted Bill so far with that side of things; there's certainly no need to doubt him now.'

'So all you'll want – apart from a nightie,' the irrepressible

Doreen joked – 'is a warm coat, sturdy shoes in case you do a lot of walking, a nice skirt and top, and a smart frock.'

Stella glanced miserably at her collection of winter clothes flung on to her bed.

'They look like a heap of rags,' she said glumly.

Doreen stubbed out her cigarette in order to examine Stella's wardrobe.

'How many clothes coupons have you got?' she asked.

'I've not had time recently to go out to the shops, so I've managed to save up a few,' Stella replied.

'Then if I were you, I'd get myself a bright woollen twinset, which you could wear with your dark tweed skirt, and a new winter frock – the rest,' she said with a dismissive gesture, 'you could sew for victory – or, in your case, darn!'

Grateful for Doreen's candid advice, Stella went clothes shopping in Manchester's C&A on her next afternoon off. Later, when she presented Doreen with her purchases, her friend was duly impressed.

'The cornflower-blue twinset brings out the blue in your eyes,' Doreen approved. 'And the plum velvet dress is gorgeous. I love the little silk collar with the satin bow.'

Opening another paper parcel, Stella added excitedly, 'And I've got a new nightie and some nylons.'

Doreen smiled fondly at her friend's radiantly happy face. 'Stop worrying, sweetheart, you look lovely whatever you wear.'

'I just want to look my very best for my Bill,' Stella said dreamily.

'You'll look like a film star,' Doreen assured her, 'Especially in that nightie,' she added with a naughty wink.

Stella did indeed feel like a film star when she stepped off the train at Peterborough Station. Though the journey, via Leeds and Sheffield, had been tediously long – stopping to give way to troop trains along the route and pulling over into obscure sidings for no apparent reason – Stella had been excited by the passing scenery: the landscape of bombed-out towns and cities changing to the rolling countryside that slowly flattened out as the train journeyed through the fertile fens. With her glorious hair falling around her shoulders and her big blue eyes sparkling with excitement, Stella drew a great deal of attention from the servicemen on the train, who offered her cigarettes in an attempt to start up a conversation. When asked, 'What's a gorgeous girl like you doing here?' Stella flashed a smile as she confidently replied, 'I'm visiting my boyfriend.'

A reply which quickly took the wind out of any further flirtatious conversation.

As the train had pulled into Peterborough Station, Stella had slipped into her warm coat, which, thanks to Doreen's generosity, was now embellished with a dark-brown fox fur. Picking up her small suitcase from the overhead luggage rack, Stella skipped off the train as soon as it stopped, then quickly looked around for Bill. Seeing him nowhere, she hurried to the exit, where she handed in her ticket; then, as she stepped out of the station, she cried out in delight when she saw her beloved waving to her from a smart military Jeep. He jumped out and ran across the road to her, arms wide open and totally oblivious to the traffic.

'STELLA STAR! SWEETHEART!' he yelled. 'Wanna ride?'

Clutched tightly against his strong chest, Stella thought she might faint with happiness and lack of air, because Bill was squeezing her so hard. Releasing her, he swung Stella in a full circle before setting her back on the ground, and then kissed her long and hard on her open lips. Tall as she was, Stella had to stand on her tiptoes to passionately return the kisses he showered on her.

'I love you, I love you, I love you!' he chanted like a wildly excited child.

Stopping his words with her mouth, she pressed her body against his, returning his kisses until they were both weak with desire. Besotted and blissfully happy, they might have stood there clasping each other for another half-hour but a bobby on the beat interrupted their romantic exchange with a sharp, 'Are you going to be leaving that vehicle over there unattended for very much longer?'

'No, sir!' Bill beamed.

Grabbing Stella's suitcase, he whisked her and her luggage into the Jeep and started up the engine; then, with one hand on the wheel and the other around Stella's shoulders, he roared away. Happy just to be close to Bill, close enough to inhale the combined smell of his favourite cigarettes and the shaving cream he used, Stella would have happily driven to the ends of the earth with him.

'Any idea where we're heading, kiddo?' Bill chuckled, as they drove out of town and headed for open countryside.

'No,' Stella replied. 'You keep telling me it's a secret, so I haven't a clue.'

'Wanna clue, babe?' he teased.

'Okay,' she giggled.

'We're heading for a city of spires and bicycles,' he informed her.

Truly puzzled, Stella echoed his words, 'Spires and bicycles?'

'Don't worry, honey,' Bill responded, as he swung on to the A1 South road. 'We'll be there soon enough.'

18. Spires and Bicycles

By the time they arrived at their destination later that afternoon, the bleak autumn light was starting to fade, and a cold damp mist rose from the river that circled its way around the city. Intrigued, Stella, in the passenger seat, turned curiously from left to right.

'Where are we?' she cried in frustration.

Pressing down hard on the accelerator, Bill took a sharp right turn, and they entered a narrow street flanked with tall greystone buildings. Bouncing over cobbles, they passed students in flowing black gowns riding their bicycles. Bill pulled the Jeep over so that Stella could take in the view. In front of her rose a magnificent towering chapel which soared high into the mauve-coloured sky, where the slow-setting autumn sun illuminated its tall spires.

'Now do you know where you are?' Bill said, grinning.

Feeling a little foolish and self-conscious, Stella shook her head.

Pointing to the chapel, Bill said, 'That's King's College – and this is Cambridge.'

At which point organ music soared out of the chapel, accompanied by the fluting sweet voices of young choristers, the combination of which sent a shiver shooting down the length of Stella's spine. Awed by her surroundings,

Stella, with tears of pure happiness in her eyes, murmured, 'I'll remember this moment for the rest of my life.'

Before they entered the University Arms Hotel, Bill handed Stella a gold ring.

'Don't get too excited: it's not the real McCoy – that will come later,' he promised. 'For now, we have to pass ourselves off as Mr and Mrs Brownlow, so I reckoned we'd need a ring to seal the deal.'

Blushing self-consciously, Stella pushed the ring on to her finger; then, while Bill signed the register, she occupied herself with gazing around the old-fashioned hotel, which (as far as she could see) was built in the middle of what looked like a vast green field.

'Strange place to build a hotel,' she remarked to Bill, as they made their way upstairs to the first floor.

'The guy on the desk said the green space around the hotel is called Parker's Piece; it's ancient common land and a public right of way,' Bill explained. 'I've booked us in for an early supper,' he said with a wink, as they walked along the carpeted landing. 'Thought we might need an early night.'

Their double room was big with windows looking out over Parker's Piece, where Stella could dimly see people hurrying along the intersecting pathways, and bicyclists whizzing along, tinkling their bells to alert passing pedestrians. Drawing her away from the window, Bill closed the heavy curtains before saying, 'Now let me finally take a long look at you.'

Removing her coat, which he threw on to the nearest

chair, he turned Stella slowly around in order to stroke her hair, her neck, her shoulders and her face.

'You are even more beautiful than I remembered,' he murmured.

Eager to touch him too, Stella reached up to sweep her hands through his thick, blond hair, after which she softly caressed his high cheekbones and strong, determined chin.

'And you are the best-looking man that ever came out of America,' she smiled.

Desperate to be close to each other, they tore off their clothes and leapt into the bed, which was cold and a bit damp. Huddling together naked, they explored each other's body, gasping and sighing in delight, and when they did make love it was slow, gentle and tender.

Exhausted after the eventful day and their love-making, Stella fell asleep with her head against Bill's warm shoulder; he remained wide awake, revelling in the sight of her long, slim body pressed against his bigger, muscular one. Winding tendrils of her hair around his fingers, Bill marvelled at the intensity of his feelings for this woman, who, less than six months ago, he hadn't even met. Her beauty took his breath away, but his feelings for her went beyond the physical. He loved her spirit, her innocence, her generosity and compassion; she was a good woman with a big heart who worked hard for her living and worked hard for her country. He realized with a jolt that he could never let Stella go, that when the war ended, or even before the war ended, if she agreed he would take her back to the States with him. Sure, it would be complicated, he thought, but, hell, he wasn't the only American Flight Engineer who had fallen in love with an Englishwoman. Official problems could be overcome; it might take time, but, if he wanted to spend the rest of his life with his Stella Star, he would make it his priority to research the protocol. For the moment, he decided, he would keep his long-term plans of marriage to himself, proposing only when the time was right; he didn't want to build up Stella's hopes, in case they were smashed by bureaucratic regulations. Gathering her warm, relaxed sleeping body close to his heart, Bill made a vow: as soon as he could he would buy his beautiful girlfriend a *real* gold ring and ask her to be his bride.

Neither of them wanted to get out of bed, and they lay tangled in the sheets, smiling and blissfully happy.

'I can't be bothered to get dressed again,' Stella groaned.

'Well, you could always go down to the dining room naked, that would take everybody's mind off their corned-beef rissoles,' Bill chuckled.

In the end hunger drove them down to the half-empty dining room, where the blackout blinds were drawn down and candles provided flickering illumination. From the menu they chose tomato soup, grilled sole, chips and peas, followed by plum tart and custard.

'Mmm,' Stella sighed, savouring every mouthful of food, which tasted even better because she hadn't been involved in any of the cooking. 'Beats tripe and onion any day.'

Bill even managed to procure a bottle of Chablis, which they polished off in no time, so he impetuously bought another.

'We're making up for lost time,' he announced, and they clinked crystal glasses and toasted each other's good health.

'Tell me about Mildenhall,' Stella asked, as they drank a bitter, chicory-based coffee in the hotel lounge lit by a roaring log fire.

As enthusiastic as ever, Bill launched off. 'It's a terrific place,' he started. 'The planes we're working on are beauties.' Bill's eyes sparkled with pride as he recited their names. 'Lancasters, Wellingtons and Stirlings.'

'Lancasters are your favourites, right?'

'The best,' he exclaimed. 'We push 'em out, good and ready for battle, but, oh my God, you should see the state of them when – and if – they come limping back. Shattered wings, leaking petrol tanks, tails blown off, windshields smashed. Seriously, you marvel that any pilot could fly such mangled wrecks back to base. Those guys are heroes,' he added emotionally. 'I tell you, a lot don't make it home, and the losses are terrible,' he said sadly. 'The awful thing is shipping the bodies of dead men back home to be buried – that's if there's a body to be buried.'

Seeing the sadness in his face, Stella gently moved the subject on to something more positive. 'Do you ever get a chance to fly your favourite planes?'

'Hell, yes! We take them on test-flights all the time, straight out over the North Sea.' Laughing to himself, he made a noise like a powerful engine taking off.

Though relieved that Bill didn't go further than that, Stella nevertheless looked anxious.

'Don't worry, honey, they're only test-runs,' he assured

her. 'And when we're not fixing planes, we're fixing the runway,' he added. 'With so many loaded bombers taking off around the clock, there's constant repair work to be done.'

'Sounds like a bit of a slog,' she remarked.

Bill gave a secretive smile. 'Occasionally we get the perks of the job.'

'Like what – a crate of Coca-Cola and some ice-cold beers?' she teased.

'That too. But, more to the point, we get to deliver planes to airbases. Only the other day I flew a Lancaster bomber to an airfield in Lincoln. Man! You should have felt the power of the engine, not to mention the width of her wings – it was one of the best flights of my whole life.' Seeing his girlfriend's eyes starting to droop with fatigue, Bill pushed back his chair and held out his hand. 'Come on, beautiful, time for bed.'

Taking his extended hand, Stella said softly, 'I don't think there's anything I'd like more right now.'

The precious days they had together passed in a blur of sight-seeing; they even got into King's College Chapel on their last night, where they listened to the evensong service sung by little boys in white and red gowns who looked more angelic than human. When Stella and Bill weren't walking by the River Cam or punting down it with a chilly mist rising, they warmed up in quaint tea shops, the Whim, on Trinity Street, and the Copper Kettle, on King's Parade, where older, bespectacled dons and fellows sat (over rock buns and anchovy-paste sandwiches) debating the works of Virgil or the complex philosophies of Heidegger and Sigmund Freud.

'I envy them their brains,' Stella confessed, as she and Bill hungrily demolished plates of baked beans on toast after spending the morning on Grantchester Meadows, which, though beautiful, was bitterly cold. 'It makes me wish I had had a better education.'

Pouring out strong hot tea, Bill asked, 'What exactly was your education?'

'Basic,' she answered honestly. 'Educated by nuns, stern scary nuns in a Catholic school in Burnley. I loved reading and writing when I was at school, especially composition, but if I was ever found with a book in my hand – wasting time reading, as my parents called it, instead of doing something useful like cleaning the windows or mopping the back step – I always got a ticking-off.'

'Aww, so you weren't allowed to daydream?' he asked sympathetically.

'No chance!' she exclaimed. 'So I used to slip into the library on my way back from the school and read anything I could get my hands on, or borrow books and sneak them into my bedroom, where I would read them at night, under the bed-covers with a torch,' she giggled.

'Wow, they disapproved that much,' he said.

Stella nodded. 'I can sort of see their point. They worked like slaves: Mum in the local cotton mill, Dad at a blast furnace on permanent night shift, making sleepers for railway tracks. They had no time for education, especially for a girl who, it was assumed, would marry and have three kids by the time she was twenty-one.'

'So how did you dodge that bullet?' he asked.

'Pig-headed determination not to go in the mill when I left school at fourteen and being quick on my feet at finding an alternative before I was press-ganged into the spinning room,' she recalled. 'I did finish up in the mill, but as assistant cook – that's how I ended up in the munitions-factory canteen,' she explained. Changing the subject, she asked, 'Tell me about you?'

'Growing up and going to school in Seattle was a happy time. I was quick to learn, curious and confident, qualities both my parents encouraged in me.' Recalling his liberal parents, Bill smiled fondly. 'Course, Dad always wanted me to join the fishing business, but Mom insisted I had a proper education before becoming part of the family firm. She was passionate about books, music and art, which I was too, but I liked skiing, rock climbing, biking and fishing a whole lot more.' He laughed. 'Let's just say that, thanks to my folks, I had a rounded education before I joined Dad on the boats fishing on the Pacific Rim – man, it was beautiful beyond words.'

Stella gazed into his rapt face, normally so vibrant and bright, now dreamy with memories.

'It's a place,' he continued, 'where the sea merges with the sky, creating a blinding blue landscape in which bald eagles mate and hunt, salmon leap upriver, bear cubs roll in the snow; and in the dark winter months the Northern Lights flicker green, purple and silver like vast fireworks exploding in the heavens.'

Stella had never heard Bill talk so eloquently or poetically. His words transported her from a tea shop in one of the oldest university cities in the world to a terrain of sea and sky that was the habitat of wild birds and animals.

'I've seen dolphins leaping and playing in front of our boats,' he continued. 'Whales, pods of them, blowing up fountains of spray as they surfaced from the deep; I've heard them at night too, deep down in the ocean, calling out to each other. More like music, it's the eeriest and most moving sound that I've ever heard in my life.' Shaking his head as if he too were surfacing from an ocean of powerful memories, he returned Stella's rapt gaze. 'One day, my darling, I'll take you there,' he promised.

On their last afternoon together they walked along the Backs; arm in arm and huddling together to keep warm, they passed the Mathematical Bridge at Queens' College, the elegant quad beside King's College Chapel, the finials of St John's College, and then, after passing red-brick Magdalene College, they followed the river and made their way home.

'It's so tranquil and removed from war – I could stay here forever,' Stella sighed.

'I wish,' he declared. 'I'm the fortunate one: this gorgeous city is only a stone's throw from Mildenhall, nearly two hundred miles from Manchester.'

Stella's heart sank as she thought of her imminent journey back to the munitions factory on the Lancashire moors.

'I can't bear the thought of leaving you, Bill,' she whispered as she quickly wiped tears from her eyes. 'I've never been so happy as I am now, here with you.'

'Stella Star, we're gonna do this again and again,' he said firmly. 'You'll come down here or I'll come up North,' he assured her. 'Occasionally we get to deliver planes to other airbases, Warrington being one of them.' Winking, he added, 'You never know – we might get a chance to revisit that remote romantic spot where we fell in love.'

Stella couldn't help but blush at the memory of their first love-making on the warm moors under the stars, close to the Japanese Gardens and Rivington Pike.

'Do you really think you might get to fly to Warrington soon?' she asked hopefully.

'I'm on the case,' he laughed. 'I can't live without seeing you, honey,' he told her passionately. 'I'll pull every string to see you.' Seeing a growing sadness in her sky-blue eyes, he finished firmly, 'Come on, Star, let's make the most of our last night in Cambridge.'

Their final meal, an absolute feast for Stella, accustomed as she was to wartime rissoles, fritters and pies, was grilled sardines, lamb chops, cabbage and roast potatoes, followed by apple dumpling and custard. Ravenous, they drank glasses of cider with their meal, then, skipping the ghastly war-time coffee which Bill simply refused to order, they drank brandy in the hotel's empty lounge, once again warmed by a crackling log fire. Tired and replete, both Bill and Stella stared at the dancing flames in the Edwardian grate, thinking the same thing: tomorrow they would part. Not wanting to voice their fears, each simply reached out to grasp the other's hand. Eventually, when their glasses were empty, Bill rose and gently helped Stella to her feet.

'Time for bed, sweetheart,' he whispered.

And together they slowly made their way upstairs.

The following morning, tired and bruised from love-making most of the night, Bill drove Stella back to Peterborough, where his mood was no longer buoyant. Pulling up at the station, he helped Stella, whose eyes were brimming with tears, out of the Jeep. His strong shoulders sagged and his eyes blurred with the tears he was struggling to hold back, their roles suddenly reversed: Stella was now the strong, optimistic one. Smiling hopefully, she whispered assurances. 'We'll meet soon, my love.'

Clutching her slender body to his, he murmured into her hair, 'You have blown me away, Stella Star.'

Utterly lost for words, they clung on to each other until the sound of the steam train preparing to depart dragged them back to reality. Hand in hand, with Bill carrying her suitcase, they walked down the platform, thick with smoky fumes from the train's belching engine. After settling her in an empty compartment, Bill returned to the platform and Stella wound down the sash window so they could kiss once more before the train pulled away from the station and the man that she simply adored.

19. Trouble in the Kitchen

In the weeks after Polly's abrupt departure following her tragic miscarriage, Ada became more hopeful about Renee's behaviour.

'She seems to have turned over a new leaf,' she told Jamie. 'More attentive,' she added.

'Maybe Polly losing her baby shocked Renee into realizing that a more solid accusation of negligence against her could lead to dismissal,' he suggested.

Ada nodded. 'And, if that happened, she might not be allowed to nurse again.'

Frowning, Jamie shook his head. 'I'm not convinced, darling. The woman's a loose cannon as far as I'm concerned.'

'Which is exactly why we have to continue monitoring her, just to be on the safe side,' Ada pointed out.

'Double-checking fellow colleagues is not part of my job description,' Jamie grumbled.

'I know, darling, but *please*, just for our peace of mind,' she asked with her bewitching smile that he could never resist.

When Ada discovered that Dora was also on the lookout for anything amiss in Sister Renee's nursing, she exclaimed, 'Oh, heavens, we're ALL spying on her.'

Dora shrugged, as if to say, 'That's her problem.'

'After her last slip-up – and that's putting it kindly,' the older nurse said – 'I think it's prudent to double-check anything Renee does.'

In Mary Vale's garden, deep in golden-red and russet autumn leaves, Sister Theresa tracked down Ada during her morning break; she found her friend standing gazing out at the waves crashing and churning on the incoming tide of the Irish Sea.

'Can I have a word with you, Ada?' she asked.

Clutching her nurse's cape around her shoulders, Ada smiled. 'Of course, dear, let's go into the summer house; otherwise, we shan't be able to hear ourselves speak.'

Sitting on the wooden bench that ran the length of the summer house, which was full of the scent of the red geraniums that trailed along the windowsills, both women gazed out over the marsh, where oystercatchers and redshanks waded in tidal pools.

'I need to talk to you about Sister Mary Paul,' Theresa immediately blurted out, as she fiddled nervously with her habit. 'I think she might be losing her sight,' she announced starkly.

Ada was shocked, her hand flying to her mouth. '*Really?*'

Theresa vehemently nodded her head. 'It's been a slow realization,' she admitted. 'When I think about it, I can date a change in her back to the spring, though for sure it's something Mary Paul would never admit to. It might be that she just needs a stronger pair of glasses.'

'Or it could be something more serious,' Ada said, wondering.

'She's constantly miscalculating distances,' Theresa continued. 'Only recently we had a mishap when she dropped a tray of pies that she was transferring from the oven to the kitchen table; she clearly couldn't see straight and dropped the lot. I'm really worried she'll have a bad accident soon.'

Slumping back against the bench, Ada listened intently to Theresa's outpouring.

'She really shouldn't be lugging heavy trays and dishes out of the oven, nor struggling to put them in when she can barely see the oven shelves,' Theresa added. 'Check her hands when you can — they're covered in burns and scalds.'

'Oh, the poor darling,' Ada cried in distress. 'She's *such* a hard grafter — she would never complain or grumble.'

'That's my point: Mary Paul would soldier on until she dropped,' Theresa agreed. 'We have to do something to help her out of what is becoming a really dangerous situation. I try my best to keep an eye on her and do more in order to lessen her load, but if I overdo it I can see that she's offended.' Getting to her feet, Theresa said urgently, 'I've left her too long on her own already — I must get back to the kitchen. Will you and Dr Jamie give some thought to what I've told you?'

Rising to her feet too, Ada replied, 'Of course, Theresa.' Then, seeing the young nun's anxious expression, she reached out to hug her. 'Thanks for alerting me. I feel ashamed that I haven't seen any of Mary Paul's symptoms myself.'

When the young nun had left, Ada strolled back across

the garden to gaze out over the marsh that was now completely submerged under the powerful incoming tide. Poor Mary Paul, she thought. Loyal, loving and utterly selfless, she would die in her tracks rather than complain. But Theresa was right: this was a matter that had to be addressed and, for the old nun's sake, the sooner the better.

Jamie, Ada, Theresa and Matron had a meeting as soon as they could in Ada's cottage garden, where they could talk privately while Catherine toddled around, pushing her little pram in which a teddy and dolly were piled. Catching sight of the little girl picking the last of the garden's flowers, and eating some too, Ada called out, 'Don't eat the leaves, darling.'

Grimacing, Catherine spat out the leaves, then continued pushing her pram around the flowerbeds.

'We must avoid making any suggestion that Sister Mary Paul should retire,' Matron started. 'The kitchen has been her realm for over thirty years.'

Theresa nodded. 'Mary Paul would be utterly devastated by the idea of retiring from her kitchen.'

'Absolutely,' Jamie instantly agreed. 'My hunch, from what Ada's told me, is she's probably got cataracts or glaucoma.'

'So it's nothing like as simple as a new pair of glasses?' Theresa asked.

'We'll only know if I can do an eye test, initially a routine examination in my surgery.'

Knowing how single-minded the old nun was, Ada said

thoughtfully, 'She'll be suspicious if we suggest she has an eye test out of the blue.'

'Then we'll have to persuade her with some flimsy excuse,' Jamie said firmly.

'And what if her fading eyesight is down to cataracts or even worse?' Matron asked.

'If that were the case, she would have to spend some time in Lancaster Infirmary having tests done and possibly treatment too,' Jamie explained.

'Who's going to persuade her to have an eye test in the first place?' Theresa asked nervously.

Jamie turned to his wife. 'Ada, of course: she's the only person in the world who will be able to coax Sister Mary Paul into doing something she absolutely doesn't want to do.'

Ada bided her time; she didn't want to broach the sensitive subject when the old nun was busy preparing a meal or clearing away. Late afternoons, when there was a lull between dinner and tea-time, were always less hectic. Entering the kitchen (smelling tantalizingly of baking scones), Ada spoke cheerily. 'Am I in time for a cuppa?'

Hearing Ada's voice, Sister Mary Paul looked up from the pastry she was rolling on the kitchen table and beamed. 'Put the kettle on, sweetheart, I'll be with you in a minute.'

Sister Theresa, washing up in the big old butler sink, caught Ada's eye and, taking her cue, quickly excused herself. 'I'll just pop into the dining room,' she said and hurried away.

Ada brewed the tea, then set the pot on the table along with cups and saucers.

'Sit down, dear,' she urged Sister Mary Paul, who needed no second bidding.

'I'll be glad to take the weight off mi feet,' the nun declared, as she gratefully accepted a cup of hot strong tea from Ada.

'Busy morning?' Ada started.

'When is it not?' Mary Paul sighed.

After sipping their tea companionably for several seconds, Ada initiated the conversation that she knew would be tricky.

'Jamie's got a busy week,' she started.

'He's such a good soul, working all the hours that God sends for us,' Mary Paul commiserated.

'He's organizing eye tests for some of the residents.'

'That's kind of him. One of the new residents has terrible eyesight; I hope he recommends glasses for her,' the nun chatted.

'So' – Ada took a gulp of tea – 'I was thinking you and I could take advantage of the opportunity and have our eyes tested too.' Seeing the nun's sudden wary expression, Ada rambled on, 'I have to admit my sight's not quite as good as it was before I had Catherine.'

'I won't have time,' the nun flatly declined.

'It'll only take a few minutes,' Ada quickly added.

Looking suspicious, Mary Paul asked, 'And what'll he do to me?'

'Just take a little peep into yours eyes with a bright light, like a torch, and he'll probably ask you to read from a chart on his wall – nothing much,' Ada assured Mary Paul, whose face had set into a determined scowl. 'Darling, please,' Ada begged with her bewitching smile that she knew Mary Paul could never resist.

Laying down her cup, Mary Paul gave a resigned sigh. 'All right, for you,' she conceded. 'But it had better not be on a Wednesday, that's my busiest morning – when the pig man comes for the slops.'

Ada and Jamie conspired to ensure that Ada and Mary Paul would arrive for their eye tests together, suspecting that the older woman might run for it if she were left alone long enough in the hospital corridor.

'I'll test you first,' Jamie suggested. 'And waffle on about your possibly needing glasses in the future; then, when you're done, I'll test Mary Paul while you're still in the room.'

'Good plan,' Ada said, smiling. 'Fingers crossed,' she added with a mischievous grin.

Everything went according to plan: after Ada's test Jamie shone a bright light in each of Mary Paul's eyes, then asked her a series of questions in rapid succession.

'Do you ever get blurred vision or see rings of light?'

Looking defensive, Mary Paul answered, 'Only when I'm tired.'

'What about headaches?'

'Sometimes, but that's nothing to do with mi eyes,' she declared.

Softening his voice, Jamie continued, 'Your eyes are sore and red, Sister, and your vision appears to be blurred and foggy. I believe you might be suffering from glaucoma.'

Visibly starting, the nun exclaimed, 'Glory be! What in God's name is that?'

'I'm not an eye specialist, but I think it might be a degeneration of the eyes; it often occurs as people age,' Jamie explained.

'It's very common, and can be treated quite easily in the hospital,' Ada quickly interjected.

'Hospital!' Mary Paul spat out the word as if it were a place of sin. 'I'll not be going to any hospital.'

Sitting beside the agitated nun, Ada gently stroked her old gnarled hands while Jamie went into more detail.

'Sister Mary Paul, if you don't have treatment, then there's a very good chance you might go blind.'

At which point Mary Paul visibly shrank in her chair. 'Holy Mother of God!'

Ada and Jamie exchanged a sympathetic look, then fell silent in order to give Mary Paul time to digest the diagnosis and the consequences of ignoring it.

'I'll have to think about it,' she eventually said.

Jamie gave an understanding smile, before he said, 'For your own sake, Sister, can I urge you not to take too long about it?'

It took an entire week of Ada's patient, gentle coaxing to win Mary Paul round to visiting the hospital in Lancaster; Ada drove her there, leaving Catherine at home with Jamie. As Jamie had predicted, Mary Paul had advanced glaucoma, and the eye specialist strongly advised urgent treatment. On the drive back to Grange, Ada was saddened to see dear Sister Mary Paul sitting shrunken and subdued in the passenger seat.

'Darling, I promise you, it will be all right. I promise I'll visit you every day and we'll take good care of you when you're discharged from the hospital.'

After gazing at the vast, sparkling sweep of Morecambe Bay as they drove past, Sister Mary Paul wiped tears from her pale milky eyes. 'I know you'll do everything you can for me, Ada dear.' Then, taking a deep shuddering breath, she blurted out what was troubling her most of all. 'But what will happen when I'm in the hospital? Who in God's name is going to cook for Mary Vale?'

20. Farm Girls

As the days grew shorter and chill winds whistled down the Borrowdale Valley, Lillian watched Daisy like a hawk; and the young mare, flourishing under her carer's attention, became devoted to Lillian. Sensing the exact time that Lillian would arrive in the yard, Daisy would always be waiting for her, nickering softly with her pretty head over the stable half-door. Hurrying to open the door, Lillian smiled as Daisy affectionately nudged and nibbled her arm, then blew softly into her hair, as if to say, 'I've missed you so much!'

Less than a year ago Lillian, watching *Lassie* in the Regal picture house, would have shed a few sentimental tears if the dog were hurt or frightened, but really, as far as she was concerned, it was all just twaddle – animals were animals, humans were humans, and the lines didn't cross. Now she knew otherwise: the lines *really* did cross. Her devotion to Daisy equalled the mare's devotion to Lillian. Major, jealous of all the attention Daisy was getting, often stamped his hooves on the straw-strewn cobbles of his stall and neighed indignantly.

'All right, handsome, I've not forgotten you,' Lillian would chuckle, as she reached over to stroke the shire's glossy neck and tickle his ears, which twitched excitedly. 'It's just that right now your lady here needs lots of care and attention,' she explained, then fed Major a carrot from the flat palm of her hand.

'Honest to God,' Sal teased when Lillian crept into bed after her regular goodnight visit to the stable, 'you'd think it was you that was having a foal, not Daisy.'

'I just wanted to tuck her up for the night and check she was warm enough and had enough water,' Lillian explained.

'You and that horse,' Mo joked. 'Joined at the hip, that's what you are.'

Though Daisy's healthy condition didn't require any visits from the vet, Robbie nevertheless regularly appeared in the yard in order to do the seasonal tasks in the farm's calendar – fortunately all paid for by the estate that owned the land rather than by Wilf, who would have let the place go to rack and ruin rather than part with a penny out of his own pocket.

Lillian loved to watch Robbie dosing lambs for worms, checking the recently castrated male calves, trimming the ewes' feet against foot-rot and a string of other routine jobs. Trailing after him, she literally learnt on the hoof about animal husbandry. She warmed to his open smile, honest brown eyes and easy-going nature. When he was out in the fields with his sleeves rolled up, Lillian admired his sturdy, strong physique and the tan he had acquired from working long hours in the sun. She always made sure there were a couple of hearty man-sized sandwiches and a mug of tea for him to enjoy while he was working. Chatting companionably in the barn if it was raining or sitting on the farm bench if the sun was out, Lillian learnt that Robbie was married but had no children. She found out from Sal that he and his wife had had a little lad who had died the previous year from meningitis.

'His poor wife took it really bad, had a breakdown and hasn't been the same since,' Sal told Lillian, who was greatly saddened to hear of the tragedy in Robbie's life.

'He never talks about it,' she mused.

'You can understand why,' Sal replied. 'I think if I was in his position, I wouldn't talk about it much either. I've heard he spends as much time as possible supporting his wife.'

'How sad they haven't had any more children,' Lillian said, wonderingly.

'I think she might be past it,' Sal answered.

Lillian sighed heavily. 'Robbie's so gentle with all the animals, I'm sure he would have been a wonderful father.'

The damp autumn weather did nothing to improve Wilf's health, which steadily worsened. Refusing to see a doctor or pay any medical fees, he typically did nothing to help himself; then, one wild stormy night after dragging himself to the pub, he had a fall on the way home and rolled into a ditch, where he was found half dead the following morning by the milkman on his rounds. At this point miserable Mrs M, long sick and tired of her husband, disappeared overnight, along with all the ration coupons she had stolen. Where she went nobody knew or even cared. With Wilf hospitalized in Penrith, the estate manager asked the Land Girls to take over the running of the farm until a new farmer was appointed, which, they were warned, would take a long time, as most able-bodied men had been called up.

'Thank God they've both gone!' Sal rejoiced as the four girls mopped and polished the filthy house until it shone.

'At least we get to make our own food these days,' Pat said cheerily.

'And buy our own food with our own food coupons,' Mo added.

'And cook fresh healthy meals,' Sal said, as she handed around warm bread that they had left baking overnight in the Aga's slow oven. 'Which reminds me, we mustn't forget to put the lamb casserole in to cook before we leave for work.'

Mo, who could never get enough to eat, quickly agreed. 'Aye, we'll need it after a day spent rounding up the sheep on the fells; it'll be nice and tasty by the time we get back.'

Happy that their lives had changed for the better, the four girls grinned conspiratorially at each other across the no longer cluttered kitchen table.

'I hope the old bugger never comes back,' Mo blurted out, as she lit up her first fag of the day.

'Which particular old bugger are we referring to?' Sal giggled.

'Both of 'em!' Mo cried.

A conscientious Pat rose from the table. 'Best be off,' she said.

Reaching up to grab some underwear drying on the maiden that hung over the Aga, Mo laughingly called after her friends, 'I'll catch you up – I can't go out without mi knickers, otherwise I might get arrested!'

*

The constant workload of the summer months had been replaced by the constant workload of the winter months, which these days was mostly centred around the beasts: cattle and sheep going to market for slaughter; and, with them gone, vast amounts of manure had to be shifted in preparation for lambing. In the barn, watched by a grumbling Sal, Lillian lovingly patted Major, who was harnessed up to the plough.

'Why can't we use the tractor?' Sal asked, as grey slanting rain started to fall. 'At least the tractor's got a roof.'

'Short on petrol,' Lillian told her. 'We've got to keep some back for emergencies.'

After a long, wet morning in the persistent drenching rain, Lillian and Sal stopped briefly to hungrily eat their cheese-and-onion sandwiches and drink tepid tea from a Thermos flask, at which point a shivering Sal, furious at the rain rolling down her neck and back, exclaimed, 'Jesus! You'd think the government would pay us more than £2 for a fifty-hour week in the freezing cold,' she scoffed. 'It's a joke!'

'You could have joined the Wrens,' Lillian reminded her.

'Not brainy enough,' Sal replied. 'I wish I'd thought of munitions work – them Bomb Girls are well paid compared to us Land Girls.'

'But if you'd done that,' Lillian teased, 'we would have missed the pleasure of your company.'

Major, eager to get back to his warm stable, tugged impatiently on his harness.

'He wants us to get a move on,' Lillian explained.

Sal rolled her eyes. 'Men!' she scoffed. 'They're all the bloody same.'

Smiling at her beloved shire, Lillian challenged her friend. 'Not my Major, he's a proper gentleman!'

Once the Land Girls were running Dobb End, they tackled the two idle sixteen-year-old lads who had been hired by Wilf to do the more mundane jobs like mucking out the cattle shed and cleaning out the hen coop. Since Wilf had been hospitalized, the lazy lads had made themselves scarce, which incensed Sal. With the bit firmly between her teeth, she tracked them down to the back of the barn having a crafty fag.

'Oi!' she yelled, as she saw them scampering away. 'Get your arses back here, right now.'

Dragging their feet, they retraced their footsteps and stood in front of a furious Sal with their scruffy heads bent.

'Listen up, you little sods,' she started. 'No more shirking. We've got our work cut out for us, farming the land and looking after the cattle and sheep. Your work's clear too. Just 'cos Wilf's laid up doesn't mean to say you're on holiday. If I catch you bunking off one more time, I'll report you right away to the farm agent who pays your wages and the local bobby for shirking your duty – do you hear me?' After both boys nodded sulkily, Sal continued, 'Now pick up them brooms' – she pointed to a pair carelessly slung in a corner of the barn – 'and sweep the yard down like you're supposed to, then clean out the coop and lay fresh straw for the hens. Understand?' Watching the boys shuffle over to collect the brooms, Sal concluded with a final scathing remark, 'There's a war on, if you've not noticed; we're digging for the nation's victory, not skiving off.'

On returning home, Sal leapt off the cart that was attached to the plough and ran indoors to check on the lamb casserole, leaving Lillian to untack Major, who was wet through and starting to steam from being so cold. After leading the weary horse into his stall, which she had mucked out and left snug with a deep litter earlier that morning, Lillian vigorously wiped Major down with handfuls of straw before throwing a thick horse blanket over his back, which she secured under his chest and tummy with leather straps. Leaving him with a manger full of hay to nibble, Lillian, her hair plastered to her face and her sodden work clothes clinging to her slim body, dashed off to the tack room to prepare a tasty bran mash for hardworking Major. She stopped in her tracks when she found Robbie sitting in the tack room warming himself by the fire, which was always kept going throughout the winter months. Puffing on his pipe, he turned to smile at Lillian.

'I didn't expect to find you here, Robbie.'

'I guessed you'd be back when it got dark,' he explained. 'I stayed on a bit longer after checking the cattle in the hope of seeing you.'

Pleased that he actually wanted to see *her*, Lillian blushed. 'Oh, that's kind of you,' she said, flustered.

'I thought we could take a quick look at Daisy,' he added.

Lillian nodded. 'Right, but first I've just got to make a

bran mash for Major – he's had a hard day working in the fields in this filthy weather.'

'You look pretty worn out too,' Robbie said, smiling. 'Trust me, I can make an excellent bran mash – get along and dry yourself off while I boil up the mash.'

Feeling a little self-conscious, Lillian went back to the stable, where she peeled off her wet overcoat, then removed her jumper, muddy trousers and boots. After slipping into the spare dungarees she always kept hanging on a hook, Lillian went back to the tack room, where she found Robbie competently stirring the mash, which smelt so good she could have eaten it herself.

'I'm starving,' she announced. 'Do you fancy some supper?'

'Wouldn't say no,' he replied.

'If you can feed Major, I'll go and find us some food.'

Hurrying across the dark yard, Lillian found Sal and Mo in the kitchen.

'Grub's up,' Mo announced.

'Is there enough for the vet?' Lillian asked. 'He's just popped by to examine Daisy and he's famished.'

'There's mash and cabbage too,' generous Mo said, as she heaped two plates with tasty lamb casserole, then added slabs of fresh bread. 'Careful you don't trip up in the yard and drop the bloody lot!' she joked.

Carrying their supper tray, Lillian made her way slowly back to the tack room, where she found Robbie making a pot of tea.

'I've fed Major – he was starving, poor lad,' Robbie said as soon as she appeared.

Quickly setting the tray on the tack-room table, Lillian urged Robbie to eat up, and the pair of them tore into the casserole, mash, cabbage and bread that Mo had provided, hardly stopping to speak as they relished every mouthful. Finally, replete and relaxed, they sat back and, after accepting a mug of tea from Robbie, Lillian lit up a cigarette while Robbie puffed on his pipe. Warm for the first time all day, Lillian sighed contentedly.

'Sometimes on cold dark nights like this,' she confessed, 'I often think I'll curl up in the straw in Daisy's stall and spend the night with her.'

'I'm not sure there'd be enough room in her stall for both of you these days,' Robbie joked, then, after tapping out his pipe, he added, 'Shall we take a look at her before I go?'

Nodding quickly, Lillian stubbed out her cigarette and followed him into the stable. Major, tired and contented, lay in his deep bedding. Daisy, starved of company all day, was eager to socialize. Neighing softly, she nuzzled the vet, who patted her gently on the flanks.

'You're looking well, lady,' he murmured, as he expertly examined her bulging belly. 'Ah ha,' he smiled. 'I can feel that foal of yours.' Seeing Lillian's fascinated expression, Robbie stepped back so she could stand where he was. 'Come here.' Positioning her in front of him, he guided her hand along the mare's side, then under her belly. 'He or she is curled up, but you can clearly make out the shape.'

Lillian's eyes widened in delight as she too traced the foal's outline.

'Oh, my God!' she whispered. 'It's amazing.'

With Robbie standing close behind her, Lillian could feel his breath on her neck as he expertly led her hand along the mare's body. When he removed his hand and she dropped hers, Lillian was caught off balance and swayed. Thinking she might stumble, Robbie caught her in his arms. The touch of him in such close proximity sent a shockwave through Lillian that took her breath away, to the extent that looking up into his tender dark eyes she had an unexpected but irresistible urge to kiss him. Luckily Robbie released his hold on her.

'Sorry, I thought for a minute there you might fall over,' he apologized.

'Yes, er, thanks,' she mumbled self-consciously.

'Well, I'd better be off,' he said awkwardly. Turning away from her so that she couldn't see his emotional expression, Robbie briefly patted Daisy. 'You're doing well, little mother, you'll have that fine foal very soon now.' Hurrying out of the stable, he called over his shoulders as he climbed into his ancient Jeep, 'Bye, thanks for the supper.'

As the sound of the Jeep's engine faded away on the night air, Lillian slumped against the nearest wall.

'What was all that about?' she asked herself.

Robbie was probably twice her age and married, but there was absolutely no doubting the physical attraction that had shot through them both like a bolt of lightning. Was it seeing him so tender with Daisy, and guiding her hand so expertly over the mare's belly, that had initiated an unexpected burst of passion in her? Older he might be, but was that part of the attraction? His powerful, commanding maturity had without question briefly over-whelmed her in Daisy's stall, and she knew that he had felt something for her too; there was no doubting the depth of emotion in his eyes or the yearning in his face. Robbie had responded to her just as much as she had responded to him. Taking a deep breath to steady her clamouring nerves, Lillian locked up the tack room and stable for the night, then headed back across the yard, thinking to herself, 'My goodness, that was a very close shave.'

21. A Flying Visit

When Stella discovered that she was pregnant, she simply didn't believe it was possible. They had had wild abandoned sex multiple times in Cambridge, but she had always been confident that Bill had taken precautions.

'I just can't be!' she had exclaimed to Doreen, who knew about her condition.

A woman of the world, Doreen raised a cynical eyebrow. 'Don't go kidding yourself, honey,' she answered realistically. 'How many periods have you missed?'

'Only one?'

'Have you had a touch of morning sickness?' Doreen further enquired.

'I've just started to feel a bit queasy,' Stella told her. Repeating what she had constantly been saying to herself, she blurted out, 'We took precautions.'

Doreen gave a laconic shrug. 'Mebbe, but accidents do happen. If I were you, I'd get on to that Yank boy of yours – the two of you have things to sort out.'

Armed with coins for the public phone that was located just outside the munitions-factory entrance, Stella entered the stuffy booth and dialled the number he had given her in case of an emergency. Taking in great gulps of air to steady her clamouring nerves, she muttered out loud, 'Oh, God, what's he going to say?'

She knew and loved Bill too well to know that he would not abandon her, but how could they make it work, when he was a Yank and she was English, and on different sides of the country as well? He might even suggest that she have a termination, which was illegal, but it still went on. Stella personally knew two girls who had gone through the grim and dangerous process of a back-street abortion. Would Bill want that – did she, in fact, want that? She had considered going home, but the thought of having a baby under her parents' roof was untenable; they would violently disapprove of her sinful behaviour and their terraced house was already bursting at the seams with Stella's younger brothers and sisters.

Sweating and trembling, Stella waited with bated breath for someone to pick up the telephone on the other end. The man who did answer took a long time to track down Bill, who had clearly come running to the phone, for he sounded breathless and flustered.

'Honey! What's up?'

In between bouts of weeping, Stella informed Bill of her condition. After what seemed like an interminably long pause, Bill's voice was clear and firm. 'Sweetheart, it's not a problem,' he said calmly. 'We'll get married.'

Completely stunned, Stella realized that this was the one option she hadn't considered.

'Get married?' she eventually said.

'Sure,' he answered with total confidence. 'We love each other – it makes sense to me.'

Now stammering and shaking, Stella babbled, 'B . . . b . . . but how?'

'Well, now, we go to a church, exchange vows and I give you a wedding ring, and BINGO! We're man and wife, Mr and Mrs Austin,' Bill laughed.

'But you're an American?' she cried.

Still laughing, Bill added, 'So? Yanks get married all the time, sometimes to beautiful English girls,' he teased.

'Bill!' she implored. 'Please be serious.'

'I've never been more serious in my life,' he assured her. 'In fact, the minute I put this phone down I'm going to start looking into it.'

Still not sure, Stella said, 'Do you WANT to marry me, Bill?' she demanded. 'Or are you just doing me a favour?'

'Stella Star,' he declared. 'I don't ever want to lose you! How many times do I have to tell you that you are without a shadow of a doubt the love of my life?'

His tender, reassuring words reduced Stella to tears all over again. 'Oh, Bill, I love you so much,' she wailed. 'But what will we do, where will we live?'

Before her decreasing pile of coins ran out, Bill said he would apply for compassionate leave right away.

'Honey, we have got a lot to figure out, and we can't do it on the phone,' he said realistically.

'I'll feel so much better when I can see you.'

'I'll come to you as soon as I can, sweetheart,' he promised. 'Meanwhile stay brave and don't panic; we'll work this out together.'

Already feeling calmer, Stella wiped away her tears.

'I'll let you know as soon as I have news,' he managed to say before the pips went.

*

Bill managed to wangle twenty-four hours leave after he and a small crew delivered a repaired Avro Lancaster to the Burtonwood base near Warrington. After getting his pass signed by an officer, Bill ran to the railway station and caught the first train to Manchester, then bused it on to the munitions factory.

Knowing that Bill was due to arrive sometime that day, Stella had worked herself into the ground preparing and refrigerating canteen meals ahead of time, so that she might be free to see Bill for the little time he would be with her.

Stella paced her small prefab flat (which Doreen had discreetly vacated for the night) like a caged animal, and, when she finally heard running footsteps on the path outside, she flung open the door and flew into Bill's arms. Burying her face against his strong shoulder, she murmured, 'Oh, my darling . . . my darling!'

'Stella Star,' he whispered, as he held her tight and inhaled the sweet smell of her wonderful golden-red hair. 'God,' he said on a long sigh, 'I never want to let you go again.' Bending, he kissed her soft red lips that readily parted to his touch. Holding the kiss until they could barely breathe, they reluctantly drew apart.

'Come inside,' she said, as she took his hand and led him indoors. 'I've got some food for you.'

Seeing the fresh home-made pasties she had prepared for him on the small kitchen table, Bill grinned. 'I'm starving. I've not had a bite to eat since I left Mildenhall at dawn this morning.'

Ravenous, he tucked into the flaky meat-and-potato

pasties. 'Thank God the trains weren't delayed – I couldn't get here fast enough,' he admitted.

Pushing his chair away from the table, he gratefully accepted the mug of strong tea that Stella offered him, but, seeing her sweet face so pale and anxious, he set it down in order to stand up and take her into his arms, gently rocking her back and forth.

'It's gonna be all right, honey,' he promised. 'Tell me how you're feeling.'

'Queasy,' she blurted out. 'I'm told that morning sickness, or, in my case, all-day sickness, can go on for twelve weeks, even more.'

'And how far gone are you?'

'Maybe six weeks – it's still early days.' Self-consciously aware that her boyfriend might be observing the changes in her body, swelling breasts and thickening waist, she added miserably, 'It wasn't meant to be like this, Bill.'

'Who cares?' he chuckled. 'I knew from the first moment I saw you in that blue silk dress across the dance-hall that I was going to marry you.'

Laughing in delight, she cried, 'Really?'

'Not a single incey-wincey doubt,' he replied, as he tenderly stroked a hand over her still-flat stomach. 'So now it looks like we'll be married sooner rather than later – what's the big deal?'

'There's a LOT to consider, Bill,' she insisted.

Unflappable, Bill unrolled his plan. 'For the time being at least my war work is here in the UK,' he continued. 'Hopefully, after we're married, we'll get married quarters close to the Mildenhall base until we can get back to the US. Don't worry, sweetheart,' he added, fondly stroking Stella tenderly on the bottom before giving her a long kiss, 'I'll take care of everything.' Suddenly rising, Bill said cheerily, 'Let's get out of here. I need a blast of good fresh Lancashire air in order to plan our future.'

Out on the cold windy moors, the couple clung to each other as they followed the narrow, winding sheep tracks that criss-crossed the hills, startling pheasants and grouse that were beginning to roost for the night.

'You know, Stella,' Bill said, as he held her hand and guided her between banks of springy heather, 'I need to be honest and tell you that I took precautions every time we made love in that Cambridge hotel, except for once,' he confessed. 'I'm so sorry, my love. I don't know quite how it happened. I thought I was dreaming that you were making love to me, you were wild, demanding and wonderful, truly I thought I had died and gone to heaven, that is until I realized I wasn't dreaming at all, it was all real – but in my delirium I didn't take the precautions.'

Stella's face coloured as she too recalled the event, which had been triggered by her waking in the night, desperate for Bill, whom she had roused and made love to while he was still half asleep.

'That was the slip-up,' she murmured.

Bill laughed out loud. 'Worth every moment, babe!'

They weren't able to walk for too long; a chilly misty darkness fell, sending them hurrying home as owls hunted over the moors and foxes barked. However, after their walk, Stella felt a lot more cheerful.

'One way or another we'll be together in the New Year, my sweet,' he promised, as they lay wrapped in each other's arms in her narrow single bed. 'We'll be Mr and Mrs Austin by the time 1944 is chimed in.'

22. Lilibet

When a gale force wind was howling down the valley and torrential rain swelling the streams and becks that fed into Lake Derwentwater, Daisy went into labour. The dramatic, stormy day started for Lillian and her friends rising as usual in the pitch dark, then spending a day up on the fells with the sheep, who needed regular check-ups after tupping. Soaked to the skin, the four girls returned home in the dark, which was descending earlier each day as autumn turned to winter.

Grateful for the warmth of the farm kitchen, they immediately stripped off their sodden outer clothes to drape on the wooden maiden over the Aga. While Sal, Mo and Pat set about supper, another variation on lamb casserole, which had been cooking all day in the Aga, Lillian (now in trousers and a fresh jumper) grabbed a raincoat and dashed across the farmyard, splashing through muddy puddles, to check up on the horses. Major greeted Lillian eagerly – her welcome appearance meant supper – but Daisy remained lying on her deep straw litter. Thanks to Robbie, who had talked to her a number of times (and in great detail) about the onset of labour, Lillian immediately knew that Daisy's delivery was imminent. Over the last few weeks signs of this had been evident: the mare's udders had filled up with milk and become engorged before a waxy yellow, honey-like secretion appeared. Entering the stall, Lillian softly stroked Daisy's bulging flanks.

'How are you, sweetheart?' she whispered.

Clearly happy to see her carer, the mare struggled to her feet to nuzzle Lillian, but then, as if in discomfort, she started to pace her stall. Lillian saw several manure droppings which she knew she had to muck out in order to keep the birthplace as sterile as possible. Briefly tying the mare up outside the stall, Lillian tidied away the droppings, then, fetching a fresh bundle of straw from the barn, she built up the mare's bedding before leading Daisy back inside. Feeling left out, Major gave a loud indignant whinny.

'All right, mister, I'll get your supper,' Lillian assured the hungry animal.

After topping up Major's manger with fresh hay, replenishing his water trough and giving him a bucket of mixed chaff and oats, Lillian mucked out his stall so he could settle down for the night. Now she needed to concentrate on Daisy, who was anxiously looking round at her flanks and trying to nibble them. As the rain thundered on the roof and the wind whistled around the yard, Lillian, knowing full well how essential privacy was to the mare's well-being, quietly observed Daisy's movements by the dim stable light. Watching from the shadows, Lillian saw the horse lie down on her bedding, then get up again and pace. Making soothing noises Lillian waited for her to settle, at which point she took the opportunity to run back across the yard to the farmhouse to grab the phone in the hallway and call Robbie.

'Daisy's started,' she cried.

Robbie's calm voice echoed down the phone, 'How is she?'

'Restless, pacing a lot, then lying down; sometimes she kicks out at her belly,' Lillian described.

'All perfectly normal for this first stage of labour. Has she urinated yet?'

'Yes, a few times,' Lillian replied. 'She lies down and lifts her tail to do it.'

'Leave her to it,' he advised. 'But stay close just in case: it's her first foal and she might need help as the labour progresses. I've got to drive over to Seatoller to see a sick cow, but I'll call in and see Daisy on my way back.'

Relief flooded Lillian, who hadn't realized up until then how scared she was by the prospect of delivering Daisy's foal by herself.

'That would be marvellous!' she cried.

'If you can, it might be a good idea to move Daisy into a bigger stall,' he suggested. 'Mares get restless during delivery; she'll need plenty of room to move around. Make sure she has a deep litter too,' he added.

'Yes, of course,' Lillian answered breathlessly.

Before she ran back to the stable, Sal made Lillian sit at the table and eat her supper, which she consumed hastily.

'You can't work on an empty stomach,' she said firmly. 'You could be out there all night.'

'You're probably right,' Lillian agreed, as she gulped down the welcome food before returning to the stable block. Daisy, now on her feet, was circling the confines of her stall. After what seemed like hours (and after William had transferred Daisy to a roomier stall), Lillian heard the welcome sound of car wheels scrunching to a halt on the farmyard cobblestones.

'Thank God, Robbie!' she cried, as she ran out to greet him.

'Let's take a look at her,' Robbie said without any preamble.

After getting Lillian to gently wash down Daisy's hind-quarters with warm soapy water, Robbie got down on his knees beside the mare in order to examine her.

'The foetal membrane is ruptured,' he announced. 'With luck she'll start presenting the foal soon.'

'Look! She's rolling,' Lillian gasped. 'Is that safe?'

'She's just trying to get the foal into the right position for delivery – Daisy knows what she's doing,' Robbie answered confidently. 'Go and make us both a cup of tea,' he suggested. 'I'll stay on here to monitor her contractions.'

In the warm tack room, where the embers glowed in the fireplace, Lillian stoked up the fire, then lit the little gas ring to boil a kettle. As she brewed the tea, she felt herself start to relax: with Robbie in charge she could now look forward to welcoming Daisy's foal into the world and hopefully learn from the experience too.

'Maybe one day I'll be as confident as Robbie,' she thought to herself.

Marvelling at the calmness of the man, his steady, unflappable manner, soft brown eyes, quick smile and gentle hands, Lillian thought Robbie was the most impressive man she had ever met. He made men like her former boyfriends pale into insignificant boys.

When she returned with two mugs of steaming hot tea, Robbie, in the narrow passageway that ran the length of the stable, pressed a warning finger to his lips.

'She's pushing the front feet out,' he whispered.

Peeping through the entrance to the stall, Lillian watched in complete awe.

'God love her,' she murmured. 'She's trying so hard.'

'She's doing well too,' Robbie continued to whisper. 'Watch carefully and you'll see the foal appears in a sort of diving position,' he explained. 'Front feet first, then the nose, followed by the head, neck and shoulders and finally the hindquarters.'

As Daisy strained to push out her baby, Lillian spoke with an emotional catch in her voice. 'It's wonderful, like a little miracle.'

Sipping his tea and not interfering with Daisy's steady progress, Robbie waited patiently for the foal to be born, and, when it was, enclosed in a translucent membrane bag which the foal broke free of almost immediately, Daisy nickered softly. As she tenderly nuzzled and cleaned her foal's face, Robbie nudged Lillian, who was raptly watching the sweet bonding going on between mother and the new-born.

'Let's leave mother and daughter to get to know each other,' he said with a smile.

In the tack room, luckily still warm thanks to the fire that Lillian had earlier banked up, Robbie explained that now they had to wait for the final stage of labour, which was the expulsion of the placenta.

'It can take up to three hours,' he warned. 'You can leave me to it, if you're whacked.'

Lillian gazed at him in utter astonishment. 'Do you really think I would leave Daisy *now*?' she cried.

Smiling at her devotion, Robbie said, 'Fine, then settle down: we could be in for a long night.'

In between regular visits to Daisy they sat on the battered old sofa in the tack room, Lillian smoking Woodbines, Robbie puffing on his pipe, talking about anything and everything. As the evening wore on, she asked, out of politeness more than anything else, after Mrs Allen.

'I hope she won't mind your arriving home in the middle of the night?'

'Harriet's used to it.' Refilling his pipe, Robbie surprised Lillian by saying, 'You've probably heard my wife had a breakdown when our son died?'

Taken aback, Lillian prevaricated. 'Er, somebody did mention it –'

'Word gets around quickly in a tightly knit valley like this one.'

Lillian was quick to remember her manners. 'I was so sorry to hear of your loss; it must have been awful for you both.'

Robbie stared for a very long time at the flickering flames before continuing. 'It was devastating. He was only six, fit as a fiddle, sharp as a razor, a son to be proud of.'

Seeing tears at the edges of his eyes, Lillian, without a moment's hesitation, gripped his hand with her own.

193

Feeling that words were heartbreakingly inadequate, she stayed in that position until he moved.

'We're thinking of adopting,' he finally said. 'Harriet's too old to conceive another child.'

'Then it sounds like adoption is your best option in the circumstances,' she agreed.

'I only hope the opportunity comes along soon,' he murmured. 'Right now, Harriet has nothing to live for.'

Hearing the tack-room wall clock chiming out the hour, Robbie rose to his feet.

'Time to check on Daisy,' he said and left the room.

Sitting on the sofa, Lillian ran through the conversation they had just had. Some people's lives are so tragic, she thought to herself. How often did she and her pals complain about early-morning starts, filthy weather, squelching mud, grumpy sheep, lambs that always insisted on being born in the middle of the night, not to mention ancient rusty farm machinery that didn't work? But they were alive; they weren't on the Front Line, lying dead in a ditch killed by a sniper's bullet; they weren't being tortured or route marched to death camps. If this was her war work, she would do it with pride and be grateful that she had food in her belly and a roof (albeit leaking) over her head.

Lillian was so deep in thought she didn't hear Robbie's hurrying footsteps. 'Come quickly,' he called urgently.

Joining Robbie in Daisy's stall, Lillian smiled at the charming little foal who was wobbling around on tall skinny legs, occasionally nudging her mother's belly in order to reach her engorged teats and feed.

Surprised by the emotion that gripped her, Lillian gulped back tears. 'Oh, she's lovely,' she gasped. 'Can I call her Lilibet, after the young Princess Elizabeth?' she asked with a lump in her throat.

Not quite as overwhelmed as Lillian, Robbie stooped in order to examine the mare. 'You can call her what you want,' he said briskly before adding, 'The placenta's out, but we have to check from its shape that it's intact. Can you take one end while I hold the other?' he asked, as he picked it up. 'If any placenta is retained in the womb it could cause an infection, so we need to be absolutely certain that the entire lot is out.'

Not relying on the dim stable light, Robbie used his torch to meticulously examine the placenta, which he suspected wasn't entirely complete.

'Damn,' he muttered under his breath. 'If she doesn't expel the rest, we're in trouble.'

'What now?' Lillian anxiously asked.

'We wait . . . and we hope,' he said grimly. 'I'm going to stay in here with Daisy – you try and get some shut eye in the tack room.'

Lillian shook her head. 'I want to be near her,' she insisted. 'I'll go over there and wait.' She nodded in the direction of the nearby hayloft.

Keen not to overcrowd Daisy's stall, Lillian nevertheless wanted to keep an eye on the proceedings. Perched on a hay bale within calling distance of Robbie, she felt her eyelids droop and, before she knew it, she fell into a deep sleep, completely dead to the world. She awoke to Robbie's urgent touch.

'Lillian, Lillian,' he murmured.

Still half asleep, she moaned, 'Mmm.'

'Daisy's just expelled the last of the afterbirth,' he told her. 'Thank God, she's fine.'

Gazing up into his smiling face, Lillian felt such an emotional rush of gratitude – this gentle, kind, clever man had stayed up all night to assist her beloved Daisy and her beautiful new-born foal. Barely stopping to think what she was doing, she wound her arms around his neck and reached up to kiss him.

'You're wonderful,' she whispered as his lips met hers.

What happened next completely took them both by surprise. The passion that simultaneously burned through their bodies was literally unstoppable. Dragging off his jacket, Robbie discarded his trousers, while Lillian wriggled out of her clothes to lie naked on the itchy hay bales. Clinging on to each other, they kissed urgently, but, as his hands travelled over her lithe, slim body, they both started to relax and, rather than rush the moment, they delighted in exploring each other. Though Robbie was twice her age, his body (as Lillian had always suspected) was strong and powerfully built, and there was a tenderness to his expert touch. Staring down at Lillian in the half-light, he could make out the excited sparkle in her big honey-brown eyes, the smile on her lips and the sweep of the smooth white column of her neck that gave way to her small pert breasts. Overcome with a mixture of desire and emotion, Robbie kissed each of her pink nipples before stroking her flat stomach, which was hard and muscular from all the physical hard work she did daily.

'Are you sure?' he asked before his need overtook him.

In answer Lillian stroked his strong back before pulling him down on to her.

'Yes, yes . . .' she moaned.

When their love-making was all over, they lay in a sleepy heap in the hay, which, though itchy, was surprisingly warm.

'Oh God,' he groaned. 'That was the last thing I expected to happen.' Though guilt was quickly overtaking him, Robbie nevertheless tenderly kissed her.

'It took me by surprise too,' she sighed, mortified now that the passion was wearing off.

'I had no idea that you felt like that about me?' he marvelled.

'I've always admired and liked you, but at the forefront of my mind you were always a married man, something I clearly forgot the minute you touched me,' she added ruefully.

'A married man and a lot older than you too,' he reminded her. Running his hands through her long, silky hair, he murmured, 'You make me feel young.'

Shocked by their actions and nervous of the consequences, Lillian held her breath as she wondered what he might say next.

'It's been a long time since Harriet and I had sex. Poor woman, Timmy dying was a death knell for our marriage. I felt so hopeless and unwanted.'

'How could it be otherwise after the loss you've both suffered?' she said sympathetically.

Gathering her into his arms, Robbie murmured incredulously, 'God, what a night this has been.'

Luckily the farm cockerel crowing in the dark before dawn brought the sleeping couple, worn out by their love-making, back to cold reality.

'I'd better get on home,' Robbie said, as he disentangled himself from Lillian's soft warm body. Quickly grabbing his clothes, he started to dress. 'Sweetheart,' he urged, 'very soon somebody's going to walk in here and find you naked.'

Groaning, she pulled on her clothes, then flopped like a bleary-eyed child against his shoulder.

'Come on,' he suggested. 'Let's check on Daisy together – then I really must dash.'

With a weak dawn light seeping into the edges of the sky, they peered into Daisy's stall, which Lillian intended to clean and thoroughly disinfect when Robbie had left.

'You're looking fine, little mother,' he crooned softly to Daisy, who was standing still while her lively foal sucked milk from her full teats. 'Good job, well done, girl,' he said, as he patted her silky neck, then tickled the foal's little ears. 'Keep an eye on her,' he said, turning to Lillian, unable now to meet her eye. 'I'm sorry about what happened,' he suddenly blurted out. 'I should have shown more self-control.'

Seeing his tense expression, Lillian gently took him by the arm.

'Robbie, we're both adults – what happened, happened,' she said, before firmly adding, 'It's our secret, and it will go no further than these walls,' she finished with a reassuring smile.

'Right,' he said briskly. 'Phone me if there's a problem.'

Realizing that their relationship was back to business as usual, Lillian responded in the same brisk manner. 'Of course,' she said in a tight clipped voice. 'Let's keep in touch.'

23. Christmas at Mary Vale

As Christmas loomed, the Mary Vale residents began to get excited about Christmas trees, decorations and exchanging simple little gifts with each other. The staff, on the other hand, were wondering how they could possibly pull Christmas off. Over a quick cup of tea in her office, Matron said, 'With Sister Mary Paul virtually retired these days, we've only got Sister Theresa in the kitchen and Myrtle the temporary part-time cook.'

Ada nodded. 'Myrtle's been a godsend, particularly as she has to cycle in from Lodore village early every morning.'

'I just hope she doesn't put in a request to take Christmas off,' Matron continued. 'We all know that Sister Mary Paul would be back in the kitchen in a blink even though she is officially convalescing.'

Ada congratulated her friend. 'Absolutely, Ann,' she said, smiling knowingly. 'If Mary Paul thought that her cooking days were over, she would be mortified.'

'Well, they are in effect, but we don't need to rub it in, do we?' Matron answered realistically. 'Dear Mary Paul – once she started to recover and her sight slowly came back, I think she was secretly relieved not to have to rush back to our kitchen, and to have the time to do the many things she hadn't got around to in years, like gardening,' Matron chuckled. 'She's replaced the kitchen with the garden.'

'She won't be doing much at this time of the year,' Ada mused as she gazed out of the window to the Home's lawns, now spiked sharp white with ice. 'She did tell me she was pleased that we had appointed a part-time cook to help Theresa, who, she had been fretting, was doing too much.'

'Wouldn't you know it, as luck would have it, we have more residents than we normally would have at this time of the year.' Matron gave a heavy sigh. 'Apart from the shortage of manpower we also have the problem of increased rationing. I don't know what on earth we're actually going to serve up to the residents this Christmas.'

Anxious that her dear Sister Mary Paul might get wind of their anxieties, Ada said earnestly, 'Seriously, Ann, we absolutely must not let Sister Mary Paul catch on to any of this. You know what she's like: if she thought we couldn't manage, she'd come storming back on a walking stick.'

Shaking her head, Matron said, 'Do you remember all the trouble you and Jamie had getting her into Lancaster Infirmary, which she saw as nothing less than a den of evil?'

Ada gave a low chuckle. 'And now sees as a place of miracles as a result of everything going so well,' she reminded her friend.

'We must leave the good soul to get on with her recovery and enjoy her gardening,' Matron concluded.

'Jamie and I could spend Christmas afternoon here at the Home and help with the cooking,' Ada volunteered. 'I know Dora and her husband plan to be here too; if they could keep an eye on Catherine, we could be full time in the kitchen – that would ease things up a bit. And I could stay on a bit longer after my shifts finish to assist Theresa with all the preparations in the week leading up to Christmas.'

'That's most kind of you, Ada.' Matron smiled gratefully. 'I'm sure with God's help we'll somehow muddle through – after all, it is only one day.'

Luckily, Myrtle had good local connections with the gamekeepers in the Lodore area.

'For a backhander, I reckon I could get hold of rabbit, maybe a pheasant or two or at least some wood pigeon, though they'll be in high demand at this time of the year,' she said knowingly. 'We could bulk up the game with onions and carrots and make tasty game pies and casseroles, served alongside roast potatoes and stuffing – meatless stuffing,' she added with a grimace. 'That should make a tasty Christmas dinner for the residents.'

Theresa agreed that it would indeed, but as she spoke her mind was already on all the other meals: Christmas Eve, Boxing Day, even New Year's Day. Sighing, she reflected on how much more stressful it was working in the kitchen without Mary Paul's vast experience and her almost miraculous ability to make something out of nothing at a moment's notice. Nevertheless, Ada was quite right: the old nun had done more than enough for her community, and it was time to pass on the baton, but to whom?

*

Waking up on Christmas morning to the sound of excited squeaks coming from Catherine's little bedroom brought a smile to both Jamie's and Ada's faces.

'She's found her stocking,' Jamie chuckled.

'Let's go and see her,' Ada said, as she reached for her dressing gown.

Jamie gently drew his wife back into bed. 'Not until I've given you a Christmas kiss, my darling.'

'Merry Christmas,' Ada whispered. 'Oh, this is so nice,' she sighed as she cuddled up to Jamie's warm body. 'We're so lucky to be able to spend Christmas together as a family.'

Using his good hand to stroke Ada's rich mahogany-brown hair off her face, Jamie gazed deeply into her wide blue eyes. 'I still can't believe that I have you and Catherine, and that we all live in the most beautiful valley in England,' he murmured. 'Every single day with her and with you is nothing short of a miracle for me.'

'Even when you're battling with teething and potty training?' Ada teased.

Jamie laughed. 'And nappy changing, washing, drying, ironing and pushing the pram for miles in the driving rain.' His happy smile faded as more serious thoughts pre-occupied him. 'Sometimes I have to stop and catch my breath when I think of all my pals still fighting this damn war: wading through mud, dying from thirst in blasted hot deserts, drowning at sea, risking their lives in fighter planes.'

Not wanting Jamie to get depressed on Christmas morning, Ada quickly interjected, 'Sweetheart, you have more than done your bit,' she reminded him.

'Though it fails to make me feel less guilty,' he replied.

The appearance of Catherine in her nightie holding a knitted toy brought them both back to the moment.

'Father Christmas brought me a pig!' she gleefully announced.

After spending a happy morning playing with Catherine and her new toys, the family set off up the farm track to Mary Vale, where preparations were in full swing. Seeing Dora standing by the twinkling Christmas tree, Catherine ran straight into her arms.

'Dodo! Dodo!' she cried.

'Little chick,' Dora said, as she swept the adorable little girl into her arms. 'Look what Father Christmas has left you, sweetheart,' she said, pointing to some parcels stacked under the tree.

As an excited Catherine scrambled to open the gifts, Dora turned to Ada and Jamie. 'I'm not on duty today, though you know me, I'll pop into the nursery soon to check the girls on the feeding rota are doing a good job,' she said with a wink. 'Don't you worry, me and mi hubby will keep an eye on the little 'un,' she added. 'You two pop along into the kitchen – Sister Theresa's in a flat spin,' she said with a grin. 'Myrtle's been bossing her about since eight o'clock this morning, and I suspect she might need a break.'

When they arrived in the steamy hot kitchen rich with the smell of roasting meat, flushed Theresa immediately excused herself, saying she had things to see to in the chapel in preparation for the afternoon Christmas service. Myrtle, who was due to leave at noon in order to join her own family for Christmas dinner, reeled off a string of instructions.

'The game casserole's ready for serving. Don't use the game pie, that'll be served tomorrow with baked potatoes. Casserole's in the slow oven, along with the roast potatoes, they're all ready to go. The potatoes in the pan on top of the oven need mashing, and the carrots and sprouts need boiling, the gravy will need warming up too. The steamed sponge is done, you'll just have to make the custard.' She nodded towards the bottles of farm milk that she had left out for them to use. 'I think that's it,' she said, as she took off her pinafore, put on her warm woolly coat and tied a scarf under her chin. 'Make sure the girls help you wash up and leave everything tidy – I don't want this kitchen looking a mess when I get back to work here tomorrow morning,' she ordered.

When Myrtle finally set off for Lodore on her old bicycle, a good five miles down the valley road, Jamie and Ada went into action.

'I'll see to the veg and spuds if you could set the tables, Ada.'

'I can get Dora and the residents to see to that,' she told him. 'Let's just both concentrate on what we have to do here.'

Tying an old cotton pinafore around his waist, Jamie suddenly said, 'Where's Sister Renee? I thought it was all hands on deck in here today?'

'She's on the wards, though thank goodness neither ward is busy right now – just a couple of patients in each. She might join us for dinner.' Then, seeing Jamie's tense expression, she smiled and said, 'Don't worry, I won't sit her next to you!'

What neither Jamie nor Ada expected when they volunteered their services that Christmas morning was to have quite so much fun. The festive excitement and the sound of carols playing out on the radio, combined with the happy chatter of the residents and the clattering of cutlery and plates in the dining room, made their chores less of a duty and more of a pleasure. As the couple worked side by side, they exchanged their own Christmas memories: Jamie's of a little boy in a comfortable, middle-class home suffering from polio; and Ada's of a large, working-class family living in over-crowded conditions with devoted parents who made sacrifices to ensure that every one of their children had a stocking at the end of their bed on Christmas morning.

'We were lucky, given the circumstances,' Ada said, as she drained the carrots. 'Nobody got left out, and there was always a good meal on the table on Christmas Day. We were so poor – God only knows how my parents managed it,' she added fondly.

Putting the potatoes he had just mashed into a large tureen, Jamie said, 'I was very much a lonely child, and weedy with it.' Looking up to smile at his wife, he added, 'I hope Catherine won't be an only child, darling.'

Grinning impishly, Ada teased, 'I think there are ways of ensuring that won't happen.'

When Sister Theresa walked back into the kitchen, she found both of them giggling,

'What's so funny?' she enquired.

Ada blushed bright pink as Jamie prevaricated. 'Oh, just something Ada said.'

Sister Theresa continued hurriedly about her business.

'Sister Mary Paul has decided she wants to join us for Christmas dinner.'

'That would be lovely,' Ada enthused.

'I'll bring her down from the convent and take her back when she's tired,' Theresa added. 'She's longing to see everybody.'

'And we can't wait to see how she is,' Jamie said eagerly.

Wiping her hands on her pinafore, Ada said, 'We'll be dishing up in about a quarter of an hour, so any time soon, Sister.'

After Theresa had hurried away, Jamie went into the dining room to add a place at the table for Mary Paul, whom he positioned between Dora and Ada. Then he rejoined his wife in the kitchen, and, wearing bright-red paper hats, they wheeled out the assortment of hot dishes.

'Careful not to overload the plates to start with,' Ada whispered. 'This lot has to feed the residents, guests and staff too. And nobody can have seconds until everybody has had their firsts,' she added firmly.

'Yes, ma'am!' Jamie joked.

As the residents streamed in, 'Silent Night' played out on the large Bakelite radio in the dining room, generating a sense of peace and happiness that was slightly marred by the appearance of a somewhat dishevelled Sister Renee. Looking flustered, she called across the room, 'Save a meal for me, please, one of the patients on the post-natal ward needs a bed-pan.'

With a large serving spoon poised in mid-air, Jamie shook his head as he watched the nurse dash off.

'Some things never change,' he muttered crossly under his breath.

'Shhh!' Ada hissed.

Lowering his voice, he added, 'Did she *really* need to share that information with the entire room?'

Luckily the welcome sight of Sister Mary Paul on the arm of Sister Theresa brought the smile back to Jamie's face. Looking much older and wearing an eye patch over her right eye, the elderly nun nevertheless beamed with joy at the sight of the assembled company.

'How wonderful to see you all,' she cried.

Ushering the two nuns to the places he had laid out for them, Jamie courteously served them both dinner.

'My goodness, what a feast!' Mary Paul exclaimed, as she took in the food on her plate with her one good eye. 'And beautifully served,' she said to Jamie, who assured her that Ada and Dora would be along to join her soon.

When everybody had been served, home-made crackers pulled and home-made paper hats donned, they tucked into their meal. Sister Mary Paul generously praised the cooks, and Myrtle, whom she had never met.

'You've all done a fine job,' she announced. 'Though if I'm honest I missed all the Christmas excitement in the kitchen – it was always one of my favourite times of the year.'

'Even with rationing?' somebody asked.

'Yes, I enjoyed the challenge,' Mary Paul answered enthusiastically.

'You were always a genius at finding a little bit of some-thing special to flavour dull food,' Ada reminded her. 'Fresh herbs, wild garlic, and tasty veg from your kitchen garden.'

'And always a sprinkle of Oxo or Lea & Perrins sauce, and mustard too, anything to liven up a dish.' Sighing, the old nun murmured, 'I wonder if I'll ever cook again.'

Quickly patting her hand, Ada assured that she would. 'But not quite as much, dearest; none of us wants to see you worn out with work at your age – we love you far too much.'

While the residents cleared away their plates, all scraped thoroughly clean, Ada and Jamie returned to the kitchen to collect the steamed date-sponge puddings and jugs of custard. As they were loading the dishes on to the trolley, Theresa appeared.

'Sister Renee has just turned up – I said I'd fetch her dinner.'

'That's kind of you,' Ada said. 'It's keeping warm in the bottom oven.'

It was only after the pudding had been served that Ada was aware of loud laughter at the end of the table.

'It's Renee,' Dora informed her. 'Some of the residents have given her a bottle of sherry.'

Unable to see from where she was sitting what was actually going on, Ada overheard some snippets of conversation.

'We know how much you like a tipple, Sister.'

'Why not have a little nip now, to keep you going?'

Catching Jamie's eye, Ada could see he was concerned, Dora too.

'I only hope she's not supping that stuff on duty,' Dora muttered crossly.

Ada's heart sank. Surely, please God, Renee would resist the temptation to drink; unfortunately it appeared not. At the end of the meal, when Ada was pouring tea for the group at the end of the table, she saw that the level of sherry in the bottle left standing on the table was nearly at the halfway mark.

'Merry Christmas, Sister,' Renee called out in a jolly voice that didn't sound intoxicated, but Ada couldn't help but notice Renee's hot, flushed face and over-bright eyes.

When Ada finally stopped serving teas, she rejoined Jamie, who was furious. 'She bloody well can't go back on duty in that state.'

'I know,' Ada agreed.

Overhearing them, Matron spoke quietly. 'I'll take over. I'm due to start my night shift at seven – a few hours more won't make any difference.'

'But you'll miss this afternoon's benediction,' Theresa protested.

Matron gave her a gentle smile. 'I'm quite sure God won't mind, Sister Theresa.'

'I could cover this afternoon,' Ada immediately volunteered.

'I won't hear a word of it,' Matron protested. 'This is your first family Christmas together; I will not have it spoilt for you.'

Sister Mary Paul, who was now tired by all the festivities, nodded in agreement with Matron.

'Think how disappointed Catherine would be if her mummy wasn't there to play with on Christmas Day.'

'Let's hear no more about it,' Matron concluded firmly. 'I'll take over from here.' Pushing back her chair, she added, 'I shall inform Sister Renee of our change of plan right away.'

Jamie and Ada watched Matron approach Renee, with whom she exchanged a few words before leaving the room. As soon as Matron had gone, Renee, without a moment's hesitation, reached out for the bottle of sherry.

'Might as well as celebrate – I've got the afternoon off.' Pouring a generous amount of the wine into her tumbler, Renee laughed gaily as she toasted those around her. *'Merry Christmas! Cheers!'*

'I can't stand this,' Jamie said through gritted teeth.

Knowing how angry her husband was and keen not to start a scene, Ada quickly got to her feet. 'Let's wash up and go home,' she urged.

'I'll come and give you a hand,' Sister Theresa said.

'No, Sister Mary Paul is exhausted: you'd better take her back to the convent and get on with your duties there.'

Throwing Ada a grateful smile, Theresa set off with the old nun who said, 'It's been lovely seeing you all together once more, but I have to admit I'm quite looking forward to a little rest now.'

Leaving Dora to take Catherine into the garden, Jamie, Ada and some willing residents washed and dried the pots and pans and wiped down the kitchen surfaces as instructed by bossy Myrtle. Finally, when everything was spic and span and after they had hung up their pinafores, Jamie turned to his wife with a hard expression on his face. 'I'd say that little exhibition out there has once and for all completely confirmed my opinion of Sister Renee: not only is she unprofessional and unreliable' – he took a deep breath – 'she is also a drunk.'

24. Counting the Days

Christmas and New Year came and went in the munitions factory on the Pennine Moors. Others might have taken a day off to celebrate but not so the bomb builders, who worked around the clock, and of their own volition put in extra hours in order to meet the bomb quota needed to beat the enemy.

'Better to be on the offensive in 1944,' the factory manager had declared to the workforce. 'Makes a nice change from the bloody defensive.'

War news at the start of January 1944 was all about successful advances. The Soviet troops' advance into Poland raised the nation's growing hopes that Hitler would soon be routed. Though Stella heard the good news, she barely had the energy to raise a smile. Her sickness had by no means subsided; she struggled throughout the day and turned green at the smell of most of the food she had to prepare, pregnant or not. Sago, boiled sprouts, and tripe and onions turned her stomach to such an extent that she had to hand over the making of those dishes to Nellie, who so far had no idea of Stella's condition.

'But she soon will,' thought Stella as she loosened the canteen pinafore tied around her thickening waist.

It was a relief to go home at the end of the day and change into something that didn't constrict her tummy or her breasts, which were tender these days. It was also a relief to be able to talk openly to Doreen, who was genuinely sympathetic to Stella's situation.

'So, what're you going to do, then?' Doreen asked, as she lit up a Woodbine.

'We'll get married,' Stella told her. 'Bill's looking into the rules and regulations.'

'And you'll move down South?'

'Yes, if all goes well,' Stella replied.

Doreen's string of questions continued. 'And when will you leave here?'

'As soon as Bill gets permission to marry me. I'll have to get a doctor's note to show to the factory manager, who will hopefully let me leave immediately.'

'I suspect he'll make you hang on until he gets a new cook,' Doreen pointed out.

'God! I hope not,' Stella exclaimed. 'I could finish up having the baby on the job.'

Doreen didn't flinch as she asked her next question. 'And you're keeping it?'

Stella's big blue eyes opened even wider than ever. 'Are you kidding me?' she exclaimed. 'Of course, we're keeping our baby; we love each other.'

Doreen raised her hand in a gesture to calm Stella down. 'Only a practical question. Lots of women in your place would be organizing a back-street abortion by now.'

'We've talked about it,' Stella admitted. 'Neither of us wants that.' Sighing she flopped down on to her narrow single bed. 'Oh, I wish I could talk to Bill. I ask so many questions in my letters to him, but it takes at least a week before I can get any answers back, and by that time I have another string of questions.'

Stubbing out her cigarette, Doreen was pragmatic as always. 'Well, at least Bill's genuine enough and wants to marry you. I can think of a few fellas that would have run a mile if they'd got their girlfriend up the duff.'

Sitting upright, Stella responded with stars in her eyes. 'I *know* my Bill wants to marry me – he would *never* let me down.'

Towards the end of January, Stella received a letter from Bill which contained a postal order for a large amount of money, enough to cause Stella to gasp in astonishment. In his accompanying letter Bill carefully explained what he wanted Stella to do with the money.

Dearest, Sweetest Stella Star,

HECK! Life is tough here at Mildenhall. We're taking new planes on test-flights, fixing old planes the Luftwaffe have wrecked and in between mending the runway, which is an ongoing operation on this base. Constant work means I never get enough time to write to you. So let me answer as many of your questions as I can before I get called away on another job. Now that I've cleared all the red tape, we can fix the wedding date for next month, any time in February when both of us are granted leave to do the deed! Can I leave it to you, sweetheart, to arrange the church or register office; not knowing dates until the last minute might result in our being the only people attending the ceremony – who cares! All it takes is a bride and groom.

You may be wondering where all the money I'm sending you has come from, and what it's for. Bear in mind that we Yanks get five times more pay than your poor guys, plus I live on an American base where most of my costs are covered so I've been able to save during my time in the UK. I've dipped into my savings too. I want you to have enough money for the wedding and all that goes with it, including a wedding dress for the most beautiful bride in the world. Whatever's left over will form our joint bank account – Mr and Mrs Austin. You gotta admit it does have a real classy ring to it!

Excited and slightly nervous, Stella set out on her next morning off to make enquiries at Manchester's register office about booking a wedding date. When she explained that she was waiting to hear back from her fiancé about exact dates, the registrar kindly explained that weddings for couples on last-minute leave were very common these days. He assured anxious Stella that when she had more precise details he would do his best to marry them on the dates they were granted.

Later, Stella spent a heavenly afternoon drifting around Lewis's bridal department in Manchester's city centre. She was captivated by the expensive and breathtaking fine silk gowns, and cheaper satin numbers in beige, cream, ivory and pure white; and she admired the fashionable broad-shoulder designs (often enhanced with shoulder pads) which plunged into sweetheart necklines and tiny, nipped-in waists. She loved the long, trailing veils in delicate lace but wondered if she would settle for a short swinging veil she'd seen on the store's mannequin, attached to a stylish

Victory Roll. Though in raptures at the satin heeled shoes decorated with tiny pearls and wonderful tiaras that glittered in the bright shop lights, Stella remained firm about not spending a penny of Bill's hard-earned money until their wedding date was set in stone. Not knowing the date was the best deterrent to buying anything in advance; her body was changing and growing all the time, and something that fitted her now might not fit her in three weeks' time. So, for the time being at least, Stella banked Bill's postal order and returned to Pendle empty-handed but in the firm knowledge that when the time came there would be plenty to choose from in Lewis's bridal department.

One week slowly followed another, and as each passed Stella yearned to hear from Bill. Counting down the days to when she would leave the gruelling canteen routine, the hard work, the heavy lifting, the tiring shifts, Stella imagined their married quarters in Mildenhall. Maybe their accommodation would be off base: a smart little bungalow or a new prefab, cheap tinny make-shift homes that were being thrown up all over the place as temporary accommodation for servicemen with families. Stella didn't care, just as long as she shared it with her beloved. They could do it up together, paint and decorate, prepare a pretty room, maybe in green or yellow, for the baby, grow flowers in the garden, even grow veg and 'dig for victory' as the populace was constantly encouraged to do.

'It will be bliss,' dreamy Stella thought.

What would her parents say when she told them of her plans to move South? So far, she hadn't said a word; like most things in her life at the moment, everything was on hold until she got the green light from Bill, and then, she thought with excitement, their plans would unfold, and they would finally become man and wife.

Stella's mood of dreamy anticipation changed as the weeks passed and there was no further word from Bill since his letter with the postal order. Seriously troubled, she poured out her fears to Doreen.

'The last letter I had from him was at the end of January – why haven't I heard again?'

As usual puffing heavily on her Woodbine, Doreen pondered. 'Could he have been posted overseas without any warning?' she asked. 'It happens,' she added.

'But surely I would have heard something by now?' Stella insisted.

'Mebbe . . .' Doreen replied. Holding Stella's gaze, she asked pointedly, 'Why don't you just phone him up? You've got a number, haven't you?'

Stella frowned. 'It's only to be used in an emergency.'

'Well, what's this if it's not a bloody emergency?' Doreen scoffed.

'I don't know . . .' Stella fretted.

Seeing Stella nervously dithering, Doreen came up with a compromise. 'Give him till the end of the week and if he's not contacted you by then phone him.'

Stella slowly nodded her head. 'All right,' she agreed. 'I'll do that.'

The end of the week came and went, and still Stella couldn't pluck up the courage to phone Bill.

'This is just bloody silly,' Doreen declared.

Gathering together as many coins as she could lay her hands on, Doreen virtually frog-marched Stella to the factory's public phone booth, where she unceremoniously hustled her friend inside.

'For God's sake, just get on with it,' she instructed. 'I'll wait here until you've finished,' she said and stood sentry by the door. 'I'm not giving you the opportunity to run away.'

Fumbling nervously with a handful of coins, Stella carefully dialled the Mildenhall base and asked to speak to Flight Engineer Bill Austin.

'Just a minute while I check, ma'am,' the American on the other end of the phone said politely. After what seemed like an interminably long pause, he said, 'Flight Engineer Austin is no longer on the base, ma'am.'

Gasping in shock, Stella felt like she had been punched in the stomach. 'He's not in Mildenhall?'

'That's right, ma'am; he's returned to the US.'

Unable to take in what she had just heard, Stella struggled to hold back a feeling of mounting hysteria.

'B . . . b . . . b . . . but WHY?'

Clearly trying his best to be both patient and polite, the American on the other end of the line asked, 'Are you Flight Engineer Austin's next of kin, ma'am?'

'I'm his girlfriend,' she answered.

'Then I'm afraid, ma'am, I can give you no further details.'

Gathering her wits, Stella quickly added, 'Wait, please wait. I'm his fiancée – we're getting married.'

'Have you official evidence of that?'

With a sinking heart Stella realized that she had no documentation to say that she was getting married to Bill.

'No, nothing,' she answered limply.

'I'm sorry, ma'am, there's nothing I can say other than Flight Engineer Austin has been returned to the United States.'

As the phone clattered from her hand, Stella fell forwards. Doreen, alarmed at the sight of her friend, who appeared to have fainted, flung open the door of the telephone box.

'Stella! What's happened?'

Supporting Stella's limp body, she tried to lead her away, but Stella, who could barely stand, kept sagging at the knees. Eventually Doreen got her to the nearest chair, where Stella sank down, covering her face with her hands and starting to sob hysterically. At her wits' end, Doreen repeated herself. 'For God's sake, what's happened?'

In shock and convulsed with sobs, Stella could barely breathe. Making soothing noises while gently stroking her friend's back, Doreen waited patiently for Stella's breathing to steady. When it did, Stella's beautiful face was ravaged with pain.

'Bill's gone,' she said in a voice hollowed out with grief. 'He's gone back to America, Doreen. He's left me.'

25. Lambing Time

Lillian didn't need to tell her Land Girl friends that she was pregnant: from the noises issuing from the bathroom every morning they guessed what was going on, plus they had seen the stars in Lillian's lovely honey-brown eyes when Robbie drove into the yard. Typically, Mo started the ball rolling, as they sat around the kitchen table drinking tea and smoking Woodbines (all except Lillian, who couldn't bear the smell of either stimulant) at the end of the working day.

'There's no point in trying to hide it,' Mo announced. 'We're not daft, and we know what's going on.'

Not mincing her words, Pat asked point-blank, 'Who's the father?'

After which Mo said, 'What're you going to do?'

Their directness overwhelmed Lillian, who briefly struggled to hold back her tears but failed miserably. 'I don't know!' she blurted out.

Taking a softer line, Sal laid a comforting arm around Lillian's shuddering shoulders. 'We're your friends, lovie, we'll do our best to help you, you know that, don't you?'

Dabbing her blood-shot eyes, Lillian gazed into her friends' concerned faces.

'Can I swear you to secrecy?'

The three girls nodded their reply.

'It's Robbie's.'

Mo rolled her eyes upwards.

'Well, we guessed that much!' she exclaimed. 'You've been mooning around like a love-sick girl for weeks now.'

Sal threw Mo a hard 'Will you shut up!' look before she enquired, 'Does Robbie know?'

Lillian intently held their gazes. 'No, and he mustn't either. He's married and his wife is very fragile. Something like this could push her right over the edge.'

Lillian's mind flew back to the harrowing conversation she had had with Robbie in the tack room, the first time they had met up after their passionate love-making in the hayloft. Having touched and kissed and caressed each other in intimate places, they now behaved like polite strangers, treading carefully around each other in order to avoid intimacy or embarrassment. Lillian had offered to make tea after Robbie had examined one-day-old Lilibet, who was thriving. After they had finished their tea and run out of conversation, Robbie, unable to keep up the pretence any longer, had opened his heart to Lillian, who listened without interruption to his tragic story. Harriet had never recovered from their young son's sudden death, he told her. They had tried to have children but without success, which had created a bitterness between them that, when combined with their inconsolable grief, became an insurmountable barrier.

'Now Harriet can't even stand the sight of me,' Robbie confessed. 'At the beginning we desperately needed each other, clung to each other for support, but as the months

222

passed the rift grew, and now we live separate lives. We don't even share the same bed any more.'

Gazing into his strong, open face, dominated by his warm dark eyes, Lillian wondered how anybody could resist a man such as Robbie, who, soft and gentle in his love-making, was clearly experienced at knowing what a woman wanted. Lillian for sure had known intense pleasure and liberating joy in their coupling, and just the sight of him now sitting opposite her set her aflame with desire.

'I don't know a way out of it,' Robbie confessed. 'I feel racked with guilt when I think about what we did, dearest Lil, but I can never regret it, or forget it,' he murmured, as he tenderly stroked a stray strand of her hair that had drifted across her face. 'You have made me want to live again.'

'How could you not feel guilty?' Lillian reasoned. 'When your wife has no joy at all?'

Robbie groaned as if in pain. 'She's suffered so much; if only I could reach her, talk to her. Grief has mangled and destroyed our marriage. Poor Harriet, medication doesn't work any more – she needs real professional guidance or God only knows what she'll do to herself.'

Alarmed by his dark words, Lillian anxiously said, 'If your wife's suicidal maybe you shouldn't leave her alone so much, Robbie.'

'I have to work, sweetheart,' he pointed out. 'As you well know, my job is completely demanding: I'm out all day, every day, and I'm regularly on call in the evenings too. I can't give up my job; it's my livelihood.'

Overwhelmed with pity for Harriet, and for Robbie

too, Lillian took a deep breath before she spoke with complete conviction. 'We should definitely stop seeing each other.'

'But we're not doing anything wrong, sitting here talking,' he protested. 'I admit I'd love to be doing more, but we both know that would be wrong.'

With tears in her soft brown eyes, Lillian sadly replied, 'Yesterday we were both caught up in the moment. You're a married man, with a vulnerable wife who might do something you would regret for the rest of your life if she were to hear of your infidelity. She's already lost one person in her family; losing another might well kill her.'

Robbie gave a deep shuddering sigh. 'You're far braver than me, sweetheart. I couldn't bring myself to say those things – I can hardly bear to think them – but you're right: we should stop seeing each other,' he whispered wretchedly. 'If Harriet found out that I'd been unfaithful to her, God only knows what she would do.'

Lillian, the stronger of the two, at least for the moment was firm. 'Go home, Robbie. Go back to your wife and forget about me.'

Dragging her thoughts back to the here and now, Lillian looked at her friends' dear faces.

'I absolutely don't want him to know about my condition,' she told them. 'It would ruin any chance he might have of saving his marriage, in fact, it would probably destroy it altogether. I got myself into this mess,' she added with a resigned sigh, 'so it's me that's got to get myself out of it.'

'Are you thinking of a termination?' Mo asked. 'One of them back-street jobs?'

Lillian shuddered at the thought. 'No,' she protested. 'I don't think I could face that; I haven't got the money for such a thing either.'

'You can't have it here,' Pat warned. 'The whole valley would know.'

'I've no intention of giving birth here,' Lillian replied. 'I'll have to go into a home, though God knows how I'll fund it.'

Lillian's determination remained firm: never once did she deviate from her decision to avoid Robbie. Knowing that he would be very much on site during lambing season, a vital part of the farm's year, Lillian made herself scarce when she heard the sound of his Jeep pulling up in the yard. Aware of her need to avoid seeing the vet, her friends took over whatever job she was doing while she fled, only to return once Robbie had left the premises.

At the beginning of March, Lillian took her savings out of her bank account. She had added every penny she had saved while working at Dobb End to it, but it still didn't entirely cover the fees for the Mother and Baby Home near Grange-over-Sands that had been recommended to her, but she had read in their pamphlet that Mary Vale had a sliding scale of payments according to the girls' financial circumstances. After phoning Mary Vale and speaking to the bursar, Father Ben, Lillian was overwhelmingly relieved to hear him say there might be a place for her in the timeframe that she required. She could hear the relief in his voice too, when she told him she could pay at least half the fees.

'We try our best for our residents, who come from all walks of life, but there are times when our coffers run low and this is certainly one of them,' the priest said in a soft, kind voice.

After talking her plans through with her devoted friends, Lillian was convinced Mary Vale was the right place to go.

'In fact, it's the only place,' she said bluntly. 'All the other Mother and Baby Homes were too posh or too expensive.'

'When will you go?' Sal asked sadly.

'Just as soon as I can get a doctor's note,' Lillian announced, pointing to her growing tummy. 'I don't want Robbie to see me like this, and the bigger I get the less work I'll be able to do.' Trying to make light of her grim situation, she joked, 'The baby's due in the summer: imagine me harvesting at eight months gone?'

'Oh, we'll miss you, kid,' Mo wailed.

'We're bound to get some other girl to replace you,' Pat grumbled. 'Some girl we can't stand.'

'You weren't that stuck on me to start with,' Lillian reminded her. 'Always telling me off for being selfish and unpatriotic,' she reminded them.

'You were a hard grafter from the start,' Pat remembered. 'And never a toff.'

'The lass before you didn't know shit from sugar,' Mo sniffed rudely. 'A right bloody dope!'

'Is there any chance you might come back to Dobb End when this is all over?' Sal enquired. 'We'll be short of a stable girl for sure and the horses will miss you.'

Just thinking of Major, Daisy and sweet Lilibet – the name she had chosen for the foal in honour of the young Princess Elizabeth, who had been called that by her affectionate grandfather King George V – made Lillian weep.

'God,' she sobbed. 'How will I ever say goodbye to them? Promise me, *promise*,' Lillian begged, 'that you will take care of them, especially little Lilibet – promise you won't let anybody hurt them.'

Her friends instantly agreed to her request – how could they do otherwise with Lillian so distraught – but, if the truth were known, they had no idea who would step into Lillian's shoes, or who in the world would love the horses as passionately as she did.

If young Lilibet hadn't contracted pneumonia, Lillian might have got away from Dobb End without seeing Robbie again. The sight of the darling foal, feverish and listless, with a nasty nasal discharge, alarmed Lillian when she walked into the stall early one freezing-cold morning. Normally the foal would be eagerly awaiting her arrival, frisking around on her long spindly legs; instead Lillian found her feebly curled up beside her mother.

'Sweetheart,' she crooned, as she felt the foal's damp hot skin and wiped discharge from her nose. Panicking, she thought, 'Oh, God, I've got to phone Robbie. I can't put Lilibet's life at risk just because I'm avoiding him.'

Trembling, she went to the phone and, after dialling

the number, she heard Robbie's deep warm voice on the other end.

'It's Lillian.'

There was an audible gasp, before he asked in a business-like tone, 'Lillian, everything okay?'

Almost in tears, Lillian spluttered out, 'Lilibet's sick.'

Robbie's immediate response before he put the phone down was, 'I'll be there right away.'

Seriously shaking in every limb, Lillian dashed to the tack room, where she found a baggy old raincoat that she draped around herself in order to hide her tummy, which, though not huge, was certainly no longer flat. Then she hurried back to Daisy's stall and crouched down on the deep straw litter to soothe mother and foal. When Robbie caught sight of Lillian bent over Lilibet, with her silky long hair framing her sweet earnest face, his heart skipped a beat. When she looked up at him, with tears in her big brown eyes, all he wanted to do was to sweep her into his arms and kiss her tears away. Steeling himself, he firmly clutched his medical bag, then crept into the stall, where Daisy affectionately nuzzled him.

'It's all right, girl,' he whispered reassuringly. 'Let's take a look at your little one.'

At the sound of his strong reassuring voice, Lillian felt her body go weak, but, like him, she concentrated on the urgent job in hand.

'How long has she been like this?' he asked.

'Since early this morning; she seemed fine yesterday,' Lillian told him.

Using his stethoscope, Robbie listened to Lilibet's heartbeat, then moved the stethoscope around the area of her chest and ribcage. Finally, looking grim he looked up. 'I suspect she's got pneumonia.'

'Pneumonia!' Lillian cried. 'How? She's never even been outside.'

'She could have become infected by inhaling dust particles, which when ingested can cause disease in the lungs.'

'Poor darling,' Lillian murmured, as she stroked the foal's soft velvety pink muzzle.

Then, looking up at him, she whispered, 'Will she make it?'

'Hopefully,' Robbie answered firmly as he got to his feet. 'Intravenous fluids and a saline mix will help her cough up the secretions in her lungs, and I'll prescribe her some anti-inflammatory drugs. Come on, Lil,' he added briskly. 'Let's not waste time.'

Lillian's heart fluttered when he called her by the name he used when they were making love, but this wasn't the time for romantic nostalgia; between them they had to keep sweet Lilibet alive.

'What do you want me to do?' she asked.

'Stay right where you are, keep her calm, keep her cool and move Daisy to another stall, just for the time being while I treat her foal.'

A long day followed, but, by the end of it, with Robbie's calm confident expertise, Lilibet was on her feet, back with her mother, hungrily nuzzling her teats for milk.

'She's going to be fine,' Robbie said, smiling.

Lillian cried out in relief. 'Thank God.'

Seeing her so tense and tired, Robbie tenderly stroked a strand of hair off her weary face. 'I've missed you.'

Lillian wanted nothing more than to fall into his arms and make love with him in the hayloft that was so close, but, if she succumbed, he would see her in her nakedness, her rounded belly and enlarged breasts. Taking a step backwards, she said, 'I'll stay with Lilibet for the time being.'

Not failing to notice how she was avoiding him, Robbie took the same line of action. 'Righty-ho, ring me if there's a problem. Goodnight.'

And with that he was gone. Staying exactly where she was, Lillian listened to his receding footsteps, followed by the sound of his Jeep driving out of the yard. When silence descended, blinded by tears, Lillian returned to Daisy's stall, where she lay down on the straw bedding beside the gentle mare.

'I'll never see him again,' she groaned.

Nuzzling her softly, Daisy seemed to understand Lillian's pain. Comforted by her warm body and the sound of her regular breathing, Lillian had a last thought before she fell into a deep dreamless sleep: 'Robbie will never know I'm carrying his child.'

26. Doreen Steps In

Stella reported in sick, and she was sick too – sick to her soul, sick at heart, devastated, bereft, abandoned and frightened. She lay on her bed for days, not eating, not sleeping, just weeping and hoping to die. It was faithful Doreen who finally sat her friend upright, handed her a glass of water and said in a voice like granite, 'You can't go on like this.'

With her head hanging limp and her glorious hair in a tangled mess around her deathly pale face, Stella whimpered, 'I don't want to live any more.'

'I can see that,' Doreen answered briskly. 'But if you carry on like this, you'll lose the baby and maybe yourself too. Is that what you want?'

Stella, who didn't know what she wanted, didn't reply.

Though her heart ached for her friend, Doreen didn't deviate from her line. 'If you want to keep the baby, you'll have to go somewhere private to have it.'

With her thoughts in chaos and her eyes red and misty from weeping, Stella could barely take in any information. 'Where would I go?'

'A Mother and Baby Home, unless you want to go home?' Doreen told her.

'I couldn't go home, not in this state,' Stella murmured.

Sticking to the facts, Doreen ploughed on. 'You've got

money – you told me Bill sent you some to be going on with.'

Stella nodded. 'It was for getting married,' she said in a sad, broken voice.

'Um, well it looks like that's not happening at the minute,' Doreen said grimly. 'So mebbe think about spending some of it on booking yourself into a home.'

Overwhelmed, Stella started to cry. 'Where?'

'Anywhere – does it matter?' Doreen insisted.

Wailing in complete despair, Stella fell back on to her rumpled bed.

'At least give it some thought,' Doreen urged. 'Go to the doctor's and get some advice; try the library too – there might be some pamphlets that you can pick up and read.'

Doreen's harsh pep talk did eventually hit home. By the end of the week Stella had dragged herself out of bed in order to visit the factory doctor who had previously confirmed her pregnancy. After examining her and instructing her to eat more, the doctor handed her a couple of pamphlets containing the names of nearby Mother and Baby Homes.

'If you can pay, you'll be in a better position to get in sooner than the women that can't,' he told her bluntly, before firmly adding, 'From the looks of you, you need taking care of – I'd look into it right away.'

Knowing that Stella, in the state she was in, could never have made the train journey from Preston to Kents Bank alone, faithful Doreen helped her pack her bags, then travelled with her to Mary Vale.

'Well, it looks nice enough,' Doreen said, as they threaded their way through a cool oak wood that led to a big house standing on a grassy promontory overlooking the Irish Sea.

In a daze Stella looked around and nodded dumbly. 'Yes,' she agreed. 'It looks nice enough, I suppose.'

Settling into a Mother and Baby Home, surrounded by women in the same boat, brought an unexpected comfort to Stella. All of them had a heartbreaking story to tell: anything from loss, fear, disappointment, hardship, rejection, abuse, even rape. Though feeling rejected and abandoned herself, Stella was grateful that (albeit briefly) she had known real love when her baby was conceived.

Gazing out of her bedroom window that looked out to the sea, Stella was dazzled by its constantly changing colours, from pewter to sparkling silver, followed by sudden bursts of blazing blue. She loved watching the sea-birds clustered on the sandbanks: long-legged redshanks, sandpipers with their piping call and red-beaked oystercatchers, all following the outgoing tide, waiting for pools to appear in which little fish and insects swarmed. Their combined calls and the constant churning of the sea were the regular melodic sounds that she fell asleep to and that she woke up to as well.

'Bill would have loved this coastline,' Stella often thought.

Over time she had worked on banishing Bill from her mind. For all his talk, he had walked out of her life with no explanation or apology. The only thing she now had of his was the money which had bankrolled her entire stay in

Mary Vale. After their baby was born, she would not have a penny in the world. Then what would she do? Have their baby adopted or try somehow to keep it? If she did that, what would she and her child live on?

When these insurmountable questions rolled around Stella's head, she forced herself to focus on Sister Ada's sound advice. 'One day at a time, dear, one day at a time.'

Stella had liked Ada the minute she opened the front door and welcomed her to Mary Vale.

Gazing into the nurse's deep blue eyes, Stella immediately felt that here was a woman she could trust. The warmth in her smile and her soft Lancashire accent reassured Stella, who had been a bag of nerves on the journey north from Preston. When her thoughts weren't on her fears and anxieties about the future, they returned like a homing bird to Bill. But, after crying what seemed like an ocean of tears, Stella bitterly reminded herself every single day: 'Bill's a dream that has turned into a nightmare; you have to forget him and move on.'

It didn't take Stella long to realize that things weren't going at all well in Mary Vale's kitchen. Though nourishing food was served at regular times of the day, it was clear from Sister Theresa's flushed face and agitated manner that the young nun was under a lot of pressure.

'Things have never been the same since the old nun, Sister Mary Paul, was forced to retire due to ill health,' a resident explained over breakfast one morning. 'We also used to have freshly baked bread, but all that's stopped since Myrtle took over; now we just have rotten old grey sliced bread,' she grumbled.

'At least you still have delicious butter,' Stella said appreciatively, as she enjoyed the rich taste of thick yellow Lancashire butter sparingly spread on her toast.

'That's from Mary Vale Farm,' the girl explained. 'We get eggs sometimes and loads of milk too.' Dropping her voice to a whisper, she added, 'I think the cook they got pro tem is overstretched; she's only engaged until they find somebody else, but that hasn't happened yet.'

Her remark set Stella thinking. She was a cook, a good one at that, and she actually missed cooking; making and prepping food was the stuff of life to her, plus she actually got pleasure from seeing people enjoy the meals she prepared.

'Maybe I could persuade the powers that be that cooking in the kitchen is just another chore.' Recalling the residents' list of daily tasks that were essential to the organized running of Mary Vale and were, in fact, one of the conditions of their stay, Stella thought to herself, 'I'd rather cook than clean the house or work in the laundry.'

With this in mind, she waylaid Sister Ada in the hospital corridor the very next day. 'I'd like to volunteer my services in the kitchen,' she said brightly.

Stopping dead in her tracks, Ada exclaimed in astonishment, '*Really?*'

Stella grinned and nodded. 'Yes, I've run two industrial kitchens, one in a cotton mill and the other in a munitions factory. Cooking here, for a relatively small number, would be a piece of cake. I've been doing a bit of snooping and gather you might be in need of a cook to replace Myrtle in the kitchen.'

'Yes, that's true,' Ada confessed. 'We have rather exploited Myrtle's generosity, but she only ever agreed to come on a temporary basis, and it's run into months now.'

'So let me help?' Stella said, smiling.

'You're here in the Home to have a baby, not slave for us,' Ada protested.

'It wouldn't be slave work for me,' Stella insisted.

'But you're going to get bigger as the months pass, dear, you'll need to rest more as your confinement approaches,' Ada said knowingly.

Laying her cards on the table, Stella said bluntly, 'You would be doing me a big favour, Sister. Cooking would fill my day and take my thoughts off other more painful pre-occupations; I'd be really grateful for a distraction.'

'Cooking three meals a day is a lot more than a distraction – it's hard work,' Ada protested. 'If your kind offer was accepted, you would have to promise not to do any heavy work. Lifting heavy buckets and sacks of potatoes could badly damage your back.'

Seeing Ada's concerned expression, Stella continued on a more persuasive note, 'We could come to an arrange-ment that suits all,' she smiled. 'Put it like this: if you can replace my daily chores with kitchen chores, I know I'll be happy with that.'

'That's a very appealing idea,' Ada agreed. 'I'll have to check it with Matron, and Myrtle too.'

'Fine,' Stella replied. 'I'll wait to hear back from you.'

Myrtle leapt at the idea of a replacement, while Matron was more cautious.

'She has paid the full fee to stay here,' she told Ada. 'It could be seen as most exploitative.'

'I agree,' Ada replied. 'But Stella's really keen – she went so far as to say she would be grateful for the work, as it would take her mind off other things. Why don't we give her a week's trial?' she suggested.

'Good idea,' Matron agreed. 'Let's see how Stella feels after a week's work in Mary Vale's kitchen.'

Stella loved her new role: it suited her down to the ground and by the end of the working day she was so tired she fell into her bed and slept a deep untroubled sleep instead of tossing and turning all night torturing herself with thoughts of Bill. Sister Theresa shyly presented her with Sister Mary Paul's old and much-thumbed recipe book, which proved to be a good place to start, but ever imaginative Stella quickly added variations and tasty alternatives: curried corned-beef balls, savoury pancakes, game pie (courtesy of the farmer's contact with the local gamekeepers), shepherd's pie, potato hash and mock roasts made from spam and fresh herbs. Stella decided that living slap-bang by the sea was something to exploit. Taking an old bike from the shed, she cycled into Grange, where she was able to buy pilchards, herrings, crab and cod. With these she made fish pie and various delicious pâtés, which were a blessed change from the endless jars of beef and fish paste that had previously graced the table every tea-time.

In the process of buying goods, Stella enjoyed getting

to know the lovely area where she now lived, and she enjoyed meeting the locals too, who were always kind and friendly. On her cycle rides into town, along the narrow sandy track that skirted the railway line, Stella keenly looked out for wild herbs, particularly wild garlic, which, once ground into a paste, could perk up any dull soup or casserole. When she arrived in Grange, Stella would prop her bike against the sea-wall and breathe in the air, tangy with the taste of salt. She loved to watch the rushing incoming tide pour inexorably over the silvery sage-green marsh, gurgling into rock pools, then, in ever strengthening waves, smash on to the shore, where hungry gulls pecked at whatever riches the tide washed in. It was at times like these that Stella felt, if not content (that would be an impossible state to achieve in her situation), then at least at peace and resigned to her fate. She had lost the love of her life and she would never see him again, but she had a child growing inside her that she had a responsibility for. When she felt her baby move, Stella wondered what would become of it; she had already discussed the future of her child with gentle Father Ben, who arranged all the Home's adoptions.

'I must do the right thing by my baby,' she told herself as she turned away from the shore and headed into town. 'The poor mite never asked to be born.'

27. Heartache

When it came to leaving Dobb End, Lillian was utterly distraught. She had imagined that her final glimpse of Robbie walking away from her would be the hardest thing to bear, but leaving Major, Daisy and frisky little Lilibet just about broke her heart. She realized too late when she walked into the stable that it was a mistake to visit them one final time. The sight of them wrung her out: Major with his big dark noble head, neighing a welcome; Daisy with her shiny silver mane and soft trusting brown eyes; and sweet little Lilibet (who already showed the same markings as her pretty mother) – all waiting expectantly for their morning cuddle and crunchy carrot treat.

Trying to greet them in the same cheery way she always did, Lillian called her usual, 'Morning!'

But when she entered their stable and Major nudged her arm for attention, while Daisy nibbled her hand and cheeky Lilibet snorted and blew into her hair, her resolve completely vanished.

'Oh, God, how can I do this?' she sobbed, as she laid her head against Major's giant chest and wept uncontrollably. 'How can I leave you all, my darlings?'

Instinctively sensing her grief, Major remained solidly still and calm, moving only to nuzzle her wet face and snicker softly. It was the same with Daisy, who, like Major, tried to absorb Lillian's unhappiness by tenderly nuzzling and nibbling her. Lilibet, on the other hand, young and excitable, just wanted to play and scamper as she did every morning on Lillian's arrival. Neighing impatiently, she pawed the ground as if to say, 'What's the matter, why aren't you playing with me?'

An emotional wreck, Lillian would never have got out of the stable if Sal hadn't turned up to collect her. Seeing Lillian's devastated face, she took her firmly by the arm. 'Sweetheart, this isn't helping things at all,' she said firmly.

'I know,' Lillian wailed. 'I love them so much; they've become like family to me.'

'Come on, let's get out of here,' Sal continued. 'You're upsetting the animals as well as yourself.'

As Lillian turned her back on the horses, they all neighed, and it felt to Lillian like they were calling out to her. All she wanted to do was to rush back to kiss and stroke them just one more time, but Sal had other ideas.

'Come on, we'll miss the bus if you hang around here much longer.'

Sal had promised Lillian that she would take her into Keswick to catch the bus to Grange-over-Sands, but then she would have to return to the farm to start her working day.

'Sorry I can't take you all the way there,' she had apologized.

'That's all right,' Lillian replied. 'It wouldn't be fair to leave Mo and Pat on their own, and with me gone your workload's already increased.'

*

On the single-decker bus that wound its way through the Borrowdale Valley, Lillian was grateful for Sal's strong presence. Everywhere she looked there were memories: the four of them cycling past the Bowder Stone in the summertime; the tiny hamlet of Seatoller, where Robbie's veterinary practice and home were; the drystone-wall sheep folds she had helped to build, now enclosing gambolling lambs and their mothers; Grange village, where bobbing daffodils bordered the river, near to overflowing its banks due to the constant levels of high spring rainfall. And surrounding all, the magnificent fells, forever rising to the highest peak. This was a landscape Lillian had known nothing of until she came (dragging her feet all the way) to Dobb End. Vividly recalling her arrival in the valley last summer, Lillian smiled to herself. Her shocked reaction to the disgusting condition of her new home, the friendship of her fellow Land Girls, the colossal amount of backbreaking hard work expected of them, being entrusted with the care of the shire horses and finally meeting Robbie – all had created an unexpected form of paradise here in this magical valley, which she now must rip herself away from. As the bus stopped and started to pick up locals, who chatted easily across the space of the vehicle, Lillian speculated: when the war came to an end and her Land Girl days were over, would she have stayed on in Borrowdale? The answer was an unequivocal yes. She would happily have spent the rest of her life breeding shire horses and working in tandem with nature, but, because of her condition, she had to leave to protect the man she loved.

*

When it came to saying goodbye to one another outside the Moot Hall in Keswick, both women wept.

'Be brave, kid, write,' Sal said, as she swiped tears off her cheeks. 'We'll miss you like hell.'

'Keep in touch, won't you?' Lillian implored. 'Let me know how things are going and please,' she begged, 'look after my beautiful horses.'

'I can't promise to meet your standards, but I'll do mi best,' Sal promised.

Before she got on the bus, Lillian leant in close to whisper in Sal's ear, 'Swear you'll never tell Robbie why I left, swear, Sal.' Seeing her friend looking distinctly uneasy, Lillian quickly added, 'What is it, Sal, what's troubling you?'

'I don't think what you're doing is fair to the vet,' Sal blurted out.

Lillian replied in a hard, steely voice, 'It might not be fair, but it has to be done. Right now Robbie must focus on his wife, not me.'

Sal looked unconvinced. 'I've heard tell the poor woman's been sent to Lancaster Asylum. The man might be in need of a friend right now.'

Lillian gasped in disbelief. 'When did this happen and why did nobody tell me?' she demanded.

Sal shrugged. 'You should know by now what valley folks are like: they look after their own kind and don't give much out to strangers. I only know 'cos I overheard somebody speaking about the vet's wife being admitted to hospital while I was queuing up in the village shop.'

'Poor, poor Robbie,' Lillian murmured.

Seeing her resolve weaken, Sal immediately said, 'You could help him, Lil, give him a bit of comfort when he's in most need.'

'NO! That would be a big mistake,' Lillian exclaimed. 'He will do far better with nothing to distract him from the important task of looking after his wife.' Repeating herself, Lillian said through gritted teeth, 'Sal, listen to me, Robbie must *never* know about the baby.'

As the bus driver started up the engine, Lillian climbed aboard, waving through the window to blow kisses to Sal, who smiled and waved back as the bus turned a corner and then she was gone.

Shortly after Lillian's departure, Robbie came storming into the farmhouse to find the Land Girls clearing away their tea.

'One of the farm hands has just informed me that Lillian's left,' he declared.

All three girls nodded dumbly.

'Where has she gone?' Robbie demanded. Seeing them all obdurately mute, he cried, 'For God's sake! Why can't you tell me where she is?'

Exchanging nervous looks, Mo and Pat turned to Sal, who went through the story that she had rehearsed several times with her friends.

'She got a call from home, bad news, she left immediately,' she told him.

Looking desperate, Robbie ran a trembling hand through his thick tawny hair.

'She must have left an address?'

Looking blank, Sal shook her head. 'No, she didn't; she said she hoped to be back in no time,' she lied.

The strain on Robbie's face slowly lifted. 'Ah, so she's coming back?'

'When she's sorted everything out at home,' Sal lied again.

Obviously relieved by this piece of information, Robbie reverted back to the reason why he had suddenly turned up at Dobb End.

'I just wanted to check on the horses,' he said. 'How are they?'

Sal pulled down the corners of her mouth. 'They're missing Lillian.'

Seeing sadness suffuse Robbie's face, Sal could have kicked herself. 'Me and my big mouth,' she chided herself.

'I'll take a look,' was all he said.

In the warm stable, with the sound of sparrows chirruping in the rafters and the horses softly moving about in their deep straw litters, Robbie could almost feel Lillian's gentle presence. His eyes instantly fell on the hayloft where they had made love the night of Lilibet's birth.

'God,' he groaned out loud as the memory of their love-making hit him like a truck.

Though still a virgin, Lillian had been a passionate, spontaneous lover, abandoning herself to Robbie, who was sensitive to her inexperience. Impatient with his caution, Lillian had pulled him closer into her body, crying out with pleasure as he found the secret parts of her that willingly opened up to him. She had been wonderful, and – overwhelmed by her youth and beauty – he had found pure joy and rejuvenation in their loving.

Even though he ached for sweet Lil, Robbie was glad that they had stuck to their promise and avoided each other for Harriet's sake, though at the moment his wife's pain and despair were well beyond his reach. The doctors at Lancaster Asylum had sedated Harriet with heavy mood-changing drugs, which they hoped would make some improvement, but, if they failed, the medics had warned him they would have to consider using electric-shock treatment. Though Robbie regularly visited his wife, she barely seemed to know him, staring vacantly out of her window. Harriet never spoke a word; occasionally she simply wept for the duration of his visit. It was a living hell to witness, especially when he could do nothing, say nothing to alleviate her agony. Sitting in silence with his wife, Robbie reflected on brave little Lillian's decision to put an end to any possibility of a relationship between them. She had been right and courageous, but her going was like another light going out in his already drab world.

'Jesus!' Sal exclaimed after Robbie had grilled them all in the kitchen. 'He wasn't for taking no as an answer; good job we had worked out a pack of lies to calm him down,' she said as she reached for her packet of Woodbines lying on the kitchen table

'You did a good job, Sal,' Pat congratulated her. 'I don't think I could have faced him down the way you did.'

'Poor sod,' Mo sighed. 'He's mad for Lil.'

'The only thing that calmed him down was you saying

Lil would be back just as soon as she had sorted out the family business; it might keep the poor man happy for a while,' Pat said glumly.

Remembering the expression on Robbie's face and the pain in his eyes, Sal shook her head. 'Not for long,' she said knowingly. 'When she doesn't show up, he'll be back, that's for sure.'

When Lillian alighted from the little local train that ran from Grange-over-Sands to Kents Bank, she – like most of the residents who arrived on foot and made their way through the little oak wood that opened on to Mary Vale's wide lawn – was pleasantly surprised. She hadn't expected such a grand house or such a breathtaking view of the Irish Sea, where gulls, suspended on the stiff sea-breeze, hovered over the waves, looking out for fish to dive-bomb. Her opinion of Mary Vale improved even more when the door was opened by a tall, slim nurse who wore her rich mahogany-brown hair tucked under a starched frilly cap. When she smiled at the newcomer, her big blue eyes sparkled. Stepping over the threshold, Lillian said, 'I'm Lillian. I think you might be expecting me.'

28. Chores

Stella's trial week in the kitchen quickly turned into nearly a month, during which time she had met Sister Mary Paul twice. Recovering from her glaucoma operation, the old nun was guided from the convent to the kitchen by faithful Sister Theresa, and once there she was carefully sat down on her old wooden kitchen chair and served tea and coconut biscuits.

'It's marvellous to meet you at last,' Stella enthused. 'I've found your recipe book really useful,' she gratefully added.

'It's well thumbed,' Mary Paul chuckled. 'But the recipes are all firm favourites with the residents, and well tested over the years. You're a bit younger than me,' she said, smiling. 'You must have added your own little bits and bobs to cheer up dull old rationed food.'

'It gets worse by the week,' Stella sighed. 'But we do our best, and this is a great part of the world for fresh produce, especially fish.'

'You're right,' Mary Paul agreed. 'And Farmer Arkwright is a saint to us with his milk and eggs and crumbly Lancashire cheese.'

'He's wonderful,' Stella enthused. 'Now that we're even getting soft fruit like gooseberries from his garden, we're lucky compared to others.'

Carefully watching Mary Paul for signs of fatigue,

Theresa was aware of the old nun's rheumy eyes gazing around her previous empire.

'You keep the place spic and span,' she congratulated Stella. 'I can smell something cooking – what is it?'

'Cheese flan with fried onions – it's tasty and it goes a long way if I serve it with cabbage and mashed potatoes.'

Mary Paul chuckled. 'I can tell you're clearly a girl who knows how to eke out food.'

Stella laughed. 'What else can a cook do in these hard times?'

Early one morning, after a busy breakfast, feeling guilty that Stella had been so long in the kitchen, Ada took the new cook to one side.

'You're getting bigger, dear; we really need to appoint another cook and let you off the hook.'

'Do so if it makes you feel better, but please,' Stella implored, 'my baby's not due till the start of July. I'm fit enough. I'm quite sure I can work for a bit longer.'

Ada looked uncertain.

'Let me check with Matron and get back to you,' she said.

'I agree it is rather unorthodox,' Matron agreed. 'Not to mention exploitative.'

'Stella insists that working in the kitchen actually helps ease her heartache,' Ada said.

'What is her story?' Matron enquired.

'She fell in love with an American airman who went back to America without even saying goodbye, and the poor girl's heartbroken.'

Matron rolled her eyes. 'An all too familiar but nevertheless tragic story,' she sighed.

'What's the best thing to do as far as her working in the kitchen goes?' Ada asked anxiously.

'I think we must advertise for a new cook because the day will come when Stella simply won't be able to cope with all that hard work; but meanwhile we must rely on Sister Theresa to monitor the situation – after all she is the one who works alongside Stella most mornings.'

'You're right,' Ada replied. 'I'd trust Sister Theresa's judgement about anything. She'll tell us when the time is right for Stella to step down, even if Stella doesn't agree with it.'

Stella was pleased to see the arrival of a young woman whose baby, she discovered, was due about six weeks after her own scheduled date. Even though they were physically a contrasting pair – tall, willowy Stella with her abundant red-gold curls and small, lean, tanned Lillian with her honey-brown eyes and delicate heart-shaped face – they quickly became friends. Their proximity to each other, with rooms on the same landing, accelerated their friendship. Though they instinctively liked each other and chatted easily, both girls held back from sharing much of their history, which in both cases was still too painful to talk about.

Stella couldn't help but laugh when feisty Lillian complained about the Home's daily chore rota.

'My Land Girl friend Mo would tell them exactly where to stick it,' she giggled. 'Never one to hold back, is our

Mo; she would have gone up the wall if she had been asked to clean out grates or work in the laundry. Yet we're used to mucking out, herding cattle, delivering lambs, worming sheep and building drystone walls,' she told her new friend, who literally gaped at her open-mouthed.

'You're pulling my leg?' Stella gasped.

'No, I'm not, that's what Land Girls do, and tree-felling and hedging and harvesting,' she continued with a rather unexpected ring of pride in her voice. 'God,' Lillian thought, sadly to herself, 'how I miss it all.'

'Well, if you ever get sick to the teeth of the chores, you could always ask Ada if you could join me in the kitchen,' Stella suggested. 'Sister Theresa helps out in the mornings, but in the afternoons she has her convent duties to attend to, so I'm always a bit pushed around tea-time.'

'That's a thought,' Lillian replied. 'I don't know how long I can stick cleaning out grates and laying fires,' she groaned.

'Give it some thought,' Stella urged. 'You know you'll always be welcome in my kitchen.'

When Stella discovered that Lillian loved walking, she suggested that they should take strolls together, either across the silvery sage-green marsh when the tide was out or along the sandy path that skirted the bay if the tide was in. It was on one of their regular walks that Lillian eventually opened her heart to Stella about her heartbreak at leaving her beloved shires. Carefully skirting around the subject of Robbie, she talked about her affinity with the horses she had left behind.

'It's not only that I worked alongside them, and, by

God, they are Trojans when it comes to work, they'll go till they drop,' she started. 'It's their trusting nature and gentle ways. They became my best friends, I simply adored them,' she said on a swallowed sob. Gazing out at the swallows screeching as they swooped out over the marsh in search of insects, she continued in a calmer tone, 'Before I was a Land Girl, I'd never even seen so much as the back end of a horse, but once I was in charge of Major and Daisy it was like a light came on in my brain. Of course, I had to be taught the basics – tacking up, feeds, cleaning harnesses, grooming, hoof-cleaning – but that came easily because I loved being with them. It was just a joy!' she exclaimed with tears in her eyes.

'Will you ever see them again?' Stella enquired.

Lillian vehemently shook her head. 'No, I can never go back there.'

Seeing the sadness in Lillian's big brown eyes, Stella desisted from asking any more questions about her Land Girl work. Instead she changed the subject.

'Have you given any more thought to joining me in the kitchen?'

'As a matter of fact, I have,' Lillian answered. 'I'm already fed up with sooty fireplaces and polishing stairs, so I'd love to if it's allowed.'

Stella beamed. 'Good,' she laughed. 'I'll ask Sister Ada if you can be my assistant.'

The following morning, after serving breakfast in the dining room, Stella approached Ada and asked if Lillian might join her in the kitchen.

'Heck, two pregnant women working in the kitchen looks rather close to slave labour,' Ada exclaimed. 'People will start saying we're exploiting our residents and that wouldn't look good.'

'As I said before, Sister, it's only another chore. You can add it to the official list of chores, if it makes you feel any better,' she suggested. 'It's not that much different from any of the other jobs that we're required to do.'

'You have a point, I suppose,' Ada conceded.

Suddenly panicked that her suggestion might land her with one of the less reliable residents rather than Lillian, Stella quickly stepped in. 'Let's try Lillian out,' she urged. 'She'll only be doing afternoon teas – let's see how that goes.'

The bond between the two women deepened as they worked alongside each other in the kitchen. When Sister Theresa departed after dinner was served, Lillian would dash into the kitchen with a cheeky smile on her face.

'Switch on *Workers' Playtime*.'

To the lilting tones of Tommy Dorsey, Joe Loss and Glenn Miller, Stella and Lillian would sing along as they washed up, sliced bread, rolled pastry and chopped vegetables. When a favourite of theirs played, they would very often break into a waltz or a foxtrot; they even tried jiving to 'Chattanooga Choo Choo', but that didn't last long, as they were both soon out of breath. Collapsing on kitchen chairs, they would burst out laughing.

'I think my dancing days are over till after this baby is born,' Stella confessed as she hugged her side. 'Far too strenuous in our condition.'

'I felt my baby bouncing around while I was dancing,' Lillian giggled. 'What silly sods we are.'

Stella's big blue eyes grew dreamy as she recalled her dancing days. 'I used to love dancing – it's how I met Bill.'

Aware that she might upset Stella by wading in and asking questions, Lillian held her breath.

'He's a wonderful dancer,' Stella continued in a soft whisper. 'But he left me.'

Lillian reached out to squeeze her friend's trembling hand. 'I am so sorry.'

Stella brusquely nodded her head as she swiped away a few tears. 'It's all water under the bridge now,' she declared, as she rose from her chair. Switching off the dance music, she added, 'I'll put the kettle on for a cuppa.'

Rising too, Lillian went back to her task of grating cheese for the macaroni dish she was making.

'Pain just breaks through in a place like Mary Vale,' she thought miserably. 'How could it not?'

So many women awaiting the birth of their babies, Lillian mused. Which most of them (her included) wouldn't even take home to bring up. The irony, she thought, was that all Robbie's poor wife ever wanted was a child of her own to love and nurture, and here in the Home were dozens of lovely babies waiting to be adopted. If only Harriet was in a sound state of mind, she could have found comfort in the babies at Mary Vale. But, tragically, Lillian feared, Harriet's days of being capable of raising a child might be behind her.

29. Seattle

In Seattle's military hospital, Bill, drowsy from pain-killing drugs, which only took the edge off the constant agony he was in, struggled to make conversation with his older brother.

'Good to see you, Pete. Mom said you'd be visiting soon.'

'Sorry it's taken me so long; you know how difficult it is getting leave these days.'

Bill gave a sympathetic smile. 'To be honest you've not missed much, just me lying here recovering from one operation after another.' Seeing his brother's pained expression, Bill quickly added, 'The medics are doing a great job, lining up physios, teaching me how to walk on one leg; they're even talking about fitting a prosthetic limb sometime in the future.'

Seeing the sheen of sweat on his brother's strained face, Pete said thoughtfully, 'Are you okay to talk? I don't want to tire you out.'

Bill nodded. 'Sure, it's good to talk, man.'

'Mom told me that the British medics who performed the amputation said it was touch and go whether you'd make it,' Pete continued. 'I can only thank God that they got you safely back home.'

'The Brits did a great job of stitching me up,' Bill reassured his anxious brother.

Catching sight of Bill's exhausted expression, the Staff Sister in charge of the ward quietly suggested that Pete should let his brother get some rest.

'Sure, sure,' Pete said apologetically, as he rose to his feet.

Holding up a hand in protest, Bill exclaimed, 'Wait a minute, buddy, I have a favour to ask you.'

Sitting back down, Pete waited for Bill to speak.

'I met a girl while I was stationed in England, the most wonderful girl, beautiful and smart, you'd love her, Pete,' Bill raved. 'We were planning to get married; then this happened. Since I was brought home, communication between us has been non-existent, and I'm desperate to hear from her.'

Astonished, Pete asked, 'Surely she would have phoned the base if she hadn't heard from you in a long time?'

Bill shrugged. 'She might have phoned the Mildenhall base, I really hope she did, but I don't know what she would have been told. I've been worried sick,' he admitted, close to tears.

Feeling increasingly hostile, Pete was thinking, 'You're worried sick, lying here crippled in a hospital bed, while a dame half the world away hasn't even bothered to make contact – gimme a break!'

'I wrote to her just as soon as I was strong enough,' Bill continued. 'But the damn letter was returned. I couldn't believe it when it landed right back where it had started. I must've been so drugged I wrote down the wrong address.' Now straining with the effort of speaking, he reached into his bedside locker. 'Here it is,' he said and produced a battered-looking airmail letter along with other newer envelopes. 'I've written her a bunch more since, this time correctly addressed,' he added ruefully. 'Would you do me a favour, buddy? Will you mail them for me?' he asked. 'I couldn't ask Mom and Dad – they made it clear from the get-go that they're not keen on me marrying a Brit.'

Thinking, 'Neither am I,' Pete nevertheless gave a curt nod as he accepted the letters from his brother.

'You know, pal,' he said tentatively, 'she may have moved on; these things happen when there's a war raging.'

'There's more to it than that, bud,' Bill said in a low earnest voice. 'Stella's having our baby.'

If alarm bells were ringing earlier in Pete's head, they were definitely clanging now.

'Oh, my God!' he thought. 'A baby would seal the deal.'

Struggling to sit up straight so he could speak more clearly, Bill added, 'As soon as I can walk, I'm going back for Stella. Even if she decides she doesn't want me any more because of this' – he nodded towards the dip in his bedding – 'I've just got to see her one more time.'

Sitting on a bench in the hospital grounds, Pete was in turmoil; he had read about grasping GI brides in the papers, British girls snapping up US servicemen and marrying them before they could say Jack Robinson! Dames cashing in on vulnerable young men far away from home.

'Jesus!' he seethed out loud. 'Once that gold ring is on their finger, they're living in the lap of luxury on a US base with better food, better housing and an altogether better life. I bet you a dime to a dollar that this Stella dame is no damn different.'

Clutching the letters in his trembling hands, Pete glared at them, considering his next move.

Now thoroughly worn out, Bill lay back against his pillows and sighed; he was so grateful to Pete for agreeing to mail his letters to Stella. Recalling his parents' stunned reaction when he had talked to them about finding Stella, he knew in no uncertain terms that they were fiercely against the relationship.

'There's a war on!' his mother had exclaimed. 'You can't possibly travel to England, son.'

His father, just as concerned as his wife, took a more radical line. 'Why chase after a woman who has never even bothered to get in touch with you?'

Bill averted his eyes from his father's penetrating gaze. He couldn't argue with him on that count.

'What if she doesn't speak to you, even if you do manage to track her down?' Mr Austin continued.

'Your father's right,' Mrs Austin agreed. 'What if she's found somebody else?'

'Then I'll have to live with it,' Bill had answered flatly.

As Bill drifted off to sleep, firm in the belief that he could trust his older brother, Pete was in the process of ripping open the battered returned letter that his brother had written.

My darling Stella Star

I don't know where to start, or how I can even begin to explain what happened to me that fateful day in February when I crash-landed my plane. The team and I had worked a twelve-hour shift on a new Tempest bomber, which I was then ordered to take up for a test-flight before the plane was despatched to face the Luftwaffe again. After quickly grabbing the usual gear – jacket, helmet, gloves and goggles – I flew the Tempest over the dense pinewoods that fringe the Mildenhall base, then briefly along the edges of the North Sea, where I didn't loiter for fear of being shot down by an enemy plane. On my return, as I made my descent into Mildenhall, a sudden wind sent the plane swinging to the right. When I tried to angle her against the wind, I put too much pressure on one of the wheels, which collapsed, and the plane began to plummet. I could barely see through the windshield, which was splattered with dark-black oil blobs, and, when I managed to squint through the little bit of windshield that remained clear, I saw that the debris from the shattered wheel had hit the left-wing, half of which had fallen away. Knowing I would have to crash-land the plane, I tried to slip through a line of trees, but the remaining tip of the broken left-wing clipped a tree and the plane exploded into a ball of fire.

I came around in a white room surrounded by doctors who were discussing amputating my leg and shipping me back home to the States. I wanted to scream out, 'NO! I can't leave my Stella.' But the words never came. Somebody must have given me a massive shot of morphine and I blacked out, but not before your sweet, beautiful face drifted before me, tumbling red-gold hair, dreamy sky-blue eyes and soft kissable lips. Honey, that crash-landing not

only cost me my leg, but it also ripped me away from you. I can
barely rest thinking of you, my precious love, all alone and in your
condition, pregnant with my baby. Please don't think I walked out
on you; I swear I would never do that. I've been pretty drugged up
here in the Seattle hospital where I'm receiving treatment and
physiotherapy, which I pray to God will get me back on my feet.
My strength is slowly returning; at least now I can actually sit up
and write a letter to you instead of falling asleep mid-sentence.

My major preoccupation these days is to find you and marry
you, my Stella Star. The only thing that's keeping me focused is
that I might see you again and we can have that life that we
planned together last summer. Please, please, write to me at the
above hospital address; when I'm discharged, which I hope will be
soon, I will let you have my home address. The most important
thing now is that we keep in touch and don't lose contact. Please,
I beg you, put my mind at rest and write back as soon as possible,
telling me where you are and how you are surviving.

I will love you forever.

Your devoted, Bill xxxxx

'Oh, my good Lord,' Pete mumbled.

Without a moment's hesitation he proceeded to rip open all the other airmail letters, which he quickly scanned, one after another.

My darling girl,

When my first letter to you came shooting back, I despaired —
after all this time I still don't know where you are or how you are,
and you don't know where I am or that I'm being treated in

Seattle hospital for a leg amputation. What a God damn awful mess. Not being able to make contact with you is driving me crazy with worry. Have you changed address or are you still at the same munitions factory where you were living and working the last time I saw you? I certainly hope you're not still working at the factory. At this stage in your pregnancy you should be putting your feet up in a safe comfortable place where you're being well looked after. I feel a total bum for not being by your side. I must find you, Stella, I must know that you and the baby are secure, so please, I implore you, contact me at the above hospital address so that we can make plans to get back together and I can take care of you and our baby.

Your loving
Bill
xxx

The message at the heart of all the letters was Bill's abject love for Stella, his overwhelming guilt at abandoning her and his utter determination, crippled as he was, to get back to England and marry her. Pete seethed at the thought of her. Months had passed and this heartless woman had done nothing to track down his brother, regardless of whether she'd received any of his letters. Not bothered to find out where he was or sent any comfort to his kid brother, nothing, zilch! What kinda woman would do that to somebody she supposedly loved? Fuming with anger, Pete leapt to his feet and walked to the nearest trash can, into which he flung every single airmail letter.

'To hell with that,' he said under his breath. 'No Limey money-grabber is going to make a fool of my kid brother!'

30. Day Off

Renee's drinking increased over the spring months due to her new friendship with Freda, the landlady of the Smugglers' Arms, just off the esplanade in Grange. In the lounge on one of Renee's days off, Freda served her guest a decent lunch of steak-and-kidney pie, accompanied by several large gin and tonics that, as the lunchtime rush wound down, Freda had liberally partaken of too. Sympathetic to Renee's demanding work, Freda had exclaimed, 'Christ! Who wouldn't need a stiff drink now and then working in a place like that?' As she sloshed another measure of gin into Renee's empty glass and her own too, she drawled, 'This one's on the house by the way, sweetheart.'

Renee in return sympathized with Freda, whose husband had run off with a barmaid half his age.

'The old bastard took all of our savings too,' Freda had tearfully confided. 'Left me here to struggle on my own,' she added and took another gulp of gin.

By the end of their first drinking session, they were firm friends and half drunk. Renee had just about managed to totter back home along the sandy track beside the railway line skirting the bay. Collapsing into bed, she had slept off her boozy lunch without anybody in the Home being any the wiser. As their friendship grew, the two women often spent their days off together, sometimes catching the bus into Morecambe or Lancaster, where it certainly wasn't the sights they were after. Once ensconced in a 'boozer', as Freda called the pubs (and she seemed to know them all), they would order large gins or a warming Whisky Mac if the weather was cool and breezy. They always had a bite to eat, a round of sandwiches or a bowl of soup, 'to keep their strength up', as Freda joked, but it was the drinking that the pair of them relished most. On more than one occasion Freda hadn't returned home with Renee. An expert at working the room, she would single out men whom she approached for a light for her cigarette, even though Renee knew she had a full box of matches in her handbag. The much-practised cigarette-lighting routine always led to another round of drinks, furnished by the gent in question, and often resulted in Renee taking the bus home by herself. As Freda put it rather apologetically, 'Sorry, sweetheart, I've had a better offer.'

Returning to Mary Vale, bleary-eyed and flushed with alcohol, Renee had had a couple of narrow escapes. The first had been when she had nearly bumped into Jamie and Ada pushing Catherine in her pram on a warm early-evening walk along the beach path. Hoping that she had seen them before they spotted her, Renee had darted into the little wood adjacent to the garden, but not before Jamie had seen her hurrying away in the opposite direction to them.

'Isn't that Renee?' he said to Ada, who was busy rearranging Catherine's bedding.

Glancing up, Ada shook her head. 'I didn't see her,' she said.

Squinting, trying to catch another glimpse, Jamie added, 'I'm sure she's avoiding us.'

Ada laughed. 'Well, it is her day off, you know. Maybe she's not in the mood for talking shop.'

On the second occasion she had returned home drunk, Renee was spotted by Matron. As she was sneaking up the stairs to her first-floor bedroom, Matron was making her way down, and the sight of her startled Renee so much she had to cling on to the banister to steady herself.

'Are you all right, dear?' Matron anxiously enquired.

Answering in the slow, emphatic manner that drunken people do, Renee slurred her words. 'Abso-lutely fine,' she drawled. 'Jush a lit-tle bit tired after my lit-tle trip to Morecambe.'

Making sure that she kept her face averted from Matron so she wouldn't let off a blast of alcohol fumes, Renee, still clutching the banister, tottered on her way. On the landing, out of sight of Matron, she swayed down the corridor, groping the wall for support.

After her excessive days out, Renee always woke up early the next morning with a thumping headache and a throat like sandpaper. Her first thought after she had gulped back almost a pint of cold water was whether anybody had seen her under the influence. When she recalled Matron's shocked expression as they crossed on the stairs the previous day, Renee's heart raced.

'It's my bloody day off,' she hotly told herself. 'I can do what I want.'

But at the back of her mind fear was growing. For all

her vows to give up drink, she was nevertheless returning to that dark, dangerous place where she had been before she left St Thomas's.

Alarmed by the increasing number of slip-ups that were mounting on her watch, Renee flopped on to her tangled, sweaty bed, where she hadn't the strength to stop the memory unspooling of when all this had started . . .

She had been drinking heavily after splitting up with her boyfriend, who had taken up with another nurse. Reporting in for duty still under the influence the next day, Renee had been doing the drugs run with a young, inexperienced trainee nurse. The controlled drug allocated to one woman in particular pain after a difficult labour had to be very carefully administered. But on this occasion, due to Renee's lack of attention, a higher dose of pethidine was administered, with very serious consequences.

Faced with accusations of professional misconduct, Renee succeeded in pinning the majority of the blame on to the innocent young nurse, who hysterically denied the accusations. Renee then fled the scene before any more scandalous claims could be heaped on her doorstep. Mary Vale had been her bolt hole, but if she wasn't careful (Renee chided herself) she would be well on the way to losing yet another position. She had seen the way Jamie and Ada looked at her, and she knew they were checking her every move; even that old fusspot Nurse Dora was on her case.

Feeling sorry for herself, Renee threw cold water on her face and brushed her hair; she had to make herself presentable for work. Grateful that she had had the foresight to iron her uniform the previous day before she went on her trip to Morecambe, Renee buttoned it up, then cinched the belt in tight around her slender waist. Tucking her abundant dark hair under her starched frilly cap, Renee checked her complexion, which looked on the sallow side.

'Too much booze!' she groaned as she gazed into the mirror on the wall. 'It's Freda's fault,' she added with a twinge of self-pity. 'She's the one who's dragged me into bad ways.'

Promising herself that she would avoid seeing Freda from now on, Renee made her way down to breakfast, where she could see climbing roses blooming around the big bay windows of the sunny dining room. Renee slipped into her cheerful nursing role, chatting to her patients, pouring hot tea into cups, handing around bread and butter while congratulating Stella on all her hard work in the kitchen.

'I hope we're not pushing you too hard,' she joked.

'I'm fine,' Stella insisted. 'Lillian's working afternoons these days – she's a big help.'

As the morning wore on and the events of the previous day began to recede, Renee began to breathe more easily. Had she got away with her drunken encounter with Matron on the stairs? Towards the end of her shift, just after she had served tea on the wards, Renee's heart sank when Matron asked for a quiet word in her office.

'Do sit down,' Matron started.

Sitting across the desk from a stern-faced Matron, Renee held her breath.

'You seemed out of sorts last night,' Matron announced.

Suspecting she might be cross-examined, Renee had been rehearsing what to say all day.

'Yes, I do apologize, ma'am. It was my day off and I went to Morecambe for a spot of sea-air.' Seeing Matron's unconvinced expression, she hurried on. 'It was there that I bumped into an old school chum who's recently married and moved North. We had tea together and, I must admit, a few drinks too,' she added with a shameful blush. 'I'm afraid I rather overdid the sherry,' she confessed. 'I just haven't the head for it these days.'

'Yes, I thought that might be the case,' Matron replied. 'What you choose to do on your day off, Sister Short, is entirely up to you; however, I cannot have a member of my staff seen to be drunk in public – do you understand?'

Looking thoroughly wretched, Renee gazed at her hands lying in her lap. 'Yes, of course, Matron. I apologize.'

Rising, Matron walked to the door. 'Please make sure that it doesn't happen again. Insobriety is completely unacceptable in an establishment such as Mary Vale.'

Sweating with relief that (at least on the face of it) she appeared to have got away with her misdemeanour, Renee returned to the wards, vowing that from now on she would stay clean and stop drinking.

'God knows, I can't afford another scandal,' she roundly told herself.

31. Summer Days

On a warm afternoon in June, Ada popped Catherine into her pram along with a few toys and a little picnic basket.

'Let's go and pay a visit to your friend Merry Paul,' she said.

'Merry Paul, Merry Paul,' the little girl babbled.

Smiling at her daughter, Ada set off down the farm track. Catherine waved to the sheep and cattle they passed, accompanied by Farmer Arkwright's fine cockerel, who liked to strut down the lane crowing and cackling, master of his own domain.

'Cockle-doodle-doooh!' Catherine echoed his shrill call.

Gazing at her daughter, who loved all animals, Ada marvelled at how quickly time had flown since she was born; in a few weeks' time it would be Catherine's second birthday; no longer a babe in arms, she was now a little toddler full of mischief and curiosity. Watching the house martins swooping in and out of their nest in the farm's many eaves, Ada considered how well sharing child-care responsibilities with Jamie was going. Admittedly they did more hours than were on their rota, but that was because neither of them could say no if there was an emergency. Sometimes after a long stint they would fall into bed straight after supper, but they were never too tired to revel in the pleasure of the other's body. Even if they were too exhausted to make love, they would at least kiss and cuddle each other goodnight, then fall asleep wrapped in each other's arms.

'And we've had the pleasure of seeing our daughter grow up,' Ada thought gratefully. 'How many couples in wartime have had the opportunity to bring up their child together?'

They had seen little Catherine take her first tottering steps; they had taught her the names of flowers and birds; they had sung nursery rhymes together and retold all of her favourite stories until they knew every one by heart. Ada could have reeled off 'The Three Little Pigs' and 'Goldilocks and the Three Bears' in her sleep. Parenting together had been a joy and a privilege, and Ada prayed there would be more babies in the future: a sweet little brother or sister for Catherine sometime soon, she hoped.

'Don't get ahead of yourself,' Ada checked herself. 'One day at a time.'

In truth, on a summer day like this in June 1944 there was real excitement in the air. The nation was lifting its weary spirit from the relentless miseries of war and beginning to hope that at last the Axis countries might be defeated. There had been great victories for the Allies recently: entering Rome and the D-Day landings on the coast of northern France had sent the nation into a frenzy. Could this war be finally grinding its way to an end? The thought of peace made Ada light-headed with relief – but how many deaths would ultimately pay for their freedom when it finally did come? Ada shuddered at the thought of how close her own beloved husband had been to death when he was serving in Tobruk: having his left hand amputated was bad enough but how much worse would it have been if he had lost his life in the desert crossfire that had ultimately sent him back home? At least Catherine had a father and she had a husband and they all had a future they could look forward to, for which Ada daily thanked God from the bottom of her heart.

They found Sister Mary Paul sitting peacefully in a wicker chair, taking a nap in the convent garden. Since her eye operation and subsequent retirement from the Home's busy kitchen, Mary Paul was encouraged to rest and enjoy the well-deserved perks of retirement. At the sound of Catherine's sweet babbling voice, the old nun's eyes flew open, and she beamed with pleasure at the sight of her approaching visitors.

'How wonderful to see you both,' she exclaimed.

Lifting wriggling Catherine from her pram, Ada deposited her in Mary Paul's arms, where she was kissed and cuddled while Ada threw a picnic blanket on to the warm grass.

'We thought we would surprise you with a picnic that Catherine and I made this morning,' she told her old friend.

'You clever girl,' Mary Paul chuckled as she tickled Catherine's little round tummy. 'You made a picnic for me?'

Giggling, Catherine nodded proudly. 'Bums!' she exclaimed.

'Buns,' Ada clarified, as she popped Catherine on to the rug along with her toys. 'Carrot and sultana buns,' she added, setting down a small plate of cakes and a flask of fresh tea. 'Just brewed before I left the cottage,' she said and poured hot tea into two little cups.

In between drinking tea and sharing out the buns with Catherine, the two devoted friends chatted companionably, and as always Sister Mary Paul couldn't resist talking about the goings-on in the kitchen.

'I do miss it still,' she confessed. 'But now that I've been away from the job for so long, I must admit I'm not quite sure I'd be up to doing it any more.'

Ada couldn't help but burst out laughing. 'You're quite right about that, dear, you wore yourself out working hard for years. Time to enjoy life and take things easy.'

'Oh, I am,' Mary Paul assured her. 'I spend a lot of time in the chapel now, and not just praying – I've been put in charge of the flowers, which I love.'

Ada shook her head. 'Trust you to find a job even in your retirement,' she said fondly.

'It keeps me occupied,' the old nun chuckled. 'I love selecting flowers from the garden, especially at this time of the year, the roses, lilies, stocks and carnations are perfect. I pick them early in the morning before the heat gets to them and arrange them for our displays on the high altar. We have so many important feast days in the month of June – Trinity Sunday, Corpus Christi, the Sacred Heart,' she explained.

'Your eyesight must be vastly improved if you've been put in charge of the chapel's floral displays,' Ada remarked.

'I can see well these days,' Mary Paul assured her. 'So well, it makes me realize just how bad my eyes were before I had my operation – I've you and Jamie to thank for that,' she added gratefully.

'And the staff at Lancaster Infirmary,' Ada laughingly reminded her friend.

Inevitably, Mary Paul returned to the subject of the kitchen. 'So, tell me, how are things progressing in the kitchen?'

'It's worked out well, actually,' Ada told her. 'Sister Theresa does a morning shift every day, then hands over to Lillian in the afternoon.'

'I don't think I've met this Lillian,' Mary Paul noted.

'She's not been here that long. She's a former Land Girl and her baby is due about six weeks after Stella's, so they'll both be hanging up their pinafores soon.'

'I should hope so too,' the nun exclaimed. 'And then what will happen?'

'We've got a new cook joining us.'

'That's good – we can't have two women working well into their pregnancies,' Mary Paul said with some relief. 'It would reflect badly on the Home.'

'I agree,' Ada responded. 'Especially so in the case of Stella, who is still doing a full day.'

'Do you know anything at all about these girls' backgrounds?' Mary Paul asked.

'No, they're both very private about their pasts,' Ada replied. 'And, as you know, I make a point of never prying,' she said with a smile.

After their picnic the two women held Catherine's chubby little hands as they guided her around the convent's flower-beds: the little girl sniffed fragrant trailing sweet peas and picked buttercups and daisies for Ada to thread into a crown. After an hour of exploring, Ada urged Sister Mary Paul to go indoors while she headed off home.

'Time for Catherine's bath,' she announced.

Pushing her daughter, still crowned with a circlet of buttercups and daisies, back up the farm track, Ada stopped for a chat with Farmer Arkwright, who produced two fresh warm eggs which he carefully wrapped up in newspaper.

'For the little 'un's breakfast,' he said, grinning.

'Chuck chucks,' excited Catherine cried when she saw the eggs.

Thanking the thoughtful farmer, Ada continued home to find Jamie in the garden picking strawberries for his daughter's supper. Stopping to watch, Ada's heart ached with love at the sight of him crouched down, searching for the ripest fruit, his thick, tawny-brown hair falling over his golden-brown eyes flecked with bewitching specks of gold.

Hearing his daughter's call, Jamie looked up and smiled.

'DADA!'

'Hello, my two favourite ladies,' he said, rising to kiss Ada on the mouth, then scooping Catherine out of the pram and swinging her round in a full circle.

'WHEEEE!' he laughed, as she begged for more.

'So where have you two been?' he enquired as he set his daughter down.

'Visiting Mary Paul in the convent,' Ada explained. 'How was your day?'

'Busy – I might have to go back later,' he explained. 'One of the residents has gone into labour and she's showing complications.'

'Can't the staff handle it?' Ada asked.

Jamie quickly shook his head. 'It's Sister Renee's shift,' he told her.

'Ah,' she answered with a knowing sigh.

Jamie didn't need to say anything further; Ada knew that if there was the slightest possibility of any complication occurring on Renee's watch, Jamie would not leave it to chance. He still did not trust the woman, and in truth neither did she.

'I'd never forgive myself if something went wrong,' Jamie admitted. 'On a night like this,' he said, as he gazed out across the valley soaked in sunlight, 'who wants to go back to work? But needs must.'

'The situation is getting ridiculous,' Ada said crossly.

Jamie shrugged. 'If we can't sack Renee, then we have to watch her for our own peace of mind – your words, sweetheart, not mine,' he reminded her.

'We can't sack her until we have proof of wrong-doing,' Ada pointed out. 'It's like we're holding our breath, waiting for a train crash,' she protested. 'Nursing shouldn't be like this.'

'Darling,' he murmured, as he pulled her close. 'Let's not spoil this moment – we have a perfect evening and a little girl waiting for her supper.'

Drawing Catherine into his arms too, Jamie carefully rearranged her crown of flowers, which had slipped down over her blue eyes.

'Now, my little princess, how many strawberries do you want?'

32. Night Duty

Having turned over a new leaf, Renee remained teetotal in the weeks that followed her ticking-off from Matron. It wasn't easy: she missed the instant pleasure alcohol provided, and she missed her trips out with Freda, who had apparently recently left the Smugglers' Arms in town in favour of a new 'boozer' in Morecambe.

'That's a relief,' Renee thought to herself. 'It's another temptation out of the way.'

Her days off were pretty dull, but at least she wasn't staggering back from the pub blind drunk any more. As a consequence of not rushing off at the end of her shift for a welcome stiff gin in the privacy of her room, Renee (with time on her hands) tended to stay on at work a bit longer, finishing off little jobs before she finally went to her room. It was something that Matron noted one day and actually thanked her for.

'You're working longer hours these days,' she commented.

Surprised, Renee gave a modest shrug. 'Oh, you know what it's like, there's always something to do,' she replied. 'I needed to get a set of instruments out of the sterilizer before I left; otherwise they would be sitting there all night.'

'I'm grateful for your thoughtfulness,' Matron added. 'But don't go overdoing it,' she ended with a warm smile.

Renee dreaded her night-shift weeks; over the years she had obviously got used to them, but, always a sensitive sleeper, she suffered from sleep deprivation, which in the past had been assuaged by sips of gin. This particular week started off well enough, but unfortunately on a few consecutive days she slept badly. No matter how tightly she pulled down the blackout blinds and drew her curtains, the slanting bright midsummer light still penetrated her room and that, combined with voices drifting in from the garden, put paid to any sleep. Starting her shift already exhausted didn't bode well. When she read up on the handover notes that Ada had left, which she *always* did these days, she was grateful to see there were no looming complications. If there had been, she knew for sure that Dr Jamie, distrustful of her nursing skills, would come running on to the ward and probably hang around there, breathing down her neck most of the night.

Patients' medication followed Renee's rounds of both the ante- and post-natal wards, then came tea or cocoa for any restless patients who needed a hot drink or simply couldn't sleep, after which Renee switched off the bright striplights that ran the length of both wards. Finally, when all of her patients were safely tucked up for the night, Renee retired to the nurses' station at the end of the ante-natal ward, which had a connecting corridor to the post-natal ward. Lit only by a small side light on her desk, the atmosphere was calm and restful; smothering a yawn, Renee started writing up her patient notes, but was disturbed by the door swinging open and Dora walking in pushing a new-born in a small mobile crib.

'Sorry to disturb you,' Dora whispered. 'But I need young Irene to give her baby a final feed; his bellowing will keep the entire nursery up all night. A feed might settle him down.'

'Okay,' Renee said, as she rose and rubbed her eyes, 'I'll take him to Irene.'

Seeing Renee's bleary eyes, Dora was immediately on her guard. 'No, that's all right, I'll pop him down there,' she said quickly.

Renee shrugged and resumed her seat. 'I don't mind either way, Dora,' she replied politely.

After waking sleepy Irene, who struggled to sit upright, Dora switched on the bedside light so that the new mother could see to feed her baby; and once they were both settled Dora hurried away.

'Please keep an eye on Irene – she can barely keep her eyes open, poor lamb – but that little lad needs to be fed if we're to get any peace tonight. I'll be back in half an hour to take him back to the nursery.'

Holding the baby, who latched on to the breast and sucked heartily, Irene forced herself to stay upright, but, inexorably, as exhaustion overtook her, she slipped down into the bed in a deep sleep.

Meanwhile Renee, with drooping eyelids, was trying to focus on her report sheets; the stillness of the dark ward, as well as the hypnotic ticking of the wall clock, completely engulfed her and she briefly nodded off too. When she awoke with a guilty start, she immediately checked her fob watch.

'Thank God,' she murmured with a heartfelt sigh.

She had only dozed for ten minutes, though that was bad enough; it could have been worse. If she had been caught asleep on Dora's return, she would have undoubtedly faced the firing squad for negligence while on duty.

Straightening her cap, Renee grabbed her torch in order to patrol the ward, which staff were expected to do throughout the night. Stopping at the foot of Irene's bed, she saw that the young woman had slipped under her sheets, where she lay fast asleep. Shining the torch over the bed, Renee searched for the baby. Had Dora come back earlier and collected him while Renee was sleeping? Surely not. If she had caught her snoozing, Dora would have definitely given Renee a roasting.

'Where's the baby?' Renee asked, panicking.

Everything happened very quickly after that. Renee threw back the bed clothes, where to her absolute horror she saw the baby squashed hard against his mother's side. Alarmed, Renee quickly picked the little boy up. Expecting him to at least squeak in protest, she gently patted him, but, getting no response, Renee shone the torch light directly into his face, which she now saw was pale and flaccid. Leaning in more closely, she frantically listened for any sound of breathing.

'Jesus! Oh, Jesus, please no.'

Irene woke up with a start. 'My baby!' she cried. 'Where's my baby? What's happened?' she demanded when she saw

Renee in the process of giving mouth to mouth resuscitation to the infant. 'What are you doing?'

Renee didn't stop for a moment, but Irene, now hysterical, was screaming, 'MY BABY! MY BABY!'

The long dark night ended with a heavily sedated Irene being removed to a private room off the main ward. The baby, who could not be saved despite the frantic efforts of both Renee and Dora, and then Jamie, who was urgently summoned, lay covered with a linen sheet. Alone in the sluice room as dawn was breaking, Dora and Jamie exchanged a grim look.

'This is exactly the kind of thing I've been dreading,' he murmured.

'Do you think Renee was drinking while on duty?' Dora whispered.

'There's only one way of finding out: I'll have to do a blood test.'

Renee, who had done everything in her power to help Irene and save her baby, knew exactly what her colleagues would be assuming: that the accident had happened on her watch because she was under the influence of booze. She had fallen asleep, which she would not easily forgive herself for, but that had not been down to drinking. Busy with patients now waking up and desperate for a cup of morning tea, Renee's brain went into a whirl of fear. Gripped with pure terror, she thought, 'I could be accused of misconduct – just like before. Maybe even manslaughter this time.'

*

278

Renee was summoned to Jamie's surgery, where, with Matron in attendance, she was questioned about the tragic events of the night.

'I did everything I could,' Renee started. 'It soon became clear that the mother had rolled over on to the baby.'

Matron gave a quick nod. 'We understand that, but, Sister Renee, what, exactly, were *you* doing at the time that Irene was feeding her baby? Dora reports asking you particularly to keep an eye on Irene because she was so tired.'

Renee's mind flew back to the dark ward and how the awful night had unfolded. 'I was writing up my notes at the nurses' station around midnight when Dora arrived pushing Irene's baby in a little trolley,' Renee recalled. 'Dora said she'd be back to collect him in half an hour.'

'Did you keep an eye on Irene while she was feeding her baby?'

Renee nodded. 'Yes, she was really tired and struggled to sit upright against her pillows, but I did see the baby latch on and start to feed.'

Matron pressed on. 'And then what happened? How long did she feed for?'

Renee gulped; there was simply no way of dodging this dreaded question. 'I can't be exact,' she muttered.

'Oh?' Matron responded in surprise. 'Why not?'

Now cornered, Renee blurted out, 'I fell asleep.'

Seeing Matron and Jamie exchanging a 'Well, wouldn't you know it' look, Renee cried out in her own defence, 'Only for ten minutes – at the most.'

'How can you be so precise about the time?' Jamie asked.

'Because I checked the time on my fob watch when I

woke up,' Renee quickly explained. 'I swear on my life it really was only ten minutes.'

Grim-faced, Jamie coldly said, 'Nevertheless, you fell asleep on duty? And those ten minutes would have been enough to save Irene's baby's life.'

Shame-faced, Renee could only nod.

'And when you woke you discovered the baby, by which time it was too late?' Jamie asked.

'I grabbed my torch and went to check on my patients,' Renee continued. 'When I discovered the baby pressed up against Irene, I realized what had happened and attempted artificial respiration, but by that time it was too late. Dora arrived about the same time too.' Batting back tears, frantic, Renee tried again to defend herself. 'I hardly slept a wink during the day of my night shift. I was worn out before I even clocked on for work. I'll never forgive myself for what happened.' Seeing the doctor and Matron exchange yet another judgemental look, Renee angrily articulated what she had been brooding about for hours. 'I simply don't understand why Dora left the child with me and asked me to keep an eye on him when, in fact, he was *her* responsibility. Why didn't she just take charge of the situation and stay with Irene or take her into the nursery to feed the baby? She must have known I had other patients to attend to as well as Irene,' Renee ended indignantly.

'But, in fact, it turns out you didn't attend to any patients at the time mentioned for the simple reason that you were asleep,' Jamie remarked.

Renee slumped in her chair. 'Yes, I was asleep, very briefly.'

*

Renee agreed to give a blood sample, which, Jamie informed her, would be sent off to the hospital in Grange for tests. After he had taken the small phial of blood, Renee turned on Jamie, saying, 'You think I was drinking, don't you?'

Trying to sound neutral but actually shaking with inner rage, Jamie answered evenly, 'We have to be seen to do the right thing.'

Tired to her bones, Renee said wearily, 'Fine. Do the right thing, but I can tell you now I was stone-cold sober. I readily admit I was in the wrong, falling asleep the way I did, but I was sober,' she insisted.

As Jamie turned to leave the room, Renee, emotionally drained, gave vent to feelings she'd been suppressing for months. 'I know what you think of me: that I'm a slacker. I know that you've all been watching me, waiting for me to make a mistake, and now I have. But I can tell you, you and your smug wife, that you have got it wrong – *I was not drunk.*'

When Jamie finally arrived home on a hot summer morning that was riotous with bird-song, he looked white and drawn. Ada (already in her uniform) was feeding Catherine porridge, and, looking up from her task, she quickly asked, 'Bad night, darling?'

Sitting at the table beside his wife and daughter, Jamie ran through the events of the night.

'Oh, my God,' Ada gasped. 'This is exactly what we've been dreading. Poor, poor Irene – she must be devastated.'

'She's sedated for the moment but every time she comes around, she's heartbroken, blames herself entirely,'

Jamie said sadly. 'You'd better get over there right away, darling. I'll take over the feeding.'

Ada hesitated. 'What about you, love?' she asked. 'You've barely had any sleep.'

'To be honest I don't think I could sleep right away,' he admitted. 'I'll be glad of a little distraction.' He smiled as his daughter sloshed porridge in her bowl. 'And this little lass is the best distraction I can think of.'

When Ada arrived for work the atmosphere in the Home, now that the news was out, was tense and sombre. After signing in for duty, Ada immediately searched out Matron, who came straight to the point.

'Renee's been suspended, at least until the test result comes through, and I've sent Dora home.'

'Who's in the nursery?' Ada immediately asked.

'Dora left a reliable resident in charge of the feeding rota until she gets back this afternoon.'

Ada said, 'You look exhausted, Ann. Go and get some rest.'

'I can't stop, Ada,' Matron fretted. 'I've so much paper-work to do and then there're the police . . .' Her voice trailed away as the terrible events of the night caught up with her. 'Oh, Ada!' she sobbed as she covered her face with her hands. 'This is terrible.'

Hurrying to her friend's side, Ada hugged Matron tightly. 'I know, it truly is awful, but we'll get through it, somehow,' she murmured.

'I dread to think what the papers will write if they should ever get hold of this story,' Matron groaned. 'We've all had our suspicions about Renee – you, me,

Jamie, Dora, even Theresa's mentioned it. We've seen it coming,' she declared. 'I have only myself to blame.'

'We all did our best to monitor Renee,' Ada remonstrated. 'But really there's a limit on how far you can go without making it obvious that you're actually policing somebody.'

'I agree with you,' Matron sighed heavily. 'If Renee was drinking on duty, she'll certainly be sacked and probably never nurse again.'

Shortly after seeing Matron, Ada hurried to Irene in her private room off the main ward. When she saw the poor, afflicted girl with her ashen face and red-rimmed eyes, her heart ached with pity.

'You poor child,' she murmured, as she sat on Irene's bed and held her trembling hands.

'I can't believe it, Sister,' Irene wept. 'I can't believe my little boy's gone. Why did I fall asleep?' she wailed. 'Why didn't I feel him right there by me?'

Luckily Jamie had left enough sedative to calm Irene down for a few more hours, but, as Ada spooned the mixture into her weeping patient, she knew Irene's tragic loss would take years to get over.

In the middle of a hectic day Matron told Ada that she had been in touch with an agency in Lancaster. 'I've put in a request for a supply nurse,' she said.

Relieved, Ada nodded. 'Good – we're going to need a stop-gap for the time being.'

Seeing the dark circles of fatigue under Matron's eyes, Ada once more urged her to go to get some rest.

'I will now that I've sorted out the agency,' Matron

agreed. Before she turned to go, she added, 'Renee's in her room, though I very much doubt she'll be sleeping.'

Renee was, in fact, sitting on a chair by the open window, blankly gazing out across the rolling emerald lawn to the Irish Sea, sparkling bright in the dazzling sunlight that danced over its rippling waves. Oblivious to the beauty before her and the perfume of summer roses drifting up from the flowerbeds, Renee thought only of one thing: her nursing career could be over because of a ten-minute sleep on duty. The accusation of being drunk on duty, when, ironically, she had not touched a drop of alcohol in months, would stick.

33. An Evening Walk

The sombre mood in the Home certainly spread into the kitchen, where Lillian joined Stella after breakfast.

'I saw Sister Theresa dashing off to the wards, so I thought you might be short-handed,' Lillian said kindly.

'We're all over the place in here,' Stella admitted. 'Theresa's trying her best to be in three places at once – in here, on the wards and in the convent.'

'I don't mind stepping in during an emergency,' Lillian said. 'What a mess it is,' she sighed. 'Poor Irene – everybody's talking about her and her little baby.'

'It just doesn't bear thinking about,' Stella agreed.

Lillian dropped her voice. 'Word's going around that the tragedy happened while Sister Renee was in charge; she's not been at work so the residents think she might have been suspended for the time being.'

'It might turn into a police matter,' Stella added. 'Whatever way you look at it, it looks bad for the Home and the staff too, who, as far as I'm concerned, have always been wonderful.' Stella set about rolling corned-beef fritters in plain flour, and her thoughts flew to the lonely woman exiled upstairs.

'God, it must be awful up there all on your own knowing that everybody in the Home distrusts and dislikes you,' she murmured sympathetically. 'She may have done wrong, but I'm actually beginning to feel sorry for the woman.'

The two women worked side by side throughout dinner, then Stella went and had a lie-down in her room while Lillian cleared away, assisted by another willing resident. Ada, passing through the dining room, saw Lillian hard at work. 'Lillian, you seem to be doing far more than what we agreed when you first started.'

'I'm fine, though I think Stella's feeling it these days. I've just sent her upstairs for a rest,' she explained.

'Well, you can both stop soon – the new cook's due at the start of next month, so you two good ladies will finally have some well-deserved time off to put your feet up while you wait for your babies to arrive.'

After Ada had left the room, her words rang around Lillian's head. 'While you wait for your babies to arrive.'

She had already talked to Father Ben about having her baby adopted. What an irony, she thought. Robbie and his wife had failed to find a child they could adopt, yet here she was, lining up strangers to bring up Robbie's baby.

'Even if I told him I was pregnant and offered him the child,' Lillian reasoned, 'Harriet is in no fit state to bring up a baby.'

Sal had regularly been in touch by letter (Mo and Pat less so), giving Lillian news of her beloved shires; she had even sent a black-and-white photo of all three of them out in the sunny meadow, peacefully grazing on the rich

286

summer grass. It was from Sal that she had learnt of Robbie's wife's worsening condition.

Of course, he doesn't say anything to us, he's a private man. Just pops in, does the job and he's off again but, as you well know, news travels fast in the Borrowdale Valley. It's common knowledge now that the vet's wife is in Lancaster Asylum, and I heard from the woman who runs Rosthwaite post office that the poor woman had attempted suicide. Luckily it didn't work – she survived – but he looks haggard these days, aged ten years since you left. The only time I see him smiling is when he's with your horses: he always feeds them carrots, whether they're in their stable or out in the paddock, and he spends time with them, patting them, stroking their ears and playing with that sweet little foal.

At this point Lillian's eyes blurred with tears. 'Oh, God,' she moaned. 'How I miss those wonderful animals, and Robbie too,' she gulped. Wiping away her tears, she continued to the end of the letter.

I'd love to come and see you soon, lovie, but you must recall how it is at this time of the year, high summer when we're busy fetching sheep down from the fells, shearing and dipping, and the hundreds of other jobs that you're all too familiar with. We've still not got a replacement for you, Lil, which is good because Mo's all set to hate anybody who might take your place. I hope you're keeping well and healthy. We miss you, kiddo.

All our love, Sal xxx

Stacking the trolley high with pots and plates, Lillian put all thoughts of Robbie to one side. She had made up her mind to pursue this course of action and she would see it through till the end; after all, she sighed, what choice had she got?

At the end of the long day Stella, much refreshed by her afternoon rest, suggested that she and Lillian go for a gentle stroll on the marsh.

'It's a gorgeous hot evening, still light and the tide's well out, so we won't get stranded,' she said.

Lillian quickly nodded. 'You're right, it will be good to get out. We don't get many days like this, best to enjoy them.'

The two heavily pregnant women cut quite a picture, both supporting their heavy tummies with a hand underneath to take most of the strain as they made their way along a twisting sandy path that led to a line of sand-dunes. Between these were dotted clear rock pools where seabirds waded and screeched at each other over tasty morsels of food they unearthed with their long curved beaks.

Settling on a little mound, the two women lay back on the soft sand, the warm evening sunlight dappling their faces.

'Ahh, this is nice,' Lillian sighed, as she closed her eyes.

'It would be nice but for this baby of mine dancing the tango,' Stella giggled, as she adjusted her body in order to accommodate the baby wriggling restlessly inside her. 'Bill was a great dancer,' she said, before she stopped herself. 'Maybe his baby has his dancing genes.'

Keeping her eyes firmly closed, Lillian let Stella do the talking.

'He's a Flight Engineer in the American Air Force.'

Stella gave a long sigh. 'Over the months here I've got used to the fact that he left me, went back to the States and abandoned me as soon as I was pregnant,' she added bitterly. 'But what I can't get used to is the thought that he might be dead,' she blurted out.

'But Bill's not even in Europe.'

Gazing into the far distance, Stella continued in a low voice. 'But what if Bill was recalled back to Europe? Flight Engineers monitor mechanical systems throughout flights and assist with take-offs and landings. With the fighting progressing the way it is, Bill's skills must be urgently needed these days. He and his team could be right in the thick of it and I wouldn't even know.' She slumped in despair. 'It's stupid, I know, but even though he did a terrible thing to me I have always imagined him strong and vibrant, out of my reach but nevertheless *alive*.'

'You still love him?' Lillian whispered.

'I think I always will,' Stella confessed. 'I wish it wasn't so. It would be easier to hate him, to forget him, but I've never known such happiness as I knew with him, and I believed him when he said he loved me.'

'So why do you think he went away?' Lillian asked tentatively. 'Could it have been some sort of misunderstanding?'

Stella gave a loud groan. 'That's what I tried to tell myself for weeks and weeks, and then I just gave up hoping.'

'And he never wrote?' Lillian asked.

'Not once, *never* – says it all, really,' Stella muttered.

Wondering if she should continue with the conversation, Lillian said cautiously, 'Did he know about the baby?'

'Yes, he was so supportive,' Stella exclaimed. 'He gave me money to arrange our wedding, I was going to move on to the US base with him.' She shook her head incredulously. 'Now it feels like a dream, and I constantly ask myself, did I imagine it?'

'Oh, I know that feeling, don't you worry,' Lillian cried.

Now it was Stella's turn to wonder how far she should go; fortunately Lillian saved her the embarrassment of having to ask questions.

'I'm ashamed to say that I fell for the local vet, who was married.' Lillian gave a weary shrug. 'There's no excuse for what we did, but his wife was suffering from severe depression after the death of their only child, a little boy. I know it doesn't make it any better – we made love once and look at me now,' Lillian added mournfully.

'And he doesn't know?'

'No,' Lillian immediately answered. 'That would have skewed everything in the wrong direction. I had to get away in order for it to work with Robbie and his wife. It was the right thing to do and I don't regret it, though I'm sad our baby will pay the price. Poor little mite didn't ask to be born and given up for adoption.'

'You're right, Lil, these babies are the innocent ones, paying the price for what we did.'

Sombre now, the two women retraced their steps back to Mary Vale and, though the sun continued to shine as it sank over the Irish Sea, they were both suddenly cold to the bone.

34. Transatlantic Journey

After his discharge from hospital, Bill spent the spring retraining in order to return to his old Mildenhall base; his squadron were keen to welcome back a trusted and highly experienced Flight Engineer, admittedly in an adapted role. Once his retraining period was completed, Bill was assigned to help fly a cargo plane, heavily loaded with food and vital equipment, across the Atlantic to Mildenhall. After he had helped land the Douglas C-47 Skytrain, Bill was relieved to be back in the country where he had not only lost a limb but also Stella, and he prayed that as soon as he could get time off from his official duties he would be able to track her down.

Thankfully his superiors were sympathetic to his plight, and as soon as they could spare him Bill was on the train north for Manchester. Bill dozed on and off when he could sit down, which wasn't very often, as the train was packed the entire length of the tedious journey; weary troops were picked up and dropped off, and they stopped for hours in sidings. From Manchester Bill took a bus to the munitions factory on the moors where Stella had worked, hoping all the way that Doreen would still be living in the same prefab accommodation that she had shared with Stella. Weary to the bone and in quite a lot of pain from his one working leg, Bill, walking with a crutch, limped to the front door and rapped on it with his knuckles. Holding his breath, he briefly wondered what he would do if the door was opened by a complete stranger. Would that be the end of the line? Without Doreen, finding Stella would be a lot more complicated. He would have to locate her parents in the hope that they knew where their daughter was, but he didn't even have their address. Hoping that his luck was in, Bill literally gasped in relief when Doreen opened the door, and an astonished Doreen gaped at the visitor on the doorstep in complete disbelief. Though she recognized him from the long-ago dance-night, she nevertheless did a double-take when she saw the same young man now leaning heavily on a crutch.

'Bill!' she cried, when she finally got her breath back. 'I can't believe it. Come in, come in,' she urged.

Grateful for the invitation, Bill made his way into the front room that doubled up as a kitchen. Seeing his weary expression, Doreen was quick to offer him a seat. 'Please make yourself comfortable.'

Wincing in pain, Bill took an upright chair and sank into it with obvious relief.

'It's great to see you, Doreen,' he said; then, coming straight to the point, he added, 'I've come looking for Stella.'

As the colour drained from Doreen's face, he panicked. 'Is she okay?'

'As far as I know she is,' Doreen answered before indignantly demanding, 'Why did you leave her the way you did, Bill?'

'I didn't leave Stella,' he insisted. 'I was involved in an accident.' He nodded towards his leg. 'I was shipped back home for specialist burns treatment.'

Seeing his ravaged expression, Doreen's heart melted, and she wondered how this really awkward situation would play out now.

'You look worn out; I'll make some tea.'

'Thanks, that would be great,' Bill replied politely before directly carrying on with what was at the forefront of his mind. 'She must be nearly due – I assume she's gone somewhere to have the baby??'

'That's right. A few months ago now,' Doreen told him as she brewed the tea.

Over several cups of strong tea and some grey sliced bread and white marg, Bill heard with horror how heartbroken Stella had been to learn of his transfer back to the States.

'Are you telling me that nobody told her what actually happened to me?' he asked incredulously. 'That I crashlanded a plane and lost a leg?'

Doreen nodded grimly. 'Stella phoned your base, but the Yank on the other end said he couldn't tell her anything as she had no proof that she was your next of kin.'

'We were getting married, for God's sake,' Bill cried.

Doreen shrugged. 'She had no proof of that.'

'So the poor kid thought I had abandoned her,' he murmured close to tears. 'Flown back home without so much as a goodbye. But what about the letters I sent to her here?'

Looking blank, Doreen shook her head. 'What letters?'

'All the letters I wrote telling her what had happened to me,' he answered frantically. 'I mailed them to this address – did you not pass them on to Stella?'

'Bill, there were *no* letters,' Doreen insisted.

Bill looked up, startled. 'But I sent so many, how could none of them show up?'

'Bill, I swear on the Bible that if any letters had arrived, I would have immediately forwarded them on to Stella. The poor girl was devastated. A letter might have given her some comfort.' Looking baffled, Doreen asked, 'Are you quite sure you posted them to the right address?'

Frustrated and confused, Bill answered, 'Sure, I'm sure. The first one was returned to sender, think I must have made a mistake with the address when I was doped up, but I've written more since and double-checked the address. I wrote to Stella often enough when I was stationed at RAF Burtonwood and Mildenhall – my letters never went astray then. I just don't understand it . . .'

'Maybe they got lost in the post?' Doreen suggested. 'It's not uncommon these days.'

Burying his head in his hands, Bill groaned like a man in pain. 'Jesus Christ . . . My poor girl. I've gotta get there right away – I've gotta see Stella.'

Seeing him sway on his crutch, Doreen advised otherwise. 'You're in no state to travel, Bill,' she said firmly. 'Book into a hotel in Preston for the night and get a train to Grange-over-Sands first thing tomorrow morning. I'll give you Stella's address before you leave. I took her there myself: it looked like a decent-enough place, run by nuns in the Lake District.'

But Bill was beginning to panic. 'I can't waste any more time, Doreen. By my calculations the baby's due soon, and for all I know Stella might well have given birth by now.'

Quickly checking her wristwatch, Doreen said apologetically, 'Look, I'm really sorry, Bill, I've got to clock on for my shift.' At that she scribbled an address on to a scrap of paper and handed it to him. 'This is where you'll find Stella.'

At the factory gates, they shook hands before they went their separate ways.

'Good luck,' Doreen said. 'Go easy on the poor kid – she went through hell.'

Sitting on the bus that wound its way along the narrow, moorland lanes, Bill's thoughts returned to the mystery of the missing letters that he had written to Stella during his stay in the military hospital and given to Pete to mail. What could have happened to them, he wondered. It was true there was a war on, but not one single letter addressed to Stella had got through. He chewed it over as the bus wound its slow way to Preston. And he thought of his brother's dismissal of any talk of a serious romance.

An alarm bell started to sound, quietly at first, but getting louder all the time. His brother had never warmed to the idea of him dating an English girl – could Pete have felt so strongly that he conveniently omitted to mail the letters in the hope that Bill would forget all about Stella? Surely to God, Pete would never do that, not while Bill was so vulnerable and learning to walk again? But he couldn't think of another explanation for so many miss-ing letters; it was just too much of a coincidence.

Suddenly overwhelmed with fury, Bill curled his fists into tight balls. 'Jesus Christ!' he fumed. 'If Pete has tried to come between me and the woman I love, I'll never for-give him as long as I live.'

35. Isolation

Renee's blood-test result was negative, proving quite categorically that she had not been drinking on the night of the tragedy.

'I might have fallen asleep, but at least I wasn't drunk,' she told herself.

The news partially vindicated Renee – it should have restored some of her low self-esteem – but her relief was offset by new information that Matron had discovered.

'I've been doing a bit of digging,' Matron privately confessed to Ada in her office.

Ada threw her a quizzical look: the thought of her religious friend turning into a detective was, to say the least, surprising.

'I've been in touch with an old friend, a woman I trained with years ago who is now a Senior Sister at St Thomas's. I know it's deceitful,' Matron added guiltily, 'but I asked her if she could find any paperwork on Sister Renee Short who recently worked there.'

'Heavens!' Ada gasped in astonishment.

'I know I could be accused of snooping, but, really Ada, I just can't allow one more slip-up to happen here in the Home.'

Ada gave a sympathetic smile. 'Did you have any luck?'

Matron nodded. 'It's not good news,' she started.

'Sister Renee was Senior Nurse on duty when a patient on her ward, in pain from a perineal tear, died of a pethidine overdose.'

Ada's big blue eyes opened wide in amazement. 'Oh, my God,' she gasped.

'Of course, there was an inquiry,' Matron continued. 'Apparently Sister Renee firmly laid the blame on the Junior Nurse who was assisting her in dispensing patients' medications. The young trainee vehemently denied the charge: she accused Sister Renee of passing the buck and insisted throughout the inquiry that she was innocent.

'How did we miss that vital piece of information?' Ada exclaimed.

'It appears that Sister Renee resigned immediately and left London in rather a hurry.'

'But her references didn't mention any of that,' Ada recalled.

'She probably presented us with older references, pre her inquiry,' Matron suggested. 'The Junior Nurse was struck off the register, but to this day, according to the information I was given, she insists that she was set up by Sister Renee.' Matron gave a long, heavy sigh, then, looking Ada directly in the eyes, she added, 'Sister Renee must go.'

Ada frowned. 'That might be tricky,' she said. 'Now that the test result has unequivocally cleared her of drinking while on duty, she would have every right to protest.'

'Don't forget we can still charge her with falling asleep while on duty – she's admitted that,' Matron reminded her in a steely business-like voice that was at odds with her nun's wimple and long black veil. 'I wouldn't want to publicize her past mistakes but if she doesn't go quietly I will.'

'I completely understand,' Ada agreed. 'We've all been on tenterhooks watching Renee for months now, you, me, Jamie, Dora; it's an impossible situation and exhausting too, not to mention rather underhanded. But really what an irony!' she exclaimed. 'When we suspected she might have been drunk in the past she got away with it, and now, when accused, she turns out to be innocent of that at least.'

'We can't change history,' Matron pointed out. 'The past will always come back to haunt you. Anyway, as I said, I'm taking no more chances with Sister Renee. I shall ask her to hand in her notice and leave just as soon as she can make alternative arrangements. Until then she must keep herself to herself: I want no mingling with the residents, and she mustn't go anywhere near any of the wards.'

'To be honest, I've overheard a number of residents saying they wouldn't want Renee nursing them after what happened; they simply don't trust her any more.'

Rising from her chair, Matron said, 'Well, it's my job to break the bad news to Sister Renee.'

Ada grimaced. 'She's not going to like the fact that we've been snooping into her past.'

Matron gave a grim nod. 'She's not going to like it at all.'

Renee was, in fact, livid.

'How dare you investigate my past!' she raged when Matron laid before her the cold bare facts of her enquiries. 'Especially after I've just been cleared of drinking, which was what you all suspected. I'll never forgive myself for falling asleep, but this is beginning to feel like nothing short of a bloody witch hunt.'

'I'm sorry, Sister Renee, you simply haven't been honest about your past,' Matron reminded her.

'I was cleared of that charge,' Renee snapped.

'The Junior Nurse you worked with at St Thomas's denies the accusation laid at her doorstep and strongly maintains it was you who administered the medication that killed the patient,' Matron said firmly.

'Of course, you would choose her story against mine,' Renee exclaimed. 'Really, I haven't got a leg to stand on: I'm damned if I do and damned if I don't.'

'You have lost a great deal of trust among the residents, Sister,' Matron continued. 'I don't think you'll find them quite as free and easy with you as they were before the recent tragedy.'

Losing the energy to protest any longer, Renee threw up her hands in despair.

'You know, I'll actually be relieved to get away from this place and everybody in it.'

'I cannot promise you a reference, Sister,' Matron told her bluntly.

'Don't worry, I'm done with nursing,' Renee hit back. 'And nuns too for that matter.'

While they waited for the arrival of the temporary nurse from the agency in Lancaster, the staff pulled together to cover Renee's shifts.

'I can get together a rota of good responsible girls who can reliably organize the feeds around the clock, which would free me up to help you on the wards,' Dora volunteered.

Ada gave a grateful smile. 'That would be good, Dora. Jamie and I can juggle longer hours too.'

'At least the new cook has arrived, which lets Stella and Lillian off the hook, so I'm sure they'd offer their services if needed,' Dora said with a smile. 'I was terrified that Stella, who's really near her time, was going to go into labour in the kitchen.'

'I really don't know what we would have done without her and Lillian,' Ada said. 'I'm going to make sure the pair of them get plenty of rest from now on.'

Dropping her voice, Dora asked, 'What do you think Sister Renee will do next?'

'I have no idea – apparently she's done with nursing.'

'That might not be a bad idea,' Dora said sharply.

'She keeps to her room all the time these days,' Ada remarked. 'I have thought of paying her a visit.'

Dora raised her eyebrows. 'I wouldn't rush into that,' she warned. 'I'm quite sure she doesn't want to pass the time of day with any of us. The residents aren't chatty with Renee any more either,' Dora added. 'She only comes into the dining room to collect her food, which she eats alone upstairs.'

Big-hearted Ada sighed. 'I actually feel sorry for Renee; it must be miserable up there all on her own.'

It was indeed miserable for Renee. Isolated and distrusted, she kept herself to herself while she fumed all the while with indignation.

'This place has had it in for me since the minute I arrived,' she thought, as she paced the confines of her hot room. 'That self-righteous Dr Jamie ticking me off for being too chummy with the patients and then his wife, Ada, having a dig at me for preferring some patients over others. Whinging Polly's wretched whooping cough didn't help either,' Renee reflected. 'I thought things would get better with her gone, but instead they got even worse.'

It was good that there wasn't a bottle of gin anywhere in sight, as Renee, in the mood she was in, might have downed the lot; she yearned for a drink but knew it would land her in even more trouble if she succumbed. Stopping to gaze out of the window, Renee caught a glimpse of the sea making its way out from high tide, leaving the marsh silvery-sage in its wake. Restless and sick of her own company, she took herself off for a walk and some much-needed fresh air.

Once outdoors, Renee removed her shoes and walked barefoot along the sandy track that wound its way around rock pools and sand-dunes. Lifting her tired face to the sun, she felt much better for being outside; she had stayed cooped up for too long. Feeling her body relax for the first time in what seemed like weeks, Renee flopped down on to the warm sand, where she lay prone. Listening to the soothing, rhythmic sound of the splashing waves, combined with the call of sea-birds strutting along the water's edge, hungry for food, Renee closed her eyes and dozed off. She came to with a start when she heard footsteps close by; with the sun in her eyes, Renee blinked as she made out one of the residents hurrying by. Thinking the woman was trying to avoid her, she waited for her to pass but instead she stopped and smiled at her.

'Hello,' she said.

With her hand shading her eyes, Renee realized that the woman was, in fact, Stella. Astonished that any of the residents even had the time of day for her, Renee cautiously replied with her own quiet greeting. She was even more taken aback when Stella continued in a normal cheerful voice, 'I was so hot I just had to get out of the Home.'

Renee nodded; she had felt the same but probably for different reasons.

'It is boiling hot,' she agreed.

'Normally I would love this kind of weather, but being this far gone it's unbearable – I feel like a kettle permanently on the boil.' Stella smiled as she sank down on to the sand beside Renee. 'So, I came out here for a paddle in the sea,' she confessed. 'Now that I'm not working in the kitchen any more, I take it easy. I enjoy a stroll every day and spend a lot more time sitting in the garden. Sister Ada says it's good for me,' she said, smiling. 'Though it does feel a bit self-indulgent doing nothing at all.'

'It is good for you,' Renee assured her. 'At this late stage in your pregnancy you should rest as much as you can. One thing's for sure, when your baby is born, you'll get very little sleep, so enjoy the peace and quiet while you can.'

Not ignorant of the gossip buzzing about the Home concerning Renee, Stella said cautiously, 'I'm sorry for all the trouble you've had recently.'

Renee wriggled uncomfortably. 'It's not been easy,' she answered diplomatically.

'When you're on the wrong side of the fence, life can be tough,' Stella responded sensitively.

Completely flabbergasted, Renee exclaimed, 'The other residents aren't as sympathetic as you, I'm afraid.'

'Each to her own opinion,' Stella reasoned.

'It really doesn't matter any more,' Renee shrugged. 'I'll be leaving soon.'

'Me too,' Stella said, as she stroked her enormous tummy sadly. 'As soon as I've got this one's adoption sorted out, I'll be on my way, though I'll miss the friends I've made here,' she confessed.

Renee stared moodily out across the sparkling sea. 'I won't miss anybody,' she thought bitterly. 'I haven't made one single friend in all the time I've been at Mary Vale.'

36. The Marsh

As the temperature rose and the heatwave continued, Bill made his way to the address that Doreen had given him. On the train from Preston with the windows pulled down, Bill gratefully inhaled the fresh salty tang of sea-air. Staring out across sparkling Morecambe Bay, where seagulls hovered on the warm air spirals, keenly waiting to dive-bomb unsuspecting fish swimming in the clear water below, he marvelled at the beauty of the place. Used to the vast stretches of the magnificent Pacific Ocean, he was charmed by the green woods and forest that hugged the coast and the misty outline of the mountains of the Lake District in the far distance.

'So this is where Stella came to have our baby?' he thought to himself. Safely away from snooping eyes and unkind gossip, she had been, he hoped with all his heart, happy in this lovely landscape and found people who would care for her and their baby too.

When Bill dismounted from the train at the tiny Kents Bank railway station, his heart began to race. Walking through the small wood that led into Mary Vale's rambling gardens, he had to stop to steady his nerves. Terrifying thoughts raced through his head: after travelling halfway across the world, would Stella even speak to him? If she had never received his letters, then who could blame her for thinking the worst: that he was a no-good bum who had abandoned her. She might have left the area already, taking the baby with her, leaving no forwarding address. Or she could have fallen in love with somebody else, somebody who was prepared to father her child. Then there was the fact that he was now a cripple, a man on a crutch, not the whole man that Stella had fallen in love with.

'God only knows how she'll react to that,' he fretted.

With sweat breaking out on his brow, Bill forced himself to stay calm. He hadn't come all this way to turn around and go home again. When he thought about what his beloved must have gone through – arriving at Mary Vale alone and in despair; walking through these very woods; crossing these green lawns; knocking at the front door – he realized that if she could do that, abandoned as she must have felt, then, dammit, he could too.

The door was opened by a tall, slender nurse with big blue eyes and a bright welcoming smile.

'Hello, can I help?'

Bill gulped. 'Hi there,' he said, smiling back. 'I've come looking for Stella Isles – I believe she might be residing here?' Seeing the nurse cautiously holding back, Bill realized that she might need more information about the stranger on her doorstep. 'I'm her fiancé,' he added. 'From the States. I've travelled here to see her.'

Ada's jaw dropped. Like many of the Mary Vale residents, Stella had kept the story of her pregnancy private; all Ada knew of her past was that she had been a cook in a canteen in a munitions factory on the Pennine Moors. Yet here was a young man, a very good-looking young man with a mop of blond hair, a disarming smile and start-lingly direct eyes, telling her that he was Stella's fiancé.

At last she remembered her manners. 'Stella is staying here with us, but I'm afraid she's not in at the moment; I saw her leave for a walk only ten minutes ago.' Realizing he was leaning on a crutch, Ada quickly added, 'You could wait in the sitting room if you like, and I could bring you some tea.'

Far too restless to sit down and wait, Bill quickly said, 'No, no, thank you, ma'am, I'll try to catch up with her. Which direction did she head off in?'

Ada nodded towards the marsh. 'That way: cross the railway line and follow the path – it winds along the coastline – but watch out for the tide, it comes in swiftly,' she advised; then, feeling a little anxious, she added a warning. 'Please try not to over-excite Stella; she's near her time and seeing you is inevitably going to be a shock.'

'I promise I'll take it easy, ma'am.'

Backtracking through the wood, Bill crossed the narrow-gauge railway line, then set off on the same path that Stella had recently taken. With the tip of his crutch sinking into the fine sand, Bill sidestepped rock pools and wading birds, all the time peering from left to right in the hope of spotting Stella. Warm in the suit he was wearing, Bill shrugged off his jacket and hooked it over his shoulder, and, as he did so, he saw a distant figure with hair the col-our of burnished red-gold, a colour he could never forget. Quickening his pace, slipping and sliding on the sand which gave way under his footfall, Bill desperately wanted to run. Impatient at his own slowness, the best he could do was to hobble quickly in order to maintain enough speed to keep Stella in his line of vision. When she dipped behind a sand-dune, Bill, terrified he might lose sight of her altogether, called out loudly, 'STELLA!'

Limping as fast as he could around the sand-dunes, he stopped dead in his tracks when he saw that Stella was actually walking towards him. The stricken expression on her face, as if she were looking into the face of a dead man, almost broke his heart. Hardly daring to speak let alone breathe, Bill stood immobile as she approached. Stopping inches away from him, so close he could see the tantalizing shape of her full pouting lips and the sweet line of golden freckles that ran along the line of her high cheekbones, she gazed at him as if in a dream from which she was terrified of waking. Reaching out to touch him, she whispered in a voice that cracked with raw emotion, 'Are you real?'

Unable to bear it a moment longer, Bill gently reached out to stroke her wonderful hair, which lifted in the warm breeze and blew across her face.

'Yes, I'm real,' he whispered.

At the sound of his voice Stella all but collapsed into his arms. Supporting her as best he could, Bill leant on his crutch and clutched Stella to his chest. Sobbing and shaking, unable to believe that this apparition really was Bill, she could only gasp, 'Don't go, please don't leave me, please don't go away again.'

Racked with guilt at what he had put her through, Bill rocked her like a frightened child until she stopped shuddering.

'I'm sorry,' he crooned over and over again. 'I never meant to hurt you, I'm so sorry. I can explain it all.'

As their raging emotions subsided, they held on to each other in sweet silence; the only sounds that accompanied their tumultuous thoughts were the shush-shushing of the restless tide and the constant call of hungry seabirds.

Speaking first, she said bleakly, 'Why did you leave me, Bill?'

Kissing her face wet with tears, Bill wondered where on earth he should start – at which point Stella spotted his crutch thrown out sideways on the sand. Staring blankly at it, she said, 'You have a crutch?'

And so he started to explain.

'My God! Why didn't anybody tell me that?'

'Doreen told me the base refused to pass information on to you.'

Surprised, she asked, 'You've seen Doreen?'

'Sure, she sent me here,' he told her. 'I wrote you, darling, lots of letters mailed to your address at the factory, telling you what had happened to me.'

'I never received any letters,' she cried.

'Doreen said the same thing: none arrived for you; otherwise she would have mailed them to you. By God, I swear I'm going to find out what happened to those letters,' he said through gritted teeth.

Stella shook her head in disbelief. 'One disastrous mess after another,' she murmured.

'A complete and tragic failure in communication,' he agreed.

'I just thought you'd stopped loving me and that you didn't want our baby.'

'Oh, my Stella darling star, I've never stopped loving you. When I think of all that you've been through, the loneliness and fear – I can never forgive myself.'

'What about you?' she exclaimed. 'If only I'd been told, I could have come to you, nursed you, stayed with you.' Starting to cry all over again, she sobbed, 'All those months wasted when we could so easily have been together, helping each other, caring for each other.'

Bill waited until she had cried herself out, then pulled her close to him.

'Honey, it's a stroke of luck that I managed to return to work over here and quickly get some time off; otherwise I would never have found you. But now we have to look to the future,' he said tenderly. 'I tell you, sweetheart, once this war is over all I want, more than anything in the world, is to bring up a family with you – if you'll have me.'

Drawing away from Bill so she could stare into his eyes, Stella steadily held his gaze. 'I've loved you from the moment I first met you, and I've never stopped loving you. I'll love you till the day I die, of that there is no question, Bill – you are my life.'

The tears that he had been holding back, all the tension and fear, the overwhelming sense of being incomplete and not good enough for this wonderful brave woman, now engulfed Bill. Overcome with emotion, he buried his face against her soft, warm breast and wept uncontrollably.

'I knew I had to come back to find you. My folks were

against it, but I just knew there would be no peace for me until I was with you again.'

'We'll get through this together, you, me and our baby,' she said, as she held his trembling hand over her burgeoning tummy, where the baby kicked and rolled. 'Can you feel it?'

Bill gasped in wonder. 'Wow! That is some hefty kick,' he laughed. Keeping his hand on her tummy, he murmured happily, 'I'll be with you all the way from now on, honey, and when you're strong and fit, after the birth, we'll settle down in married quarters on Mildenhall base, if that's what you'd like?' he added anxiously.

As she reached up to kiss him on the lips, her eyes shone with joy. 'I'd like that more than anything.'

Walking back over the marsh, each of them supporting the other, they talked non-stop about the past and the future: their wedding, the baby, the Home and Stella's friends there.

'I'll introduce you to everybody when we get back,' she promised. 'Maybe Matron can put you up in a guest room in the convent for the time being.'

At which point Bill laughed out loud. 'Man, that beats it all, me staying in a convent – with nuns, for crying out loud!'

Before they left the marsh together, Stella turned to look back on it, throbbing in the golden heat of the late summer day, a day that had given her back a future.

After her brief encounter with Renee on the marsh, Stella found herself defending the woman the very next day when she heard residents in the dining room criticizing the suspended nurse.

'She's better off in her own room – at least she can't hurt anybody up there.'

'She's always been a flighty one: look what happened to Polly's baby, now this with Irene. It's not good practice – the Home should kick her out before Mary Vale's good name gets tarnished.'

'Actually,' Stella said from the other end of the dining table where she was buttering her breakfast toast, 'I think you're all being a bit hard on Sister Renee.'

'You wouldn't say that if you'd lost your baby,' one indignant girl exclaimed.

'That's true,' Stella admitted. 'But the Home is short staffed, and she'd been working very long hours,' she pointed out. 'You never know, you might be grateful for Sister Renee in an emergency.'

'I don't think so,' growled the angry resident. 'I wouldn't trust her as far as I could throw her.'

37. Call the Midwife

For an all too brief few days that hot summer, the marsh proved to be their bolthole, a place where they could go and occasionally cross paths with a family of rabbits or a flock of honking geese. Bill and Stella rekindled their passion and commitment in their own private paradise during Bill's term of compassionate leave. Barefoot, wearing cool cotton smocks with her hair hanging loose, Stella loved to lie on her back with her head in Bill's lap, he (much cooler these days in cotton shirts and slacks) usually holding his hand over Stella's tummy in order to feel their baby's wriggling movements. On more than one occasion Stella talked to Bill about his amputation.

'Believe me I was drugged up to my eyeballs, but I heard what the medics said, that my leg would have to come off. I wanted to scream out, "NO!" But I passed out in seconds and didn't really come around, not in real terms, until I was in the military hospital in Seattle.'

'Did anybody in the military hospital talk to you about a prosthesis at some point in the future?' she asked.

'Sure, we discussed it a lot, but my damaged leg has got to thoroughly heal below the knee first,' he explained. 'Only then will it be strong enough to support a prosthesis, but the medics are hopeful – I'm young and strong and damn well determined that it will happen,' Bill assured Stella.

Smiling at his optimistic determination, Stella kissed him full on the lips.

'If you want that, Bill Austin, then I have no doubt that it will happen.'

Pulling her closer for more kisses, he passionately murmured, 'You make me feel stronger by the day. Every minute with you is a tonic, an affirmation that life with you will always be good whatever fate throws our way.'

'I'd say life has thrown a heck of a lot at both of us already,' Stella pointed out. 'But, look, we're still here, together again, thank God.' She groaned as horrible memories from the past flashed through her mind. 'I thought I would die without you, Bill.'

'You're safe now, my Stella Star,' he whispered before asking cautiously, 'Before I came back, what were you planning on doing after the baby was born?'

'I'd arranged with Father Ben to have it adopted; he'd lined up a nice childless couple in Preston.'

'Adopted?' he exclaimed.

'What else could I have done?' she exclaimed. 'I had no means of bringing up a child on my own, my parents would never have accepted it, and you had seemingly walked out of my life. I was going out of my mind,' she confessed. 'The baby, the very last thing of you that I had, I was planning on giving away to strangers.'

Seeing her getting distraught, Bill quickly said, 'Well, thank God that's not on the cards any more.' Looking at her, he anxiously asked, 'Have you cancelled any legal arrangements you might have made with Father Ben?'

'Of course,' she assured him. 'I immediately told him

of my change of circumstances, and he was genuinely delighted for me and will do his best to place another baby with the family as soon as he can.' Stella's sky-blue eyes looked suddenly sad and troubled. 'I'm so lucky, Bill.'

'Funny kind of luck,' he teased.

'What I mean is I've got you, and our baby, and a future, which a lot of the Mary Vale residents haven't got. Some of them are so young and ignorant they don't even understand how a baby even started to grow inside them; one poor kid was raped.' She sighed. 'I know Lillian's dreading parting with her baby, but she's in the same place as I was when I thought I was on my own.'

Recalling the small pretty dark girl that Stella had introduced him to, Bill nodded. 'She seemed like a nice woman,' he responded.

'Yes, she's lovely,' Stella agreed. 'I wonder how her life will pan out after her baby's born?'

They often fell asleep in the hot sunshine, Stella curled up with her head on Bill's chest, and both would wake up bleary-eyed, dazzled by sunlight, always incredulous that they weren't dreaming, that they really were together. On one afternoon, seeing the tide making its way in, Bill gently pulled Stella to her feet.

'Come on, sweetheart, time to get you home before they think we're stranded on the beach and call out the life guards.'

Laughing, Stella leant against him, but the slippery silver sand underfoot caused her to lose her balance and she fell back on to the ground. Grabbing his crutch, Bill held out a hand to raise her but when he saw the horrified expression on Stella's face he cried out in alarm. 'Stella! What is it? What's up?'

'I felt a rush of water between my legs when I fell over,' she gasped. Seizing his outstretched hand, she struggled to her feet. 'My waters must have broken – we need to get back to Mary Vale right away.'

Supported by Bill, Stella made slow, lumbering progress back along the track. Concerned that the turning tide might start to speed up and cut them off, Bill longed to pick her up and run back to the Home with her in his arms, but, as it was, all he could do was to gently encourage her to keep moving. As the tide started to lap into the rock pools, which quickly filled up, Bill began to panic. 'Oh, God if it comes in any faster, we really will be marooned on the marsh till morning.' At which point, to his absolute relief, Bill spotted Renee, who was also hurrying down the track but coming from the opposite direction. Raising his free hand, Bill yelled, 'Hello there!'

Seeing Stella pale and tense, with her body leaning heavily against Bill's, Renee instantly guessed what might have happened. Like Bill, she was all too well aware of the swiftness of the incoming tide and the very real urgency of getting Stella to safety as quickly as possible.

'Let's support her together,' she suggested to Bill, before speaking calmly to Stella. 'Put your arms around both of us, sweetheart, let us take the weight.'

Weak and afraid, Stella nodded and did as instructed, and between them Bill (with great difficulty) and Renee half lifted Stella, carrying her swiftly off the marsh. When they came to the level crossing at Kents Bank Station, where a train blocked the crossing point, Bill groaned out loud. 'Jesus! Can we go around it?'

'No, we'll have to wait for it to move on,' Renee told him. 'It shouldn't be long.'

Just as soon as the steam train puffed on its way, they hobbled over the track; then, when they reached the small shady wood adjacent to the Home, Renee said, 'Stay with her while I fetch a trolley.'

Resting against a stout tree trunk, Bill held Stella close, all the time stroking her hot cheek. 'You're gonna be okay, kiddo,' he soothed.

In no time at all, Renee reappeared, wheeling a full-sized hospital trolley on to which Stella was quickly settled. Seeing the feverish activity taking place in the garden, a number of curious residents had gathered in the hallway.

'Make way,' Renee said with authority as they pushed a path through the gawking girls. 'We need to get Stella on to the ward.'

Exchanging dirty looks, some of the residents started to grumble.

'Shouldn't you be handing her over to a proper nurse?' one sneered. 'Someone more fit for the job than you?'

Renee stopped dead in her tracks, with flaming cheeks and trembling hands. 'Get out of my way.'

The insolent resident faced Renee, who did not flinch from her angry gaze.

'You could be reported for this, you know.'

'Renee's only trying to help us,' Stella, prone on the

trolley, cried out, at which point Bill, covered in sweat and sick with worry completely lost his temper. 'Will you get the hell out of our way!' he shouted.

Shocked at his angry tone, the residents finally made a space for the trolley to pass through. As the ward door closed shut behind them, Renee threw Bill a grateful look.

'Thanks,' she said a little shyly. 'I'm unused to having an ally these days.'

Stella reached up to touch Renee's hand. 'We're grateful for your help, Sister.'

When Ada saw Renee pushing Stella on a trolley on to the ward with Bill limping in their wake, she raised her eyebrows in concern.

'Stella's okay,' Renee quickly said. 'Her waters broke while she was out on the marsh.'

'I was worried about getting stuck out there with the tide coming in,' Bill added. 'Sister Renee helped me carry Stella back here.'

Quickly looking down at the newly arrived patient, Ada asked, 'How are you, dear?'

Lifting her head, Stella gave a weak smile. 'My back really hurts, and my tummy feels like a tight drum,' she replied.

Beginning to feel awkward that she was in a place that was officially now out of bounds to her, Renee muttered self-consciously, 'I'd better be off; you're in safe hands now, Stella.'

Stella looked from Ada to Renee and back again, and in a split second she made a decision that took everybody by surprise.

'No, please, Sister Renee, I'd like you to stay with me and deliver my baby.'

Haunted by guilty memories, Renee vehemently shook her head. 'I don't think that's such a good idea, Stella.'

Stella's response was simple and direct. 'Please, Sister, I trust you.'

Knowing this wasn't the time to beat about the bush, Renee came straight to the point. 'You know I'm suspended, Stella, because I fell asleep on duty the night that Irene lost her baby. You'd be wise to let Ada take over from here.'

Stella's sharp cry of pain brought everybody back to the task in hand. 'Argh!' she cried. 'Can we please just get on with delivering my baby!'

Turning to Renee, Bill bluntly stated, 'She needs your help, Nurse.'

In a highly charged moment, intuitive Ada quickly assessed the situation; the last thing she wanted was to upset an already over-wrought patient.

'Over to you, Sister Renee,' she said decisively. 'I'll be close by if you should need me.'

At the end of that very hot day, with the moon sailing high over a tranquil sea, Stella gave birth to a bouncing baby boy with the lungs of a young lion. Renee expertly delivered the baby and, once she had cleaned and weighed him, she wrapped him in a blanket and placed him in Stella's arms.

'Congratulations,' she said warmly.

'Oh, he's so beautiful,' Stella sighed as she kissed her baby's damp dark hair. Turning to Bill, who had joined her, she started to say something but stopped when she saw tears streaming down his exhausted face. 'Darling, what is it?'

Completely overcome, Bill sobbed. 'You must have been so brave and strong, I don't know how women do it, it's nothing short of a miracle,' he said incredulously. 'And you, Renee,' he said, as he gazed in awe at the midwife. 'God only knows why you're suspended; beats me how anybody could doubt your professionalism, after everything you did for Stella today.'

Taken aback, it was now Renee's turn to fill up; this was praise she had never reckoned on. Flustered, she replied in a choked voice, 'It was a real pleasure – Stella's a natural. Now, if you'll excuse me, I'll leave you in private for a few minutes.'

Bill frowned as he watched her go. 'What's the story there?'

Stella pressed a finger to her lips. 'Long story, I'll tell you later.'

In the empty sluice room Renee quickly wiped away her tears; Bill's kind words and Stella's gratitude had completely overwhelmed her. Renee allowed herself a moment of pure pleasure: just when she thought she had come to the end of her midwifery career, she had delivered a healthy baby into the world without a single hitch.

'Maybe I should rethink my future,' she thought with a smile.

Back on the ward, Bill was tenderly examining each of his son's little fingers and toes. 'He's perfect, just perfect.' With tears of joy in his eyes he continued, 'I never thought when I was all those months in hospital that I would be here when our baby was born – it's more than I could ever have wished for.' Turning from the baby to the mother, he leant in close to kiss Stella's soft lips. 'Thank you, Stella Star, for my beautiful son.'

38. Sal

Stella's safe delivery of a son made Lillian intensely aware of how close she was to giving birth herself, but, unlike Stella, she certainly wouldn't have a man at her side to support her through the trials of childbirth. Remembering how gentle and loving Robbie had been when he had delivered Lilibet, how patient and attentive with Daisy – just thinking of his concerned brown eyes, soft gentle voice, and strong hands – made Lillian's insides melt.

'Poor darling,' she thought. 'He had so much to put up with, yet he always had all the time in the world for animals in need of his help.'

Recalling how much the shires had loved him brought tears to Lillian's eyes; she could still picture how the three of them neighed excitedly at the sound of Robbie's Jeep pulling into the yard, or how they trotted eagerly across the paddock to greet him, knowing he would always have a carrot for them and a cuddle too.

'How could you not fall for a man like Robbie, somebody you could trust with your life? How sad that his wife had lost that bond with him,' Lillian reflected.

Thinking of Harriet always made Lillian feel glad that she had made the momentous decision not to take her relationship with Robbie any further. Making love with him once had been emotionally unparalleled; if they had continued as lovers, she knew that she would never have been able to let him go.

'Kill it dead before it grows out of control,' had always been her hard line.

Lillian didn't want to live with the knowledge that she had broken up an already delicate marriage. With time, she prayed that Robbie and Harriet's relationship would heal, though sadly they would never have another child of their own to replace the one they had lost.

When Lillian was allowed to visit Stella on the post-natal ward early the next morning, she was impressed by how strong and happy the new mother was. Holding her baby to her breast, where he suckled greedily, Stella told her visitor how wonderful Sister Renee had been throughout her delivery.

'From the moment she helped us out on the marsh till the moment he was born she never put a foot wrong.'

'Well, that's good to know,' Lillian replied. 'This might just swing the residents' opinion of her.'

Stella gave an excited smile. 'I hope so. She looked genuinely delighted when she delivered our little boy; Bill was impressed by her too. I really hope things work out well for her,' she added anxiously.

Smiling at the now sleepy baby, Lillian asked, 'Have you decided on a name for your son?'

'Ryder,' Stella proudly announced. 'It's Bill's second name, after his grandfather.'

'Ryder . . .' Lillian murmured. 'I like it, very unusual.'

'We're both determined to get married soon,' she told

her friend excitedly. 'My parents have said they'll come and as a mark of our gratitude we've asked Sister Renee to be our witness. Bill and I hope you'll come too, if you can manage it?' she added, eyeing Lillian's large tummy.

'I'd be delighted,' Lillian responded. 'Heavens!' she laughed. 'It's all happening for you, Stella.'

After seeing her happy friend, Lillian walked out into the garden, where she sat glumly on a bench and stared out to sea. Though she was genuinely pleased for Stella, who deserved some joy after what she has been through, Lillian nevertheless felt troubled and rather tearful.

'God in heaven, what am I going to do with myself once this baby is born?' she groaned out loud.

Under her instructions, Father Ben had already drawn up the adoption papers for her baby, and now it was just a question of waiting for the birth, after which, once she was fit enough, she would catch a train back to Blackpool and pretend nothing had happened to her in the time she had been away. Female conscription was still under way, so she would have to report back for duty, but the idea of being a Land Girl again filled Lillian with gloom.

'Maybe I should apply to work in a munitions factory next time around.'

Deep in troubled thought, Lillian didn't even notice somebody striding across the lawn towards her. When a shadow fell across the bench, making her start and look up, she was astonished to find herself staring into the smiling face of one of her Land Girl friends.

'*Sal!*' she exclaimed in complete delight. 'How marvellous

to see you,' she cried, as she leapt from her seat and flung her arms around Sal's neck.

'My, Lil, you've grown,' Sal said and stepped back to admire Lillian's huge pregnant tummy.

Lillian nodded. 'I know, I'm all baby,' she agreed. 'It's because I'm so small,' she explained. 'The bigger women in the Home don't show anything like as much as me.'

'You look like you might pop soon,' the irrepressible Sal joked.

'Weeks, rather than months, now,' Lillian said, as she sat back down and patted the seat for Sal to join her. 'Tell me your news – how are Mo and Pat?'

'The same,' Sal said, grinning. 'Though Mo's found a fella. I tell you,' she added, dropping her voice, 'if she's not careful she'll end up in here with you. The pair of them are at it like rabbits!' she laughed.

Unable to contain her curiosity a second longer, Lillian cried, 'And the shires, how are they?'

Sal, pausing before she spoke, made Lillian's stomach lurch. 'Are they all right?' she gasped.

'A local lad from the village has been put in charge of them, but he's not a patch on you. Poor things look proper scruffy these days, covered in mud and muck; I've hardly seen him groom them yet.'

Looking stricken, Lillian whispered, 'Does Robbie visit them?'

'Aye, when he can,' Sal answered warily.

'What do you mean, "when he can"?' Lillian enquired. 'He regularly used to call in and see them when I was around.'

'Robbie's not been at Dobb End recently,' Sal answered cautiously. 'Or any other farm for that matter.'

Seeing Sal's nervous expression, Lillian knew something was wrong. 'Out with it, Sal, what's up?'

Shifting awkwardly Sal started. 'I didn't want to write and tell you the news. I thought it would be too much of a shock, you being in a delicate condition, and I certainly didn't want you reading about it in the papers.'

By now Lillian was holding her breath. Covering her mouth with her hand, she cried, 'Is he all right?'

'He is,' Sal answered grimly. 'But his wife's not.'

'Harriet! What's happened to her?'

'I'm so sorry, love, to be the one to tell you this, but she took her life last week.'

Feeling like she was going to keel over, Lillian gripped the bench. 'Oh, my God!'

'She hanged herself in the asylum,' Sal continued. 'Poor woman, she must have been in such a state to do a thing like that.'

Shocked rigid, Lillian simply couldn't speak.

'You should see the state of Robbie,' Sal added. 'Imagine having to live with two family tragedies like that for the rest of your life; I really don't know how he'll cope.'

'Robbie,' Lillian sighed, as tears flowed unchecked from her eyes. 'He tried so hard to help her, but Harriet was clearly beyond all help.' Stopping suddenly, she glanced up at Sal. 'You haven't told him about me, have you?'

Sal shook her head. 'No, I haven't broken my promise, if that's what you mean, though to be honest I can't think why you're keeping it a secret from him now – after all, what's the poor man got to live for?'

'No, Sal!' Lillian protested. 'I can't tell him now. It would be wrong when he's in such emotional turmoil, like blackmail.'

'That's just ridiculous!' Sal exclaimed.

After having a welcome cup of tea with Lillian in the Home's sitting room, Sal set off back for Rosthwaite.

'I can't be gone for too long, it's not fair on the girls,' she explained.

Lillian nodded. 'I remember what it was like,' she said, smiling wistfully. 'Never enough hours in the day.'

'Take care, lovie, and good luck with the baby,' Sal said, as she hugged Lillian goodbye. 'We still miss you, and we always will.'

Standing on the station platform, Lillian waved her friend off before turning to retrace her steps to the Home, where she had yet to do her chores. Thinking of the cleaning tasks ahead of her, Lillian didn't flinch, in fact, she welcomed them: right now she wanted to obliterate all thought of Robbie and his wife from her mind. Any task would be welcome; she would happily scrub, mop and polish until she dropped, just so long as she didn't have to think of all the heartbreak Robbie was going through and the beautiful horses she had cared for, now abandoned and unloved.

By tea-time Lillian was on her knees; she had thrown herself into every chore and successfully managed to shove all thought of Robbie to the back of her mind. Now she was starving hungry and her back was aching after so much stooping and bending. Hurrying into the dining room buzzing with the assembled residents' chatter, she gratefully sank into a chair. After downing several cups of hot strong tea, Lillian filled her plate with spam and lettuce sandwiches, which she gratefully devoured. All chatter stopped when Renee walked into the room to collect her tea and sandwiches; catching sight of the residents' dirty looks and surreptitious nudging, Lillian was suddenly gripped with a rush of anger. The ongoing resentment of her fellow residents suddenly incensed her.

'Renee's paying the price for her wrongdoing,' Lillian thought hotly. 'And pretty soon she will have left Mary Vale altogether.'

Remembering Stella's kind words for the disgraced midwife, Lillian heard herself suddenly calling out, 'Would you like to sit down, Sister Renee? There's a chair free next to me?'

Looking astonished, Renee paused. 'Yes, please, Lillian, I'd like that very much.'

As the silent residents gaped at her, Renee sat down and accepted the cup of tea Lillian poured out for her, then she took several sandwiches from the serving platter.

'Stella's doing well,' Lillian said loudly. 'Did you hear what they called the baby you delivered?' she added pointedly.

'Yes, I did. It's a very unusual name, rather sweet, don't you think?' Renee replied self-consciously.

Passing the sandwich platter around the table, Lillian said, 'Come on, help yourself, ladies. I wouldn't want any of you to go hungry.'

As the buzz of chatter started up again, Renee threw Lillian a grateful smile. 'Thank you,' she said. 'And I don't just mean for the food.'

'You're most welcome,' Lillian said, smiling back.

Biting into her sandwich, Lillian thought sadly of poor Harriet, and she was glad that she had just now reached out to a woman in need. There was already enough unhappiness in the world without adding more.

39. A Slip-up

Even though Robbie had known his wife had a precarious hold on life, he had always hoped that she would pull through; but, clearly, she had seen no way back; she was done. The inquest had attracted newspaper reporters, who wasted no time in getting the story into the local press, making Robbie's working life hell. In the valley he was protected by people who looked after their own kind; everybody knew what the vet and his wife had been through and, though they might gossip between themselves, the gossiping stopped right there. Now it seemed to Robbie that the whole of Westmorland knew all about his private life, past and present. There was nowhere he could go to hide his hurt and the overwhelming sense of shame that he had utterly failed the woman he had married.

Though he had had little time to spare while Harriet was at her worst, Robbie was determined to check up on Lillian's shires after the inquest into his wife's death. Visiting her horses was one of his few remaining comforts; they reminded him so much of the laughing, beautiful girl who had lifted his heavy heart and made him feel young again. Dearest darling wonderful Lil – why had she disappeared the way she did? No note, no message, nothing, just gone like a dream in the morning. However, when

Robbie finally did get around to seeing the horses, he was outraged at their neglected condition. Wasting no time in tracking down the idle lad supposedly in charge of the horses, Robbie grabbed him by the scruff of the neck.

'What the hell are you playing at? Muck out the stable NOW – clean straw, fresh hay in all the nets and freshen up their water buckets.'

Leaving the boy to get on with the jobs he had ordered to be done, Robbie led all three horses into the paddock, where in the cool evening air he patiently examined each of them in turn.

'My God, Lillian would be heartbroken if she could see you now,' he murmured sadly, as he brushed them down to remove the embedded mud and grime.

Responding to his concern, all three vied for his affection. Feeling their velvet-soft noses nuzzling at his chest, Robbie gave up any attempt to groom them and instead gave them all a cuddle.

'I know, I know,' he crooned as he slid his hand down Daisy's scrawny neck. 'You miss her too.' Turning to Major, whose huge brown eyes seemed to speak of his misery, Robbie whispered, 'I'll try and sort something out for you, big fella – you can't go on like this.'

Instinctively sensing Robbie's sadness, Major neighed softly, at which point Lilibet, fed up with being excluded from the conversation, shoved her nose in Robbie's face and blew in his hair. For the first time in weeks Robbie burst out laughing.

'Little monkey!' he cried, as the affectionate foal licked his hand.

After giving all three shires cuddles, carrots and finally a thorough grooming, Robbie returned to the stable in order to examine the stable boy's work. Ordering him to clear up the stinking droppings left on the stall floor, Robbie declared, 'If I find those animals lying in their own filth again, I'll tan your hide – do you hear me?'

'Yessir,' the terrified lad replied.

'Get yourself home, and be back here by six tomorrow morning,' Robbie snapped. 'These animals need feeding and grooming before they're sent out into the fields.'

Afraid of getting a clip round the ear hole, the lad ran off, leaving Robbie to smoke a pipe of tobacco in the farmyard, where he was found by Sal, only recently back from Mary Vale.

'Oh, hello. I'm just popping in to see the horses. I promised Lillian that I'd check on them as soon as I got back.' Slamming a hand to her mouth, she quickly corrected herself. 'I mean, er . . . I promised her a few months ago that I'd keep an eye on the horses,' she said, flustered.

The vet had not missed a trick. 'You just said, and I quote, "that I'd check on them as soon as I got back". Got back from *where*?'

All day long Sal had doubted the wisdom of Lillian's determination to keep her whereabouts and her condition from the vet; she even recalled the actual words she had said to Lillian's face – 'After all, what's the poor man got to live for?'

Lillian had been adamant, but on the journey back Sal had got to thinking: it was all right for Lil to take up a position but she wasn't the only person in the game; a woman had died, a baby was on its way and the man at the centre of the drama was oblivious to the fact that he had even fathered a child.

Seeing her faltering expression, Robbie took a few steps closer. 'You've seen her, haven't you?' he insisted. 'For God's sake, Sal, I'm in agony here,' he implored. 'If you know where she is, I beg you, *please* tell me; I've got absolutely nothing else to hope for.'

The sight of the poor man bowed with pain and remorse brought tears to Sal's eyes. How could she justify denying him the truth?

'Yes, I have seen her.'

Robbie's head snapped up. 'Where?' he cried.

'She's in Grange-over-Sands,' Sal told him. 'In a Mother and Baby Home run by nuns.'

Turning a sickly white, Robbie grasped a fence post for support. 'A Mother and Baby Home?' he gasped. 'Why?'

Trying not to smile at his question, Sal raised her eyes to the skies. 'You're the vet – work it out.'

At which point Robbie swayed. Rushing forward to catch him in case he fell to the ground, Sal said, 'Lil begged me not to tell you, but after what you've been through you deserve to know the truth; she's pregnant with your child. That's why she left in such a hurry: she didn't want to make your life any harder. But it's a bit late for that now,' Sal ended with a sad sigh.

Gripping her hard by the shoulders, Robbie was so choked he could barely speak. 'How is she?'

Sal grinned. 'Blooming, I'd say! Go and see for yourself.'

*

With his mind in turmoil, Robbie hardly slept a wink. First thing the next morning he was in his Jeep driving south as fast as the rickety old vehicle would go. Peering at the scrap of paper that Sal had thrust into his hand, he read out loud: 'Mary Vale, Kents Bank, Grange-over-Sands. God, she's been so near – all these months and I never knew,' he marvelled.

All the pieces now fell into place: Lillian's sudden departure, and all the mystery surrounding it. Robbie had never understood how she could have left her beloved horses the way she did, it was so out of character, but now he saw that Lillian hadn't really had a choice. If she had hung around any longer, he would have guessed her condition and that would have inevitably complicated the situation. Lillian had had to get away from Dobb End before Robbie realized that she was pregnant with his child.

As the hilly mountainous landscape fell away, to be replaced by small farmsteads and little villages dotted with fields, Robbie's thoughts shot off in an entirely different direction.

'Will Lillian even talk to me when she knows what happened to Harriet?' he fretted. 'She might think it was my fault, that I brought on my wife's death; there's every reason to think that she might not even trust me any more.'

The thought of Lillian bearing his child made his head spin with joy, but would Lillian allow him to be involved in the child's upbringing? Was she even planning on keeping the baby? He could only hope. There were no answers to the questions that teemed in his head, just confusion and fear of rejection. By the time Robbie had located the

Home and parked in the driveway, he was shaking with nerves. Taking deep breaths to steady his chaotic thoughts, he politely announced himself to the young nun who opened the door to him.

'I'm here to see Lillian Latham.'

'And who should I say is calling?' Sister Theresa enquired.

'Robbie Allen – we worked together when she was a Land Girl in the Borrowdale Valley some time ago,' he explained.

'She's with the doctor right now,' Theresa told him. 'Would you like to wait in the sitting room?'

The thought of meeting Lillian in a public place horrified Robbie, who shook his head. 'No, if you don't mind, I'll take a stroll to stretch my legs,' he quickly said.

'She should be done in half an hour,' Theresa added.

Walking quickly away from the Home, Robbie took a turn off the garden path that led on to a quiet farm track. Once he was out of sight, his shoulders sagged, and he gratefully leant against a drystone wall that bordered farm fields laid out like a neat green patchwork quilt. Lillian had picked a lovely place in which to wait for her baby, Robbie mused, as he lit his pipe and gazed out at the sheared sheep with their well-grown lambs no longer clinging to their mothers' sides but running and frisking in the summer meadows. The area had neither the grandeur of the Borrowdale Valley he had just left, nor its majestic mountains and tumbling waterfalls, but it had a soft, rolling gentleness that was easy on the eye, and the ear too, he thought, as he listened to the warbling exchange of birds in the nearby wood. After tapping out his pipe, Robbie continued down the lane, passing a cottage where a little girl and her mother were picking flowers in their pretty garden.

At the end of the lane, Robbie wondered about walking into the wood, but, fearful of missing Lillian, he quickly retraced his steps and headed back up the track – then he froze. Heading towards him was Lillian herself, her sun-streaked hair blowing around her face and her hands supporting the huge weight of her burgeoning tummy, which dramatically contrasted with her small, delicate frame. Looking around in confusion, as if she expected somebody to appear and explain to her how Robbie could possibly be standing in front of her, she spluttered nervously, 'How did you find me, Robbie?'

Almost too scared to speak, Robbie took a cautious step forward. 'Sal told me.'

Lillian let out a resigned sigh. 'I thought as much. She came to visit me yesterday; I had a feeling that her resolve was slipping.'

'I think she just feels sorry for me,' he muttered miserably.

Now it was Lillian's turn to take a step closer. 'I feel sorry for you too, Robbie, I'm sorry for your terrible loss,' she whispered. 'All the time I've been here I've never stopped hoping and praying that things would get better for you and your wife . . . but instead it looks like they just got worse. Poor Harriet,' she murmured.

'Even though she lost the will to live a long time ago, it was still a terrible shock.'

Unable to see the man she loved so broken, Lillian hurried to his side. 'Oh, Robbie,' she cried.

Grabbing hold of her as if she were a lifeline, Robbie pulled Lillian close to his chest and held her there like he would never let her go.

'Darling, why did you go away like that, why didn't you tell me?' Sobbing, he laid his head on her slender shoulder, where he wept out the misery of the last few months. 'I've missed you so much.'

Overwhelmed by the tidal wave of his feelings, Lillian stroked his hair as she kissed away his tears. Afraid that he might have overstepped the mark, Robbie slightly drew away. 'I'm sorry,' he murmured. 'I've said too much.'

Gripping him firmly by the hand, Lillian said, 'Can we walk back to the garden? I can't stand for long these days and we *really* need to talk.'

In the empty summer house overlooking the Irish Sea, they sat on the wooden bench where they talked for hours, interrupted only by Sister Theresa, who appeared with a tray of tea and sandwiches.

'You've missed dinner, Lillian,' she said shyly. 'I've brought enough for your visitor too.'

After the food had been consumed and Robbie was a bit calmer, he took both of Lillian's small hands in his own and said, 'Darling Lillian, please tell me your plans for our baby.'

'Well,' she started cautiously, 'I'm in the process of having it adopted.'

'Is that what you *really* want?' he murmured.

Tears welled up in Lillian's brown eyes. 'Of course not, Robbie,' she exclaimed.

'Sweetheart, more than anything else in the world I want you to keep this baby and, if you'll allow it, let me help you bring it up.'

Lillian gazed at him in joyful disbelief. 'Of course, I'd love that, Robbie. I never wanted to part with my baby in the first place.'

'You won't have a thing to worry about,' he promised, as he pulled her close. 'I'll take care of everything, financially and practically. I'll support you in a way I've not been able to up until now.' In a rush of utter devotion, he gazed into her dreamy brown eyes. 'Tell me, Lil, is there anything you urgently need?'

In answer Lillian burst out laughing. 'Yes. Stop squeezing me so hard,' she begged 'The baby is kicking so much I'm afraid I might give birth on the spot!'

Gently releasing her, Robbie, swept up in the moment, was unable to stop himself kissing Lillian tenderly on the lips. Drawing away from him, Lillian said, 'Actually, there is something you can do for me, Robbie.'

'Anything, sweetheart,' he said impetuously.

Mischievous Lillian answered with a bubble of excitement in her voice. 'You can take me to see my horses!'

40. Honeymooners

Even though Stella's wedding party would consist only of her parents, Sister Renee and Lillian, there was much excitement in the Home surrounding the event. As food was passed up and down the dining table during meal-times, Stella was bombarded by residents' questions.

'What will you be wearing?' somebody asked.

'Bill's bought me a nice cream silk suit which I'll wear with a straw hat trimmed with a cream ribbon, and new white strappy shoes too,' Stella answered excitedly.

'Where will you have your wedding do?'

'At the Smugglers' Arms off the esplanade in Grange, though there'll only be a few of us.'

'I heard tell that Sister Short is one of your guests?' one girl slyly asked.

'She certainly is – Bill insisted on it,' Stella told her staunchly. 'We have so much to thank Sister Short for.'

A few hours later, in the privacy of the sunny garden, Lillian sat beside Stella, who was concentrating on breast-feeding baby Ryder.

'Bill's already put in a request for married quarters on his base,' Stella said excitedly. 'So we'll start married life in a new home.'

'And when are you leaving?' Lillian asked.

'Straight after our honeymoon night at the Smugglers' Arms,' Stella blushed. 'It's all arranged. Ryder's going to stay in the nursery with Dora so there'll be no interruptions.'

'No getting up in the night and feeding?' Lillian said, smiling.

'I've sorted all that out with Dora so hopefully Ryder won't miss me too much. Anyway I'll be back the next day to pack up here. Never mind me, though,' Stella said, changing the subject. 'Tell me about your visitor,' she said with a grin.

Knowing how news of Robbie's visit had spread through the Home, Lillian gave a happy little laugh.

'Robbie wants me to keep the baby and he's asked if he can help me bring it up,' Lillian exclaimed.

'That sounds like a serious proposition,' Stella smiled. 'I'm really happy for you, lovie.'

'That Robbie found me and wants me to keep his baby is more than I ever dared dream of,' Lillian admitted.

'I know that feeling. I thought I was hallucinating when Bill appeared as if from nowhere,' Stella agreed.

Both women, brimming over with joy, smiled at each other.

'I never thought when I arrived here that I would ever see Bill again,' Stella declared.

'And I thought I would never see Robbie again. Life has a wonderful way of working itself out,' Lillian laughed. 'I don't know what the future holds for us – the poor man has been through so much, and it won't be easy for me – but, for now, being able to keep his baby and knowing Robbie will be involved is enough.'

Staring thoughtfully down at her chest, where her son was happily suckling, Stella murmured, 'I just hope I can squeeze into the nice suit that Bill bought for me. I used to be so slim but now with these breasts I barely fit into anything.'

Smiling at Ryder, who grew bigger and stronger with every passing day, Lillian said, 'All in a good cause.'

'That's what Sister Renee says,' Stella added. 'She's been a real help to me, you know, not just over the delivery but advising me and explaining everything that happens after the pregnancy. She's a really good nurse – a loss to Mary Vale, I'd say.'

'I thought the Home might have reconsidered their decision after seeing how well Sister Renee handled your delivery,' Lillian replied.

'She showed them her worth in the end, even though everybody was watching her, waiting for her to make another mistake,' Stella said crossly. 'But really who would want to work in an environment where you were distrusted? Best for her to move on and start afresh – I know I certainly would.'

Stella's wedding took place as soon as Bill was granted more time off work – thankfully his colleagues were so sympathetic to what he'd been through that they moved heaven and earth to make that possible. It took place in the register office in Grange, and afterwards the small party had a pleasant meal in the Smugglers' Arms, now run by a landlord who wasn't, as Renee noted, as keen on the bottle as the pub's old landlady. With their son safe in Dora's care, the newly marrieds were free to relax and enjoy their wedding night, and, thanks to a combination of Bill's money and everybody else's pooled ration coupons, a good meal was laid on for the guests: local roast pork, freshly grown carrots, peas and new potatoes, followed by a gooseberry fool. Throughout the meal Bill made sure everyone's glass was topped up, stout for Stella's parents, a modest sherry for Stella and Renee, and beer for himself.

At the end of the meal, the groom rose to his feet to make a speech. Raising his wife's left hand, he kissed the golden band he had only recently put on her finger. 'Ours has been a long journey, one on which we both thought we had lost each other forever.' Taking a breath to steady his emotions, he continued, 'God brought us back together and now, with His blessing, we can look forward to a future neither of us imagined possible. To my darling, beautiful bride, Stella, Mrs Austin.'

'Cheers,' the wedding party chorused. 'Good luck!'

When the meal was concluded, Lillian and Renee set off back to Mary Vale, leaving Stella hugging her parents, who were struggling to hold back tears.

'I feel like I'm losing you forever,' Stella's mum cried.

'Mum, we'll still be in the same country,' Stella pointed out. 'I'll write, and send photos of Ryder. You never know, you and Dad might get the chance to pop down South and visit us soon.'

After her father had hugged her tight and her mother kissed her for the last time, Stella's parents boarded a train for Burnley.

'Bye, good luck, safe journey!' they called through the

open window, as the train belched out a thick cloud of black smoke before chugging out of the station.

Wiping tears from her eyes, Stella turned to Bill. 'I feel like one part of my life has ended and another has just begun,' she said, as memories flooded her mind.

She had grown up in Lancashire, in a closely knit family, all of whom (apart from her dad) worked in the mill, which dominated the entire community. She could even recall the sound of clogs clattering on the cobbles as the mill hooter sounded out and workers changed shifts. Her primary school had been a little red-brick building, and she had played hopscotch in the school yard, where the rain regularly washed away all the chalk markings Stella had painstakingly drawn on the flagstones. She had frequently walked on the moors, first as a child with her parents, then, as she grew up, with her friends, exploring the wild countryside; and, the best time of all, introducing Bill to the Japanese Gardens on Rivington Pike, where she had given herself completely to him one extraordinary summer night. Now it seemed like time had turned full circle: she had let go in order to move on to the exciting future which beckoned like a seductive dream.

Seeing Stella's thoughtful expression, Bill pulled her close and kissed her. 'Don't worry, sweetheart, you know I'll always take care of you and our baby.'

'I know you will, Bill,' Stella answered with complete certainty. 'There's no doubt in my mind about the choice I've made: I want to be with you, Mr Austin, forever and ever.'

Standing on the platform, they kissed like the romantic lovers they were.

'And now,' Bill murmured into Stella's blazing golden-red hair, 'the time has come for a bit of privacy, don't you think?'

And so, in the big double bedroom of the Smugglers' Arms, Bill and Stella rolled into each other's arms, and, though things were physically different from their previous times together, the chemistry between them still sparkled. As Bill kissed her naked body, Stella forgot about her stretch marks and post-baby tummy and gloried in Bill's tender touch as he reconnected with her body, which ached for him, as it always had done. And Bill, who had previously worried about the changes in his own body, like Stella, forgot his fears. Stella's tenderness and passion eased his self-conscious state; her love restored him, making him feel like a whole man again, which (if that were possible) made him love and desire her even more than before. As the sun set over the Irish Sea and the moon rose silvering the gentle waves of the incoming tide, the newly-weds, entwined in each other's arms, fell into a deep sleep until the dawn light woke them.

'This is the face I want to wake up to every morning of my life,' Bill said, as he traced the line of golden freckles that speckled Stella's small nose with his index finger.

'And these are the lips I want to kiss every night before I sleep,' she whispered, as she reached up to kiss him.

Pulling her on to his broad chest, Bill laughed with sheer joy.

'Oh, my darling, what a life we're going to have together,' he declared. 'I'll take you to places that you've never even imagined, islands where the sea meets the sky and mountains that reach higher than the clouds.' Gazing down at Stella, he kissed her on both cheeks and then on the mouth. 'We'll raise a family, you and I,' he promised. 'One day we'll live by the ocean: I'll fish for a living and little Ryder will have brothers and sisters to play with.'

Snuggling up close to her husband's warm chest, Stella smiled. 'Until that moment comes, my darling,' she murmured, 'living with you and our baby in married quarters on the Mildenhall base will suit me just fine.'

41. The Visit

A couple of weeks after Stella's departure, Lillian told Ada that she was planning a short trip to Keswick.

'Robbie will pick me up and drive me there; I'll be back in time for supper,' she explained.

Ada, who had been introduced to Robbie and liked him very much, looked doubtful.

'Really Lillian?' she asked. 'I'm not at all sure I like the idea of your gadding about the countryside at this late stage in your pregnancy.'

'Oh, Sister Ada!' Lillian declared. 'I've been cooped up here for months now; this is the first opportunity I've had for a change of scene. It'll do Robbie good too,' she added. 'Take his mind off his troubles.'

Knowing of the tragedy that had occurred in Robbie's recent life, Ada gave a sympathetic smile. 'I can see your point, but bouncing around in a van on bumpy roads won't be good for you, Lillian,' she pointed out.

'It's a Jeep actually and they're not bumpy roads, they're all tarmac,' Lillian explained.

Eventually Ada reluctantly agreed to Lillian's excursion. 'If you're not back by supper-time I'll raise the alarm,' she concluded firmly.

*

On the day planned for the excursion, Lillian was excited to see Robbie arrive as she waited on the drive.

'You look lovely,' Robbie said, as his eyes swept over her radiant face.

'I feel huge,' Lillian moaned, after he had helped her into the passenger seat. 'This smock is the only thing that fits me these days.'

'Dearest, you'd look lovely in a sackcloth,' he murmured. 'The minute you've had the baby I'll buy all the summer dresses my clothing rations will stretch to,' he promised.

Lillian shivered with pleasure; his words made her feel wonderful, though she had no idea how things were going to work out between them once the baby was born. Sitting as close to him as she could, she inhaled the combined smell of his pipe tobacco and the old familiar tang of antiseptic soap.

'I'm so happy to see you,' she whispered, unable to stop herself from kissing his freshly shaved cheek.

'And I have barely slept a wink, young lady, thinking of our baby.'

Driving along the road to the North, Lillian's smile widened as they wound their way through Windermere's grey narrow streets, then headed up to Grasmere, passing the rock formation that was known as the Lion and the Lamb, which could distinctly be seen from the road far down below. Robbie pointed out the majestic outlines of Helvellyn to their right and the Langdale range to their left.

'One day I want to take you up there,' he announced. 'I

want our baby to grow up loving this landscape as much as I do,' Robbie added passionately.

'Did your son love walking?' Lillian asked hesitantly.

'Yes, he loved it, from being a toddler. Harriet wasn't so keen, but Timmy and I did some easy walking routes together; we went fishing too, in the becks and lakes. He was a real outdoor boy,' he finished fondly.

Relieved that she had broached the sensitive subject of his past, Lillian for the moment left it at that, but she was determined that Robbie's former life would not be bundled away in a place at the back of his mind. He had loved a woman before her who had given him a son; respect needed to be paid to both their memories and she for one was determined to do that.

'Almost there,' Robbie announced as they drove past the stone circle on the outskirts of Keswick, dropping down into the town before driving around Lake Derwentwater, then on to the Borrowdale Road. Lillian wriggled like an impatient child in her seat.

'Oh, I just can't wait to get there, Robbie.'

It was on their approach to Rosthwaite that Robbie thought he ought to prepare Lillian for the changes she would see once they reached the Dobb End stable. Keeping his eyes on the narrow twisting roads, he said, 'I have to warn you, darling, that the horses are not as fit as they were when you left them.'

'Sal mentioned that to me when she visited,' Lillian replied. 'I was so upset, Robbie.'

'They were left in the charge of a stable lad who, well, to be blunt, neglected them,' Robbie told her. 'It all happened over the few months when I was going back and forth to Lancaster visiting Harriet. Because of the circumstances I was barely working at all, but when I did have a bit of free time, I drove over to see how the shires were and, to be honest, I got a terrible shock when I saw the state of them.' Seeing her anguished expression, he quickly added, 'I took the matter in hand, threatened the lad with a good thrashing if he didn't do his job properly, but the poor things have had a tough time,' he concluded.

When they arrived at the farm, Robbie helped Lillian out of the Jeep and, linking her arm in his, he led her to the paddock, where he had turned the horses out that morning. Hearing the sound of the Jeep pulling up, all three animals trotted to the fence, tossing their heads and eagerly awaiting Robbie's arrival. What none of them could possibly have expected was that Lillian would be with him. Smelling her from a distance, they began to neigh shrilly and impatiently pawed the ground. Seeing Major, Daisy and darling Lilibet, with the sunlight dappling their skinny shanks and lack-lustre manes, brought a rush of tears to Lillian's eyes; hurrying towards them, she extended her hand and, whispering softly, almost crooning, she stroked each in turn. Fondling their manes, running her hand along their backs, she felt the changes in the horses' bodies as well as saw them.

'You poor, poor darlings,' she whispered, as she tickled their ears and stroked their velvet-smooth muzzles. 'I should never have left you; I've missed you so much.'

With Daisy and Major on either side of her, nuzzling her arm and blowing into her hair, Lillian could see that

Lilibet was looking a bit left out. 'Come on, poppet, I love you too,' she beckoned. In a rush of enthusiasm Lilibet bounded forward to be at Lillian's side, but in doing so the gangly foal bumped hard into Lillian's burgeoning tummy.

'Ouch,' Lillian gasped.

'Are you all right, dear?' Robbie cried.

'Fine,' Lillian assured him, then, turning her attention to Lilibet, she gave her the cuddle she had been waiting for.

Leaving Lillian for ten minutes, Robbie went to fill up the horses' water buckets and collect a bundle of hay for them to enjoy in the paddock. After distributing the hay between the horses, he turned to see Lillian bent over.

'Darling, what is it?' he cried, as he hurried towards her.

'I've got really sharp shooting pains in the base of my back,' she explained, as a sweat broke out on her brow.

'Show me exactly where?'

'Right here,' she said, guiding his hand down to the base of her back.

'Let's get you indoors,' he said, as he led her to the tack room, where he quickly fetched her a glass of water.

'The pains are in my tummy too,' Lillian groaned as she bent over to clutch her belly. 'Is there anywhere I can lie down?'

Though the farmhouse was only across the yard, Robbie knew that three women shared one bedroom. Keen she should have some privacy, he said, 'The hayloft is close by. I've got a couple of clean blankets in the Jeep, and I could settle you there, if you didn't mind?' he suggested cautiously.

Relieved, Lillian instantly agreed. 'Yes, that's all right.'

'Wait here – I'll go and get the blankets,' he quickly said.

Running to the Jeep, Robbie quelled the panic rising within him. 'You've delivered sheep, puppies, kittens, calves and foals – you can certainly deliver a baby,' he firmly told himself, but emotions overrode practicalities. 'But this is *my* child, my baby – what if I make a mistake, what if I get it wrong?'

Grabbing the blankets, he ran back to the stable, where he settled Lillian gently down on the blankets laid out on the floor of the hayloft.

'Ahhh,' Lillian sighed as she felt her body relax a little. 'This is much better.'

Briefly leaving her, Robbie dashed back to the tack room and phoned the local doctor. He wasn't home, so he left an urgent message with his housekeeper; then, picking up his medical bag, he returned to Lillian, propped up against a hay bale, grimacing in pain. Wide-eyed, she stared at him. 'It's started, hasn't it?'

'Yes, it's started,' he answered calmly. 'I've phoned the doctor in Rosthwaite, but we can manage just fine for the time being. Are you quite sure you're all right here, sweetheart?' he asked.

Lillian smiled tenderly. 'This is where our baby was conceived,' she replied. 'It isn't a bad place for it to be born either.'

Kneeling down beside her, Robbie wiped her long hair off her pale face. Filled with turbulent emotions, he couldn't stop himself from saying what he'd been longing to say all day.

'I love you so much, dearest Lil. I'll take care of you, don't worry.'

Lillian responded with a loud yelp. 'OWWW!'

'The contractions are getting closer together, which is unusual for a first baby,' Robbie said, as he checked his watch, waiting to see how long the contraction would last. 'You're in the early stages still,' he told her. 'But they will speed up, so in between your contractions you must try to conserve your strength. I'll help you with your breathing.'

Remembering how wonderfully patient and instinctive he had been with Daisy during her labour, Lillian was filled with confidence. She knew she couldn't have been in safer hands. As the contractions increased, Lillian's waters broke. Not wanting to leave her lying in wet clothes, Robbie hurried into the farmhouse, where he spotted a clean nightdress drying on the wooden maiden suspended over the Aga. Snatching it up, he returned to the hayloft.

'I don't know who this nightdress belongs to,' he confessed.

'From the size of it,' Lillian said, smiling as the gown swamped her, 'I think it's Mo's.'

'I need you to lie back now, sweetheart, so I can examine you,' Robbie instructed.

'Everything is fine,' he assured her, though he didn't add that, from the look of things, there was still a long way to go.

As the afternoon wore on, Lillian began to get tired; the contractions were stronger and more frequent, but she didn't appear to be making much progress. Afraid that he would actually have to help the baby out, Robbie telephoned the doctor again. When he came back, he found Sal by Lillian's side.

'I saw the Jeep and came looking for you but found Lil instead,' Sal explained.

Relieved to have company, Robbie gave her a welcoming smile. Seeing his anxious face, Sal suggested he take a break and make himself a cup of tea while she stayed with Lillian. When they were alone, Lillian gave her friend a knowing look. 'I know you told him.'

Sal didn't flinch from the truth. 'I'm sorry for breaking my promise, but I felt it was the right thing to do.'

Lillian smiled. 'It was, and I'm grateful that you did.'

They got no further: a contraction gripped Lillian, who arched her back to ride it out. Clutching Sal's hand, she flopped back as the pain eased away and she could breathe evenly again. The afternoon seemed endless, and the increasing contractions were beginning to concern Robbie.

'I'm worried the baby's stuck,' he whispered to Sal, who went pale. 'I'm going to try to turn it. I'll need clean towels, a lot, and hot water – can you go and quickly get them for me?'

Sal nodded and ran off to do as instructed; meanwhile weary Lillian was rolling in constant pain.

'Darling,' Robbie whispered, 'when Sal comes back, I want you to lie as still as you can in between your contractions. It's really important, as I'm going to try to turn the baby.'

Arranging clean towels under Lillian, Robbie carefully

washed his hands in hot soapy water and, after waiting for another contraction to pass, he spent several minutes expertly manipulating Lillian's taut tummy until he was happy with the baby's position. With expert skill he turned the baby and, to his intense relief, it then took only another twenty minutes or so for the baby to make its appearance. He waited for the baby to take its first breath and, when it did with a loud cry, colour and life rushed into its face.

'*A girl!*' he cried, '*A girl!*' Tears of joy and relief rolled unchecked down his cheeks.

Propping herself up on her elbows, Lillian cried too, overcome with emotion. 'Is she all right?'

It was at this point that the doctor arrived.

While the doctor was attending to Lillian and the new-born, Robbie, euphoric but completely exhausted, stood puffing on his pipe in the stable yard while Sal (in shock) smoked one Woodbine after another in rapid succession.

'Oh, my God,' she murmured. 'I've never experienced anything like that in the whole of my life.'

After thanking Sal for all her help, Robbie hurried back to the doctor, who had washed and wrapped the new-born in a clean towel. Settling the baby in Lillian's arms, he congratulated Robbie on a difficult delivery.

'You did well,' he said wryly, before he left the new mother in peace.

Gazing into her daughter's milky-blue eyes, Lillian felt such a surge of unconditional love that she was completely engulfed.

'She's so beautiful,' she whispered, as she gently felt the silky texture of her baby's downy hair.

'She's perfect,' Robbie agreed; then, looking around the hayloft, he added, 'We can't stay here all night: you and our little girl need a nice warm bed.'

Lillian looked aghast. 'We can't drive all the way back to Mary Vale now!'

Kissing his daughter's pearly-pink fingernails, Robbie smiled. 'Of course not, my darling . . . I'm taking you home.'

Utterly exhausted, Lillian hardly comprehended his words. 'Home?'

'Darling Lillian, I can't hold back my feelings, not now, after bringing our daughter into the world. Please, will you marry me and stay with me forever?' Robbie begged.

Too weak to speak, Lillian could only nod, as tears of pure joy rolled down her pale cheeks.

42. All Change

When Lillian didn't return by supper-time, Ada chastised herself.

'I knew I shouldn't have let her go,' she exclaimed.

'I thought she was just going for a day out.'

'She was,' Ada agreed. 'But she's still not back and it's gone seven o'clock.' Pausing to think, she added, 'Her boyfriend must have a phone – he's a vet, vets always have phones.'

Unfortunately, it turned out Robbie had never left his phone number with the Home.

'Maybe our local vet will have it,' Matron suggested. 'Let's give him a ring and find out.'

The Grange vet did, in fact, have Robbie's number, but when Ada dialled it, she got no reply.

'I can't go home until I know that Lillian's safe,' Ada insisted when Matron urged her to leave.

Fortunately for weary Ada, Robbie phoned the Home about an hour later to update them.

'Where is Lillian now?' Ada gasped.

'At home with me, tucked up in bed with our baby,' he added proudly.

Smiling with relief, Ada updated Matron. 'Thank goodness for that – at least I can rest easy now that I know she's safe,' Ada said, as she reached for her cape.

'With all the worry about Lillian, you haven't forgotten that tomorrow is Renee's last day?' Matron reminded her.

Ada clapped a hand to her mouth. 'I had forgotten,' she cried. 'Don't worry, I'll have it at the forefront of my mind when I start my shift tomorrow morning.'

'Heavens!' Matron exclaimed. 'There have been a lot of comings and goings recently.'

Ada smiled and shrugged.

'That's Mary Vale for you – never a dull moment.'

Back at home, Jamie had put Catherine to bed.

'We've been playing outside, first in the garden, then when it got really hot, we went paddling in the beck. Catherine loved it, she even gave her teddy a bath!' he told his tired wife, as they ate a late supper of sausage, beans and mashed potatoes.

'Let's go into the garden where it's cooler,' Ada urged. 'It's been so hot all day, I feel like I've been cooped up indoors for most of it.'

In their pretty cottage garden, which still held the sweltering heat of the long August day, they inhaled the intense fragrance of blossoming honeysuckle and white jasmine, combined with the heady smell of stocks and tall lilies. Sitting on the bench, with her head on her husband's shoulder, Ada sighed. 'Oh, this is nice.'

In contented silence they watched the first stars prick the navy-blue night sky, where a new moon, as pearly-white as a baby's fingernail, sailed out from behind the clouds, shedding silvery light on to the nearby woods in which nightingales called back and forth to one another.

357

Ada was the first to speak. 'I still can't get over Robbie's safely delivering her baby.'

'Well, he is a vet after all,' Jamie pointed out.

'He's taken mother and baby back home with him for safekeeping,' Ada said, smiling. 'Don't you think that's sweet?'

'I'd do exactly the same thing if it were me,' Jamie agreed. 'So Lillian might not come back to Mary Vale?'

'I certainly wouldn't if I were her. I mean, why would she go to all the trouble of coming back here, only to put her baby in the nursery, when she could be living in the home of the man she loves?' Dog-tired but reluctant to leave the lovely evening light, Ada reminded her husband of Renee's imminent departure.

Lighting up a Capstan cigarette, Jamie said, 'She's certainly a lot more motivated these days. I suspect she's off the booze.'

'Pity she can't stay on now that she's a reformed woman,' Ada murmured.

'After all that we've been through,' he cried. 'Are you mad, darling?'

'Better the devil you know than the one you don't,' Ada answered.

When Ada arrived for her shift the following morning, Matron beckoned her on to the ward. 'I've just spoken to Lillian on the phone,' Matron exclaimed. 'She wanted to assure us all that she is absolutely fine.'

'Oh, that's marvellous. Did she talk about the birth?' Ada asked.

'She said it was long, but Robbie knew exactly what to do, as he had delivered so many animals in the past.' Matron chuckled. 'I'm not sure how foals and sheep compare to a human baby, but I suppose in the end it's all the same process.'

'Well, I'm thrilled everything is all right,' Ada responded. 'But I do think that when Lillian is on her feet again, she and her baby should come back here for a final check-up, so she can be officially signed off, if that's what she wants.'

Matron nodded. 'I quite agree. Let's give her some time alone with her new family, but for now we have other, more immediate things to attend to. Would you mind being in the office when I talk to Renee later this morning?'

'No, of course not,' Ada replied. 'Though, to be honest, I am dreading it.'

Matron raised her eyes as if to say, 'Me too.'

In the end Renee was actually quite gracious.

'I've arranged for a friend to pick me up; we're planning to take a brief holiday in Scotland before I return to London.'

'Have you any plans for future work?' Matron asked cautiously.

'I'm going to give it some thought while I'm away,' Renee replied. 'And, by the way, just for the record,' Renee said, as she rose to go, 'I have completely stopped drinking. I realize now that nursing is not a profession where you can mix business with pleasure.' Standing upright, Renee said, 'I wouldn't say it was easy, but it was worth it.'

*

Later that day, as Ada was walking with Catherine (now a rebellious two-year old who refused point-blank to go in her pram) along the farm track, she spotted Renee standing by a smart car. A young man, busy loading suitcases into the boot, exchanged some remark with Renee, who threw back her head and laughed. Seeing her former colleague happier and more relaxed than she had been in months, Ada silently wished her luck.

'Mama, Mama,' Catherine called out. 'Chuck!'

Ada turned to see the farmer's cheeky cockerel, clucking proprietarily, strutting ahead of them, lord of all he surveyed. When she turned back again, Renee was gone.

43. Making Plans

Robbie and Lillian named their baby daughter Rosemary. The three of them together were like a fairy-tale family; when Robbie wasn't kissing his daughter, he was hugging Lillian, and when she wasn't kissing Robbie, she was cradling her baby.

'It seems wrong to be so happy,' Lillian said, as she pushed sweetly sleeping Rosemary in her brand-new sparkling Silver Cross pram that Robbie (the besotted indulgent father) had bought, along with cosy bedding, terry-towelling nappies, little white cotton nighties, shawls, bootees, and even a tiny lace bonnet threaded with pink ribbon.

'I agree,' Robbie replied. 'Especially when I thought I would never be happy again.'

Lillian stopped to ask him the guilty question that was forever whirling around in her thoughts. 'What do you think people say about us, living together as we are now?'

Knowing exactly what was on her mind, Robbie's eyes met hers. 'Don't think I haven't thought the same thing. Valley folk have got to know you, Lil, they've taken you in. Plus it's wartime – if ever there were a time to grab happiness while you can, this has got to be it. With luck, time will heal the rest,' he smiled, adding, 'Believe me, there's always another bigger newer drama unfolding in the valley that will take gossips' minds off me and you too.'

With his free hand Robbie pressed Lillian to his side. He recalled lying in bed with her that morning, when he hadn't been able to stop himself from running his hands over her small body, which was still strong and muscular from her Land Girl labours. Though her breasts were bigger and her tummy rounder these days, these changes made her, if it were possible, even more beautiful to him.

'Dearest Lil, I know you've been erring on the side of caution, but it really is time to start thinking about setting a wedding date – a small, intimate affair, just us, the vicar and a few friends.'

'But first we have to take Rosemary to Mary Vale,' Lillian reminded him. 'I promised Sister Ada on the phone that I would visit with the baby, whom she's longing to see.'

'She deserves that,' Robbie said, smiling, 'after all we put her through on the day Rosemary was born.'

Just thinking how skilfully Robbie had delivered their child into the world made Lillian's honey-brown eyes sparkle with pride.

'You were so calm,' she told him.

'And you were so brave,' he replied.

'And Sal was *so* terrified. I really thought she would faint clean away when Rosemary finally appeared,' Lillian joked.

Following the course of the full bubbling beck that ran alongside the lane, Lillian and Robbie, laughing and chatting all the way, walked to the village of Rosthwaite, where Lillian immediately quickened her pace.

'Be quick, darling,' she impatiently begged.

Knowing that the bottom of the pram was loaded with carrots, Robbie threw her a teasing smile. 'What's the rush?'

In answer came the combined shrill neighing of three very impatient shire horses running the length of their paddock.

Lillian nimbly ran ahead of Robbie in order to greet the horses. Leaping over the farm gate, she gave a soft whistle; then, holding out her hands, she embraced each in turn.

After putting the break on the pram, Robbie leant over the gate to help Lillian feed them the carrots. 'Wait your turn, Lilibet,' he chuckled, as the foal, who now had the same pretty silver markings as her mother, pushed and jostled for more.

Stroking their silky manes that lifted in the warm breeze, Lillian glowed with pleasure at the sight of her beloved horses, who looked happier, healthier and certainly smarter since her return to the valley.

'Major isn't as solid in the back quarters as he was when I was in charge,' she observed. 'God only knows what that idle lad fed the poor beasts,' she fumed. She was still livid with the boy who had neglected his charges.

'Don't worry, darling, with you back in the saddle, the three of them will be the size of gable ends in no time,' Robbie teased. 'But be aware,' he said in a mock strict voice, 'a woman who has only recently had a baby and is still breast-feeding can only do so much.'

Turning her doting attention to Daisy, Lillian stroked the gentle mare's neck and ears. 'Lovely lady,' she whispered. 'It's fun being a mum, isn't it?' she giggled.

In answer Daisy turned around to nip her cheeky foal, who was trying to push her mother out of the way so she could have all of Lillian's attention.

'It will be much easier when they're stabled next to us at home,' Lillian said. 'I'll be able to wave to them from my bedroom window,' she laughed.

'Let's get their stable built before you start inviting them into the house for tea,' Robbie joked. 'Though you're right, love, it will be far more convenient to have them grazing close to home and nice for Rosemary too,' he added with an indulgent smile. 'She'll probably want her own little pony soon.'

Laying her head against Major's dark sturdy neck, Lillian inhaled the strong musky smell of his warm body.

'I never want them out of my sight again,' she declared passionately. 'I understand they're needed for the war effort and they'll have to continue to work for the farm agent, but I'll make sure I keep an eye on what they're doing and with whom; I'll make sure they're never mistreated again!' she vowed. 'And when they come to retirement age, hopefully, I'll be able to buy them and we can all live together, side by side, for the rest of our lives,' she concluded happily.

'Lucky that you already own Lilibet,' Robbie said, grinning at her.

Lillian threw him a grateful smile. 'Thanks to you, darling, the best wedding present a husband-to-be could give his bride.'

'It was a complete stroke of luck finding out that the agent was planning to sell Lilibet,' Robbie added. 'Can you imagine coming down here one morning only to find her gone?'

'I'd have had a fit and Daisy would have been heartbroken,' Lillian cried.

Seeing his daughter start to stir in her pram, doting Robbie urged Lillian, 'We need to get home, Lil, unless you fancy feeding your baby in the paddock with the horses?'

Climbing back over the gate, Lillian giggled. 'After giving birth in a hayloft, I wouldn't give two hoots about breast-feeding in a field.'

After helping Lillian over the gate, Robbie lifted her into his arms and kissed her.

'I thought you might say that,' he teased. 'You wild and wonderful woman!'

Their final visit to Mary Vale was hectic but great fun. First, they had to load Rosemary into the Jeep, along with all the baby paraphernalia that went with transporting a new-born. Then there was the drive there, with Robbie trying to avoid all the potholes in order not to disturb his slumbering daughter. And, finally, the great excitement of their arrival brought most of the residents and half the staff on to the drive in order to catch their first glimpse of Lillian's tiny baby.

'Ooh, she's gorgeous.'

'The spit of her lovely mum!'

'You didn't really have her in a hayloft, did you?'

'You look marvellous, the picture of health.'

Showered by compliments and congratulations, Lillian was touched by the residents' warm words and affection. It brought back a stream of memories of her time in the Home: some awful ones, like when she was struggling with her misery at leaving Robbie and the horses, and wondering what she would do once her baby was born;

others happier, like working with Stella in the kitchen and their long walks out on the marsh in the unforgettable summer that they had shared together. She was delighted when Ada handed her a letter from her friend.

'It only arrived this week,' Ada told her.

Sitting on a bench in the garden that was now beginning to show its first soft autumn colours, Lillian eagerly read the letter while she breast-fed her baby. Stella's happiness and excitement bubbled out of the pages as she described her new life down South.

Hi Lillian,

We've finally settled into our new life at Mildenhall, where Bill's working on the base, while Ryder and I enjoy our lovely family bungalow that's situated beside Thetford Forest. We wake up to bird-song every morning, owls hoot at night, and when Ryder starts to crawl, he'll have a big garden to play in. The journey down to the South was hectic, with Ryder feeding every four hours in hot, packed trains, but somehow we managed.

Over the last few weeks Bill confessed that he was, in fact, relieved that we have this time together in Mildenhall, as he was worried about introducing me too quickly to his family, particularly his brother, Pete. It turns out that Bill entrusted Pete to post the letters he wrote to me when he was having treatment in the Seattle hospital. None of Bill's many letters ever arrived so, determined to get to the bottom of the mystery, Bill wrote and asked Pete point-blank what he had done with them. Cornered, Pete admitted he had dumped them all in a rubbish bin. He said he didn't want his brother marrying a money-grabbing Limey! It's lucky that Bill and Pete are half a world apart, otherwise there would have been an enormous fight. As it is, I suspect it will take Bill a long time to trust Pete again. It was a pretty nasty thing to do. It makes me feel relieved that we're starting our married life in England and not in America, which is where we'll travel to once the war's over. At the rate things are going right now, with the US troops mounting the Siegfried Line campaign in western Germany, and Operation Market Garden under way, we could be celebrating victory very soon. What a blessing it will be to bring our babies up in peacetime.

My other news is that Bill's amputated leg is healing well, and he's already being considered for a prosthesis, which is simply marvellous. Ryder grows big and strong, I love him more with every passing day, and Bill is the most wonderful father in the world. We are so lucky to have each other, sometimes I have to pinch myself to believe my luck.

You must have had your own baby by now. I hope all went well for you, Lil? Please keep in touch: we went through so much together, and I would hate to lose contact with you. Maybe one day, when this war is over, and it looks like it soon might be (please God), we can meet up and swap stories of our lives as conscripted women during the war, who came to be working in a kitchen alongside nuns.

Lots of love and best of luck,
Stella

Touched by Stella's letter, Lillian carefully folded it before she changed breasts so Rosemary could continue to feed. Seeing Robbie approaching with a welcome cup of tea, she smiled at him.

'It must be odd for you to be back here,' he said, as he settled down beside her.

'Very odd,' she admitted. 'I never thought I'd leave here with you by my side and a baby in my arms to keep,' she murmured, snuggling close to his warm, strong body.

'It's a nice place,' he observed. 'The staff clearly care for their patients and their babies too.'

'They're a great team,' Lillian said unconditionally. 'Especially Sister Ada and her husband. He's the doctor who examined me when we arrived this morning,' she explained. 'He said I was in tip-top health and the baby is too,' she added proudly.

Seeing his daughter getting fidgety, Robbie held out his hands to take her. 'May I hold her?' he asked.

Handing the baby over, Lillian buttoned up her dress, then sat back and watched Robbie cradle his daughter in his arms.

'She's so perfect,' he murmured, as he kissed her little fingers. 'I love her to distraction.'

Before they set off for home, Lillian and Robbie asked Ada if she and her family would attend their wedding. A delighted Ada immediately accepted. 'Catherine will be thrilled too,' she said.

'She can be my little flower girl, if she'd like that?' Lillian suggested. 'It will be a quiet affair,' she said, lowering her voice. 'It would be disrespectful to have a big do in the circumstances.'

'We'd be delighted to join you,' Ada promised. 'See you on your wedding day,' she cried, as she waved the happy couple and their baby off.

44. A Valley Wedding

On the morning of Robbie and Lillian's wedding day, it wasn't the bride who woke up in a flat spin but the groom. Throwing off the bed-clothes, Robbie sat bolt upright on his side of the bed and took several deep breaths.

'Darling,' he eventually blurted out. 'Are you quite sure you want to marry me?'

The sleeping Lillian, who had been up half the night feeding Rosemary, was lost to the world. When Robbie turned to her, his tense expression melted into one of pure and abject love. His darling, his very-soon-to-be wife, was fast asleep on her side, curled up like a child, with her long, light-brown hair tumbled around her small, heart-shaped face. As he stared at Lillian, his heart contracted: she had been through so much and given him so much, culminating in the best gift of all, a child. After Timmy died, Robbie never thought that he would hold a child of his own in his arms again, but here was sweet Rosemary, in a little crib in a corner of the room, a daughter to cherish and glory in as she grew up. He simply didn't deserve this rich harvest of joy. Bowing his head, Robbie prayed that Harriet, poor tormented woman that she had become, would be at peace with their son and forgive him for seizing happiness and a new life.

Lillian stirred and woke up to find Robbie with his hands clasped and his eyes closed.

'Darling, what is it?' she blearily asked.

Opening his eyes, Robbie stroked her warm cheek. 'I'm just happy,' he whispered. 'And a bit overwhelmed. Lil, sweetheart,' he started hesitantly. 'Are you sure you want to marry me? I really would understand if you wanted to change your mind. If you wanted a younger man more worthy of you.'

Before he said another word, Lillian pulled him down on to her naked body.

'Robbie Allen, will you please shut up? I don't want another man, younger or older, taller or smaller, fatter or thinner, richer or poorer. The only man I want is YOU!' Giggling, she wrapped her arms around his neck. 'Now kiss me before I have to see to your daughter.'

While Robbie was organizing Rosemary, Lillian managed to squeeze into one of her pre-pregnancy crêpe tea dresses, a pretty forget-me-not blue number with a blowzy top and pearls buttons down the front. Leaving her hair long and loose, she inspected her happy face in the mirror in the bedroom. Gone were the days of glamour girl Lil, made up to the nines, hair dyed and dressed like a film star. This radiant woman needed no make-up, her honey-brown eyes sparkled with love, her smile was wide, and she glowed with joy. Skipping downstairs in her new black suede sandals that fastened around her narrow ankles, she was surprised not to find Robbie in the hall.

'Hello there, where are you?' she called.

'Out here,' he replied from the driveway.

Expecting to find Robbie waiting in the Jeep with Rosemary, Lillian stepped outside to get the shock of her life. Robbie was standing before her holding on to Major and Daisy, who were harnessed to a pretty little open-topped carriage decorated with red, white and blue ribbons. Neighing excitedly at the sight of their beloved mistress, the two shires, and Lilibet tied securely by a lead rope to the rear of the decorated carriage, tossed their heads and pawed the ground.

'Robbie?' Lillian started but words failed her. Hurrying forward to pet the horses, she saw Rosemary, snugly wrapped in a shawl, settled in a little straw basket on the passenger seat. 'How did you manage all of this?' she gasped.

'It was nothing short of a route march, I can tell you,' Robbie laughed as he spoke. 'I paid that idle lad at the stable to bring the horses over here first thing this morning, groomed and fed, then, while you were making yourself beautiful, I popped the little one into a basket and harnessed the horses to the carriage I borrowed, which I secretly decorated last night with coloured ribbons. Piece of cake,' he joked as he threw up his arms. 'We couldn't get married without our extended family, could we, darling?'

'It's the very best present you could give me,' Lillian cried, as she leapt into the carriage and placed Rosemary's cosy basket on her knees. Grinning, Robbie, in the driver's seat, twitched the reins and the wedding party set off for Rosthwaite village just down the road.

*

Mo, Pat and Sal had forgone their dungarees and instead, dressed in their best and wearing flowers in their hair, were waiting for the bride and groom along with several friends from the valley, plus Ada, Jamie and Catherine, who had driven up from Grange that morning, and Lillian's parents, who had arrived early from Blackpool. Wearing a pink party frock, Catherine excitedly hopped from foot to foot, and when she saw the horses approaching jingling their shiny harnesses she squeaked in delight.

'CLIP-CLOP! CLIP-CLOP!'

Seeing the small crowd awaiting their arrival, Major and Daisy put on a great show. Tossing their heads, they drew to a halt when Robbie pulled on their reins; then, standing tall and strong, with the slanting sun gleaming on Major's ebony-dark coat and Daisy's bright contrasting silver mane, they waited patiently as the bridal party stepped down.

'Pretty, pretty horses,' Catherine cried, as she walked closer to admire them.

The stable lad had been paid half a crown to supervise the horses while they were in church.

'Take good care of them,' Lillian instructed with a glint in her eye.

'Aye, missis.'

When the vicar appeared, the bride and groom led the procession into the tiny slate-built chapel with the guests following behind them, Ada bearing Rosemary in her arms. After Robbie and Lillian had exchanged rings and vows, man and wife emerged into the sunshine to showers of rose petals. Photographs that would decorate their family sideboard for decades to come were taken of

Robbie, Lillian and Rosemary, accompanied by the handsome shires and pretty Lilibet, who completely stole the show that gloriously happy day.

After the wedding, the newly married couple led their guests to the Scafell Hotel, where they were served good local ale, egg-and-cress sandwiches and a wartime version of wedding cake (with no eggs) in the hotel grounds. All too soon the afternoon celebrations came to an end and one by one the guests, after passing on their best wishes, drifted away. When it came to saying farewell to Ada, Lillian thanked her from the bottom of her heart for all the professional care she had received while she was a resident in the Home.

'You were so kind to me, to us all, in fact,' Lillian said gratefully. 'And Dr Jamie too. It was the hardest decision of my life to book myself into Mary Vale, but in retrospect I think it was the wisest.'

Jamie laughed as he replied, 'It was your husband who did all the hard work in the end. I didn't have a hand in your delivery, but I'm glad you were happy in our care.'

'I don't think I've ever been as terrified in my entire life,' Robbie confessed. 'Give me a horse or a cow any time,' he joked.

'Each to his own,' Jamie joked back. 'I'll stick with humans.'

After waving Ada and her family off, Lillian bid her Land Girl chums a fond farewell. 'I'll come and help you with the shires whenever I can,' she promised.

'Don't be daft,' Sal cried. 'You've got a family to take care of now.'

'You keep forgetting, Sal – the horses *are* my family,' Lillian reminded her.

Trotting home in the carriage, with the sun sinking over the fells, Lillian cradled her baby in the curve of her arm, leaning her head against her husband's shoulder. With a heart brimming with gratitude, she murmured, 'Robbie, we should thank God for this wonderful day.'

'Our wedding day,' Robbie answered with an emotional catch in his deep voice.

Tenderly wrapping the warm shawl more closely around her sweetly sleeping daughter, Lillian whispered, 'The happiest day of my life.'

Leaning over to kiss the top of her head, Robbie smiled. 'Just one of many, *many* more to come,' he promised.

Epilogue

Another couple, also driving home, were enjoying the beauty of the fells and valleys around them. With Catherine fast asleep on the back seat, worn out by playing with Lilibet, Ada reflected on the summer they had spent together.

'It's been a summer of many surprises,' she said. 'All the trouble we had with Renee, then poor Sister Mary Paul losing, then regaining, her sight, followed by Stella's American romance and now Lillian's wedding.'

Jamie chuckled. 'One thing's for sure, you never know what's coming next at Mary Vale.'

'Well, there is one thing that I *do* know is coming next.'

'Don't tell me – Matron's retiring?' Jamie teased.

'No, it's what's coming next for *us*.'

Concentrating on taking a steep bend, a preoccupied Jamie said, 'What about us?'

'Pull over, darling,' Ada suggested.

Parking the car by the roadside, which edged a forest loud with the call of roosting songbirds serenading each other to sleep, Jamie anxiously turned to his wife. 'Ada, what's going on?' he asked.

Smiling, Ada reached up to kiss him. 'I'm pregnant,' she said.

'WHAT?' he spluttered. 'Are you sure?'

Taking his good hand, Ada ran it over her tummy. 'I'm a midwife,' she replied. 'I'm quite, *quite* sure.'

Pulling Ada into his arms, Jamie wept for joy. 'A baby, another baby!'

'A baby, please God, born in peacetime,' Ada added with tears of hope in her blue eyes.

Acknowledgements

I couldn't have completed this book without the professional expertise of Dr Aditi Vedi, Consultant Paediatric Oncologist at Addenbrooke's Hospital, Cambridge. In her sunny garden, surrounded by her lovely babies Aditi patiently talked me through and advised on the many medical issues I address in *A Mother's Love*, paying special attention to medical conditions at the time of the Second World War. I'll be forever grateful to you, Aditi. I'd like to thank Selwyn Image (Cambridge) for cups of tea and glasses of wine that always accompanied my visits to pick his brains on anything to do with the war; from rationing to the North Atlantic Blockade, Bomber Command, American airbases and Pearl Harbor, Selwyn always had the answer. You're a star, Selwyn. Particular thanks to Donna Poppy, my copy-editor at Penguin; thank you, Donna, for your amazing memory and meticulous eye for detail. I am so lucky to have you! For my wonderful editorial team at Penguin Random House I have nothing but praise and respect – Rebecca Hilsdon and Clare Bowron, you are not simply my editors, you are friends who I trust and admire. Long may this lovely relationship that we three share last. Finally, with a full heart I want to thank all the millions of conscripted women who fought for their country during the Second World War, and all wars in fact. This army of women, like Lillian, Stella and Ada who I write about in this book, turned the world upside down with their strength and determination; they are a ceaseless inspiration to me. God bless them all, living and dead.

A Daisy Styles Original Recipe

Traditional Lancashire Parkin

Nothing beats a traditional Lancashire parkin – a rich sticky cake that's great to finish off a teatime meal with the family.

We used to take thick sticky wedges on picnics and eat them sitting on the moors with skylarks singing overhead. Happy days!

Makes 20 slices

INGREDIENTS

225g fine/medium oatmeal
225g self-raising flour
225g brown sugar
pinch of salt
½ teaspoon mixed spice
1 tablespoon ground ginger

225g butter or margarine
125g black treacle
125g golden syrup
2 eggs
50ml milk

TO MAKE

1. Preheat the oven to 150–170°C/gas 2–3.

2. Put the oatmeal, flour, sugar, salt, mixed spice and ground ginger in a bowl and rub in the fat.

3. Add the treacle, golden syrup, eggs and milk.

4. Mix the heavy mixture well.

5. Place in a small roasting tin lined with greaseproof paper.

6. Bake for 1 to 1½ hours.

7. Keep the parkin in the roasting tin for several days before cutting into thick wedges.

8. Store in a tin until ready to serve – enjoy!

READ ON FOR A SNEAK PEAK
OF DAISY STYLES'S NEW NOVEL

CHRISTMAS
with the
MIDWIVES

COMING 2022

1. Nurse Libby Godburgh

Knowing that she had a full day ahead of her, Libby was out of the family farmhouse just after dawn. With her long, Titian golden-red hair flying around her sweet, oval-shaped face, dominated by big violet blue eyes that could drift from dreamy to thoughtful in a matter of seconds, Libby stopped in her tracks when she saw her father at the back door with his tall, muscular bulk. Clearly he had been up even earlier than her.

'Dad,' she exclaimed with pleasure.

'I wanted to say goodbye, pet,' he said with a tender smile. 'I'll be thinking of thee, little lass.' A catch in his husky voice, he held his arms out wide to her. 'Come and give thee owd dad a big hug.'

Running into his embrace, Libby nestled against his broad body which always smelt of sheep, pipe tobacco and engine oil.

'I'll write, Dad,' she murmured.

'Aye, you'd better,' he chuckled, 'or your Mam will raise hell.'

Exchanging a conspiratorial smile, Libby nodded. Nobody knew better than the pair of them how uppity Mrs Godburgh could get if she felt neglected.

'I'd best be off to market; sheep are loaded up and restless with it. We're proper proud of you, our lass,'

Mr Godburgh said as he gave his daughter a final hug and a flying kiss. 'Take care of theeself, my pet.'

After watching her father drive the farm truck away, loaded with yearlings to sell at Kendal market, Libby ran across the farmyard to the stable block located next to the paddock, which was neatly hedged-in by ancient drystone walls. When her fifteen-hand silver-grey fell pony heard her steps ringing out on the worn flag floor, he popped his head over the stable door and neighed shrilly at his mistress.

'Morning, sweetie,' Libby murmured fondly as she stroked her beloved pony's long silky mane. 'Big day today,' she said while she slipped an old leather halter over Snowball's neck then walked him across the farmyard to the paddock, tying him to a post and giving him a net of fresh hay, which he immediately tugged and nibbled at.

Once Snowball was contentedly settled, Libby set about grooming him for the journey south. After using a curry comb to loosen the dirt in his coat, Libby vigorously brushed him down with a dandy brush, before applying regular sweeping strokes with a soft body brush. The regular rhythm of the brush across the pony's silvery bright rump, neck, chest and withers gradually calmed Libby's nerves. Feeling his mistress relaxing against him, Snowball nuzzled his velvety nose against her flat, muscular tummy.

'We're going to a new home today,' she whispered. 'We're going to Mary Vale.'

Just saying the words made Libby's pulse race. 'Mary Vale,' she repeated the name softly.

Libby would never forget her first sight of the Home for unmarried mothers and their babies, set on a high rocky trajectory overlooking the vast majestic vista of Morecambe Bay. It was a beautiful, old red-brick house, and at this time of the year covered in riotous Virginia creeper, its vivid autumn-red colours blazing gold and scarlet in the intense afternoon light. The house faced due west with breathtaking views of the turbulent Irish Sea that rolled in alternating shades of silver and grey towards the distant horizon before disappearing in a shimmering haze of iridescent blue. Closer by, a vast sage-green marsh hugged the coastline which was washed by the incoming tide twice a day. On the afternoon of Libby's memorable interview for a midwife vacancy, she had stood transfixed watching the many squawking, squabbling seabirds wading in the shallows of the marsh: red shanks, oyster catchers, sandpipers, dunlins and piping curlews waiting expectantly for food; and crustaceans, worms and molluscs washed in by the tide.

Quite unlike her usual confident, buoyant self, Libby that afternoon had been a bag of nerves. This was her first real job interview, her first real challenge. Though she had done well throughout her nurse's training course at Lancaster infirmary and excelled on the midwives' course that followed, she had never faced an interview panel who might for all her fine qualifications reject her in favour of somebody with far more experience. Realistically, it had to be said that she didn't have much, apart from the work on the wards and community nursing twice a week, which had formed part of her course.

'Somebody older and more experienced will definitely stand a better chance than me,' she recalled thinking to herself, but then her father's staunch words of support on the morning of her interview came back to her.

'You'll be alreet, lass, just be yourself.'

Approaching Mary Vale's imposing front door Libby had taken deep breaths, then thrown back her slender shoulders and knocked firmly. A plump, smiley-faced nun immediately flung the door open.

'You must be here for the interview?' the young nun said with a such a warm smile that Libby immediately smiled back. 'Come on in, I'm Sister Agnes,' she continued in the same warm vein. 'I'd offer you a cuppa and a few oat cakes, fresh from the oven, but Sister Ada and her husband, Dr Reid, are waiting for you in Matron's office.'

Intrigued Libby said, 'It's unusual these days having a husband and wife team working together on the same premises?'

Sister Agnes positively glowed.

'Yes, for sure. Dr Reid is our resident doctor and Sister Ada is Senior Staff Nurse. They work in shifts so there's always one of them about the place. We're blessed to have them both with us at Mary Vale.'

Following the kindly, chatty nun down a corridor with floors so highly polished the wooden tiles reflected the dust motes floating in the air, Libby was led into an office where the interview panel were assembled. Libby would never forget how warm and welcoming the staff had been when she walked into the room, flushed with nerves. Comfortable though the atmosphere was, the questions the panel threw at Libby were demanding. Had she nursed patients on the post-natal ward suffering from puerperal fever? Yes, she had. Had Libby ever attended the birth of twins with complications? Yes, in the first year of her midwifery training. She managed to answer all the questions as best she could and when given the chance, told them all about her community work in Lancaster too.

By the end of the interview – which was brought to a halt by an urgent call requesting Doctor Reid's presence in the delivery room – Libby's big, violet blue eyes were alight with passion and a small excited smile played around her full mouth.

'Would it be useful for you to know something about the history of Mary Vale, Miss Godburgh?' Matron asked as the interview came to a close.

'Yes, I'd love that,' Libby enthused. 'It's such a beautiful place in a lovely setting.'

'Well it isn't just in its present guise that Mary Vale offers sanctuary to those in need; it has in fact done so for centuries.' As Matron spoke, her face lit up with pride. 'The building stands on the foundations of an ancient Cistercian priory and for over a thousand years, it was a stopping place for pilgrims en route to Furness Abbey. Pilgrims crossing the Irish Sea landed at Heysham, then they were led safely across the bay on donkeys by guides who knew the whereabouts of the treacherous tidal quicksand which claimed many innocent travellers' lives. After being safely delivered to the abbey, they were given food and a bed for the night before they went on their way to Furness early the next morning.'

Pleased to see Libby so enthralled, Staff Nurse Ada, who had the loveliest dark blue eyes, leaned forward. 'We like to think we carry on that great tradition of giving sanctuary to all those in need, especially to the desperate women who arrive here in great distress.'

'Thank God for such a refuge,' Libby said earnestly.

'Just like the Cistercian monks, we never close our doors to anybody.' Matron smiled. 'We're funded by the convent of the Sisters of the Holy Mother, which is right next to us; they in turn are funded by rent they obtain from farmland and property. Believe me, we are by no means a rich foundation. Our burden is eased when we admit self-funding residents; their fee pays for the non-funded residents who are very often homeless and destitute.'

'It would be hard to turn away such women,' Libby said compassionately.

'We don't,' Ada assured her. 'But it does make life hard when we barely make ends meet.'

Picking up on Ada's comment Matron chipped in, 'We depend a lot on the charity and kindness of our local community, who are generous in their gifts of food, and we have our own farm nearby run by Farmer Arkwright, who keeps us well-stocked in milk, some eggs and local cheese, sometimes meat, and an endless supply of fresh vegetables, which he himself grows for our own specific consumption.'

'We don't go hungry!' Ada joked. 'Not with the loving community that we're so grateful for.'

Libby shuffled nervously in her chair. 'Er, would you mind if I asked a question?' she blurted out.

'No, not at all,' Matron said kindly.

'You talk about "community", which I have a great interest in.'

The two women behind the desk turned curious eyes on Libby who by now was on the edge of her chair.

'As I mentioned earlier, I have some experience of community nursing and I have a real passion for it. I saw so many poor pregnant women give birth in awful conditions in Lancaster, in homes barely less than hovels, surrounded by little toddlers in rags crying out for food which their poor mothers couldn't begin to find for them. It was heartbreaking.' Libby paused. 'The fact is those women needed more care and professional help than any of the women I was nursing on the wards – they and their families were virtually on the street. Quite a few died and so did their babies, but some fared better due to our intervention. I love working with women in need and making a difference to their lives,' she explained. 'I was just wondering . . . I hope you don't mind my asking, but is community midwifery ever something that Mary Vale might consider taking on?' She stopped herself, wondering if she'd gone too far, but she could only see warmth and interest in the eyes of the two nurses. Though Libby's question struck home, Matron's response was cautious.

'To be honest, community midwifery is not something we have had the resources for so far but it is certainly not something I would object to. Of course, any changes in our policy are always ultimately determined by our Reverend Mother.'

Not wanting to dash the hopes of such an enthusiastic young midwife, bright-eyed Ada interjected. 'We're a forward-looking team at Mary Vale. I would like to think your experience of community midwifery would interest the staff here, Miss Godburgh.'

Feeling self-conscious and still anxious she might have over-stepped the mark, 'Put her big foot in it', as her mother would have chided, Libby nevertheless couldn't stop herself from speaking her mind.

'Thank you. I suppose I just think that God is telling us something – if they can't come to us then we must go out to them.'

Stunned and touched by Libby's sheer force of will, Matron and Ada stared at each other. Without a word, each knew exactly what the other was thinking – here's a young woman who is more than a nurse: here is a bright, brave Mary Vale crusader! Though touched by the young woman's compassion, Matron again erred on the side of caution.

'It's a worthy idea for serious consideration,' she diplomatically concluded.

Recalling how she had waited tensely over a week to hear back from Mary Vale, Libby vividly remembered the day when the letter from the Home finally dropped on to the farmhouse doormat. Trembling as if it were a bomb about to go off, she had backed away.

'Mam, what if it's a rejection?'

Ever the pragmatist Mrs Godburgh had said, 'Well, lass, there's only one way to find out.' Picking up the letter she handed it to her daughter who resolutely shook her head.

'No, Mam, you read it.'

Hardly daring to breathe, Libby watched her mother tear open the envelope. When she glanced up there was a glow of pride in Mrs Godburgh's eyes.

'You've got the job,' she had announced. 'You start next week, lovie.'

Filled with jubilation and relief, Libby had grabbed her poor mother around the waist and jigged her up and down their flagged kitchen floor until they were both breathless.

'I'm going to Mary Vale,' starry-eyed Libby had announced.

Time had flown in a whirlwind of frantic preparations and now here she was a week later, tacking up and simply raring to go. Suddenly aware that she had been so deep in thought that she had actually stopped grooming Snowball, who was now indignantly blowing into her hair, Libby giggled. Tickling his little pointy ears, she laughingly apologized.

'Sorry sweetheart,' she murmured.

Reaching into her tack box for the hoof pick, Libby methodically cleaned out each of Snowball's hooves in turn, a procedure he liked a lot less than grooming. Just as she was finishing her task, she spotted her mother approaching out of the corner of her eye. Knowing full well that her mother tended to chide rather than confide when she was anxious, Libby braced herself.

Typically, Mrs Godburgh came straight to the point. 'I don't see why you have to do it this way, lass.'

Concentrating hard on brushing out Snowball's long, thick tail that almost swept the ground, Libby respectfully held her tongue.

'You could always go over to Grange in't truck when your dad gets back from't market in Kendal.'

Libby exclaimed so loudly Snowball snorted in surprise. 'Mam, by the time Dad gets back from Kendal the truck will be swilling in sheep muck. We'd have to spend an hour hosing it down before I'd even think of putting Snowball in it.'

Having lost the battle to persuade her daughter to travel in relative style Mrs Godburgh pursed her lips before turning her frustration to another source of contention.

'Why in heaven's name you have to take that pony with you when you're starting a new job beats me. What will folks think when you fetch up looking like a tinker on a pack mule?'

Seeing her dear mother's troubled expression, Libby laid aside the hoof pick and gently drew her into her arms.

'Stop worrying, Mam,' she said softly as she swiped a strand of grey hair off her mother's worn cheek. 'I asked Matron's permission to stable Snowball at Mary Vale. They've been kind enough to sort out grazing and stabling for him with the local farmer. It's not a problem, I promise,' she soothed.

Sighing heavily Mrs Godburgh stared into her daughter's wonderful violet blue eyes that had melted her heart the moment she had given birth to her wild, wilful, passionate daughter. Ever since she was little, Libby had never wavered in her determination to do whatever it was she had set her mind on. Whether it was learning to ride at three years old to competing with her three older brothers in fell-running competitions and fox hunting, Libby never took on a secondary role; in fact, she often excelled over her brothers, particularly in the schoolroom. Libby had a passion for learning. Though immensely proud of her beloved daughter, Mrs Godburgh regularly despaired of Libby's unconventional attitude which was at logger-heads to her own.

'I don't see why you can't travel to your new place of work on the Lancaster train. You could wear that smart navy barathea suit we bought you last Easter and take a suitcase instead of a blinking saddle bag.'

Knowing her mother was not going to stop, devious Libby used decoy tactics.

'Could you pack a few butties for the journey, Mam?'

Alert to the soothing, practical task of nurturing, Mrs Godburgh jumped at the opportunity to busy herself.

'Cheese and pickle or spam?'

'Cheese, please,' Libby replied with a grin.

Mrs Godburgh bustled off, leaving Libby alone to finish grooming Snowball.

'Are you ready for an adventure, handsome lad?' she said as she wiped his face with a clean, damp cloth.

Sensing his mistress's palpable excitement, Snowball gave Libby an affectionate nudge in the chest. Smiling, Libby bent to plant a kiss on his soft muzzle.

'You didn't think I'd leave you behind, did you, sweetheart?'

Libby couldn't have picked a better day to make the fifteen-mile journey to Kent Banks. After kissing her mother goodbye and promising to write regularly, she mounted Snowball, who impatiently tossed his silver mane, keen to be underway. Leaving the twinkling blue waters of

Windermere behind, Libby trotted along the track where a low-lying autumn sun turned overhead oak and beech leaves to burnished gold. On their way to Cartmell, they passed the little village of High Newton and the shadowy outline of Hampsfell before stopping beside a clear, gurgling beck where Snowball could quench his thirst. Sitting on the riverbank beside her pony, Libby enjoyed the sandwiches her mother had so carefully prepared. Libby felt a great surge of love for both of her parents: they had always encouraged her to follow her own path even if it came at a high price, like leaving home in order to do her training. Libby knew that they had secretly hoped that she would return to Newby Bridge to work and marry a local lad and bring up a family that they could enjoy in their old age.

Libby gave a guilty sigh, poor things, yet another disappointment, she thought. Not that she disliked the idea of men and courting but growing up with three older brothers had left her with no romantic notions about the opposite sex. She enjoyed their company and relished the physical challenges they took on together. From fell running to mountaineering she could compete with any lad in the valley, but romance had barely touched her. The closest thing had been a kiss on the lips from a boy at school whose advances had left her stone cold. If the truth be told, when most of her girlfriends were experimenting with make-up or sewing dance dresses, Libby made it quite clear she wanted no distractions from her studies, which were paramount to her. Gazing adoringly at Snowball, who was snapping his tail to ward off flies, Libby said out loud, 'You're the only fella I want, lovie.'

Wiping crumbs from her jumper, she gave her pony the apple her mother had packed for her, then mounted up. Pressing her thighs firmly into Snowball's stout belly, she moved forward, ambling along the bridle path lined with horse chestnut trees heavy with conkers glowing in the autumnal light.

Some hours later, Libby arrived fresh faced and breathless at Mary Vale, with her tumbling golden-red hair flying in complete disarray about her tanned face. She lithely dismounted and rang the bell, holding on to Snowball's reins. Though warned that Libby would turn up on horseback, Ada immediately burst out laughing when she opened the door to her new colleague and saw Snowball standing before her shaking his long mane.

'Welcome to Mary Vale!' Ada exclaimed in delight.

Giving a loud snort, cheeky Snowball inched forwards to brush his soft muzzle against Ada's arm.

'You're a friendly boy,' she murmured, as she caressed his warm, silky neck. 'My little girl is going to love you.' Turning towards Libby, Ada added, 'You must be starving. Tea time's at five, but I can fetch you a cup of tea and a sandwich from the kitchen, if you like?'

Though Libby was indeed starving she shook her head.

'Thanks, but I'd like to untack Snowball and settle him down for the night, if you don't mind?'

Recalling the arrangements that had been made with Farmer Arkwright, Ada quickly nodded her head.

'Of course, the farm's just down the cobbled lane at the

back of the house, you can't miss it. I know Alf's already sorted out a stable for Snowball, and the grazing land is close by,' she went on. 'In fact the fields back on to my cottage, so I hope we'll be seeing a lot of your pretty pony.'

Gathering up the reins, Libby sprang back into the saddle.

'I can't wait to see it. I won't be long,' she promised with her widest smile.

'If I'm on the wards when you get back, Sister Agnes will see you to your room,' Ada quickly added.

'I'm so excited,' Libby blurted out happily.

Catching her mood Snowball gave a shrill neigh.

'It sounds like you both are,' Ada joked as she waved them off.

Watching them trot off towards the back of the house, Ada felt a deep sense of contentment; a dynamic, youthful, compassionate nurse with an irresistible wide grin was exactly what Mary Vale needed.

When Alf Arkwright heard the clip-clop of horse's hooves on the cobbles, he laid aside the pitchfork he had been using to muck out the cow byre to go and greet his visitor. The sight of eager Snowball tossing his mane as he quickened his pace in anticipation of a filled hay net made the old farmer chuckle.

'Welcome, miss,' he rumbled as he helped Libby dismount.

'Pleased to meet you, Farmer Arkwright,' she politely started.

'Alf'll do, lass,' he told her. 'I've got a stable ready for yon one,' he said as he nodded at the pony. 'Now't special, but it's dry and warm, and more to the point not far from't big house where you'll be living.'

'I couldn't be more grateful, Mr . . . er, Alf,' Libby gratefully exclaimed. She could see the small, snug stable just off the main yard, with a little tack room adjacent to it.

'Untack the beast and we'll get him into the paddock. He'll be wanting a roll after that long journey.'

Wide-eyed Libby gazed at him in amusement.

'A roll is exactly what he wants,' she agreed. 'How did you even know that?'

Alf let out a loud, deep laugh.

'I know about hosses; I've kept 'em for years.'

Glancing around Libby asked, 'Have you any here now?'

'Aye, th'owd shire, Captain. He's in't paddock yonder. He'll be pleased to have a bit of company.' Alf cautiously eyed Snowball who was considerably younger than Captain. 'Just so long as he minds his manners.'

When they turned Snowball out in the paddock, Alf's old horse ambled over and nudged Snowball's rump.

'Aye aye.' Alf grinned as he watched the two animals cautiously circumnavigating each other. 'Looks like they might be pals,' he said with some relief.

Libby's gaze drifted across the farm fields, neatly hedged with drystone walls, and towards the imposing sight of Mary Vale, presently basking in the last of the day's rosy gold light.

'Hopefully,' she smiled to herself, 'it will be more than Snowball who makes friends at Mary Vale.'

*

Once Snowball was comfortable, Libby made her way back to the Home where sweet Sister Agnes was waiting for her with a welcome cup of tea and a cheese sandwich.

'Tea's at five, corned beef fritters and roasted parsnips, followed by a nice apple crumble,' she said with undisguised relish. 'Just what you need after your long journey.'

Sinking her teeth into the delicious, tangy Lancashire cheese Libby said, 'It wasn't long really, though we did stop a lot to admire the scenery, especially around Cartmell Priory.'

'That's a gorgeous place of worship,' Agnes enthused.

'And the view when we dropped down into Grange from the top of the hill was wonderful. The tide was way out, so we had a brilliant glimpse of Morecambe Bay, it went on for miles and miles, all silvery-blue and grey,' she ended wistfully.

'Oh, it's a beautiful part of the world there's no doubt about that, God's own country,' Agnes declared. 'Now, when you're done, I'll show you to your room before I fetch in the tea.'

Springing to her feet, Libby followed Sister Agnes up two flights of highly polished stairs to the second floor which was reserved for staff accommodation. Once inside the large corner room at the end of the corridor, Libby spun around in order to examine every aspect of her new lodgings. With its two large bay windows facing south and west, the room was suffused with the last rays of the low setting sun. Out of one of the windows, Libby could see the vast sweep of the Irish Sea presently at full ebb while the other window looked out over the rose garden which sloped down to the marsh and sea birds settling down for the night. As she stared out, a barn owl swooped out of a small wood and circled the silvery marsh where darkness was swiftly falling.

'This is lovely,' Libby joyfully declared. 'Absolutely perfect!'

DISCOVER MORE FROM

DAISY STYLES

The Bomb Girls

On an ordinary day in 1941,
a letter arrives on the doormats
of five young women, a letter which
will change everything…

The Code Girls

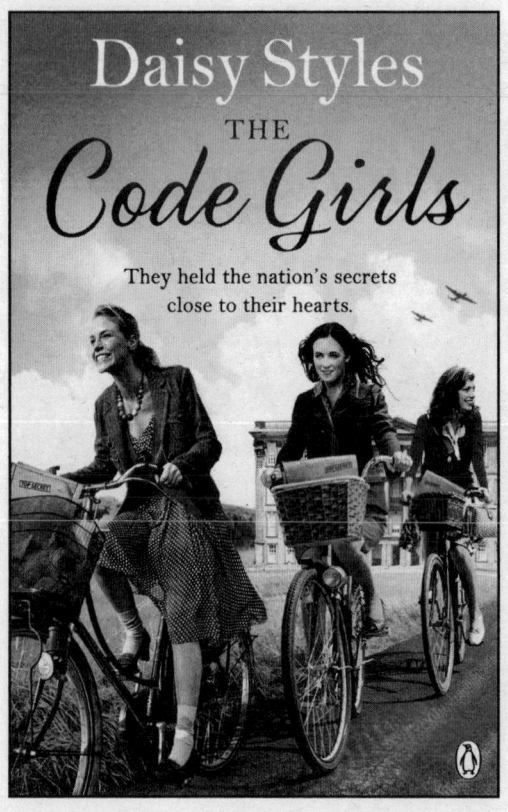

Can four girls protect a
whole country?

The Bomb Girls' Secrets

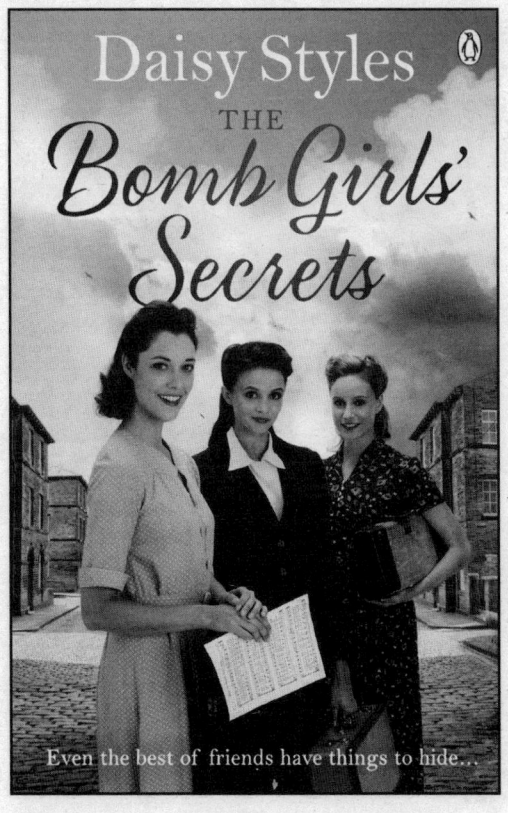

In the Phoenix Munitions Factory
everyone has their secrets . . .

Christmas with the Bomb Girls

In times of trouble,
can wishes come true . . .

The Bomb Girl Brides

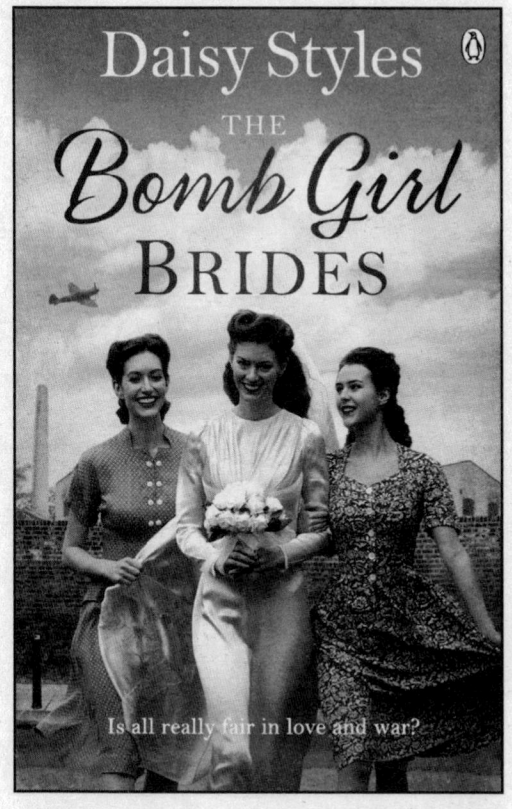

It's 1944 and Britain is a country at war. The young women of the Phoenix Munitions Factory are giving their all to the cause, but romance is beckoning . . .

The Wartime Midwives

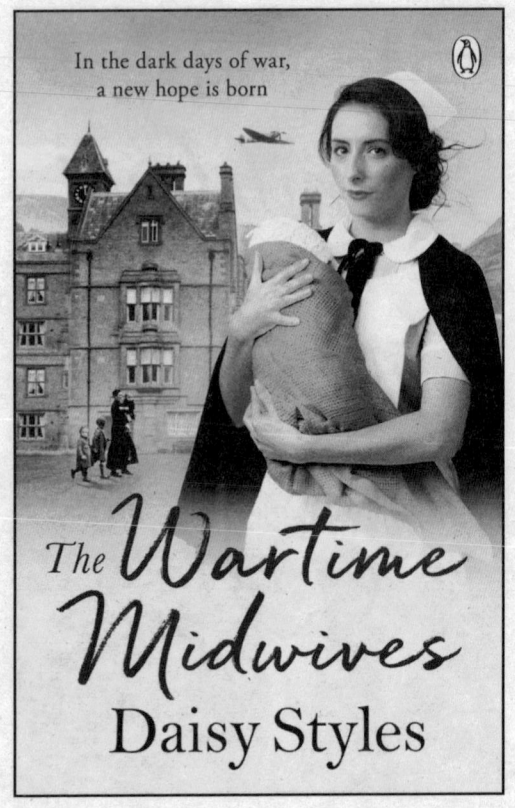

In the dark days of war,
a new hope is born

The Wartime Midwives

Daisy Styles

In the dark days of war a new
hope is born . . .

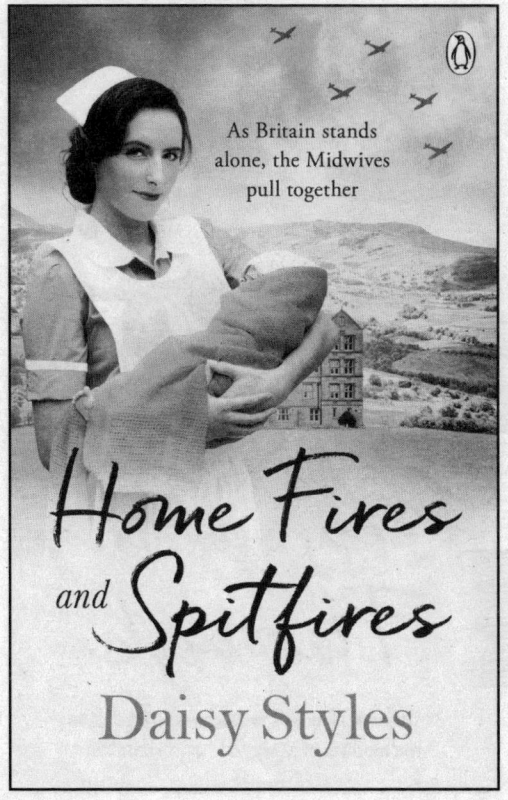

As Britain stands alone, the Midwives pull together

Home Fires and Spitfires

Daisy Styles

It is June 1940, and as the bombs fall, the women at home must dig deep . . .

Keep Smiling Through

Daisy Styles

The Wartime Midwives series

Keep Smiling Through

As the dark clouds of war descend over Britain,
the mothers of Mary Vale must stand tall

The Lake District, 1942. The women
at Mary Vale Mother and Baby Home
must pull together during their
darkest hour . . .